Modern Mythology

Modern Mythology

By
Jay Dubya

Published by
Bookstand Publishing
Morgan Hill, CA 95037
3564_2

Copyright © 2012 by Jay Dubya
All rights reserved. No part of this publication may be reproduced
or transmitted in any form or by any means, electronic or
mechanical, including photocopy, recording, or any information
storage and retrieval system, without permission in writing from the
copyright owner.

ISBN 978-1-61863-130-5

Printed in the United States of America

Other Books by Jay Dubya

Adult Fiction
Black Leather and Blue Denim, A '50s Novel
The Great Teen Fruit War, A 1960' Novel
Ron Coyote, Man of La Mangia
Pieces of Eight
Pieces of Eight, Part II
Pieces of Eight, Part III
Pieces of Eight, Part IV
The Wholly Book of Genesis
The Wholly Book of Exodus
Thirteen Sick Tasteless Classics
Thirteen Sick Tasteless Classics, Part II
Thirteen Sick Tasteless Classics, Part III
Thirteen Sick Tasteless Classics, Part IV
So Ya' Wanna' Be A Teacher
Frat Brats, A 60's Novel
Maimed Mauled Mangled Mutilated Mythology
Fractured Frazzled Folk Fables & Fairy Farces
Fractured Frazzled Folk Fables & Fairy Farces II
Nine New Novellas
Nine New Novellas, Part II
Nine New Novellas, Part III
One Baker's Dozen
Two Baker's Dozen
Random Articles and Manuscripts
Suite 16
Time Travel Tales

Young Adult Fantasy Novels
Pot of Gold
Enchanta
Space Bugs, Earth Invasion
The Eighteen Story Gingerbread House

Contents

Description

Modern Mythology is a collection of fifteen imaginative stories having mythological themes and also possessing interesting mythological allusions and characters. Humor is represented in "Olympus Lives" and in "Olympus Lives, Part II." Anachronism is depicted in the stories "Immoral Immortality," "The Seven Statues," "The Heroic Belt," "Greek Statutory Law" and in the very intriguing exploit "Mythology Economics." Conflict and action/adventure situations dominate the tales "The Amazon Sorority," "Perseus, II" and also "Twelve Modern Labors." The presentations "Excavations" and "Ice Ages" involve rather amazing archeological discoveries from ancient times. Finally, mystery and suspense can be found in "The Oracle," in "Marvelous Modern Mythology" and in the creative rendition "Accidental Coincidence."

"Olympus Lives"

Mt. Olympus has been a source of awe and inspiration since ancient times. Situated between Thessaly and Macedonia, the massive mountain rises to a celestial peak that towers nearly ten thousand feet above the Earth. From prehistoric times up to the present age shepherds have loyally tended their bleating flocks near the mammoth wonder's base. *Olympus's* grassy slopes gradually surrender to snow-clad crags when human eyes observe its grandeur from a distance. *Mt. Olympus's* glorious crest is often shrouded by a veil of fog or by a mystic halo of clouds, thus adding to its general mystique.

The majestic peak was thought by ancient Greeks to be the very center of the then known world. Many believed the mountain's spectacular summit to be the official residence of the twelve Olympian gods. Poets and bards imagined that splendid white marble palaces were supremely situated atop the fabled mountain's stately crown.

The decline of Greece as a dominant ancient civilization occurred when the power base of the *Western World* shifted from Athens to Rome. Knowledge of the ancient cultures had been almost completely forgotten during the *Dark Ages*. But then the *Renaissance*, the *Age of Enlightenment* and the *Industrial Revolution* had drastically altered man's methods of thinking, working and recreating. By the time of Shakespeare mythology had diminished in prestige when compared to more modern *Globe Theater* comedy and tragedy play presentations. And later in human history science and technology became the most powerful cultural forces of the twentieth century.

Men are no longer fearful superstitious creatures. Mortals have evolved into haughty, proud and ambitious beings who can invent computers that are smarter than Apollo, who can build skyscrapers that would give Hephaestus an inferiority complex, and who can generate atomic energy that would make Zeus's thunderbolts seem like mere child's play.

Ancient beliefs handed-down from classical bards have now been reduced in importance by modern education. Anything not originating from science and technology is subject to cynicism and doubt. Materialism and humanism are presently contributing to the decline and fall of classical wisdom. Homo sapiens don't have time for imperial Zeus and whimsical Hera anymore. Instead the fickle species reveres plasma-screen televisions, automobiles, computers, the *Internet,* music disks and thousands of other prized technology "things."

Contemporary humans have become hedonistic pleasure machines worshiping wealth, mobility and convenience, the triplet decadent offspring of the *Industrial Revolution.* Compare those ideas to what Zeus and the Olympians had to offer mortals: poverty, travail, sacrifice, punishment and misery. Modern men have little time for ancient gods and *their* mercurial propensities. Their new religion is science, and science has made mankind selfish, defiant, independent and agnostic.

Greek mythology has suffered a terrible demise over the past two millennia. Children prefer believing in fairies, dragons, magic, witches and sorcerers rather than in Poseidon, Hades, Ares, Apollo and Athena. But a little known esoteric fact is fully and astutely comprehended by a small nucleus of "New Age" mystics. The Olympian gods of antiquity are indeed still alive.

Mt. Olympus's present facade suggests a rather lazy august serenity. Neither mortal nor immortal activity seems to be existent anywhere on its placid surface appearance. The mountain's noble tranquility reflects the notion that the Olympians have either perished or have evacuated the entire vicinity. Presented herewith is accumulated documentation to the contrary.

A vast network of silver labyrinths has been built inside the noble mountain. The immense passageways are coordinated with a maze of marble tunnels. The internal city of *Olympus* is so self-contained that its immortal inhabitants need never venture outside its perimeter. The well-concealed fortress grants refuge from humans to eccentric Zeus and his divine family. The Olympians are served by legions of appreciative and well-fed slaves, who have been generated and bred from Mediterranean ancestral stock. The loyal descendants of the original servants have been in the imperial gods' service several centuries before Julius Caesar's Rome.

Zeus's very colossal resplendent palace dominates the subterranean Olympian Empire, which is lit by millions of candles burning in golden sconces and by thousands of brilliant torches attached to sturdy ivory holders embedded in the marble walls. The magnificent edifice towers over the other lesser gods' smaller-but-impressive gleaming structures. But the impeccable central temple is the property of the king of gods. Zeus's singular mansion has marble and bronze floors, golden ceilings and it also flaunts glittering platinum roofs.

One side of Zeus's incredible temple looks like the original Athenian *Parthenon*, only ten times as large. Another side is similar to King Minos' former great palace at Knossos on the island of Crete, a third side is like Priam's much-heralded castle at Troy, and the fourth is comparable in design to the famous Oracle's shrine at Delphi. Ornate Corinthian columns and incredible statues of major and minor gods and goddesses have been erected everywhere inside the fantastic edifice. A gallery on the right side of Zeus's palatial residence leads to a special chamber, the official meeting place of the Olympian Council.

The Olympians have reluctantly relinquished the Earth to mortals over the last two millennia. When men built factories in the nineteenth century their knowledge of chemicals, compounds and combustion greatly surpassed even the greatest achievements of the proud immortals. The divine ones, under the aegis of Zeus, now borrow ideas and constantly steal patents, just to play catch-up with mankind's formidable ingenuity.

Electricity is satisfactorily generated inside *Mt. Olympus* by an underground river's waterfall turning rudimentary turbines. The kinetic energy eventually produces sufficient light for streets, parks, gardens and buildings. The principles of the gasoline engine, stolen from old Henry Ford blueprints, enables Hephaestus to power underground "mass transportation" to shuttle slaves from one palace to another.

"It's a good thing we gods are immortal," Zeus had told Ares at the last Council meeting, "or else we would suffocate to death from all this terrible subterranean air pollution."

Zeus owns a fleet of seventies-styled Cadillacs and Lincolns but the other gods, depending on their rank in the divine pecking order, must drive Olympian renditions of Fords, Chevrolets and Pontiacs. Television units have recently been installed but the gods must watch black and white '50s reruns imaginatively siphoned from nearby Greek satellite transmitters. "Man has gone from slave, to nuisance, to rival, to conqueror," Zeus lamented to Hera the night before his next scheduled Council forum. "His vast achievements have vastly eclipsed those of the immortals."

"We definitely need more spies out there stealing their technology," the queen goddess recommended. "Maybe Hades could lend us Benedict Arnold, Nathan Hale, Francis Gary Powers and Mata-Hari's services."

"We can't even keep up with what these remarkable creatures had accomplished in the early twentieth century," Zeus confessed, "and now, with the advent of atomic power, Star Wars' technology, the *Internet* and space travel, let me tell you Hera, those insane humans scare the living Hades out of me!"

"The once-obedient children of Arcadia have gone from your humble servants dressed in tawdry rags to being the insane terrors of the Universe," Hera added.

"Prometheus and I molded those miserable creatures from mud, do you hear me Hera, m-u-d," Zeus angrily emphasized. "Those first men were puny. I should have snuffed them out right then and there before they had a chance to make fire and weapons. Now I must rely on *them* for such crazy things as shampoo, dog food and tacos. By Cronus, how I love Mexican tacos! And burritos and enchiladas are quite tasty too!"

"Zeus, when can I have my first Lexus automobile?" Hera inquired. "I hear from Hermes that they're really beautifully designed."

"Whenever Hephaestus or Hermes can steal the plans," the Lord-god answered in a disgusted tone of voice. "It seems that's your only hope of ever getting one."

Olympus still has many time-honored laws. One edict dating back to the genesis of intelligent life states that once man has acquired certain knowledge, a new skill or a useful secret, then the gods would never take it away. But the discovery of electricity, the evolution of telecommunications, the creation of the microchip, the practice of biochemical warfare and the detrimental influence of *MTV* have all given the Olympians gross inferiority complexes.

The gods are now paranoid and refuse to confront men directly because the divine ones now feel inadequate to *their* creation. Zeus and company evade contact with their former suppliants at all costs. Even Zeus has a phobia of humanity. The Olympians' energies are now exclusively devoted to subversive tactics, sabotage and counter-intelligence. Their prime goal is to have men quarrel and battle among themselves, or as Athena aptly calls it, "a basic divide and conquer defensive strategy."

"Father, if we could get men fighting each other," Athena mentioned at family discussion time at the great marble-slate dining room table the night before the upcoming Council meeting, "then mass discord could possibly trigger the fall of human civilization."

"Yes," Hera alertly agreed, deftly preempting her depressed husband, "the gods could enter the vacuum caused by world chaos and then again assume absolute power on Earth."

"Then I could swiftly regain dominion of the Earth *and* the sky!" Zeus exclaimed. "Our regal glory would grace this despicable planet once more. Our authority would again reign supreme and unchallenged!"

"I sure hope we can steal *MTV* and *VH-1* before the humans stupidly eradicate themselves," Athena complained. "I want to see what this disco stuff is all about and what this Fleetwood Mac group looks and sounds like. I don't even know what the Beatles or the Rolling Stones look like. But I like their music cassettes I hear on my new tape player that Hermes stealthily pilfered for me and conveyed here to *Mt. Olympus!*"

"Athena, that is exactly what's wrong with immortal children nowadays," Zeus quickly admonished. "I mean, you've been a child, my child, for over three thousand years now. Don't you get it! You idolize these pathetic humans, but *they're* supposed to be worshiping *you*! Athena, I'm warning you, stop acting like a spoiled childish Greek geek!"

"Daddy, I also happen to like soap operas, poodle skirts and *Disneyland!* Gee, I hope my adolescent hormones kick in soon. Three thousand years is a long time to wait," Athena said before she effortlessly raised her body up into the air and then effortlessly drifted into another section of the fabulous palace.

The Olympians knew and preserved a few secrets that still gave them some distinct advantages over mortals. One was the elixir nectar and ambrosia, the drink and the food of the gods. Even that wonderful knowledge was in danger of being discovered by, as Zeus aptly called them, "those treacherous monstrous creatures living on Earth."

"Hera, genetic research done down in those weird rooms the mortals call laboratories is analyzing the structure of the complicated *DNA* molecule," Zeus informed his lovely spouse. "I created life, and I have no idea what in Sparta a *DNA* molecule is! I mean, all I said was 'Let there be a little person version of an Olympian that will be a mere mortal to serve the gods.' I mean, I never said anything about the existence of a silly trivial *DNA* molecule!"

"Zeus, when can I get a credit card?" Hera inquisitively asked. "I'm tired of these obsolete tunics and cumbersome sandals I've been wearing now for over three thousand years. Then I could shrink down to a diminutive five-foot-six-inches in height, go to malls disguised as a svelte lady and enthusiastically purchase some new modern clothes at my leisure."

"Hera!" Zeus hollered. "You aren't listening to me as usual. This repulsive race I had created is on the threshold of mastering a synthetic formula for immortality. They don't even waste their precious time trying to find nectar and ambrosia anymore. They want to do *it their* way just like that Frank Sinatra crooner fellow sang about!"

Zeus sadly missed his former personal involvement in human history. He used to enjoy interfering with men's goals and manipulating their destinies. When the mighty King God didn't do it himself, he cleverly used surrogates like his wife Hera, like Ares, god of war, or like the Fates and the Muses to do his wicked bidding.

"Remember the good old days, Hera," Zeus fondly recalled as he sat erect on his golden throne. "Men were our puppets and we pulled the strings. Remember all the fun we had producing and directing the action-packed scenes of the *Trojan War*."

"Do I?" Hera nostalgically recalled. "We staged the whole *Odyssey* as if the thrilling adventures of Odysseus were strategic moves in a silly chess game."

"You've done it again, my dear wife," Zeus complained. "Mortals invented chess, not us. That's what really grieves me about them. They invent more than we create. They seem to have more imagination and motivation than we gods do."

No doubt, Zeus and his Council felt exceedingly threatened by humanity's recent arrogant insurgence, especially ever since the introduction of the microchip. At first the gods ignored man's stubborn quest for intellectual independence. But over the past two millennia, mankind's indifference to the gods has evolved into "unbearable insolence." The very evident defiance had reached intolerable proportions. The gods, especially Zeus, no longer felt rivaled. They now feel imperiled and overwhelmed. Their former egocentric self-concepts have been atrophying into a malaise of "abundant poor self-esteem." Zeus now despised the Earth dwellers' apathy towards their Principal Creator along with his hating their "atrocious disgraceful irreverence" towards the Olympians in general.

Every hundred Earth-years, ever since the reign of Julius Caesar, Zeus has convened his Olympian Council to discuss in detail current events and to analyze the gods' progress and their particular strategies. Plenty had happened in the last century to cause the gods much alarm. Nuclear weapons, spy satellites, space exploration, cable television, new medical technology, computers, the *Internet*, jet airplanes, cell phones and the automobile were just some of the accomplishments down on Earth that had easily surpassed anything the gods could collectively conceive or invent.

The Olympians' game plan was rather simple. They believed they should live in isolation until mankind imminently terminated its existence through war, decadence, rap music lyrics, drug abuse and by means of death resulting from excessive body piercing and flesh mutilation. The Mt. Olympus gods are presently plotting sinister schemes to accelerate mortals' inevitable downfall from power.

Zeus's Council assembled on the evening of December 31, 2000 and the important conclave was about to convene. Aphrodite and Athena wore glamorous yellow and purple silk tunics of different designs and also flaunted stunning diamond diadems on their heads. Hera was dressed in purple and wore a brilliant sapphire and ruby tiara. Ares, Poseidon, Hermes and Apollo sat at the other end of Zeus's long gold, emerald and marble table that was elaborately trimmed with embedded ruby and sapphire gemstones. Dionysus and Hades were exchanging anecdotes as they stood next to their topaz thrones that had soft velvet cushions. Hephaestus, the lame blacksmith god, was the last to enter the chamber and eventually find his ruby throne.

The meeting room was dazzling in appearance. The huge chamber had more sparkling jewels inserted into its walls and ceiling than the total number of rare gems in all the world's jewelry stores put together. Zeus soon called the meeting to order by hurling a wicked thunderbolt at an enlarged black and white photograph of Manhattan. The lightning bolt immediately obliterated the city's skyline. The other gods ceased their prattling and rather quickly came to attention.

Artemis was the only major deity absent from the Council. Zeus had given her permission to go on a rare hunting mission to Ethiopia to capture an elusive beast called *Big Foot*. Zeus believed Artemis's story, even though the goddess knew all along that the difficult-to-capture creature would more likely be found in Saskatchewan than in Ethiopia. The enactment of such a wondrous feat would definitely boost Zeus's ego, but only Artemis knew that it "ain't gonna' happen."

"My fellow immortals," Zeus prefaced his dissertation, "we need discipline amongst our own ranks to soundly defeat the scourge that currently plagues us on all major continents. My biggest mistake was modeling the human mind after my own."

"My dear Husband," Hera haughtily interrupted, "you should be edified. After all, every achievement man enjoys is indirectly *your* achievement because their minds are really reproductions of your most noble genius."

Zeus raised his massive white eyebrows, shifted about on his gigantic elevated golden throne, smiled briefly at Hera, and then proceeded with delivering his prepared text. "Fellow deities, I regret ever giving mortals intelligence, cunning, courage and stubbornness. These bold, brazen vermin, er, I mean creatures have, believe it or not, ascended to a level worthy of our admiration and also if I might add, our condemnation."

The other Olympians in attendance nodded their heads in tacit agreement. Zeus proceeded with his didactic rhetoric, which his speech-maker Apollo had actually prepared on the backside of a scroll that had been positioned on an easel directly to the Lord-god's right.

"Initially we had derived amusement from watching their blunders and their folly," Zeus pointed out. "Man's futile effort to merely survive was indeed a novelty to behold. The fools feared us, worshiped us, respected us and sought our divine protection. We even gave the mendicants a benign code of ethics to practice based on moderation, just to safeguard them from engineering and executing their own self-destruction."

Everyone seated in the magnificent chamber concurred with Zeus's excellent assessment. The Council gods were now all anxious to give their reports and get the meeting over with so that they wouldn't have to witness Zeus lose his temper or hear his dictatorial rhetoric for another hundred years. Hera wanted to read the latest *Hollywood* tabloids, Athena wanted to listen to her disco tapes, Hermes wanted to study how *Federal Express* and *UPS* operated, and Aphrodite wanted to look at the centerfold in the latest available copy of *Playgirl Magazine.*

"Yes, my fellow Olympians," Zeus sorrowfully continued, "I fondly recall brave men like Odysseus, Agamemnon, Achilles, Orpheus, Perseus, Hercules and Daedalus. They paid homage to *us*. They demonstrated fortitude and mettle in their behavior. The men of Homer's time were what I had in mind when I molded the first puny Arcadians out of clay. Now, I regret that I had molded a vile curse that has viciously haunted me for over three millennia."

"Yes Your Grace," a drunken Dionysus interrupted, "now-a-days *Arcadians* are those young obnoxious humans who play pinball and video games."

"Enough of your inane juvenile drivel Dionysus," Zeus commanded. "Show me more respect and maturity."

Ares could not control his temper any longer. He cleared his throat and stood up to be recognized. "Your eminence, if I may say something significant," Ares courteously requested. "I believe our problems all began with the activities of that treacherous traitor, Prometheus."

Zeus became enraged at the mention of *that* reprehensible name. "Don't ever even think about that insolent obscene Titan again. Prometheus had egregiously violated Olympus's most sacred rule!" Zeus blasted out so loudly that he shattered the crystals in an overhead ostentatious-looking chandelier.

"That only male gods could be promiscuous?" Hera defiantly asked.

"No!" Zeus screamed. "The undeniable rule that gods should never give men tools or bestow on them knowledge. Once man acquires a gift, it should not be taken away. Oh, how I regret ever establishing that error-laden mandate around the time of Medusa's demise caused by that intrepid fiend Perseus."

"So what?" Athena challenged. "Men got fire, men stayed warm. Big deal! Prometheus felt sorry for them and did them all a giant favor, in fact a Titanic favor."

"Athena," Zeus said while shrugging his shoulders, "men did not learn how to make fire on their own. Prometheus gave them fire and taught them how to make it. After they acquired knowledge of fire-making men radically changed from savages figuring out how to survive to creatures having free time to think. Humans then used fire to combine copper and tin to make bronze and after men knew all about bronze, they made weapons from bronze. Soon the wretches had swords, helmets and shields. *Thinking* was the true beginning of man's insubordination to the gods. Thinking is what made the race rebellious!"

"Where is Prometheus right now?" Ares fearfully asked.

"Yes, he's no longer chained to *Mr. Etna*," Hera confirmed.

Zeus explained that Prometheus had to be moved to a less conspicuous location after humans had invented the camera. Pictures would have been taken, and eventually, Prometheus would have been interviewed by the media and by television talk show hosts. The humans would naturally feel sympathy for Prometheus and next try to liberate him from his shackles. "My eternal command would have been reversed by stupid human compassion and intervention," Zeus protested. "I could have never lived with *that* sort of disgrace. Prometheus is now imprisoned in a dungeon a mile beneath this very room."

"King Zeus," said Hades, "you are too kind in describing the human vermin."

"Hades my brother, you take care of the underworld and the afterlife, and let Poseidon and me take care of the rest," Zeus sternly answered. "But I must say I am deeply angered by human conceit. I did not create men for us gods to envy *them*. Their token remembrance of us is limited to naming rockets and planets in honor of our Greek and Roman appellations," Zeus acknowledged. "The planet Pluto honors you, dear Hades, Mars honors Ares, Mercury honors Hermes, Venus honors Aphrodite, Neptune honors Poseidon, and of course, Jupiter, the largest planet in the solar system pays homage to me, Zeus."

"Don't forget the summer and winter Olympic Games too!" Apollo reminded the presiding god.

Poseidon was just as perplexed as his brother Zeus has been ever since the time of Homer. "Unfortunately," Poseidon stated, "earthlings have forgotten the original purpose of the Olympic Games, to praise and worship *us*, the Olympians. Now they egotistically carry on our proud games to sanctimoniously edify themselves! How spiteful and inconsiderate!"

"Enough of this lousy hollow shallow sentimentality!" Zeus thundered. "Our Golden Age is long gone but let's not lose our focus. The purpose of this meeting is to contrive a plan to restore our glory. I'm going to call upon each of you to report your activities of the past hundred years. Hermes, we'll start with your indispensable testimony."

"Thank you, Your Excellency," Hermes commenced. "I am saddened to report that the earthlings have learned to build great machines that enable them to fly three times faster than the speed of sound. These jets, as they call them, could fly ten times faster than any god in this room. Just yesterday I was almost rammed out of a cloud by something called a Boeing 747. The wings almost fell off my helmet from the turbulent air currents that resulted from the near tragedy."

Zeus stopped Hermes' monologue and told him to refrain from his personal experiences and to stick to telling exactly how the messenger god had thwarted "the decadent descendants of Pandora and Epimetheus." Zeus then politely cracked a small smile for the first time in seventy decades, and Hermes felt safe proceeding with his most demonstrative presentation.

"As the official messenger god," Hermes declared, "I have tried contaminating communications on Earth. But I really got aggravated when the *United States Mint* discontinued the Mercury dime. They removed my image and put someone by the name of Franklin D. Roosevelt on the coin instead."

"You're deviating off course once again, but tell us Hermes, what did you do to get even with the dastardly humans' mint?" Zeus asked.

"Thousands of people living down on the planet's surface overreact to one another by imitating the violence I make them see on television," the messenger god informed the Council. "Negative behavior in movies, newspapers, rock n' roll and rap music on the radio and TV, and also what people see on *Action News* have all contributed to man's moral corruption. It's only a matter of time before Earth cultures will disintegrate from hedonism and a lack of civilization."

"I strenuously object!" Athena loudly disagreed. "What's wrong with television, *MTV* and *VH-1*? And please tell me, what the heck is rap music? I'd like to listen to it and see if it is enjoyable and pleasing to my ears."

"Nothing is wrong with *MTV*, my dear daughter," Zeus replied. "It's all right for the gods to be decadent. What Hermes is saying is that he is trying to use decadence to have mankind self-destruct. I feel a terrible migraine coming on. Continue please, won't you Hermes?"

"I'm glad to say, if I might use a popular human expression, that we're 'all on the same wavelength'," Hermes laughed. "Thanks to depravity in the mass media, there are more crimes than ever down there on Earth. Misdemeanors and felonies are rampant everywhere. Weaker-minded unscrupulous men and women are mimicking the random violence they see enacted on television and in the movies. Arson, theft, homicides, muggings and greed are undoubtedly on the rise."

Hermes also predicted that he believed the avaricious species residing down on Earth would be extinct in another hundred years. The messenger god finished his report by promising that the Olympians would soon live in the sunshine once more because events were happening fast instead of slow as they had in the *Dark Ages*, before men had electricity and when peasants were too cheap or too poor to use candles.

"And if *we* don't come to power again?" Zeus challenged. "What then?"

"Well, I could always get a job with *FTD Florists* delivering red roses if things really get rough," Hermes cleverly responded. "That might be the start of a budding career."

Poseidon was the second deity on the agenda. He had a very haggard expression on his hoary wrinkled face. The sea god raised his rusty bronze trident to get everyone's attention. King Neptune's role in the Olympian conspiracy was restricted to the oceans' floor. Poseidon was Zeus's favorite brother who introduced him to the pleasures of Maryland crab soup and *Bumblebee* tuna fish. The king-god held the marine sage's advice and friendship in high regard.

Poseidon possessed a very strong resonant voice because he would always inadvertently gargle salt water whenever he slept and snored on coral reef beds at the bottom of the oceans. He had become quite laconic over the centuries because it is hard talking to anyone seven miles below the *Pacific Ocean* because there aren't too many people or gods living or traveling even five miles underneath the shallower *Atlantic*. The sea god sounded rather pessimistic as he began his oration.

"My fellow deities," Poseidon prefaced, "I have relentlessly encouraged through mental suggestion that humans should pollute the oceans. This will have a devastating effect on the delicate balance of nature. It will undeniably change weather patterns and there will soon be destructive hurricanes, typhoons and monsoons all year round to frustrate the vile Earthlings."

"Excuse me Poseidon," Hera spoke-up in defense of logic, "but if *you* contaminate the ocean, isn't the sea *your* home? Aren't you ravaging and destroying your own environment?"

"Hopefully," Poseidon said, "there will be enough left to work with after the catastrophe so that I and the sea nymphs, Charybdis, and Triton and all the rest of my submerged gang can start from scratch all over again."

"Continue, my dear brother," Zeus commanded. "My wife is a little wet behind the ears when it comes to matters of the sea," the King of gods laughed. All the chauvinistic male deities roared with delight while the lady deities frowned and grimaced, all sharing Hera's humiliation.

"When the oceans are adequately polluted," Poseidon proceeded, "fish and aquatic vegetation will die by the billions. Whales are already in short supply in three oceans right this minute. Other sea creatures are already classified as endangered species. Soon the reckless race of men, by virtue of their avarice, will become an endangered species too," the sea god declared.

"Very perceptive, promising and inspirational my astute brother," Zeus commended, "because I know that even land animals are in jeopardy of extinction. Humans are happily trashing-up their fresh water rivers and lakes. My dear brother, is there anything else you'd like to contribute?"

"As a matter of fact there is," Poseidon indicated. "I really loved the movie *The Poseidon Adventure*. The humans still remembered my glory by naming the film after me. And I'll bet you didn't know that I was instrumental in the sinking of the *Titanic* and the *Lusitania*, even though those stupid humans down on Earth credit a dumb iceberg and an errant torpedo for causing those particular calamities. And I also hated that Jacques Cousteau jerk, who incidentally now is in my brother Hades' custody. He had the audacity to name his research ship *Calypso*, plagiarizing right out of Homer's *Odyssey* the goddess that offered dastardly Odysseus immortality," Poseidon vehemently complained. "And then Cousteau was brazen enough to invent the aqua-lung. With advanced SCUBA equipment men can now stay underwater almost as long as I can. Even I must surface occasionally to check out some pretty sirens and hot-looking sea nymphs basking on rocks."

Zeus told Poseidon that he was deviating from *his* report and that the sea god should forget his likes and dislikes and refrain from discussing *his* personal opinions. "Stick to the facts!" Zeus objected. "This meeting ought to be over in less than one human month!"

"Thank you for pointing out my mental weaknesses and faulty habits," Poseidon admitted. "Those vain creations of yours have built dreadful battleships and submarines. I now feel very leery and uncomfortable swimming about in my native environment. Many smaller channels of water are completely unsafe to enter. I have a scar on my left arm from a wayward harpoon and one on my right shoulder from a ship's propeller. And those new-fangled jet skis are drivin' me absolutely nuts!"

The sea god then related that in 1995 he had to scramble behind a coral reef when a Russian submarine fired two torpedoes at him. "It required all my nautical skill to avoid being blown all the way to Neptune," Poseidon wryly reported.

The other Council gods gave Poseidon their approval by heartily clapping their hands. Zeus thanked his brother for his vigilance while experiencing "dire straits."

"I too fear the pestilence Prometheus and I have carelessly created," Zeus indicated. "What's to stop the human idiots from discovering *our* present location and demolishing *Olympus* with a megaton nuclear bomb? And it might not even be a legitimate government that does us away, either! It might be some maverick Arab terrorist group out to make a name for themselves!"

Throughout his three millennia reign Zeus had always been chauvinistic, even three thousand years before Napoleon's cavalier general, Nicholas Chauvin appeared on the Earth. The King-god preferred masculine domination of the Universe, as long as *he* was the chief male and overlord. Goddesses were always subordinated to gods' whims. That was why Hermes and Poseidon's presentations were scheduled before any female deities could address the Council. Feeling satisfied that male dominance had been effectively asserted, Zeus asked his wife to articulate her clandestine activities during the past century.

The beautiful queen goddess stood and then broadly smiled. Hera's pearly white teeth added power to her wonderful charm. Her grace was matched only by her guile and sagacity. The queen's hypnotic eyes communicated her shrewdness, and her haunting voice exuded charisma. Everyone, including Zeus, sat captivated on his or her throne, virtually hypnotized by the influential goddess's overall radiance.

"Thank goodness the humans' calendar still recognizes the month of June, named after my Roman name Juno," Hera irrelevantly began, "and they still honor Ares with March, Mars being our war god's Roman designation," the chief goddess indicated.

"Humans love war!" Ares yelled. "They are lost without it. That's precisely why mankind will remember me until the bitter end! And I almost have to admire them for it!"

14

Everyone cheered Ares' appropriate remark. Even the gods enjoyed fighting among themselves more than they relished cooperating with each other. They regarded sharing as being "a petty human enterprise unworthy of pursuing."

"My beloved husband and fellow deities," Hera saluted, "I have been extremely busy this past Earth century. I have adopted 'a novel sociological approach.' To use the enemy's lamebrain terminology, 'I am currently involved in the spread of mortal misery.' I once read that fairly magnificent passage in the *New York Times.*"

"Could you be more specific in describing your recent activities?" Zeus requested.

"Certainly my ethereal spouse," Hera kindly obliged. "By convincing women that they must have equal rights, I have sowed the seeds of distrust between the sexes. Most men now fear their mates more than they fear the scheming of other men. Now that's what I call progress!"

"My dear wife," Zeus interrupted, "make sure you restrict this dangerous women's liberation business to Earth. It could cause real problems up here inside *Olympus.*"

Hera waited until the other gods stopped their cackling and their rude chattering. "I am proud to announce the deterioration of families all over the globe. Conflict abounds everywhere on all continents. Separations and divorce are rampant. Infidelity is everywhere. It's actually growing at epidemic proportions," Zeus's intelligent wife reported. "The basic moral fabric of earthly societies is being slowly-but-surely eroding away. In another hundred years I confidently predict that lesbians will rule all families, clans, tribes, men's clubs and nations!"

Hera paused to evaluate the extent of her impact on her receptive audience. Seeing that her power had its usual bewitching effect, she proceeded with her spellbinding dissertation.

"Men are already disenchanted with their spouses, who aspire to surpass them in every area of achievement. Since women now work they are no longer dependent on their husbands. They are becoming *independent* of male authority," Hera insisted. "Millions of wives now cheat on their already cheating husbands. Jealousy and spite are flourishing with the obvious collapse of male family and workplace jurisdiction. This new mass conflict will make Lenin and Marx's class conflict of the nineteenth century look like an elementary school picnic. Soon there will be global pandemonium, not between countries or alliances, but between men and women, both inside and outside of the family structure."

"Forget Lenin and Marx," Athena impertinently interrupted. "What about Lennon and McCartney?"

"Silence daughter!" Zeus nastily boomed. "Either respect your parents or go to your temple and pray!"

Almighty Zeus also felt a bit threatened by his controversial wife's insistence on women's liberation in addition to Athena's quite apparent defiance of his almighty autocracy inside his family's structure and also at centennial Council meetings. He also believed that Hera was giving women mental powers that when coupled with female physical attributes, would eventually overwhelm all males, gods included.

"Hera, I think you're giving women too much guile to complement their sexual allurement," Zeus challenged. "That is a very volatile combination."

"Indeed, my dear sage Husband," Hera promptly proceeded, "earthly women, just like men, are seeking variety with the opposite sex. They are responding to my mental transmissions like hungry bees lusting for honey. Quarrels, fights, suspicions, accusations and domestic violence abound. Eventually family unity will rot away," Hera elucidated.

"Is that good?" Apollo interrupted. "Is family disunity a blessed event?"

"Yes, because the ingredients of lust, disloyalty, insincerity and infidelity have been added to my subversive recipe," Hera answered. "In the end, physical sex will be the deciding factor and since women usually have and control what men want and need, women will stack the deck, and those same powerful women will deal the cards while they hold all the aces and all of the trump suit. Now do you see the wisdom enveloped in my scheme?"

Athena and Aphrodite gave Hera a standing ovation while the male gods, including Zeus, passively clapped their hands in mock applause.

"My effervescent wife, thank you for your dramatic and very animated presentation," Zeus praised. "Your graphic exposition was laden with truth and marvelous half-truths. At this time I would like to make a public confession to this Council."

The assembled gods suddenly became absolutely silent. The colossal opulent meeting chamber was as quiet as the deepest unexplored tunnels of Hades. The Council had never before heard Zeus apologize for anything. His will had always been paramount and his guilt had always been cunningly concealed. The other gods leaned forward to hear every syllable.

"I suppose it's more of an admission than an actual confession," Supreme Zeus clarified, much to everyone's disappointment. "Nevertheless, you are all aware of its reality. In the past I have been unfaithful to Hera. Those minor affairs were but casual, token, spur-of-the-moment romances I had had with only a handful of mortal women, or should I call them incidental encounters with two handfuls of mortal women," Zeus indicated by raising all ten massive fingers directly before his crimson face. "At any rate, those incidental rendezvous' trysts have haunted my vulnerable conscience for centuries. Hera, I hereby beg forgiveness for three thousand years of foolish indiscretions."

"Let there be soap operas!" Athena called out.

Hera blew a kiss at her philandering husband and the Council of deities laughed in unison for the first time since the emergency session they had held in late 1492 about some dis*oriented* fellow named Columbus discovering America.

Hephaestus, husband of Aphrodite and the lame forger of metals, who still made bronze helmets, swords, and shields for the Olympians, was the next speaker on the agenda. He rose slowly because of his disability. The blacksmith god spoke in a very deliberate manner. His words reflected his skepticism with the ineffective way the Olympian campaign against humanity had been progressing. His speech's content did not share the contrived optimism of the other more theatrical immortals that had already spoken.

Zeus hoped that Hephaestus's address would be brief. He did not want the hammer and anvil god's lethargic and pessimistic mood to become contagious. The Council was already too jittery as far as the King god was concerned.

"I regret to report that humans are doing all sorts of fantastic things with metals and alloys," Hephaestus drearily began. "Their incredible discoveries have made my greatest attainments seem like mere child's play. I have borrowed many of their brilliant methods and have implemented them in my furnace room two thousand feet below this hallowed chamber."

The ugly lame deity went on to explain that he had difficulty keeping up with the latest scientific technology. Hephaestus then asked Zeus to requisition an updated computer system in the next fiscal budget so that the beleaguered blacksmith could keep up with the latest advances in metallurgy. The bronze forger had gradually entered the iron and steel ages and he needed more technical machine assistance to produce more mechanical inventions. The blacksmith god testified to the Council that computers had "memory banks" full of valuable information that could close the enormous "technology time gap" between Earth and *Olympus* to only a hundred years.

"Maybe I could arrange to have Bill Gates and Stephen Jobs help you out?" Hades, the always-somber Lord of the Underworld suggested to Hephaestus. "Once they get to Hades, I'll immediately transfer their ghosts to *you* to labor in your boiler-room as your private slaves. In a matter of nine short decades Hephaestus, you'll be fully automated!"

"These confounded-but-determined Earthlings," Hephaestus continued, ignoring Hades' constructive suggestion, "they have developed many practical uses for new metals like steel and aluminum. I've finally gotten the making of steel down to a science, but aluminum needs much more research and application. I'm trying to get two spirits, Edison and Carnegie to leave the bleak Underworld of Lord Hades and help me out."

"Are you into heavy metal?" Athena asked.

"Heavy metal? What do you mean?" inquired the befuddled blacksmith god.

"Heavy metal rock groups," Zeus's daughter clarified. "Haven't you ever heard of Metallica and Led Zeppelin?"

"Athena, you said you haven't heard that kind of trashy music ever being played!" Zeus chastised. "And besides, even I know that a blimp must have either helium or hydrogen inside and not something heavy like lead."

Athena did not want to make an embarrassing public confession in regard to acid rock music. "No Father, I haven't exactly heard the trashy music, but I've *heard about* the rock groups that sing the trashy music," she nervously stammered.

"Please forgive my obnoxious daughter, Hephaestus," Zeus commiserated. "Please continue with your irrelevant, er, I mean informative presentation. But make it short and sweet. I feel a triple migraine and an upset stomach coming on."

"These irascible humans, King Zeus," the charcoal-skinned god commented, "they use metal wires to send messages and information around the world at the speed of light. They have developed alloys it would take my overworked staff, consisting of three imbeciles and two morons, a million years to duplicate. The mortals' initiative is dauntless and relentless. No obstacle seems to thwart or handicap them," the crippled god regretted.

"Is there no hope?" Hera asked. "Have we been demoted to incompetent victims? Minor actors in a bad theatrical play?"

"Our only hope," the blacksmith god said, "is that the pollution from the numerous industrial smokestacks disrupt the precious atmosphere the humans have to breathe. Already they've created a deleterious 'greenhouse effect' that is warming the seasons and quickly melting the polar ice caps. Cities will be deluged from rising oceans and seas by the time the next Council meeting convenes. That is the only cheerful news I can presently relate."

"You've done an exceptionally admirable job Hephaestus against very staggering odds," Zeus commended. "Keep things under surveillance. At our next banquet we can celebrate our ultimate victory over those repugnant mortal overachievers. My will shall be vindicated!" Zeus prophetically bellowed.

"When are we gonna' eat?" Athena restlessly asked. "I'm getting tired of nectar and ambrosia all the time. I wanna' have some custard, hot dogs, French fries, pizza, popcorn and enchiladas for a change."

"My neurotic Daughter," Zeus answered, "you're beginning to be corrupted by those despicable land beings. You're enunciation is grotesque and quite atrocious if I may add."

"Sorry Daddy, but I wanted to *chow down* before I *chill out*! Get it, Amigo?"

The rest of the Council members cringed down in their seats at Athena's blatant defiance to her almighty father's assumed authority. No one dared to utter a word.

"My dear misguided Daughter," Zeus petulantly chided, "please do not embarrass me in front of our extended family. And for *your* information, we shall feast right after our meeting. And it's gonna' be nectar and ambrosia instead of pizza and burgers, and the music is gonna' be flutes and harps instead of Guns n' Roses and the Beach Boys, ya' dig baby!" Zeus yelled in mock imitation of his offspring's jazzed-up lingo.

Zeus's mental equilibrium had also been intimidated by a "political invention" of modern-day man commonly called "Constitutional Democracy." The practice of freedom had made men enterprising, individualistic and independent. Liberty automatically fomented disrespect for monarchy, for autocracy, for aristocracy, for dictatorship and for ancient gods.

"Fellow gods," Zeus said and lamented, "who would have thought that such fantastic achievements could have blossomed from man's feeble and humble origin? These crazy bizarre men have demonstrated tenacity and stubbornness that we all should fear. They thrive on continuous catastrophe and adversity. They welcome tragedy. I have created monsters down on Earth, a menace far worse than all the minotaurs, gorgons, centaurs, cyclops and Titans put together!"

As weary Hephaestus and playboy Apollo began to doze off, Zeus expounded on his cynical observations. The King-god eloquently explained that his spirit had become fatigued from lack of human worship. "I need sacrifices, lots and lots of sacrifices to bolster my deflated ego," he confessed and confided. "Apollo, are you ready to speak to the Council?"

Poseidon gave Apollo a sharp nudge to the ribs with his tarnished bronze trident. The god of music and medicine blinked his eyes, and then he banged into Hephaestus, waking him up also. Apollo awkwardly stood to give the Council his disclosure.

"The past fifty years Ares and I have collaborated in furtively assisting the humans in their deployment of nuclear weapons," the sun god assertively admitted. "Several atomic bombs have already been dropped on Japanese cities. I foresee a massive global debacle is looming on the horizon."

"How do you know this?" Hera asked. "From your famous *Oracle at Delphi*?"

"No Your Majesty, I went to see a tarot card reader at a rural carnival in upstate New York," Apollo answered.

"Were you on official Olympian business in New York?" Zeus stormed. "I don't want my treasury paying for unnecessary expensive side trips!"

"Why certainly, King Zeus," Apollo apologized. "You all know how I love music and how music is in *my* jurisdiction and in my realm of expertise. Well, I was attending an important concert at the *Apollo Theater* in Harlem and that's how I wound-up at the tarot reading in upper New York State."

"Well all right," Zeus grumbled, "your excuse is a valid one. Proceed with your talk but make it as brief as possible."

"Ares and I had caused a terrible explosion to happen in Russia at Chernobyl, and we had orchestrated a near miss at the Three Mile Island's atomic energy plant in Pennsylvania,"

Apollo proudly informed the Council. "But then clever American scientists figured out our in-genius subterfuge at the last minute and thus averted a nuclear meltdown."

"Wow!" exclaimed Athena. "That big explosion would have been *dynamite*!"

"Child, stop your repulsive stupid harping!" Zeus thundered.

"I don't play the harp but I want Keith Richards to teach me the electric guitar," Athena answered. "I really like the way he moves his fingers."

"Forgive my reckless daughter's impulsiveness, Apollo," the Chairman of the Council counseled. "As you can plainly observe she's going through the rebellion phase of teenage maturation."

"Anyway Lord Zeus," totally unfazed Apollo conscientiously proceeded, "nuclear arsenals are presently being accumulated in many *Third World* countries. Being the sun god, I have learned all about fission and fusion and their horrific destructive consequences. Worldwide detonations of hydrogen and atomic bombs will bring about an unimaginable nuclear holocaust. When the radiation fallout gradually clears, the Earth, or what's left of it, will be *ours* to govern over again."

"Bravo," Zeus loudly applauded as the other Olympians politely clapped their hands. "Now Ares, please give us *your* thoughts and general strategies."

"I support Apollo's convictions about the future demise of those feckless Homo sapiens," Ares concurred. "Our star will rise from the ashes of destroyed human civilization like the legendary Phoenix. Man has authored his own self-destruction. His societies will be obliterated by military science's awesome advanced weaponry. Those unfortunate individuals that survive will be relegated to slaves designated to serve us."

The appreciative Council members warmly applauded Ares' encouraging speech. The Olympians were finally organized in a dedicated crusade against their chief nemeses.

Ares then told of his specialty, arranging invasions and revolutions through the power of mental suggestion. When men saw other men involved in carnage, they would become influenced by their observation and then mimic the heinous deeds. According to Ares, men were "stupid chimpanzees" who instinctively imitate one another, so once one major nation attacks another world power, the whole planet will be doomed to disaster by "the basic deployment of man's propensity for duplication and retaliation."

"Ares, your arguments make much sense and are most persuasive," Zeus acknowledged. "These devilish humans behave like hyperactive monkeys all because of some fellow named Darwin, who taught them that they actually came from monkeys. It makes a lot of sense doesn't it, 'monkey-see, monkey-do'? And it would make a whole lot more sense if I hadn't created the dangerous species in the first place!"

"Yes my Lord," Ares acceded, "and Apollo and I have used suggestion and persuasion to cause a number of brutal battles in the last hundred years. *World War I*, *World War II*, the *Vietnam War*, the *Korean War*, the *Gulf War*, need I identify more international conflicts? We've been very busy this last century."

Aphrodite, goddess of beauty, was the next speaker slated on Zeus's agenda. Her external enchantment disguised the cunning that dwelt deep inside her scheming heart. The skilled mistress of deceit claimed that she had been concentrating her efforts on decaying the morals of men, women and children. She desired to cripple human emotions, just like her grotesque-looking husband Hephaestus ironically had been crippled physically.

"I shall continue to debilitate humanity with my secret stealth," Aphrodite predicted.

"You're always coming-up with lame ideas," Athena annoyingly criticized.

"Malice and slander will dominate the vile creatures," Aphrodite uttered while ignoring Athena's annoying juvenile prattle. "With the help of my loyal associate Eros, prostitution, homosexuality and pornography are rapidly proliferating."

"Now you're talkin'!" Apollo hollered a little too-loudly without realizing his subconscious fascinations or his sudden impact on the other assembled gods.

Aphrodite stated that she relied heavily on the primitive instincts that often guided the mortals' compulsive behaviors. She claimed that first she affects their "lower minds" with erotic fantasies. Then she "mesmerizes their vulnerable senses with passion. "Perverting the species is very simple once you utilize those very effective methods," the goddess of love and beauty professed and related.

"Bravo, bravo!" Zeus raved. "Tell us more. I'm actually getting aroused by your vivid descriptions."

"The sight of a lady's ankle would be enough to arouse my husband," Hera laughed. "He's easily influenced by even the most casual of suggestions."

"Forget the ego! Eros and I focus on stimulating the libido," Aphrodite continued. "We've also done a lot to lower the world's population by promoting gay rights and gay conventions. Homosexuality, when you think about is, is really a form of sterility. Eros and I look at it as a method of birth control. Gays don't reproduce by natural means. And so," Aphrodite editorialized, "homosexuality is good for the rule of *Olympus* because fewer humans on the planet translates into less headaches for the gods!"

"Thank you lovely Aphrodite, thank you very much for your valuable insights. And it all started on our wonderful Greek isle of Lesbos!" Zeus observed and reminded his colleagues. "Now let's hear some intoxicating remarks from our cohort Dionysus, our usually intoxicated god of wine and merriment."

"Thank you my Lord Zeus for your splendid introduction," Dionysus slurred in a drunken tone. The erratic god held a golden goblet of red wine, which he drank from between rambling sentence stutters and mumbles. Dionysus wobbled back and forth from right leg to left to right again, staggering, slurring and blubbering his way through his comical oration.

"Fellow Olympians," my *back is* killing me," the zany fool said. Everyone at the meeting hooted and hollered in response to the egregiously ludicrous pun. "I'm happy to report that over twenty percent of the Earth's doomed population can be classified as chronic alcoholics," Dionysus hiccuped. "Half the soldiers in the Russian Army are hooked on phonics, er, I mean vodka. And recently I have diversified my clandestine activity into drug addiction. Marijuana, cocaine, heroin, opium and morphine are in plenteous supply all over the blasted planet," sputtered the tottering Dionysus. "The world is becomin' sicker by the minute, thanks to little old me and heroin."

"What's wrong with a *little* heroin?" Zeus challenged.

"Nothin' at all," the crocked wine god answered and then loudly burped. "Now Joan of Arc, that was a little heroine."

Everyone seated around the table laughed incessantly, even Zeus upon his elevated golden throne. Dionysus belched twice and then he adroitly imbibed another serious mouthful of "vino."

"Drug addicts need lots of money to feed their lousy habit," Dionysus informed the Council. "They gotta' commit crimes like robberies, thefts, looting and burglaries just to keep their' habit goin'. My powerful drugs and alcohol schemes have guaranteed the future of anarchy and the future of chaos, I'm quite happy to report."

"Dionysus, quit your *whining,*" Athena laughed. "Your cup spilleth over!"

Dionysus burped again, quite loudly. "How would you like if I came to your side of the table and my throat suddenly made your nice yellow and purple tunic partially burgundy," the absurd drunken god threatened.

"Now, now! We don't need any additional embellishment from you Dionysus!" Zeus exhorted, standing and waving his hands in the air to subdue the boisterous laughter prevalent in the sacred chamber. When order was finally restored, Dionysus resumed his extemporaneous discourse.

"All I gotta' say Lord Zeus is that almost as many people are addicted to and killed by legal pharmacy prescription drugs than are eliminated by illegal drugs," the perpetuator of festive occasions divulged. "I have nothin' more to say except what modern day sailors yell when they enter their submarines. Down the hatch!" Dionysus enthusiastically exclaimed as he swallowed the remainder of his delicious wine.

Hades, morbid god of death, was the next speaker slated to expound at the royal symposium. The pallid-faced king of the afterlife had sunken gray eyes and colorless lips that magnified his gloomy personality. Hades addressed the Council in his familiar macabre, miserable, wretched voice. Several of the gods began squirming on their velvet cushions in response to hearing his haunting monotone.

"The bright reflections in this Council chamber hurt my eyes," Hades said, "so I'll try to abbreviate my remarks."

"You're finally seeing the light!" Athena blurted out without heed or discretion.

"Silence Daughter!" Zeus shouted. "Any more uncouth outbursts from you and I'll see to it that my brother Hades gives you a hundred year tour of his subterranean kingdom. Now dear Brother, you may continue your evaluation of current events."

"It is good to get away from my drab home once in a while," Hades observed and shared. "Immortality can be a very boring and tedious thing when you happen to be the eternal custodian of the dead. Like you, King Zeus, I too am concerned about the brash mortals studying the *DNA* molecule, whatever the Hades that is! If man learns immortality, it would put me completely out of business. On the other side of the coin, my death business is prospering. My kingdom Hades itself is overcrowded."

"How do you now transport the ever-increasing multitude of deceased souls to Hades?" Ares asked. "Do you now have mass transportation?"

"Loyal Charon and his employees currently operate a fleet of twenty-four motorized barges to ferry souls across *River Styx* from the world of the living over to the abysmal catacombs of Elysium," Hades explained.

"Wow! If I visit you in Hades dear Uncle, can I get to meet the Grateful Dead?" Athena adolescently asked. "I've heard all about Jerry Garcia."

"Athena!" Zeus un-affectionately yelled. "I'm warning you for the last time. Interrupt Hades once more and you're outa' here and grounded, meaning that you'll no longer be permitted to fly for five Earth years. During that period I'll send you down to the dark Underworld without a skeleton key to get out!"

"I was wondering," Hera revealed to get her husband's mind off of disciplining Athena, "are Al Capone and Frank Nitty in Hades? They were pretty big *underworld* figures when they were alive, weren't they?"

"Hera, sometimes you're worse than Athena when it comes to making and vociferating total nonsense," Zeus loquaciously corrected. "Stop making a travesty out of my dignified conclave! Now please continue, my dear Brother before lightning strikes twice, once at Hera and the second time at Athena."

"Thank you for re-establishing order," Hades assented. "We recently had to make extensive additions to the Elysium sector. Ten thousand new acres of daffodils had to be planted to accommodate the ghosts of the happy dead," the death god declared in his dismal listless voice.

"Athena would ask you if there are any '70s Flower Children resting there in Elysium, but since she is not allowed to talk I'll exercise my franchise at this forum and ask the question for her," Hera stated with a weak smile.

"Yes there are," Hades admitted, "and most of them that attended the Woodstock concert are already dead from drugs and from alcohol abuse. Now those mentally deranged hippies can frolic or sleep with Elvis, John Lennon, Otis Redding and Frank Sinatra just about any time they like. I'm still trying to figure out that Otis Redding fellow. He doesn't do anything except keep sitting at the dock of the Styx."

"Well then," Zeus wondered out loud, "what about the Area of Atonement? Is that district still being utilized effectively? It's probably filled to capacity."

Hades reported that the Area of Atonement was where the most rapid growth was taking place. The punishment zone had to be quadrupled in size to accommodate the billions of souls that required purification by fire. The god of death informed the Council that a dozen new tunnels had to be burrowed deep into the Earth's mantle during the last century. "This accommodation problem is expanding exponentially," Hades lamented to his peers. "It's all quite ironic when one takes the time to analyze it. The more immorality that thrives on Earth, the greater the Area of Atonement must become. The more sinful mankind becomes, the more exhaustive my labor and responsibility," the melancholy Hades acknowledged. "That guy Hitler set me back a full century. If the earthlings have any new incidences of mass genocide and world destruction on the horizon, a tremendous nightmare would ensue. I'll be backlogged for the next hundred million years."

"That's perfectly all right," Zeus replied. "You have the resolve to handle it. But tell me Brother, what about Tantalus and that deviate Sisyphus? Are they still down there atoning?"

"Indeed they are," Hades attested, "but they have filed grievances along with another dissident soul named Lazarus of Israel. They're all complaining about the lowlife spirits from the Woodstock generation partying all the time and listening to loud music and they think my administration must terminate it," Hades related. "Tantalus still stands hungry while chained in his pool being tantalized by overhead fruit. When he bends down, the water filters out of the tub. When he reaches for a banana or an apple, it disappears from sight. I believe that Hephaestus did a great job designing *that* particular punishment."

"How about my favorite soul, poor Sisyphus?" Hera wanted to know. "Is the poor spirit still engaged in performing his eternal punishment?"

"Truculent Sisyphus still must roll his huge boulder up the steep inclined plane for all eternity. After it tumbles down from the force of gravity," Hades said, "old Sisyphus must repeat his monotonous task over and over again until the end of infinity. As you all are well aware, the impudent fool had surrendered his free will when he died."

"Wow!" Athena howled. "I wonder if Mick Jagger knows that Sisyphus was *the first* Rolling Stone? That might have been the real beginning of rock and roll!"

"Athena, I can't tolerate any more of your inane juvenile quips!" Zeus stormed. "Now go to your palace immediately. And don't listen to any of your repugnant Elvis or Buddy Holly music tapes or call Ethiopia long distance and talk to Artemis's friends on the telephone. Your long distance calls are putting a strain on my royal treasury! Now get along dear, or I *will* place you into Hades' exclusive custody!" Zeus boomed.

Athena stood up, curtsied mockingly to her parents and as she left the splendid Council Chamber the girl yelled out to her father, "You Ain't Nothin' But a Hound Dog!"

Zeus shook his head in total dismay. "It's a good thing my immature daughter is only allowed to listen to dead artists' music," the troubled King God qualified. "When the punk rockers, the hip hoppers and the rappers start to die off in large numbers, I'm going to need a new set of eardrums. This rock and roll music is corrupting Athena's morals and making me want to abdicate my throne," Zeus bitterly grieved, momentarily losing his train of thought. "Now where were we? Oh yes, finish up my dear Brother."

"You're absolutely right in your assessment of the younger generation, King Zeus," Hades agreed with a lugubrious expression on his visage. "These horrendous humans have the mental appetites of miniature gods. Could you imagine what would happen if they all were fifty foot tall like us? There would be no Earth left to burrow tunnels into!"

"What about your expense budget?" Zeus inquired. "Are you staying within *our* guidelines?"

"Well, let me tell you my Lord," Hades stated with his cold metallic gray eyes focused on his almighty brother. "The bookkeeping has become a major mammoth problem. I'm just getting computerized and I do have two intelligent spirits named Newton and Einstein helping me to become more organized. Unfortunately the task at hand is quite overwhelming and formidable."

"Enough of your myriad difficulties," Zeus insisted. "What about your successes?"

"On the other side of the ledger," Hades declared, "I've discovered many neat new ways to cause the phenomenon the human's call death." The underworld god then admirably differentiated between new methods of accidental death and new techniques of suicide and other forms of deliberate deaths. "Many of these lackluster mortals have a low tolerance for emotional anguish. They lack coping skills, become easily frustrated, and then go out and spontaneously kill others before they terminate themselves," Hades reported to the Council. "They now call these types of executions 'going postal.' The death business is booming, even much better than the cannon business ever was," Hades finished.

Zeus finally slowly stood from his ornate throne to provide his assessment of the past hundred years. His sixty-foot-tall form towered over the others still seated at the resplendent marble gold, and emerald table trimmed in various shiny jewels.

"I must admit," Zeus sincerely summarized, "my soul still craves tribute from the humble creatures I had molded out of mud and dust for *our* benefit. But regrettably. man's science has been a terrible threat to the gods. Let it now be a vicious curse to the mortals!"

The Council delegates cheered and shouted accolades at their arrogant leader and mentor. The King-god held his hands high above his regal head for quiet.

"When I had Pandora's Box constructed," Zeus prefaced, "I filled it with hate, famine, war, disease, pestilence, despair and death, all specifically designed to encumber the mortals. I beg your forgiveness for also placing the gift of *hope* into that historic chest. *That* foolish act constituted a pretty large mistake on my part."

"Your daughter Athena calls Pandora's Box a *hope chest*," Hera flamboyantly cackled.

"Wife, let me finish my solemn speech and then we'll have time to feast and gossip," Zeus mildly reprimanded. "I must congratulate all of you for I have found *your* illustrious presentations most illuminating. I promise you that we Olympians shall again have dominion over what is rightfully ours, over what I have unselfishly created."

Zeus went on to explain to his Olympic family that the materialistic world the earthlings had built was too complex for even the gods to comprehend. "Things were much easier to understand in the good old days when Jason, Perseus and Odysseus roamed the Earth. All we had to govern over then was land, wind, fire, water, sky, monsters and mortals," the King-god nostalgically recalled.

The Sky-god culminated his concluding remarks by saying that mortals had besieged the Olympians with too many inventions and discoveries. The Lord-god Zeus had created all the electrons, protons, neutrons and atoms without even bothering to name them. But the upstart "scurrilous mortals" had analyzed and changed those same atoms and molecules by reorganizing them into amazing compounds that confound even the advanced reasoning of the now-threatened immortal gods.

"My fellow gods and goddesses," Zeus continued, "robots, androids, radioactivity, dynamite, nuclear bombs, laser beams, telecommunications, credit cards, it's all just too mind-boggling! And add to *those* complex creations ideas like capitalism, socialism, communism, democracy, science, technology and rock and roll music, and suddenly our former simple pastoral lives have become all too wickedly complicated. Science has become the mortal's new god, and I don't relish that abomination one iota!"

The other Olympians enthusiastically applauded Zeus's perceptive observations. The King-god thought it most appropriate to dismiss the parley on a more positive note. "My Loyal Family, I must commend all of you for your dedication to my supreme authority. I personally cherish your superlative labors and your steadfast faithfulness. The next great upheaval is most certainly within our grasp," Zeus emphasized as he dramatically raised his two clenched fists to chest level. Then the Chief-deity delivered his final comment.

"Let our greatest opportunity not slip away into the clutches of infinity. We must initiate a violent counter-revolution. I officially adjourn this Council until July 1, 2100," the Sky-lord thundered with new-found hope and energy.

"Immoral Immortality"

The four *Rowan University* professors were returning south to Glassboro from a teacher union seminar given at the *College of New Jersey* in Trenton. While traveling south on *Route 73* near the town of Berlin, Henry Chapman, a U.S. History and Political Science instructor suggested that he and his colleagues should stop for an early supper.

"Good idea Hank," Lester Schaffer agreed. "My stomach's growling as if there's a bear inside. I'm so hungry I could eat a moose. Well, a chocolate mousse, anyway," the zany Mathematics Professor declared.

"You're the driver Hank," Vince Olivo, a distinguished-looking Grammar and Writing authority chimed-in from the back seat. "I'll have to venture anywhere your discretion takes us."

"The Pallas Diner is two miles up ahead at the Berlin Circle," suggested Anotal Suez, a widely acclaimed *Rowan* Music Professor sitting next to Dr. Olivo. "It's got a decent reputation for steaks and seafood at affordable prices along with a variety of other terrific dishes on its menu."

"How come it's not called the Palace Diner instead of Pallas Diner?" Les Schaffer reflexively asked. "Is that some sort of discrepancy?"

"Because the owner is a Greek and named his establishment after Pallas Athene, goddess and protector of Athens way back in the glory days of antiquity," Anotal confidently explained. "The Parthenon up on the Acropolis was constructed during the Golden Age of ancient Greece. The architecture's inspiration was the impeccable goddess Pallas Athene."

"How do you know so much minutia outside the realm of music?" Hank Chapman asked his acquaintance. "I have trouble remembering the generals at Bull Run, Gettysburg, Vicksburg and Antietam. And the south won at the first battle of Bull Run because the northern army was *as slow as Manassas,*" the effervescent history professor jested while deftly implementing a rather clever play-on-words.

"I'll have to remember that one the next time I pour some molasses on my pancakes," Vince Olivo indulgently laughed. "Hank, your foolish sense of levity is sometimes wittingly senseless!"

"Say Anotal, I'm with Hank about you," Les Schaffer humorously interrupted. "You seem to know a lot of academic trivia outside your field of knowledge for a fellow that was named after an important strategic canal! Could you expand on how you know so much data that isn't related to music?"

"Oh, I do plenty of reading in my spare time," Dr. Suez readily replied. "I'm an expert on virtually everything and an authority on almost anything that's purely academic. I am especially well-versed in medicine, poetry and in astronomy, particularly our nearest star the sun, which has always fascinated me," Anotal immodestly added.

"Hey Hank, there's Pallas Diner halfway around the circle!" Les Schaffer indicated from the front seat passenger side. "It's time to feed our faces!"

The driver pulled into the restaurant's recently resurfaced parking lot. Chapman stopped his aqua Honda sedan between two parallel lines and the four men got out of the reliable vehicle. The honorable gentlemen ascended the classy diner's marble steps and Les Schaffer opened the glass door leading into the foyer. A beautiful marble statue guarded the eating establishment's front entrance.

"Wow, a magnificent statue of Venus!" Hank Chapman exclaimed. "She's a real beauty even in this crazy day and age we're living in."

"That's an amateur representation of Aphrodite and not Venus!" Anotal immediately corrected. "Aphrodite was the sacred goddess of beauty in Greek mythology and her counterpart Venus was the Roman substitution for the love deity in *that* culture's religious tradition."

"Well then Anotal, who is that marble figure standing over there in the other corner of the vestibule?" Hank innocently asked.

"That's certainly a mold-cast model of Athene, but in Roman mythology her counterpart would be Minerva," Dr. Suez lectured without the aid of a lectern. "Unfortunately, today the Roman names are much more popular than the original Greek identities."

"Suez my friend, you probably don't realize it," Vince Olivo courteously stated, "but you speak of these defunct deities as if they're your close acquaintances. If you can get me a date with either Aphrodite or Athene and not their dusty skeletons or their marble statues, I'd be much obliged!" the confirmed bachelor said with a broad smile.

A pretty brunette hostess showed the four new arrivals to an empty booth, and after studying the menu and ordering "a late lunch," the professors began discussing the boring seminar on retirement investment options and health care benefits they had recently attended. Soon however the conversation switched to political science, Hank Chapman's forte.

"Tell me Anotal," the gadfly history researcher implored, "what would Socrates and Plato have to say about boring union seminars and about white marble statues of scantily clad Greek goddesses adorning diner foyers? I understand that both critics despised bureaucracy and female nudity too!"

"Socrates and Plato were both stupid imbeciles that didn't have a clue about the topic of excellence, about feminine beauty or about true wisdom," Anotal emphatically professed. "Mediocrity was *their* watchword even when Plato and his mentor Socrates challenged the shallow hypocrisy of the sophists."

"Anotal, you speak of Socrates and Plato as if the sages were both your personal adversaries," Lester Schaffer marveled and questioned. "How could you condemn their great contributions to *Western Civilization?* Are you speaking from envy or jealousy? Why do you have so much contempt for them? Have you no respect for the dead?"

"Those two clowns were absolute idiots!" Professor Anotal Suez stubbornly maintained. "I have read Plato's *Republic* numerous times and also diligently studied the moronic Platonic Dialogues where Plato attempts to celebrate his contemporary Socrates as a heroic benefactor of philosophy. Plato's poor writings and Socrates' foolish speeches are all a bunch of rubbish, plain and simple!"

"How could you possibly make such an unwarranted assertion?" Vince Olivo aggressively challenged. "Surely Anotal you must be making light of the two eminent founders of certain academic disciplines. Anotal, are you acquainted with a scholar at our university named Daphne Agora?"

"The attractive Ancient History instructor with the conceited attitude?" Dr. Suez answered.

"Yes," Professor Olivo confirmed. "She could defend Plato and Socrates to the hilt and make mincemeat out of your inane generalizations and criticisms."

"And I'll wager a hundred dollars that you Dr. Suez couldn't even manage to get an ice cream parlor date with the gorgeous prudish woman," Les Schaffer chimed in. "The two of you would hardly be compatible according to any zodiac combination matching I know of. And besides that, Daphne Agora might be a lesbian!"

"I'll also wager a cool hundred dollars," Hank Chapman enthusiastically offered. "What about you Vince? Want to make some easy money?"

The English Rhetoric Professor contemplated the temptation and then vociferated, "I'll also gamble a hundred bucks. That's three hundred saying that Anotal couldn't get to first base with the enchanting Dr. Daphne Agora."

"Okay foolish gentlemen, I wholeheartedly accept your daunting proposal," Dr. Suez very seriously mentioned. "I'll effortlessly sweep the defiant woman right off her dainty feet with my magical charm."

"It's a deal!" Hank Chapman indulgently laughed. "It's such a fabulous consideration. Anotal Suez doomed to failure! How funny can it get? Ha, ha, ha!"

After the four fatigued men's dinners had been served, the conversation next focused on the nature of the universe and then to analogous historical events. Hank Chapman was responsible for generating most of the radical topic transitions.

"Speaking of ancient mythology," the history and political science professor prefaced, "the zodiac constellations are named after legendary heroes and various creatures from ancient civilizations. But science has replaced astrology as the fundamental basis for understanding the complex nature of our galaxy and the functioning of the universe itself'."

"To a certain extent," Anotal instantly disagreed. "For what the ancients lacked in knowledge they more than made up for in wisdom."

"I thought *you* had just insisted that Plato and Socrates were total jerks, and now you're defending the ancients as great benefactors to modern science and civilization!" Vince Olivo pointed out to Dr. Suez. "I think your statements Anotal are both contradictory and ambivalent. Wouldn't you agree with my plausible assessment?"

"When I had alluded to the ancients," Anotal defensively responded, "I was referring to the ideals endorsed by ancient immortal Greek gods and not to the vanities of immoral men. The Olympian gods epitomized the pursuit of perfection whereas *our decadent age* encourages the pursuit of happiness. That is the essential distinction between then and now. Poseidon, Hades, Zeus, Hermes and the rest of the Olympians all sought achievement and explored glory in their own impeccable ways."

"But man's modern technology has given us computers, cable television and fantastic automobiles," Les Schaffer effectively argued. "How could the Greek gods ever have contemplated such brilliant innovations? The Greeks fabricated their gods in man's image!"

"What you speak of Lester is emblematic of mere knowledge and has little connection with actual wisdom," Anotal maintained. "Man still has the blight of war, new grotesque diseases, animosity towards his neighbors and every other negative thing that originally flew out of *Pandora's Box.* Little has changed over the past thirty centuries in the area of human wisdom. All man has learned how to do is manipulate his environment through inventions and knowledge while he has neglected the advancement of what I call 'genuine behavioral progress.' My colleagues, that is the essential difference between then and now!"

Hank, Les and Vince respected their eccentric colleague's very obvious mental capabilities and were in awe of his wild outlandish comments. Several years before their present exchange Anotal had warned his associates to avoid attending a North Jersey union conclave. The event had been scheduled to take place at *Paterson State University* on September 11th, 2001. The three skeptics had not heeded Dr. Suez's sage advice and were caught in massive traffic jams on the *Garden State Parkway* and on the *New Jersey Turnpike* all the way from Wayne to Glassboro.

And then once when Hank Chapman had called Dr. Suez "a soothsayer" he had demanded that "the prophet" provide proof by auguring the outcomes of certain forthcoming sports events. Anotal had accurately predicted the participants, the scores and the victors in the 2001 World Series a full three months ahead of time. The three suspicious professors discredited Anotal's exceptional ability and called the apparent uncanny phenomenon "bizarre coincidences," "demonstrable psychic voodoo" and "amazing and lucky clairvoyant feats." Soon dessert was served and the rejuvenated men rekindled their stimulating intellectual discourse.

"I believe that the universe is made up of integrated mathematical truths," Lester Schaffer attested. "Remember when

Anotal claimed that something unexpected would occur on *9-11* and then hit the identity of the 2001 *World Series'* champions right on the head, well it is my contention that everything happens as part of some inexplicable arithmetical formula. We only see bits and pieces of the colossal puzzle but ignore all of the prominent factors in the complicated given equation."

"Please Les, would you mind explaining yourself less vaguely without putting your wide foot inside your big fat mouth?" Hank Chapman requested. "You tend to be quite nebulous at times."

"Okay Hank, *9-11* occurred on September 11th. 9 plus 1 plus 1 equals eleven. September 11th was the 254th day of 2001. 2 plus 5 plus 4 comes out to eleven," the mathematics instructor seriously disclosed. "New York City has eleven letters and so does the words *The Pentagon*. New York was the eleventh state admitted to the new democracy. The *Twin Towers* were vertical parallel skyscrapers that stood side by side forming the number 11. Afghanistan is a word composed of eleven letters. Ninety-two passengers were aboard Flight 11. Nine plus two amounts to 11, and sixty-five victims were traveling on Flight 77. Six plus five is equivalent to eleven. Do you cynical gentlemen now see the merits of my universal mathematical hypothesis?"

"Yes, quite astounding when you consider all of the unique circumstances," Vincent Olivo concurred as he performed a simple mathematical procedure on a Pallas Diner napkin. "And after September 11th there were an additional 111 days left in the calendar year. I do believe you have something relevant there Dr. Schaffer."

Professor Hank Chapman figured that he could contribute significant evidence from history to substantiate Lester Schaffer's remarkable arithmetical claim. "What about the Kennedy and Lincoln assassinations?" he asked the other intrigued informal forum members.

"Well Hank, what about the comparable items concerning the dual historical tragedies?" the mathematics guru questioned his social science associate. "What are the basic outstanding similarities?"

"Well, Lincoln was elected to Congress in 1846 and Kennedy exactly a hundred years later in 1946," the social studies expert maintained. "Abraham Lincoln was elected President in 1860 and a century later John F. Kennedy was elected to the highest office in 1960. Both men were shot on Fridays and both Presidents' wives lost a child while living in the *White House*.

Lincoln had a secretary named Kennedy and Kennedy had a secretary named Lincoln. And Lincoln was shot inside the Ford Theatre in downtown Washington and Kennedy was riding in an open Lincoln in Dallas when he was assassinated. As you know, Lincolns are made by the Ford Motor Company."

"Wow!" Vincent Olivo exclaimed. "And both Presidents were shot in the back of the head while their grieving wives witnessed the abominable acts taking place. There evidently are many incredible coincidences!"

"And don't forget the vital mathematical aspects," Lester Schaffer insisted as he attempted bringing the debate back to objectivity. "Both assassins had *three* names, John Wilkes Booth and Lee Harvey Oswald and both Booth and Oswald were each killed before ever being convicted of political murder in a government trial."

"And don't forget other historical parallels," Professor Chapman reminded his attentive listeners. "Lincoln was shot in a theater and fled to a warehouse and Kennedy was shot from a warehouse and then Oswald cowardly sought shelter and escape in a theater. And in addition," the history authority excitedly elaborated, "Abraham Lincoln's successor was Andrew Johnson born in 1808 and John Fitzgerald Kennedy's replacement was Lyndon Baines Johnson, who entered this very violent and confusing world in 1908. Say Anotal, you've been mighty quiet during this most compelling dialogue. What do you think about all of these incredible relative facts and statistics?"

"My intuition dictates to my consciousness that there is extraordinary profound truth in Professor Schaffer's arithmetical theory," the sly maverick and sometimes aloof pedagogue concluded and enunciated.

"Give us some justification of your claim!" an adamant Les Schaffer demanded of the inimitable Anotal Suez. "As a dedicated mathematician I need to have valid and reliable quantitative proof!"

"Okay Lester, if you insist," Anotal casually acceded. "Here's a bona fide hundred dollar bill. Go alone this evening to Bally's Casino and step up the aisle to the seventh roulette wheel on the left from the boardwalk entrance. Do not play any rows or wager on black or red numbers. Instead buy and put a one hundred dollar chip down on number nine and then parlay your winnings onto number eleven. See what happens and then report back to me."

"You gotta' be kiddin'!" Dr. Schaffer politely objected. "Why should I waste a silly trip to Atlantic City and squander your hard earned money in a dumb spin of a roulette wheel. It just defies logic and reason. It goes drastically against the most extreme odds! Now I think you've absolutely fallen off your rickety rocker!"

"Could Lester have an objective Atlantic City eyewitness?" Vince Olivo pleaded. "I'll be glad to accompany him on this most peculiar enterprise."

"Count me in too!" Hank Chapman energetically volunteered. "I can't wait to prove you wrong Anotal! You've really painted yourself into a precarious corner this time!"

"Why most certainly!" Professor Suez cooperatively acquiesced. "Three dumbfounded fools are much better than one. But remember gentlemen, after Hank drops me off at my place tonight, the three of you agnostics will have to travel with dispatch to Bally's Casino to conduct your field experiment in advanced celestial mathematics. Now let's pay our bills and exit this majestic marble and tile eatery."

At 10:30 that night Anotal Suez was watching a *History Channel* cable special about the battle of Thermopylae where three hundred courageous Spartans led by King Leonidas admirably held off a vital "hot springs" pass from the Persian Immortals under the dominion of King Xerxes. 'They don't make warriors like those three hundred valiant Spartans anymore,' the *Rowan University* professor decided. 'I don't know why Ares didn't directly interfere with the outcome of that particular engagement. The outnumbered Spartans had a philosophy that if they didn't come home victorious carrying their shields, then the defeated soldiers had to be transported back to Sparta dead on their shields. How wonderfully noble and worthy of praise their fighting spirit was!'

Just as the Spartans were about to be showered by a plethora of Persian arrows on the television screen, Dr. Suez's telephone rang. The euphoric caller was none other than Professor Lester Schaffer.

"Calm down Les so that I can comprehend what you're saying," Anotal recommended. "Now please tell me in a rational plausible manner exactly what has made you so utterly exhilarated."

"Anotal, everything at Bally's happened just as you had crazily prophesied," the math wiz began. "I played nine and won big and then parlayed the total on eleven. Everyone at the wheel including the croupier thought that I was insane, even Vince and Hank," the caller panted. "And when the spinning ball landed squarely on number eleven, all of their mouths were agape. The pit boss came over with an astonished look on his face wondering how I had performed the mathematical impossibility. And then fifteen minutes later he very reluctantly handed me a crisp new check in the outrageous amount of $125,500.00."

"What are the odds of doing it once?" Dr. Suez patiently asked.

"Thirty-five to one!" Les exclaimed. "But to achieve those formidable odds twice in a row on two different numbers is virtually astronomical in magnitude. I wish I had the entire event filmed on video. I would show it over and over again until the tape broke."

"And what are you going to do with your prodigious winnings?" Anotal calmly inquired. "Donate the money to your favorite charity?"

"No Sir! I've decided to split the proceeds four ways among you, Vince, Hank and myself'. I could use a new car with my trade-in and then have enough left to underwrite a Vegas vacation."

"Thanks for your kind and generous endowment!" the music professor matter-of-factly acknowledged. "But Les, I want you to know that I overcame even greater odds than you did tonight at Bally's."

"Could you identify exactly what you are describing," Dr. Schaffer requested.

"Why certainly Les. I recently gave Professor Daphne Agora a surprise call after researching and then locating her number in the faculty directory," the classical music connoisseur disclosed. "And guess what? Daphne's consented to going out on a date with me and she thinks I'm rather suave and intelligent."

"Well congratulations Anotal!" Lester boisterously boomed. "That *is* quite remarkable! Where are you taking her?" Schaffer wondered and asked. "She looks like she'd be a little too fussy and way too fastidious for my taste in women."

"To the Philadelphia Zoo," Dr. Suez succinctly replied. "Daphne told me that she loves animals, especially carnivores and reptiles."

"Well dear friend, let me tell you that this has been a most festive and joyous evening for all of us," the caller concluded.

"Thanks again for those terrific mysterious gambling tips. You ought to be a feature on Ripley's *Believe It or Not*! Goodnight now!" Click.

The following Saturday Anotal pulled up to Daphne Agora's Glassboro condominium in his sky-blue 1988 Dodge Aries. The music professor hopped out, ambled up the straight flagstone walkway and rang the appropriate doorbell. After being greeted by his lady date, Daphne locked her front door and the pair stepped to Anotal's vintage automobile. The driver gallantly opened the passenger-side door for his date for the afternoon to enter and gracefully sit down.

"Why do you drive such an old car Professor Suez?" the querulous woman curtly chided. "Surely you could afford either a 2004 Honda or Toyota."

"I'm fascinated by Greek culture and ancient myths," Anotal answered as he turned the key and fired up the ignition. "Ares was the god of war and Aries as in *Dodge Aries* is the zodiac constellation for The Ram. A-r-i-e-s was the closest that I could come to A-r-e-s, so I'm stubbornly keeping this old sluggish dilapidated puddle-jumper until it can no longer mechanically function on the highway!"

"I think you're just fabricating all of those esoteric academic references because you're aware that I'm a professor of Ancient History and now you're vainly trying to score some favor points with me. I'm wise to your unscrupulous devious tactics Anotal Suez, and quite frankly, I'm hardly impressed!"

"Okay, you win Daphne. I was just going to reveal that I am a good acquaintance of Ares, the god of war, but I now see that I can't deceive you in any way. Your reputation among the male faculty members is that you are tough as nails and you're convincingly exhibiting that stellar persona right now. Are you an Aries?" the music prof' coyly asked as he turned left from *322* onto Delsea Drive.

"No, I'm a zodiac Gemini," the pretty-but-haughty woman facetiously answered.

"I see, your birthday is anywhere between May 20th and June 20th. I'm a Leo," Anotal lied.

"That means that you were born between July 22nd and August 22nd," Daphne stated, demonstrating her mastery of astrological time divisions. "Really Dr. Suez, perhaps you shouldn't endeavor dazzling me with your great acumen in legends and myths. Consider changing the subject to another one of your trite venues."

"Okay Dr. Agora, did you know that this highway is appropriately called Delsea Drive because it takes summer vacationers that come from Delaware through Glassboro down to the shore. It goes from Delaware into Glassboro and then down to the sea at Cape May, hence the word Delsea."

"I believe we should return to the topic of the ancient world," Daphne suggested, intentionally showing her familiar haughty contrary side. "I find *that* discipline area much more interesting than hackneyed etymologies."

Anotal turned up the tape player volume, which featured classical renditions of Wagner's "Ride of the Valkyries" and a powerful version of "Thus Spoke Zarathustra." Little Conversation ensued between the polarized pair until the Dodge Aries passed by the architectural splendor of the *Philadelphia Museum of Art* situated on an elevation above the bank of the Schuylkill River.

The driver lowered the volume on the tape player and spoke to his rather apathetic passenger. "The art museum is my favorite building in all of Philadelphia," Anotal divulged. "Its majestic columns are designed and constructed in the tradition of the Athenian Parthenon situated at the summit of the Acropolis. It's the most picturesque setting in all of Philly'!"

"I know, next you're going to tell me all about the vertical Ionic columns and how Greek they look!" Daphne reactively criticized.

"You can't trap me Professor Agora," Dr. Anotal Suez fired back. "I'm not one of your lackluster undergraduate students. Those stately columns are more akin to Doric pillars like the ones on the Parthenon than they are to the standard Ionic design. You must admit that the columns are more Doric than they are either Ionic or Corinthian!"

"Tell me some more trivia about the art museum," Daphne implored in a semi-demanding tone of voice. "You seem to know as much about ancient architecture as I do and I'm a highly qualified Ancient History professor."

"The art museum was founded in the year 1876, but the newer structure we just passed was erected in 1926 to 1928," the driver stated as he skillfully wove his vehicle in and out of heavy Philadelphia highway traffic. "The most wonderful part of the architectural masterpiece is the sculptures of the Greek gods and goddesses on the north side. Phidias himself would be green with envy just observing and admiring them. The museum is quite comparable in exterior design to an ancient Greek temple."

"Very captivating indeed!" Daphne concurred. "And are the appealing sides made of yellow-shaded marble? I never heard of pure yellow marble."

"No, the museum's façade is composed of dolomite that had been delivered all the way from Minnesota," Anotal elucidated. "The total appearance makes the edifice one of the most spectacular architectural wonders in the modern world. It's a tremendous tribute to the nobility and resplendence of the omnipotent Olympian gods."

"Perhaps we should have toured the inspiring art museum instead of visiting the Philadelphia Zoo," Daphne reconsidered. "Your research into the history of the building far supersedes my general knowledge of it. You're beginning to affect my psyche Anotal Suez. Not every man can establish a fluid channel of communication with me. Congratulations for being temporarily successful."

Soon the driver steered the sky-blue Dodge off the crowded *Schuylkill Expressway* down the Girard Avenue exit ramp until he came to 34th Street, the location of the world renowned Philadelphia Zoo. After parking his vintage vehicle, Anotal escorted his finicky date to the ticket booth pavilion, purchased two admissions and then the couple entered the asphalt promenade that spiraled between the various sturdily constructed animal exhibits.

"I simply love it here because the creatures are displayed in simulated natural habitats," Daphne snobbishly opined. "That sort of presentation shows virtual authenticity. The zoo takes all precautions for duplicating environments ranging from tropical jungles to adverse arid deserts. There's almost as much art shown *here* as there is at the art museum."

"Quite brilliantly put my dear Daphne!" Anotal rather impetuously praised. "Now what species do you prefer seeing first? Mammals, Reptiles or Amphibians."

"I think that Mammals would be a very good choice," the sophisticated lady professor declared. "Since *we* are mammals, let's now investigate mammals."

"Well then," Anotal answered, "would you like to see Ungulates, Primates or Carnivores?"

"What are Ungulates?" Daphne asked in a baffled tone of voice.

"They're hoofed animals like zebra, gazelles and horses," her date explained. "Even a rhinoceros is classified as an Ungulate even though it looks more like a Pachyderm."

"I think carnivores would be my first desire," the very discriminating woman replied. "I'm fascinated with tigers, leopards, panthers, lions and bears, as long as I can observe them from a safe area."

The couple was gradually gaining compatibility as Daphne began admiring Anotal's extensive warehouse of infallible facts on just about anything and everything. The pair eagerly toured the Carnivora House, the Bird House, the Primate-Tree-Serve, the Amphibian House and the Pachyderm House. After buying some tasty refreshments from a zoo fast food concession, Daphne preferred viewing the Reptile House next.

"Right after we wolf down our hot dogs and wash down our *Cokes*," her date promised. "Then we'll check out some lizards and snakes." Soon the pair entered the portals of the aforementioned Reptile House.

Walking midway through the magnificent setting, the two touring professors heard shouting and screaming down the aisle, the clamor originating from the other end of the congested chamber. An enormous python had managed to exit its confinement and was harassing and intimidating several frenzied tourists, who were erratically scurrying and evacuating the Reptile House in all imaginable directions.

Without wasting a precious second, Anotal leaped onto the huge reptile's back, and with an exertion of massive strength he intensely squeezed the scaly creature's neck with great dexterity. The snake hissed and twisted, attempting to coil around its antagonist and then constrict its attacker, but in a matter of thirty seconds Anotal had not only strangled the monster to death but had also snapped its neck with the great force exerted by *his* clenched fists and powerful fingers. Everyone that had witnessed the incredible demonstration gasped at the savagery of it all and then warmly applauded the triumphant "beast killer." A confused zoo attendant came over to investigate the cause of the incident.

"Sir, you possibly had just saved someone from being severely crippled or killed," the uniformed man appreciatively said. "The zoo and its staff are deeply indebted to you!"

"Even though the python is regarded as an endangered species," a higher-ranking zoo employee added, "under the circumstances you sir bravely acted in self-defense to protect yourself and other visitors. The zoo will not press any charges against you, Mr…"

"Mr. Suez," the reptile conqueror sternly answered. "Anotal Suez. I used to wrestle ferocious anacondas down in Venezuela so this python was really no match for me. And I know a certain trick I often used to kill the gargantuan snakes from my experiences along the Orinoco. I've also tamed similar beasts in Brazil while on an expedition along the muddy Amazon. I suppose it was just an example of fortuitous serendipity that I just happened to be present in this specific place at this particular time."

"Well obviously Mr. Suez," the second very impressed employee uttered, "the Philadelphia Zoo is obliged to thank you for your intrepid response under what I can only describe as extreme duress. Thank you very much."

The next morning the muscular music professor received a phone call from Hank Chapman. "Hey Anotal, what's this I hear from Daphne Agora that you single-handedly strangled and mangled a giant python that was terrorizing innocent tourists at the Philadelphia Zoo? Is this true?"

"That's a gross hyperbole!" Dr. Suez modestly answered. "It wasn't that big of a snake or that big of a deal. Women always tend to exaggerate about things like that. They have a propensity for getting over-emotional. I didn't do anything sensational that you, Les or Vince wouldn't have done under similar circumstances."

"Okay then, you've overwhelmingly convinced me," the history instructor conceded. "Now Les, Vince and I want to take you out Saturday afternoon to dinner so that we can officially recognize your valuable insights pertaining to certain gambling hunches. What's your preference?"

"How about either the reputable Oceanos Restaurant over in West Berlin or the Adelphi over in Woodbury across from the Deptford Mall. My car will be in the shop at *Midas Mufflers* getting a new exhaust system so one of you will have the responsibility of getting us safely to either place and then back to Glassboro. What's your choice between my two suggestions?"

"I think the Adelphi would be par excellence," Professor Chapman automatically articulated. "That saves me a bumpy ride in your archaic Dodge Aries. I hope you're getting new shocks put into that old decrepit chariot of yours."

"No, just a brand new Midas exhaust system," Dr Suez admitted. "And pick me up around two in the afternoon on Saturday. I'm working on a very intricate musical composition I plan to get published and want to get it completed sometime Saturday night. And then Sunday afternoon I have an important dinner date with Daphne."

"Okay, we'll pick you up at two on Saturday and dine at the Adelphi according to your wish," Hank confirmed. "See you then. Got any more sure-shot gambling tips?"

"No Hank, not right now. I don't want to jinx either you or me with your continued good fortune. Just be content with your substantial bonanza and be happy with your current good health. Hubris and greed often lead to self-destruction. So long for now Hank." Click.

On Saturday afternoon the four opinionated professors were enjoying delicious meals at the popular Adelphi Restaurant Bar and Grille. The music professor was trying his best to act nonchalant about his amazing intervention into what could have potentially evolved into a tragic zoo development.

"Sometimes life is like taking a small ship sailing between Scylla and Charybdis," the eccentric music mentor observed and stated. "An individual sometimes finds himself vacillating between danger and jeopardy and must make an unenviable choice. I had only acted in instinct at the Philadelphia Zoo. It was simply a situational reaction that required little or no thought or preparation," the enigmatic music professor editorialized. "A deer or a squirrel would have run away from the hissing python, but humans have evolved beyond the elementary *cause and effect* thought patterns that dominate animal life. *We* can reverse that behavior into becoming *effected by a cause*. I didn't run away. I basically was intellectually stimulated to *effectively* and rationally respond to an impending emergency."

After the dining party had thoroughly discussed Anotal's phenomenal heroics at the Philadelphia Zoo, the conversation assumed a more erudite philosophical twist when it turned to the topic of immortality.

"Speaking of animals," Vince Olivo transitioned, "I've read in *National Geographic* where animals live anywhere from ten to fifty years. I'm sure glad I'm a human and get to stay around for a few more decades than an alligator or a crocodile, that is, if I have a normal longevity."

"A common dog lives an average of thirteen years," Les Schaffer contributed, "and I read where certain types of condors get to fly around in the sky for fifty-two years. Those seem to be in the same number-range as Vince had identified."

"Well now fellas'," erudite Anotal Suez promptly interrupted, "an elephant lives an average of sixty years and red and blue macaws enjoy sixty-four years of existence on this planet. But certain box turtles can live to be a hundred and twenty-five years if not abused or mistreated."

"You must spend a good deal of your leisure time reading encyclopedias and a plethora of non-fiction books," Hank mildly balked. "And Anotal, how come you don't seem to age like the rest of us mere mortals? You've been on our faculty now for thirteen years and you look just as vernal as when I had first met you. What's your secret?"

"Well Professor Chapman," Dr. Suez coyly responded with a wry smile upon his countenance, "in addition to an occasional good lobster I also consume small quantities of my favorite drink and food, nectar and ambrosia. That's what makes me virtually immortal!"

"You're developing a healthy virile sense of humor," Les Schaffer complimented his strange *Rowan University* faculty peer. "Anotal, you seem to have an illustrious cryptic answer for just about everything."

"Perhaps our science department should study the box turtle and figure out a way of increasing the human life span," Vince Olivo proposed. "The longevity secret might lie in the creature's genetic composition. Perhaps Owens over in biology could get a grant to study all of the various implications."

"I suggest that *you* stick to your students' sloppy and inferior English compositions," Anotal lightheartedly advised his English Department colleague. "You're much more competent in your own area of expertise than you are awkwardly cavorting around in the more demanding scientific realm."

"Now Anotal, you had told us several weeks ago that Socrates and Plato were complete imbeciles," Hank Chapman remembered and declared. "If my memory serves me right, Aristotle was the genius that had classified animals into each phylum zoologists and biologists study today. Is Aristotle a doltish nincompoop too?"

"Beyond the shadow of a doubt," Dr. Suez instantly replied, much to the amusement of his enthralled audience. "Aristotle knew as much about music as today's rap chanters and about as much about medicine as that lame-brained fellow Hippocrates did. The only major thing Aristotle ever did was to teach young Alexander of Macedonia the art of greed and how to go out and savagely conquer the ancient world."

"You tend to be more than a trifle antagonistic and petulant this Saturday afternoon," Les Schaffer injected into the lively symposium. "What's wrong with rap singers?"

"Their music isn't music at all!" Anotal barked back quite perturbed. "It is dissonance, chaotic repetitious mind-controlling stupidity! Rap is like looking at a rainbow having only one color. The lyrics have little or no variety in musical scale. The words reflect no intellectual merit and there are no instruments played except maybe a dull redundant drumbeat," the music instructor zealously maintained. "The rapper's voice is monotonous and does not ascend to any soprano or alto tonal modulations. The entire presentation is inadequate inferior gibberish, absolute rubbish lacking necessary depth and quality, yet young people are influenced to believe that the gross travesty known as rap is a viable form of musical expression. What a grotesque pity!"

"Waitress, we'd like to order dessert now!" Les Schaffer signaled and bellowed. "Now Anotal, I too share your acrimonious feelings about rap singers. But please tell us more about this esoteric nectar and ambrosia business," the mathematics pedagogue jovially insisted. "I'd like to be around to see another age of cultural enlightenment where college students will again be enchanted with geniuses like Verdi, Brahms, Beethoven, Bach and Mozart."

* * * * * * * * * * * *

On Sunday afternoon Anotal drove his repaired sky-blue Dodge Aries to a Glassboro florist to purchase a dozen roses. Such extravagance was contrary to Suez's frugal nature but Daphne Agora was no ordinary female specimen. While the floral shop clerk was organizing Anotal's order, the customer glanced at a commercial golden rendition of a Greek god speeding along his merry way with inordinate dispatch.

"That's the ancient god Mercury," the chatty shop attendant informed his amused sole patron. "He's the floral industry's rapid delivery symbol."

"It's really the Greek god Hermes," the astute music professor corrected. "Mercury is the Roman counterpart of the Greek deity Hermes. So Hermes would be the most accurate nomenclature to use in describing him."

"Whatever you say Sir," the accommodating cashier harmoniously compromised. "I'll have to remember *that* vital fact and politely admonish my boss the next time he uses the improper name."

Next the usually passive music professor motored over to Daphne Agora's condominium to honor the dinner engagement he had proposed to the austere Ancient History professor. Anotal exited his light blue automobile, sauntered up the familiar straight flagstone walkway and rang the doorbell three times.

"Oh, what really beautiful red roses!" Daphne exuberantly exclaimed in utter surprise and totally out-of-character emotion. "I'll have to put them in a suitable vase. Thank you so much for your thoughtfulness!"

After the gorgeous flowers had been neatly arranged in a desirable vase, the music instructor and his attractive brunette companion left the well-decorated and warmly furnished condominium. Daphne locked the front door and the pair strolled arm in arm to the escort's nondescript Dodge Aries.

"The sun's really bright this afternoon!" Daphne commented as she entered the vintage automobile.

"The sun's not only the source of all earthly energy," her didactic date lectured, "but I assure you Daphne it is also the origin of all truth and inspiration on this diabolical Earth. If it weren't for our nearest star, only bacteria and other resilient hardy microorganisms could exist on this rather despicable mediocre globe."

"Your words are virtually poetic even though your opinions being expressed are borderline sarcastic," Dr. Daphne Agora appreciatively lauded and simultaneously verbally assaulted. "You seem to be an authority on everything including the sun. Quite frankly, I find you more dynamic and puzzling with each successive contact. Please elaborate on your sagacity about the sun."

After forty-five minutes of conviviality Anotal steered his substandard automobile into the Radisson Hotel parking lot on *Route 73* in Mt. Laurel.

"This is the Wyndham Steak House that's located inside the Radisson," the driver communicated to his receptive passenger. "It has the finest grilled lamb chops, salmon, rib eye steaks, surf and turf and filet mignon around. Tonight my dear Daphne you'll be treated and entertained like a goddess."

"Your charm is beginning to erode my resistance," the lady professor admitted. "I'm already lightheaded without even imbibing any champagne."

After wining and dining for two solid hours, the music professor enticed his lady friend up to an elegant suite he had specially reserved at the Radisson. Another bottle of champagne was ordered and subsequently delivered to the door, and then after an hour of reminiscing, conversation magically changed into romance. Then after making his conquest in seduction, Anotal Suez hopped out of bed and anxiously began dressing.

"Where are you going darling?" Daphne questioned, almost in a daze. "Let's snuggle up together again. This comfortable bed is so exotic and elegant!"

"I've accomplished my objective," Dr. Suez bluntly replied, "and now it's time for me to pursue other romantic challenges. You were a difficult quest My Lady, but now Daphne I must explore other rigorous relationships with the opposite gender."

"What do you mean!" a jilted Daphne Agora yelled as she pulled her satin covers up to conceal her healthy exposed breasts. "Of all the unmitigated audacity!"

"Enough of your belligerent condescending attitude!" Anotal screamed at the now almost-hysterical woman cursing a slue of invectives from the king-size bed. "I told you I would treat you like a goddess, a promiscuous goddess at that, and so I have honored my pledge up to this point."

Then the now-irate music professor peered into a mirror, and his business suit instantly sparkled and then glistened and soon his black polished shoes disappeared. Then the man miraculously transformed into the Greek god Apollo wearing golden sandals and a sublime white gold-trimmed tunic.

"Now let your mortal eyes behold who I really am Daphne!" Apollo turned and boomed in a deep mellow voice. "I am truly the enlightened god of art, music, medicine and the sun!" the renowned chariot master loudly exclaimed to the horrified woman. 'She has not yet figured out that Anotal is my mother Latona's name spelled backwards and that Suez is my father Zeus's designation reversed also. And yes, Latona is the proper Roman name for the Greek appellation Leto.'

And then, without any further utterance or gesticulation, Apollo pointed a finger at the still-astonished Daphne Agora now lying petrified in the huge luxurious bed. An aura crystallized around her and much to the lady's dissatisfaction, she was swiftly beamed outside the Radisson Hotel where she miraculously reappeared as a laurel tree situated on the main entrance lawn.

'Another laurel tree right here in somnolent Mt. Laurel, New Jersey!' Apollo mused as he again admired his divine countenance in the room's gold-framed wall mirror. 'I had easily performed *that* deed just like I had turned another Daphne into a laurel tree many centuries ago in mythology, or should I say *history?* At any rate, I also killed a savage python at Delphi before my sacred Oracle had been established there. I suppose that a reliable axiom of life is that history is destined to repeat itself!'

The handsome Greek god exited the Radisson's third floor room, took the elevator down to the lobby and soon was the subject of patrons' laughter and gossip as Apollo proudly stepped by the registration desk and paced out the hotel's electronic front doors.

Apollo conscientiously scrutinized his wristwatch that was in the shape of an ancient sundial, took a glimpse of the newly im*planted* laurel tree, looked-up to the clear heavens and let out a rhythmic whistle. Soon an immense white flying horse descended from the twilight sky and majestically landed on the hotel's asphalt driveway, amidst a gathering of fifty or so bedazzled gawking bystanders.

"Well, I guess it's time for me to assume another identity in another time and place!" Apollo dynamically related to the still-flabbergasted crowd of well-dressed shocked gossipers. "It's indeed time for Phoebus Apollo to establish himself in another century and artfully entice another Daphne, and if the occasion arises, slaughter another python. Come Pegasus! Take me to Mt. Olympus where I can freely replenish my dwindling supply of nectar and ambrosia! And you may take the scenic roundabout route if you wish."

The muscular gleaming god then nonchalantly mounted the fabulous obedient white-winged stallion, who immediately raised its noble head and gently ascended-up into the dusky sky. The magnificent creature and its eminent rider triumphantly circled above the Mt. Laurel Radisson Hotel and then wonderfully disappeared over the western horizon in the direction of the setting sun.

"The Seven Statues"

American life had been good to Nikos (Nick) Mitropoulos. His father Dimitri was a Greek immigrant' who had arrived in the United States in the spring of 1953, worked as a diner dishwasher and later steadily advanced from short-order cook to the title of head chef. In 1975 Dimitri had saved enough money to purchase the then defunct Midway Diner located on a major traffic artery, *Route 30* in Hammonton, New Jersey. Then the entrepreneurial Dimitri gambled in business, took out a mortgage on his accumulated equity and within two years refurbished the newly named Silver Dollar Diner's interior and exterior with expensive tile walls and marble floors. In June of 1993 Dimitri succumbed to lung cancer, and Nikos inherited a very lucrative business that was complemented by a powerful stocks and bonds' portfolio.

Nikos was a firm believer in the American free enterprise system and the ambitious fellow was a loyal advocate of his father's conviction that the United States was the land of boundless opportunity. After paying off his diner renovation loan in 1997 Nikos formed partnerships with other sons of Greek immigrants and acquired controlling interest in seven diners all over South Jersey in towns bearing the names of Mays Landing, Williamstown, Vineland, Egg Harbor City, Berlin, Atco and Turnersville. Workaholic Nikos soon learned to balance labor with leisure.

In 1998 Nikos Mitropoulos took a break from his business responsibilities and vacationed in Greece. In Athens he reunited with (and several months later) married Penelope Papuldopoulos, his grammar school sweetheart. The proud diner mogul then brought his beautiful wife to the United States. Good fortune was smiling on the industrious Greek immigrant's son.

In late February of 2002 Nikos and Penelope had booked a June Bermuda cruise out of New York aboard the *Pacific Princess*, better known as *The Love Boat*. Over the years Nikos and Penelope had become good friends with Frank and Carolanne Imhoff, the owners of a prominent furniture store in Burlington, New Jersey. The two couples were excited about their *Atlantic* excursion to the scenic islands acclaimed for having picturesque emerald green harbors and magnificent white and pink sandy beaches.

"Frank," Nick said over the telephone, "when are ya' goin' to send your interior decorator down to Hammonton to put together my new sun room scheme. I've just landscaped the garden outside and Penelope and I need an attractive room overlooking our back lawn to entertain guests and important business clients. I figured I'd remind you of your commitment to the project."

"Nick, I'll have my man Tony at your place evaluating the situation right after we return from Bermuda," Frank Imhoff promised. "He'll color-coordinate and arrange everything and then we'll order the sofa, chairs, wallpaper, tables, accessories and matching rug. The whole package should be installed by early August at the latest. You have my word!"

"Well Frank, I want you and Carolanne to think about something else besides furniture," Nick Mitropoulos insisted. "I'm having seven statues of Greek gods standing on pedestals arranged in a semi-circle in the center of my backyard garden. The expensive statues will be facing the new grand room that you're coordinating. So please bear that idea in mind Frank when you come up with vibrant fabrics, paintings and drapes."

"I'm already being inspired by your description but I hope the lawn statues are made of white marble," Frank answered. "That's an easy neutral color to contrast items with."

"Yes Frank, as a matter of fact they are," Nick proudly replied. "I'm having them made from genuine imported Greek marble. There's nothin' fake or artificial about them. They're being shipped from California this week," Nick proudly bragged, "and I've already contracted a Williamstown mason who had worked on my original Hammonton diner to get the statues set up and solidly cemented to the pedestals. I mean Frank, the white marble is from the hills of Attica and it's the same material that had been used to construct the magnificent Parthenon up on the Acropolis!"

"That freight bill from California must be out of sight," Frank remarked with admiration. "That's what I like about you Nick. When you want something, money's no object!"

"True," the Greek diner capitalist replied with a smile on his countenance. "But you must remember that Greek history and Greek mythology are very important parts of my cultural heritage. Now that I can afford to have authentic-looking marble statues in my lush garden," Nick explained and paused, "I'm going to combine artistic aesthetics with environmental beauty. I had Louie Cappuccio do the landscaping," the diner-chain mogul related to his friend. "Louie calls the arrangement of trees and shrubs 'a *treatment!'* What a word, 'treatment', ha, ha, ha! That treatment cost me a hundred and eighty-five thousand bucks. But I gotta' admit that my back lawn now looks pretty spectacular and exotic, almost like a botanical garden!"

"Those nifty seven white marble statues must've cost you just about as much as your landscaping did," Frank Imhoff guessed and stated. "I'm sure there aren't too many back lawn statues around this neck of the woods exactly like them."

"I'm not saying any specific quotes on them," Nick ambiguously and evasively responded. "It's my little secret, but between you and me I'll have to open another diner just to pay for the detailed craftsmanship. Ya' know Frank, those statues are sculptured! They weren't manufactured out of any cheap assembly line molds!"

"That's just great! I'm happy for you!" Frank sincerely congratulated over the telephone. "Carolanne and I will see you and Penelope at our place at noon on Sunday. My son Glenn will drive the four of us to the Westhampton Bus Terminal. The *Pacific Princess* is scheduled to leave the 55th Street Pier at four. That gives us about two hours of free time on the ship before our bon voyage out of New York," Frank elaborated. "But first we have to pass through customs so we gotta' first catch the bus at Westhampton in order to catch the ship out of New York. Just make sure you're at my place in Burlington by noon and leave the rest to me."

"Terrific Frank!" Nick exclaimed. "Penelope and I will be at your Mill Road home promptly by noon on Sunday. Have a choice bottle of *Merlot* ready to officially christen our *Atlantic* cruise to Bermuda!"

"No problem Nick!" Imhoff amenably agreed. "I have a case of your favorite vintage sitting in a large rack down in my wine cellar. See ya' on Sunday June 23rd."

On Sunday after church service Nick drove Penelope in their blue *Lexus* thirty miles from Hammonton to the Imhoff's Mill Road estate in Burlington City. After Nick and Penelope Mitropoulos arrived at their destination the couple discussed with eager anticipation their upcoming cruise with Frank and Carolanne and in the process the four managed to consume a bottle of vintage Merlot while casually chatting. After Frank and Carolanne's son Glenn drove the four enthused passengers in the Imhoff's spacious *Chevy Suburban* to Westhampton, the four loaded their luggage into the awaiting bus's cargo area and were soon off heading north on the *New Jersey Turnpike* with their objective being the 55th Street Pier on the *Hudson* in midtown Manhattan.

The famous ship's departure from its berth was a happy one with confetti and streamers being tossed from the *Love Boat* onto the pier below. The *Pacific Princess* was gently pushed from its mooring by a tug and the harbor pilot escorted the famous cruise liner down the *Hudson* past the inimitable New York City skyline. Mixed emotions of joy and bitterness filled the hearts of all six hundred and fifty passengers aboard the splendid vessel.

"That big vacant spot in lower Manhattan is where the twin towers used to be," Frank Imhoff solemnly indicated to his three traveling companions. "Things have really changed since *9-11* of 2001," the furniture store merchant acknowledged as the two couples stood on an outside deck at the bow of the majestic cruise liner. "Isn't it ironic that the same three numbers are present in *9-11* and in the emergency phone number *911*!"

"Security is now the watchword in this country!" Nick agreed. "There are international terrorists everywhere. But I must also caution you that there are local terrorists all over this great land that hate themselves and hate everybody else living in towns and cities all across this blessed country," the Greek diner tycoon elaborated and editorialized. "It seems that danger is destined to be everywhere, even in a wonderful place like Bermuda. We have to be cautious no matter where we travel."

"Look, there's landmark *Ellis Island* and behind it the *Statue of Liberty*," Carolanne noticed in a cheerful voice that melted away everyone's melancholy. "I'm prone to motion sickness. How long will we be out in the *Atlantic*?"

"A day and a half to Bermuda," Frank authoritatively informed. "Let's go up on the Lido Deck and have a late lunch buffet before all of the complimentary food is gone. Then we gotta' unpack our things before we have to assemble for the standard passenger life-preserver drills."

"Good idea to empty the suitcases first!" Nick suggested. "Frank, you're so damned organized. I've always envied you for that! Now just don't forget to have your interior decorator Tony over to get my new grand room fully coordinated."

"I guarantee to have him there if you agree to buy our table a bottle of Merlot for supper!" Frank merrily pledged and negotiated. "If you could afford seven exotic Greek statues along with exclusive state-of-the-art landscaping, then a bottle of vintage wine should be no sweat for a person of good taste such as yourself!"

"You've got yourself a deal Frank!" the Greek restaurateur amiably reciprocated. "In forty years we'll all be comfortably and eternally resting in the cemetery so we might as well enjoy ourselves right now while we're here and still breathing. How's that for a suitable philosophy to live life by?"

That evening the two couples dressed casually for the supper that was served in the Coral Dining Room, several floors below *their* Aloha Deck staterooms. The voyagers were served a selection of sumptuous meals by headwaiter Carlos, assistant waiter Luis and a conscientious novice experiencing his first cruise, George. After the main meal had been consumed the accommodating attendants kept coming back with an assortment of tempting dessert delicacies that pleased everyone's palates.

"These waiters really know how to practice their profession," Frank perceptively observed and shared. "They're hustling for some big tips at the end of the cruise and I'll wager they're gonna' get them. Nick, this meal rivals those at Tommy G's Gourmet Restaurant over in Burlington. If I recall Carolanne and I took you and Penelope there' once," the retail furniture distributor reminded his close friend and *his* wife.

"Oh yeah, I remember now," the diner tycoon recollected and verified. "That's the fancy place that was converted from an old bank into a ritzy food joint. You reserved 'The Vault Table' for us. That was really a unique dining experience with the four of us having a gourmet meal inside a former bank vault with all the safety deposit boxes still there in the walls. How could I ever forget that?"

"Frank and I have a surprise for you," Carolanne disclosed to Nick and Penelope. "Do you remember meeting Bill Burns and Jerry Gares, those college professor friends of ours?"

"Sure, nice guys. They were at a couple of parties at your place. Isn't Jerry your brother-in-law?" Nick asked Frank.

"That's right!" the furniture store proprietor quickly acknowledged. "Bill and Jerry are both professors at *Camden Community College*. Anyway Carolanne, tell Nick and Penelope what those crazy guys are up to!"

"You'll never believe this," Carolanne prefaced with a broad grin, "but Bill and Jerry like to travel together because their wives are beach fanatics always sunning themselves down in Wildwood and in Stone Harbor. Since those two brainiacs hate the beach, they're touring museums in London right now as I speak and they're taking a special flight from England to Bermuda to meet up with us Wednesday night for dinner at the *Hamilton Princess Hotel*. Isn't that absolutely wild!" Carolanne marveled and asked. "Bill and Jerry are going to make a special trip and land in Bermuda just to have dinner and cocktails with the four of us. Now if that's not the nuttiest thing you've heard in a long time, then I don't know exactly what is!"

"With husbands like those two unpredictable guys," Frank lustily laughed, "Irene Gares and Fran Burns are much safer wading around in the surf at Wildwood. Say Nick, tell us all about those nifty seven marble statues you ordered for your fabulous garden. They sound mighty fascinating and have sparked my curiosity."

The diner kingpin took a sip of Merlot and related to his captivated listeners his passion for Greek mythology, how he loved the Olympian gods and how he professed the values and life-lessons many of the ancient myths had taught him. Carolanne was quite intrigued by Nick's revelations and asked her loquacious friend what his favorite Greek myths were.

"Well, I especially like the story of Sisyphus," the suddenly excited Greek/American citizen revealed. "Sisyphus tricked the Olympian gods and because of *his* excessive pride and evil scheming, the gods had the prankster punished forever. The conniver had to roll a huge rock up an inclined plane in Hades for the remainder of time. Every time Sisyphus was about to complete his arduous task and roll the gigantic stone over the ramp's summit," Nick elucidated and chuckled, "it would tumble down again and he'd have to start the job all over. This story has significant moral implications. It teaches young people that ya' must respect and honor the laws of the gods or face the dire consequences."

"It's sort of like a fable with a moral attached," Penelope explained to the Imhoffs. "The ancient Greeks had no *Bible* to learn Commandments and life values and the like, so they had masterminded wonderful stories like the *Iliad* and the *Odyssey* epics along with a collection of marvelous myths to transmit positive culture and beneficial attitudes to the next generation. Many of the ancient myths possessed ethical lessons that in

58

olden times were seriously studied and conveyed as models of behavior worthy of imitation."

Carolanne Imhoff was enamored with Nick's devotion to mythology and insisted that he describe another of his cherished tales from antiquity. Mitropoulos was more than glad to comply with his friend's wife's unsolicited request.

"Well, another interesting story involves a gifted young sculptor named Pygmalion living on the island of Cyprus," Nick stated before sipping some mellow Merlot. "The devoted artist hated women, thinking that his love of his work was enough to get him through life. Even a gorgeous woman he considered to be an annoying distraction from his heartfelt craft."

"I vaguely remember the myth from high school literature," Carolanne modestly volunteered. "How did Pygmalion learn *his* moral lesson?"

"Yeah, tell us what special values that story imparts," Frank Imhoff coaxed. "I could always use a little more morality, especially while enjoying delicious Merlot!"

Nick proudly smiled and stared at his three listeners, amazed and delighted that Carolanne and Frank desired to know more details about a story he admired so much. "Pygmalion intensively labored in his workshop and created a magnificent statue of a woman that was so beautiful that even the goddesses of Mt. Olympus would've been envious of *her*. The artist instantly fell in love with his statue creation that obviously was incapable of loving him back. What great anguish his saddened heart suffered!"

"What happened next to Pygmalion?" Frank anxiously asked before imbibing another gulp of savory Merlot. "I must apologize for my academic ignorance. I've never been good at intellectual stuff but this particular story has somehow peaked my interest."

"Well Aphrodite, the goddess of love and beauty deliberately encountered Pygmalion," Nick continued his authoritative discourse, "and she granted him his wish. One night Pygmalion leaped up on the pedestal of the young woman statue he had formed and kissed her stone-cold lips. She then transformed into a lovely maiden Galatea, and the lonely sculptor at last no longer despised females and immediately found the love of his life, thanks to Aphrodite's personal intercession!"

"I've remembered what I wanted to say now," Carolanne anxiously interrupted. "The *Broadway* musical *My Fair Lady* is based on the famous Pygmalion myth. Professor Henry Higgins transformed a Cockney girl named Eliza Doolittle into a glamorous charming woman just to win a bet. The movie version starred Rex Harrison and Audrey Hepburn. But Nick," Carolanne curiously continued, "is this Pygmalion myth why you feel a need to have seven Greek statues as the centerpieces of your new garden?"

"Why, in a way yes!" Nick laughed. "Now that you've mentioned it I never thought of *that* particular relationship, but Carolanne, I think you've accurately hit the nail right on the head. Bravo for you Carolanne! I think you would've made an excellent world-famous psychologist or psychiatrist. I hereby propose a well-deserved toast to Carolanne Imhoff!"

Everyone seated at the Coral Restaurant table raised and then clinked their long-stemmed wine glasses. After desserts had been served and devoured, the couples strolled the entire Promenade Deck perimeter, checked out the ship's glitzy casino and then enjoyed rum-based tropical cocktails in the very intimate Pirate's Cove Lounge.

"Don't forget to set your watches back one hour!" Frank reminded his three jovial companions. "We're heading east and Bermuda time is one hour later than eastern standard time."

"That's right," Nick chimed in. "The islands are six hundred miles due east of North Carolina. I read in a brochure where they're the northernmost coral islands in the world."

"And I thought that Bill Burns and Jerry Gares' were the real college professors," Penelope giggled. "Carolanne, I think that our husbands missed their true callings as accomplished geography instructors!" she continued while winking at Frank's convivial wife. "What time do we arrive in Bermuda?"

"We're slated to disembark at St. George's at 1 p.m. on Tuesday. That gives us all day Monday at sea," Nick informatively replied. "And guys, don't forget to be my guests at the Hammonton Lions Gold Raffle Dinner next Monday night, July 1st. I've reserved a table for my favorite friends."

Monday June 24th the four avid vacationers spent actively partaking of the many passenger privileges and accommodations the *Pacific Princess* provided. The two adventurous couples had an ample breakfast in the Coral Restaurant, strolled to their rooms, changed into swimwear and then ventured out to the sundeck and found four beach recliners conveniently situated near the top-deck pool as the Love Boat headed southeast towards "Paradise."

"The ocean water is the bluest I've ever seen," Penelope said as she applied suntan lotion to her already tan legs. "It's more beautiful than a picture postcard!"

"Don't forget the gala stage show tonight in the Carousel Lounge," Carolanne reminded her brunette traveling colleague. "They're giving a tribute to *Broadway* show tunes to commemorate New York City."

"Ship performers really work hard for their money," Nick contributed and opined. "Most of them are very talented but unfortunately few ever make it to the big time. But I gotta' commend them for their dedication. They live their great dream daily and sing and dance their hearts out."

"That's right!" Frank congenially concurred. "Many of the performers have different job assignments on the ship besides entertaining the passengers at show time. I noticed that the girl who had led us through the ship's emergency drills yesterday is also the assistant social director and besides that," Imhoff expounded, "she's a marvelous singer and dancer listed daily in the ship's morning newsletter."

Just before 11 a.m. on Tuesday morning Nick spotted a Bermuda island in the distance. The channel into St. George's was very narrow and the *Pacific Princess* only had a ten-foot-clearance on both port and starboard sides through treacherous cliff embankments and rocks while majestically sailing into the port's harbor. A town crier dressed in a British colonial uniform rang a welcoming bell and greeted the ship by yelling out from the rocks on the starboard side, "*Pacific Princess*, welcome to St. George's Bermuda!" His booming-but-friendly salutation was followed by a loud blast from an authentic-looking cannon that sent a cloud of smoke billowing into the air. The small cumulus then gently wafted toward the enthralled passengers witnessing and snapping pictures of the event aboard the arriving cruise vessel.

The Mitropoulos and Imhoff couples spent the afternoon enjoying an informal sightseeing tour of King's Square and later traveling by motor coach to visit such historic attractions as the Unfinished Church and Fort St. Catherine. The late afternoon was squandered away by ambling around the St. George's colonial-styled downtown square, window shopping on Duke of York Street and learning about the desperate struggles between early Spanish and British exploring expeditions attempting to seize strategic military control of the local islands. The four tourists were particularly fascinated with their final trek through King's Square where they took several rolls of film of each other locked in colonial-era stocks and then the travelers attentively listened to a comprehensive historical narration on the famous "ducking stool."

"Maybe Congress should re-introduce some of the drastic punishment methods effectively used in the past," Frank facetiously chuckled. "You can ask any successful Wall Street executive! Being in *stocks and bonds* in the twenty-first century takes on a whole new meaning than it had in the more austere sixteenth and seventeenth centuries."

"And did you see that ducking chair!" Nick boisterously laughed. "If a woman was even suspected of gossiping, let alone infidelity, they plunged her into the water for everyone to publicly mock and scorn the offensive shrew!"

"How embarrassing that indignity must've been! The woman might've been completely innocent!" Carolanne adamantly objected.

"Embarrassing yes, but the method was also quite useful as a deterrent!" Nick pontificated. "People back then abided by the established rules and laws, and if they didn't show self-discipline and restraint, they were publicly jeered and humiliated! Back then the ends justified the means!"

"No thank you my dear husband! I much prefer living in the year 2002!" Penelope asserted while thoroughly endorsing Carolanne's more humane position on the matter of public mortification. "Thanks to the advancement of psychology, certain things are more civilized nowadays."

"There's a jetliner about to land at the airport!" Nick pointed out as he deftly changed the subject while pointing to the cloudless azure sky. "The only airport on the Bermuda islands is over there on that patch of land called St. George's Parish, so that's where Bill and Jerry will be landing from London!"

That evening the four dressed-up for the Captain's reception, which was followed by the traditional formal dinner. Frank and Nick wore black tuxedos and their wives were clad in elegant evening gowns. Later the four ascended the stairs from the Coral Deck to the Fiesta Deck where Nick approached the purser in order to make an important long-distance phone call.

"Oh, isn't this just wonderful!" Penelope excitedly told Carolanne. "This reception counter and lounge area is the exact same setting often seen as background on *The Love Boat* TV show. I used to watch that terrific program and its reruns all the time! Believe it or not the series was extremely popular back in Greece!"

"You're right Penelope now that you've mentioned it!" Carolanne instantly recognized. "And the Carousel Lounge, the Pacific Lounge and the boutique shops are almost identical to the familiar sets often viewed on the show. I still can't believe that we're cruising on the one and only *Love Boat!* And coincidentally, this is its last *Atlantic* cruise. I've read where the ship's been bought by a European company and will be soon cruising the Mediterranean.*"

Nick removed a business card from his wallet, received the phone from the purser and provided the operator with the telephone number of Tom Larson, the Williamstown stone mason he had contracted to cement the seven Greek statues to their white marble pedestals.

Much to the caller's disappointment no one was home at the Larson residence so Nick left a message on the answering machine. "Tom, this is Nick Mitropoulos from Hammonton. I'm callin' ya' from Bermuda. Make sure you arrange the seven statues in a semi-circle facing the outdoor pool and bar. Leave a space of five feet between each pedestal. And don't forget where I live, 37 Greco Court just off Golf Road," Nick emphasized. "The house key is under the side-laundry room doormat. I'll be back in town on Sunday night, June 30th and my wife and I will be thrilled to see the statues in place. Good luck!"

On Tuesday evening the four voyagers were entertained by a comedian, by a pop singer and by a variety of dancing routines provided by the ship's dozen talented performers. After the stellar show Nick returned to the purser's desk to once again call Tom Larson.

"Tom, this is Nick again. Did ya' get my earlier message? How ya' doin'?"

A shocked expression suddenly appeared on the caller's face. "No wonder why you sound so upset Tom. Tell me all about it." After listening to a depressing three-minute oration Nick said, "Sorry to hear that Tom! But thanks for still plannin' to install the pedestals and the statues. I'm glad to hear they've been delivered safe and sound to your Williamstown warehouse.

Hope to see you Monday night at the Lions Club Gold Raffle Dinner. I've bought tickets for you and Betty. Good luck to you Tom, and sorry to hear the bad news!"

"What's up?" Frank asked Nick. "Did something tragic happen to Tom or his wife?"

"Something bad happened to both of them!" the Greek tourist disclosed. "When Tom and Betty were out to dinner, vandals broke into their house, drank all their whiskey and then ransacked the entire place, smashing windows, mirrors, glasses, bottles and just about everything else. Damage is estimated to be over thirty thousand dollars. What an ugly mess!"

"Is Tom too upset to install the statues?" Penelope curiously asked. "He might change his mind and wait until he's a little more emotionally stable after that terrible ordeal he and Betty experienced."

"He said he would show-up on Thursday and supervise his crew," Nick informed, shaking his head in disgust and shock. "That Tom's one heck of a guy. Here his place is in shambles and he still promises to have the statues in my garden done by the time I return from Bermuda."

"And you say he's going to the Hammonton Lions Gold Raffle Dinner too?" Carolanne marveled and added. "You never told Frank and me that."

"Yes, in fact Tom and Betty will be sittin' at the same table as *we* will be," Nick reported. "I had bought ten tickets to the charity affair. I was going to have Tom and Betty's attendance as sort of a surprise for you and Frank but since this unfortunate disaster at *his* home has turned up, I had to spill the beans and tell you two about the Larsons attending the Lions Club dinner."

"Well, tomorrow evening we'll meet-up with Jerry and Bill at the *Princess Hotel,*" Penelope reminded the others at the table, trying to change the conversation to a more pleasant topic than frightening house vandalism. "Let's retire early so that we're well-rested to be able to do all of tomorrow's activities."

The *Pacific Princess* sailed from St. George's at seven a.m. on Wednesday and several hours later promptly moored at Hamilton at nine. The morning proceeded without incident for the four adventurers. After a nourishing breakfast Fran and Nick studied a detailed map of the downtown shopping area. The men then left their spouses, who intended doing some light shopping on Front Street at world-renown stores Trimingham's, Calypso and the Irish Linen Shop. Nick and Frank hiked four blocks to the Hamilton Public Library on Queen's Street to use *Internet* computers to check the early morning stock prices in London and Frankfurt.

"Everything is so clean and well-maintained on these islands," Nick told his loyal companion. "It's about as close to Utopia we can experience on this beautiful Earth."

"Sure is," Frank suavely verified. "And as a former interior decorator turned furniture store owner I just love the various pastel shades used on the exteriors of the shops and houses. I especially like the bright yellow facade on the Calypso Store. The whole island is appealing and cheery!"

"I read where all buildings on the island must be constructed out of cinder-blocks made from coral rock," the Greek diner owner explained. "It's illegal to use wood as a building material in case a hurricane ravages the islands. And Frank," Nick garrulously continued, "notice that most of the houses have those white roofs with drains that collect water going down into cellar cisterns," Mitropoulos elucidated. "Fresh water is at a premium here in Bermuda and the practice of conservation by all residents is an absolute must."

On late Wednesday afternoon Nick and Frank were the talk of Front Street, which had been cordoned-off to allow street foot traffic while promoting a festive pedestrian promenade replete with street vendors and kiosk merchants selling various foods and souvenir items. The two enterprising Americans showed-up for the occasion in formal Bermuda outfits with navy blue blazers, matching knee-socks, white shirts with identical red, white and black polka dot ties, black spit-shined dress shoes and navy blue Bermuda shorts. The two show-offs were asked to pose for photographs taken by other tourists, who were both amused and impressed by *their* regal appearances.

Nick examined his *Rolex* and determined that it was time to saunter to the *Hamilton Princess Hotel* where they were scheduled to rendezvous with Professors' Bill Burns and Jerry Gares. "It's time to hit the pavement and honor our supper commitment," the diner tycoon related to Frank. "I've booked reservations for a table for six and also reserved tickets to a stage show. Now all we have to do is meet up with those crazies Bill and Jerry."

"How far is the *Princess Hotel* from where we are on Front Street?" Carolanne inquisitively asked. "My feet are getting tired and my energy level is not the greatest."

"I figure about five or six blocks west," Nick estimated. "It's certainly within walking distance. I studied a map and Front Street becomes Pitts Bay Road just past the Chamber of Commerce Building," Nick convincingly continued, "and Frank told me our college professor friends are stayin' at the *Elbow Beach Resort* and are gonna' take a taxi over to the *Princess.*"

The *Princess Hotel* was indeed an exquisite-looking edifice with a rich pastel pink exterior and handsome mahogany-paneled walls inside. Bill and Jerry were patiently standing there already waiting to reunite with their four erudite friends at the main entrance.

"Things have really changed here on Bermuda," Professor Bill Burns joked tongue-in-cheek. "They'll obviously let anybody into this place now-a-days."

"Good to see you fellas'," Nick gleefully remarked. "Of course you guys know Carolanne and Frank."

"Frank's my favorite brother-in-law," Jerry Gares facetiously snickered and joked, "and with a guy like Frank around, I don't need another obnoxious brother-in-law besides him. He's enough of a challenge to contend with."

"This has got to be the craziest thing I've ever heard of," Penelope said after taking pecks on the cheek from the men stopping off in Hamilton while en route to Philadelphia from London. "Landing in Bermuda just to have a few drinks, eat a meal, see a show and then staying one night before flying out the next day is not your typical everyday behavior. You two itinerants sure have a flair for the unusual!"

"If it was a typical thing," Bill Burns theorized and expressed, "then it wouldn't be extraordinary enough for anyone to talk about. I'm hungry. Let's eat and then we'll have time to reminisce."

A matre'd showed the six visitors to their reserved table in the stately Three Crowns Restaurant. Wine was ordered before the shrimp cocktail and cherry-stone clams' appetizers. Then the entrees were selected and prepared to order. Congenial exchanges were bantered for the next half-hour and the conversation soon focused on nostalgically recollecting shared past adventures.

Finally as the six drank vintage Merlot and feasted on surf and turf, crab-meat and filet mignon, the conversation quickly shifted from the fabulous Bermuda weather and downtown Hamilton to Nick Mitropoulos's love of Greek mythology.

Frank insisted that the flamboyant restaurateur tell everyone seated at the table a fresh Greek myth.

"Tantalus was the son of a mortal woman and of Zeus, king of Olympus and god of the sky," Nick began his exclusive narrative. "Tantalus was favored on Earth by ordinary mortals, who admired the great one's enthusiasm and generosity. Tantalus was invited to feasts sponsored by Zeus, who allowed his offspring the privilege of eating nectar and ambrosia, the delectable drink and food of the gods that made them immortal."

"Wasn't that a violation of the rules of Mt. Olympus?" the very knowledgeable Penelope asked her husband. "Nectar and ambrosia were secrets to be kept by the gods and not to be shared with half-gods like Tantalus. But I suppose the almighty deities could break their own rules if they wanted."

"Please Penelope, permit me to continue," Nick admonished his wife with a contrived frown, much to the elation of his four friends. "One day Tantalus gave a tremendous banquet at his palace for the divine Greek gods. He had just murdered *his* son Pelops, boiled him in a colossal-sized kettle and while acting quite obnoxiously and egotistically in the presence of his divine guests," Nick emphasized, "Tantalus served Zeus and the other great gods his son's flesh, with the evil intent of making the Olympians practice primitive cannibalism."

"Did Zeus and the other gods ever find out they had been hoodwinked?" Bill Burns asked while being fully familiar with the incredible tale. "This Tantalus fellow sounds like an ancient psychopath. I don't think they had trained psychiatrists way back then to analyze wackos and deviates."

"Yeah Nick, what happened next?" Jerry Gares demanded to know, pretending to also being ignorant of the weird story. "They didn't have any mental hospitals for sick deranged psychos back then either, did they?"

"Hey, wait a minute!" Nick protested. "Are you guys pulling my leg, or what? You're both prominent college professors and you're now acting like you've never heard of this famous myth? Give me a break!"

"No," Bill Burns confessed. "I'm a math' and calculus instructor, and Jerry here is chairman of the college's computer department! Mythology is not part of *our* expertise." Everyone listening got a good chuckle from Professor Burns' timely gem of explanatory information.

"Ha, ha, ha!" Nick heartily laughed. After finishing his draught of Merlot and then pouring some more into his tall-stemmed glass, the Greek entrepreneur resumed his oratory. "Anyway, the immortal gods knew of Tantalus's private evil and over-confident plan. For deceiving the gods Tantalus was removed from his palace and forced to spend all eternity in Hades doing a very monotonous punishment," Mitropoulos relished and related. "He had to stand chained to a post in a chest-high tub of water, always thirsty. When his parched mouth bent over to drink the water, the liquid funneled out of the huge drum. Then food and fruit would appear over his head, and when Tantalus would reach-out for an apple or a banana, it too would automatically disappear or would be wafted away by wind. That wicked cycle was repeated over and over again," Nick informed his attentive listeners. "It was Tantalus's penalty for attempting to trick the gods into doing a very ungodly act."

"And that's precisely where our word *tantalize* comes from, *his* name!" Penelope smartly educated the four others.

"And as you can plainly see, it was wrong to mess around with the Greek gods and to defiantly disrespect them," Nick seriously conveyed to his fellow diners. "In the end the evildoer was always rightfully condemned to an unhappy eternal afterlife of sacrifice and misery as Tantalus had discovered!"

Carolanne then insisted that Nick tell Bill and Jerry about the seven handcrafted statues, which the likeable center-of-attention immediately promised he would. "But first, I want to remind Bill and Jerry that they're both gonna' be my guests Monday night at the Hammonton Lions Club's annual Gold Raffle Dinner. You guys attended last year and said you wanted to bring Fran and Irene again as my personal guests this year."

"That's really great! I already have the date circled on my calendar," Bill Burns commended Nick. "You can show the six of us the seven Greek statues in your new garden on Monday night before or after the big dinner. Where is the Lions Gold Raffle extravaganza going to be held?"

"At Kerrie-Brooke Caterers on *Route 30,* better known as the White Horse Pike," Nick stated quite matter-of-factly. "The same place as it was last year. Now let me tell ya' about those seven Greek statues I'm havin' Tom Larson erect in my new gardens. Incidentally, Tom and his wife Betty are gonna' also be my guests on Monday night. I've reserved a table for ten. Since I'm a past president of the town's Lions Club," Nick eloquently proceeded, "I feel obligated to ensure the Gold Raffle fundraiser's success. Proceeds go to help Lions' sight and hearing projects across New Jersey and in the community."

"Say, what's the entertainment going to be after dinner tonight?" Bill innocently asked after being somewhat bored with his host's monotonous monologue. "Jerry and I could use a little additional diversion since we've already diverted ourselves from London to Hamilton!"

"A stand-up comedian followed by a talented magician," Penelope answered.

"Come to think of it," Nick said, "Tom Larson is goin' to have to be a *magician* to get those seven statues erected after havin' the misery of seein' his home wrecked by vandals. There're more barbarians cavorting around out there in society today than there were in ancient Greece! Now let me tell you two newcomers about my newly acquired seven marble statues."

On Thursday morning Jerry and Bill hired a taxi, which then transported them from the Elbow Beach Club Resort to the Bermuda Airport in St. George's Parish. At noon the *Pacific Princess* raised anchor and headed on an hour and a half excursion for its last Bermuda' destination, the West End Royal Naval Dockyard, which had been converted into an attractive gallery of retail shops, food concessions and historic and cultural museums. The mixture of buildings bore the designation *Bermuda Arts Centre.* The highlight of the tourist attraction for the four tanned vacationers was the Dolphin Quest Aqua Marine area, which consisted of five pools of water where brave tourists in swimsuits were instructed how to share space and eventually swim and communicate by touch with seven very passive and well-mannered dolphins.

The *Pacific Princess* eased out from its Royal Dockyards' mooring berth at noon on Friday, and the two merry-but-tired couples endured one rough night at sea where Nick had to summon the ship's doctor to administer Penelope an injection in order to avert additional seasickness. By morning, Penelope Mitropoulos felt almost back to normal, although she only drank tea for breakfast.

"Carlos, Luis and George really treated us with great hospitality throughout this voyage!" Nick said to Frank. "They were very cordial and helpful!"

"What kind of tip should we leave each?" Frank Imhoff asked. "After all, they did treat us like royalty."

"Let's each' give Carlos a hundred-and-fifty bucks and Luis and George a century note apiece!" Nick suggested. "I think that would be fair compensation for their terrific services. And it's not that we can't afford that kind of generosity, either!"

"I wholly endorse your recommendation!" frugal Frank Imhoff reluctantly acceded. "That Baked Alaska on top of that Cherries Jubilee dessert last night convinces me that *you* are right on the money about the compensations."

The *Statue of Liberty* and *Ellis Island* (symbolizing freedom of speech and freedom of enterprise) never looked so impressive to the four returnees as the ship sailed northwest into New York Harbor. And as soon as the *Pacific Princess* approached the *Verrazano-Narrows Bridge* stretching from Staten Island to Brooklyn, tears formed in Nick Mitropoulos's eyes when he again perceived the Manhattan skyline with the twin towers missing.

Frank Imhoff sensed his friend's melancholy and said, "Nick, look in the distance over to the right. That's the old Coney Island parachute jump ride. I used to take the subway out of Manhattan with my Burlington High School buddies and visit Coney Island during its heyday, ride the Cyclone roller coaster and then walk the boardwalk trying to meet all eligible girls. What great fun teens had back in the late '50s and early '60s! They were such innocent times for a kid to grow-up and I wish I could relive them!"

Glenn Imhoff was waiting with the *Chevy Suburban* at the Westhampton Terminal for the bus to arrive from New York's 55th Street Pier. The luggage was neatly packed into the vehicle's rear compartment and the four fatigued voyagers were happy to be back on good old United States' soil.

On Monday night, July 1st Frank and Carolanne Imhoff showed up at Jerry and Irene Gares's residence in Edgewater near the *Delaware River* to drive thirty miles southeast to Hammonton and be Nick and Penelope's guests at the annual gala Lions Club Gold Raffle Dinner.

"Well Jerry," Frank affably said to his jovial brother-in-law, "at last we're gonna' see those special seven white marble statues Nick's been jabbering and bragging about. We certainly don't want to disappoint our host. Remember to make a big fuss over the marble figures."

"Knowing Nick, they're probably authentic-looking right down to the last muscle and ligament," Jerry Gares predicted.

"Our friend will go to any length or to any expense just to get exactly what he wants. Nothing stops Nick Mitropoulos for very long. That's what I admire most about him! His tenacity!"

"I hope those male statues are wearing tunics or something!" Irene Gares laughed. "I still possess a degree of modesty even in this anything goes age of hedonism."

"Are we going to meet Bill and Fran Burns at Nick's place or at Kerrie-Brooke Caterers?" Carolanne inquired. "I don't remember hearing where!"

"At Nick's place!" Jerry affirmed. "Bill and Fran are driving over from their home in Blackwood and not from their seashore place in Stone Harbor."

After Frank drove his *Suburban* off of Valley Avenue down Golf Road to Greco Court, he pulled into the U-shaped cement driveway at number 37, Nick and Penelope Mitropoulos's opulent residential palace.

"Nick had bought all eight lots on the cul-de-sac so that his family would have total privacy," Jerry related. "Nick's a strange guy in some respects. He loves the people that patronize his diners but our friend also loves being isolated from them when they aren't paying customers."

"I suppose he has to deal with the random public at his many restaurants," Carolanne conjectured and related, "and sometimes a person reaches his or her saturation point. Frank and I know how Nick feels about dealing with the general public simply by managing *our* one and only furniture store."

Betty and Tom Larson and Fran and Professor Bill Burns were already at Nick and Penelope's Greco Court mansion when the Imhoffs and the Gares rang the front doorbell. They were enthusiastically greeted by Penelope, who escorted the four into the yet to be furnished grand den overlooking Nick's newly landscaped garden.

"This new room is absolutely breathtaking," Frank Imhoff immediately observed and praised. "Gorgeous California red cedar wood beamed ceiling, oak floor with maple wood plugs, waist' high birch wood cabinets along the wall and pinewood trim around the abundant array of full and half-length *Andersen* windows. And those overhead trapezoid windows really complement the room's overall appearance," the very impressed interior decorator complimented. "I'm absolutely delighted with this splendid room! I already have a vivid idea in my mind of the right Oriental rug and of the exact mauve soft leather furniture that would easily blend-in perfectly with this very appealing great room."

"Nick, you look a little glum!" Jerry Gares perceptively remarked. "Is everything all right?"

"Come outside to the garden," Tom Larson requested. "Then Nick will show and explain to everyone why he's a bit depressed today."

Everybody anxiously stepped out to the newly landscaped garden that was actually more of an arboretum featuring over one hundred different varieties of trees, flowers and shrubs. In the center of the sublime garden was a miniature marble Greek-temple bar accompanied by eight white marble stools. Not far away from the pillared-bar stood seven awesome white marble statues standing on white marble pedestals, which were aesthetically situated on marble bases.

"Look at this fantastic outdoor bar designed like a Greek temple!" Bill Burns genuinely exclaimed. "It looks like it belongs on the Acropolis next to the Parthenon!"

"It's modeled after the Nike Temple," Nick solemnly and proudly informed his guests. "Nike was the Greek goddess of victory. I love the temple-bar that Tom and his crew have put together for me but I'm a little bent out of shape about the seven statues."

"They look pretty sensational to my eyes!" Jerry sincerely praised and shared. "I wouldn't mind owning just one of these fabulous beauties!"

"Well, someone in the shipping department of the company out in California made a major mistake with the pedestals," Tom Larson explained with a reddened face that honestly expressed his personal embarrassment. "Nick will explain the true nature of the dilemma! I haven't the heart."

The disconsolate host explained that the seven statues were perfect and that *he* was satisfied with their craftsmanship and general appearance. The problem was with the names carved on the seven pedestals. "Look here," Nick pointed out in a disgusted tone of voice. "The name on the pedestal says 'Jupiter', but it oughta' say Zeus. Jupiter was the Roman chief god and Zeus was the king of the Mt. Olympus Greek gods!"

"Oh, now I see," Carolanne caught on. "And this fellow with wings on his helmet and on his sandals should be the Greek god Hermes and not the Roman god 'Mercury' as *he* has been accidentally labeled."

72

"And this statue holding the trident that says 'Neptune' should have 'Poseidon' carved on it," Penelope pointed out, "and this one that has 'Heracles' on it should have the name 'Hercules'! How could anybody make such a dumb blunder getting their Greek and Roman mythologies confused?"

"And 'Bacchus' here should be 'Dionysus', the Greek and not the Roman god of wine," Nick related to his audience in a rather disgruntled and disappointed tone of voice, "and 'Pluto' over there should be 'Hades' and good old 'Mars' ought to be 'Ares'. Now how could those California shippers have screwed up big-time like this? This is definitely an example of employee incompetence!"

"I must confess," Tom Larson disgustedly admitted, "I didn't know the difference between the Greek and the Roman god names on the pedestals until Nick turned green and told me of the lousy shipping error. Some guy in the company's shipping department had sent the wrong pedestals with the wrong pictures to identify and misrepresent the right gods with the right pedestals. I actually believed that the statues had been erected properly until Nick had brought the unfortunate discrepancy to my attention. What a horrible disappointment!"

"And Tom, after your Williamstown home had been ransacked," Jerry Gares sympathetically noted, "your mind wasn't exactly looking for statue name irregularities. You were just concentrating on following directions and assumed that everything planned was manufactured to Nick's specifications and then efficiently shipped from California to Jersey."

"And I had to be away in Bermuda!" Nick lamented and complained. "I couldn't wait a week and then notice the mistake exactly when the statues were being delivered here. I suppose I'm a victim of my own impetuousness! I've always hated procrastination and now I've inadvertently punished myself because of it. I should've never assumed that things would've automatically been done right!"

"It's nothing that can't be readily solved," Tom Larson diplomatically assured the perplexed owner of the house. "I've already contacted the company out in Los Angeles and they're gonna' send a shipment of the desired Greek pedestals out later this week. It's a good thing I didn't cement the statues to the pedestals. I wanted to first make sure Nick was satisfied with them," Larson explained to the other guests. "At least I did one thing right!"

"Look, let's forget about it for now!" the frustrated diner tycoon entreated. "Damaged property can always be replaced but good friends can't be. Let's have a few cocktails from my new out-door temple-bar and then we'll head over to Kerrie-Brooke and have some fun at the Gold Raffle Dinner."

The five couples had a terrific time at the Lions Club Gold Raffle Dinner. Nick was fortunate to win a five-thousand-dollar consolation prize in the elimination drawing and the good-hearted Greek immediately presented the check to a very surprised Tom Larson. "Here, take this Tom," Mitropoulos sympathetically and sincerely said. "Thanks for being my guest at the Gold Raffle. I know the insurance company is gonna' send an adjuster to pay for the vandalism to your home and you'll never get back full value. This five thousand should help compensate for the difference!"

"Thanks a lot Nick!" Tom happily acknowledged. "I don't know of too many people who would genuinely display similar generosity! I assure you Nick that this money will be well-used for domestic necessities!"

While Nick and his friends were celebrating at the gala Hammonton Lions Club Gold Raffle Dinner, seven motorcycles pulled into a remote dirt trail that led into a woods situated behind the resplendent mansion at 37 Greco Court. Tank, leader of "The Fugitives," a notorious Williamstown biker gang gave the signals for his intimidating disciples to halt and then to shut off their *Harley* hogs.

"Why did ya' take us to this friggin' woods?" Bruiser, Tank's ill-tempered first lieutenant asked. "I just wanta' get drunk. I'm allergic to poison ivy!"

"Listen stink bomb!" the scar-faced Tank reprimanded Bruiser. "I staked this special hit out yesterday and learned at a local gas station that the dude that owns the dump we're gonna' raid is at a big local shindig tonight. In fact, all of the bigwigs in Hammonton are not home tonight because they're attendin' the big Lions Club charity affair! The town's all ours to ransack, you dumb knucklehead!"

"Where'd ya' get the info' about this creep's pad?" Chains, the third toughest punk in the gang inquired. "Tank, how'd ya' know where it was?"

"Remember that neat vandalism gig we just pulled over in Williamstown," Tank told his half-dozen overzealous malicious apostles.

"Yeah, a guy named Larson. I believe Tom Larson was his scummy name," Knuckles recalled as he cracked all eight of his finger knuckles simultaneously. "We pulverized and ob-*litter*-ated his place, that's for sure! But what does Larson have to do with this Hammonton gig?"

"Ya' got a good memory Bozo!" Tank chided and ridiculed Knuckles. "Well, the guy that owns the place we're goin' to plunder tonight called Larson while I was drinkin' bourbon in the dumb dude's kitchen. The caller was such an imbecile that he left his name and Hammonton address on the answering machine. Was he friggin' stupid or what?"

"Wow!" Grunge butted in. "This guy deserves to have *his* palace vandalized. What do ya' say Punk?"

"Let's first see what kind of whiskey this rich freak drinks!" Punk encouraged his very anxious colleagues. "Then we'll get nasty and raunchy and tear the whole dump apart!"

"Okay idiots! Let's attack this rich dude's crib!" Tank convincingly commanded. "It's time to get some kicks. We'll break in from the back yard."

The seven unsavory grizzly-bearded derelicts followed a dirt path through the woods and arrived at a seven-foot-high red cedar fence that surrounded the perimeter of Nick Mitropoulos's inimitable garden, temple-bar and accompanying swimming pool. One by one the diabolical biker criminals awkwardly clambered up and tumbled over the temporary obstacle. Each nefarious intruder plunged into exotic shrubbery on the opposite side, doing instant damage to a holly bush, a dwarf Japanese maple, a dogwood tree and to three rhododendrons.

"Hey guys, check out the wild fancy bar with all the white pillars!" Tank indicated to his fanatical followers. "This guy must be a pillar of the community, ha, ha, ha! It looks like Caesar's tomb or Caesar's Palace or something like that!"

"Let's get drunk on the jerk's booze and then we'll trash his house worse than the one we just did over in Williamstown," Bruiser suggested.

"The pad's probably wired with a silent alarm to the cop station!" Tank theorized and mentioned. "Instead, let's get drunk and then trash the guy's garden, temple-bar and then demolish those seven expensive statues over there. Then we'll blow this joint after stealin' all the guy's *Southern Comfort* and *Jack Daniels*!"

The seven giddy trespassers imbibed nearly a bottle of whiskey each and then recklessly staggered around the garden, breaking tree limbs, smashing glasses and then managing to all together lift and finally overturn the magnificent and opulent heavy white marble temple-bar. The obnoxious rowdy bikers were indeed quite proud of the widespread devastation they were causing.

"Okay you amateur hoodlums," Tank boisterously criticized, "let's each knock a statue off of its platform. This mission is gonna' be the best one yet! I can't wait to bust *Jupiter's* chops!"

The seven vile interlopers approached the seven immaculate white statues. Each brazen villain unzipped a side pocket to *his* black leather motorcycle jacket and removed a spray paint can. Then the gang's chieftain gave his belligerent disciples some final instructions.

"We'll first do some professional graffiti," Tank militantly ordered, "and then we'll topple the freakin' statues. Too bad we forgot to bring a sledgehammer to crumble these expensive figures into powder. Who the hell is this stupid *Jupiter* jerk anyway? Is *Jupiter* another planet or what? Ha, ha, ha! This marble idiot does look like he's out of this world! Ha, ha, ha!"

"Look at Neptune getting' ready for dinner!" Knuckles laughed. "That fork he's holdin' could be a dangerous *unconcealed* weapon! Ha, ha, ha!"

"Okay men," Tank yelled, "on the count of three we all, *hic,* spray these ancient dipstick dudes until there ain't no more paint in the cans! Are ya' turkeys ready? One, two…"

Before the seven intoxicated plunderers could utter "three," the white skin represented on the seven statues instantaneously turned to flesh-color. Each god then hopped in unison off of *his* marble pedestal and each immediately grabbed an astonished drunken unruly biker by the throat. Then the now-animated antagonized Greek gods (with the incidental Roman names) each separately lifted one of the seven nefarious astonished bullies up into the air.

As the groggy and astounded bikers gagged and choked, each god justly punished *his* chosen adversary. All six gods and demi-god (Heracles or Hercules) suddenly shot up to a height of twenty-foot-tall, holding their respective gasping bikers suspended in the air with determined superhuman grips. Pluto (Hades), god of death flung Grunge through the air in the direction of the kidney-shaped swimming pool. The unfortunate biker's head crashed against the diving board, instantly snapping the degenerate's neck.

Mercury (Hermes), the messenger god used his winged sandals and rose a hundred feet into the dark night sky. Beneath an almost full moon the deity dropped Punk like a bomb into the center of the overturned marble-temple bar, causing multiple internal injuries and a very slow death. The handsome mythological messenger god then gracefully and adroitly drifted down to the ground, landing with the greatest of ease.

Stimulated by Mercury's improvisation, Bacchus (Dionysus), imaginative god of wine reached down with his free left hand and picked-up a half-full bottle of vodka. The deity shoved the bottle's neck down Knuckles' throat, and after the vandal frantically gasped for air, the infuriated god tossed the helpless biker into the shallow end of Nick Mitropoulos's swimming pool where the ill-starred victim suffered broken legs and finally drowned from the bottle's delicious intoxicating contents.

Mars (Ares), god of war then flipped Bruiser high into the night air twenty-feet or so above the three-story-home's orange tile roof, and in one very impressive motion, took an arrow from *his* quiver and then aimed his bow. Ares fired an accurate dart at his plummeting target, hitting Bruiser directly in the center of his chest and immediately sending his prey's black soul directly to Hades (the Greek after-world) to join Sisyphus and Tantalus's illustrious company.

Neptune (Poseidon), inspired by what his eyes had beheld squeezed and twisted Chains into a knot and then flung the modern barbarian high above the abode's roof. The god of the sea carefully aimed and threw *his* trident, which quickly penetrated Chains' abdomen. The mighty thrust immediately killed the very petrified biker, who ultimately fell and collided against Knuckles bobbing remains on the fringe of the swimming pool.

Finally Jupiter (Zeus), king of the gods, flipped totally perplexed Tank high into the lower atmosphere and sent a lightning bolt piercing into and through the gang leader's heart, immediately terminating *his* motley earthly existence once and for all. The seven Greek gods with Roman names quickly looked at each other, smiled, shrank down to six-foot in height and then each hopped back onto *his* individual pedestal. Within thirty seconds, each god's skin changed from flesh-color back into hard white marble.

* * * * * * * * * * * * *

At midnight Nick, Penelope and their guests returned to 37 Greco Court after feasting and reveling at Kerri-Brooke caterers. The cheerful diner operator deactivated the alarm system before entering his posh residence. Penelope, Carolanne, Fran Burns, Irene Gares and Betty Larson stepped from the massive pink marble-floored foyer through the library and then into the newly constructed den. They exited the grand room to the back garden and soon the five women emitted a series of shrieks and screams that startled the men, who were still chatting in the ornate foyer. Nick, Frank, Jerry, Bill and Tom all rushed to the backyard garden to learn the source of the hysteria.

The women were still gawking, crying and wildly shouting in response to the horrible carnage their eyes had perceived. The Hammonton Police Department was immediately notified of the "massacre on Greco Court." Soon four police cars, a state trooper's cruiser and three town rescue squad ambulances were on the "crime scene."

"Do you know any of these dead persons?" Lieutenant Kevin Santora asked the mansion's owner.

"Dead persons did you say!" Nick Mitropoulos angrily challenged. "They aren't dead persons. They're dead animals, vandals, filthy human scum that were ransacking my garden!"

"Mr. Mitropoulos," Detective Mark Frederico said, "please calm down and get a grip on your emotions. We know you're under great duress at the moment! Please try and be more cooperative! We have to figure out the cause of these bizarre deaths! Now kindly calm down and cooperate!"

"Mr. Mitropoulos, do you know any *one* of these dead persons?" Lieutenant Santora repeated.

"No Officer, I don't associate with biker gangs or villainous hooligans and the like," Nick all-too-honestly replied, "and I don't know any of this bloody human trash clutterin' up my garden! I find your questions insulting and preposterous!"

"Mr. Mitropoulos, for your own sake, please refrain' from name-calling. Everyone is a suspect until we catch the culprits that committed this atrocious mass murdering!" Detective Frederico warned.

"Oh great! These worthless scumbags climb over my fence, ransack my exotic garden, destroy my white marble Nike bar and now you're investigatin' why these important citizens have been killed on my property!" Nick strenuously objected. "I can't help it if I'm not as politically correct as you guys are!"

"Be careful of what you say!" Lieutenant Santora cautioned. "Anything you utter or mutter could be held against you! How do you know *they* climbed over your fence?"

"How else could they have gotten into my garden? I don't see any damned parachutes lying around!" Nick stubbornly retorted. "What kind of Mickey Mouse investigation are you' officers conducting, anyway! I wanta' call my lawyer and get his opinion before I answer any more of your lame irrelevant questions. I wanta' talk to your boss, the Chief. He's a regular at my Hammonton diner and I know him pretty well! In fact I was just in his company over at the Lions Club Gold Raffle!"

"Lieutenant, the coroner's people are here now to conduct their own probe into the murders," Patrolman Angelo Ingemi announced to his superior.

"But what about the vandalism!" Nick yelled at the still-stunned police investigators. "The lowlife creeps have done over fifty thousand dollars worth of damage to my property!"

"Mr. Mitropoulos, nothing like this has ever before happened in the town of Hammonton," Detective Frederico informed the very distraught homeowner. "We're investigating what happens to be a very mysterious mass murder here. Your insurance company will take care of the property damage. Property can be replaced but people can't," the department's veteran detective sanctimoniously preached. "We must always value lives over property. Now please try to be more rational and objective. Mr. Mitropoulos, we know you and your wife are under extreme emotional stress right now!"

"Whoever killed these seven pieces of trash did society a big favor!" Nick yelled as his wife and Tom Larson attempted escorting him back into *his* mansion. "They've never done anything constructive or beneficial in their damned lives! They're disgusting drug addicts, avowed alcoholics and destructive savages dedicated to violence. And *you* cops happen to feel sorry for this fecal matter human garbage!" the very upset Greek/American criticized as he was tugged from his vandalized garden and then quickly ushered inside his mansion.

Finally Jerry, Bill, Tom and Frank managed to gently pull Nick into the new "grand room" where the group then watched the police and the county coroner's staff' conduct their comprehensive investigations.

"Have you ever seen anything as gruesome as this in all your years on the force?" the stunned assistant county coroner asked Lieutenant Santora.

"No Sir I haven't!" the still-shocked officer confidentially admitted. "One guy is shot with a strange-looking ancient arrow and another guy is killed with a giant three-pronged solid bronze fork that's deeply lodged inside his guts! It's definitely the weirdest evidence I've ever gathered! It's all sort of surreal."

"And," the baffled assistant coroner added, "our preliminary findings reveal that one guy is apparently dead from electrocution and another homicide victim, the one with the vodka bottle shoved down his throat is dead from drowning. Not drowning from water while floating in a swimming pool, mind you. I mean the man has drowned from an excess of vodka in his lungs. Of course," the assistant coroner qualified, "I make these remarks strictly off the record because they haven't been confirmed by a thorough battery of laboratory forensics soon to be conducted."

Inside the mansion's grand room Tom Larson put an arm around Nick Mitropoulos and attempted to comfort the still highly disturbed and traumatized man. "My house has been ransacked too, Nick," Larson said in an effort to emotionally connect with and console his wealthy acquaintance. "I know exactly how you feel about your garden and about that dead biker scum layin' out there."

"Thanks Tom," Nick responded in a more conciliatory voice than the vehement one Mitropoulos had previously exhibited and directed at the police interrogators. "I appreciate your moral support. I just have no regard for wicked people that get satisfaction from destroying the property and lives of others!"

"Nick, do you still want me to go forward and order new pedestals with Greek names on them instead of the Roman names you now have?" Tom Larson asked. "I'm sure the California' firm we dealt with has the right pedestals in stock! We'll just have to get the ordering numbers correct this time."

The incensed diner mogul stared out of the six full-length grand room *Andersen* windows into the chaotic investigation being performed in his exotic garden that contained more expensive shrubs and trees than would be found at the average retail nursery. Nick focused *his* attention on the seven statues having Roman designations beneath them in his cherished "Greek garden."

Mitropoulos's intense contemplation and scrutiny led to several amazing discoveries. Neptune (Poseidon), god of the sea was no longer holding his trident in *his* right hand, and Mars (Ares), god of war, now had two arrows in his marble quiver instead of the three that had been inside the stone pouch that same afternoon.

Nick Mitropoulos slowly turned to the Williamstown stonemason and prudently said, "No Tom, I think I'll keep these seven pedestals even though they have Roman names instead of Greek ones inscribed on them. The Roman names have protected my home very well from being abused and ransacked, and I don't want to offend the gods, if you know what I mean! I must respect *their* wishes!"

Tom Larson peered out at the seven lifeless bodies in and around Nick's kidney-shaped swimming pool. Then Larson appreciatively studied the splendid seven marble statues in wonder. "I'm a very superstitious man too," the accomplished mason confidentially divulged, "and believe me Nick, I know exactly what you mean and where you're coming from! There just might be such a thing as almighty justice after all!"

"The Heroic Belt"

Mr. Thomas Farley loved ancient history, particularly the significant cultural contributions the Greeks had made to Western Civilization in the areas of science, education, architecture, literature, athletics, government and philosophy. The Hammonton High School social studies teacher was fascinated by everything Hellenistic from the Olympian gods to the *Persian Wars*, from Aristotle to Socrates and from the Oracle at Delphi to the celebrated Olympic Games.

Now that the New Jersey instructor was retiring as of July 1, 2003 after thirty-five years of dedicated service and now that his wife was hanging up her diploma after thirty challenging years of instructing at the Winslow Elementary School in Vineland, the two could finally relax from their arduous careers and reward themselves with a "two-week Greek dream hiatus."

"Well Doreen," Tom began as the couple packed their final suitcase for the next morning's drive from 127 Woodlawn Avenue to New York's bustling *Kennedy International Airport*, "let's not forget our passports and photo *IDs*. Airport security is pretty rigid after that terrible *9-11* catastrophe."

"Yes dear," Doreen answered as she neatly folded the next to last of Tom's shirts before placing the item in the gray *American Tourister* luggage piece opened on their bed. "All of that airport precaution is for *our* own protection. It must have been much safer getting from village to village in ancient Greece. If anyone should know about that, it certainly would be you!"

"Traveling was always a difficult thing, especially in ancient times," her husband glumly replied. "Oxcarts had trouble fording rivers and were often cumbersome being tugged by animals up jagged mountain paths. And as I always told my college prep' Ancient History classes, three-fourths of Greece is covered by limestone mountains that are extremely hard to ascend. And coincidentally, the hundreds of islands that dot the Aegean and Ionian Seas are actually the exposed peaks of submerged mountain ranges."

"I suppose the mountains were where the Greeks got the marble to build all of those magnificent temples and statues," Doreen conjectured and replied as she deposited the last article of clothing in the final gray suitcase.

"Yes and I can't wait to visit the *Parthenon* up on the Acropolis," Tom stated with more than mild anticipation. "I've been waiting to do that pilgrimage ever since college. I've been talking about it to my students for the past three and a half decades but never had the opportunity to ever see what I was discussing. Now's my big chance."

"Now please just wait a minute Tom," Doreen objected. "I was only a second grade teacher all those years and the subject matter you're throwing at me is a little more advanced than phonics or grade-school math' ever was. It's like you're speaking another dialect of English with that sophisticated terminology you just mentioned about a *Parthenon* and an Acropolis. Please downshift to my knowledge level."

"Sorry dear Wife," Farley apologized with a broad grin. "I should have realized I was getting a little too far ahead of myself'. The Acropolis is a flattop mountain in the center of ancient Athens and the *Parthenon* is the splendid architectural masterpiece built on the Acropolis to honor Athena, the protector goddess of the city. Roughly translated into English the word Acropolis means 'city in the air.' Just think of *acro*bat and metro*polis* to remember that academic idea."

"Why did the Athenians construct this so-called city in the air?" Doreen Farley inquired. "Wouldn't it have been much easier to build the temples on flat ground level? That would seem to make much more sense."

"Yes it would have upon first impression," her spouse agreed. "But the Athenians were very worried about invasions from nearby Asia Minor and the people believed they could defend their city's most sacred buildings from a higher elevation. Throughout history," Tom lectured, "the soldiers and armies occupying the high ground always maintained a distinct advantage during a battle."

"Well then, did the Athenians have any important structures built on the low ground?" Doreen queried. "It seems peculiar that an advanced civilization would build everything in consideration of being attacked. Then everyone would have lived and worked on mountain peaks. Why were the Greeks so defensive-minded? Were they paranoid?"

Tom reflected for a moment to garner a feasible explanation to Doreen's inquisitiveness. He had assumed that his mate had a fundamental background in history but apparently she had forgotten much information from her high school textbooks and from her college elective course preparations. "Well now, the Athenians of Plato's time had a busy marketplace beneath the

Acropolis called the Agora," the history scholar revealed. "Not all of the famous temples were situated on the Acropolis. For example, the Temple of Apollo and the Temple of Ares were constructed next to shops known as stoas. The Odeion was a theater in the Agora's center, and the Fountain House was where people would come to get their daily water supply. Several key government buildings were also a part of the Agora complex."

"I guess that's where Socrates and Plato would hang out?" Doreen speculated and asked. "The two thinkers had to do something to pass the time without any televisions, computers, telephones, *VCRs*, radios or stereos around to keep them occupied."

"Correct!" her husband gasped while feigning amazement. "The Agora was not only a marketplace where food and goods were bought and sold but it also was the center of gossip and discussion for the entire city. Many philosophers would congregate there and then stroll up to the Acropolis to admire the *Parthenon* and the even more exquisite Temple of Athena Nike," Tom explained. "Many statues of Greek gods lined the Agora, and later in history the Romans probably modeled their famous Forum after the renowned Athenian marketplace. Although the Romans were great conquerors, they were better borrowers than inventors. The Greeks had the Romans beat when it came down to artistic imagination and ingenuity."

"Why do you love the Greeks so much after talking about them in classrooms for thirty-five years?" Mrs. Farley inquired. "One would think that the novelty would have worn off by now! Doesn't the subject bore you after so much repetition?"

"The Greeks were the first genuine European civilization on the face of the earth," the husband matter-of-factly declared. "We owe everything from democracy, theater,' drama and from justice to scientific logic to that marvelous creative culture. You name it, art, music, biology, and mathematics' as well as all the other subjects taught in modern-day schools have their roots in Greek thought and in Greek tradition. I suppose even phonics and simple addition and subtraction originated in and around Athens too," Tom elaborated. "It all started in ancient Greece, a land no bigger than Kansas or Nebraska strategically wedged between the Mediterranean and the Black Seas. And Doreen, that's why I'm thrilled to death to be able to visit the country and view its spectacular ruins and historic places. Do you now understand my motivation to go there?"

"What did the Greeks call all those that were not of their culture?" the wife curiously asked. "Geeks?" she laughed.

"Barbarians!" Tom bluntly articulated with an exaggerated giggle. "And the Greeks preferred drinking wine diluted with water as their main thirst-quencher. Anyone caught drinking milk was scorned and ridiculed or maybe even ostracized. Milk was regarded as a drink worthy only of animals, slaves and barbarians."

* * * * * * * * * * *

The *United Airlines* flight from *Kennedy International Airport* had a refueling stopover at London's *Heathrow* and then the 757 continued onward to its glorious destination, Athens, Greece. The Farleys were now immensely enjoying their smooth flight over and across the European continent.

"I'd have liked to have stayed in London a few days and view Buckingham Palace, Parliament, Big Ben and the Tower of London up close," Doreen regretted. "Now there's an old city rich in tradition too."

"And don't forget Piccadilly Circus, 10 Downing Street and Trafalgar Square," her husband authoritatively added. "But if this Greek vacation works out without any major complications we'll schedule England sometime next summer. I'd love to attend a concert at the Albert Hall. We're probably flying over southern France right now without even talking about the sights of Paris. But I can't wait to see the impressive ruins of enduring structures built during the *Golden Age* of Pericles."

The jumbo jet landed at *Athens International Airport* on schedule and after passing through customs with their five burdensome luggage pieces, the couple located an accommodating driver whose jitney transported them to the front entrance of their attractive hotel just off Piraeus Street, within walking distance of Monastiraki Square.

"The Piraeus is where Socrates would often walk to from the Acropolis discussing topics like justice and honesty with fellow philosophers," Tom excitedly related to his somewhat attentive wife. "The Piraeus is about five miles away from Athens and was and to this day *is* the port leading into the main part of the city. Doreen, I don't expect you to be as enthused about being here as I am."

"You know so much about this place even before touring it for the first time!" Doreen marveled and related. "Maybe you should write a textbook on the subject when we return to the States. That should keep you busy on the computer for a good while."

The travel agent had arranged a host of side trips to supplement the Farleys' whirlwind Athenian vacation. In the next several sultry days the couple had toured the Agora ruins and then ascended steps up the steep hill to the Acropolis, a ten-acre plot featuring the remains of the once resplendent *Parthenon*.

Other wonderful bus and plane side excursions were taken after the third day in Athens. Those trips were to Delphi to visit the site of the Oracle and the original Olympic Games, to Knossos, Crete where the Farleys viewed and took photographs of King Minos's excavated palace' ruins, and then to Mycenae, the legendary city of King Agamemnon, leader of the 1184 BC Achaean expedition that according to legend defeated the powerful city of Troy.

Of course, Tom told his wife all about the valiant heroes Achilles and Odysseus, and how the cunning King of Ithaca imaginatively thought up the idea of the wooden horse that led to Troy's demise. And the husband eagerly related other popular myths about ancient Greek champions to his patient wife, such heralded champions as Perseus, Atalanta, Theseus, Jason and Hercules. It was as if Mr. Thomas Farley was again teaching his Ancient History course on location at Hammonton High School to his now captive audience of one.

On the day before the couple's scheduled departure from Athens, the pair decided to curtail their exhaustive sightseeing activities. Mrs. Farley elected to shop with Mrs. Betty Ingemi, an American tourist she had met at the hotel. The women desired to purchase some souvenirs in the many ritzy stores between Omonoia Square and Syntagma Square.

"Doreen, you and Betty can do your shopping together," Tom suggested. "It's very safe in *that* section of Athens. As for me, I feel a bit adventurous so I'll take a stroll over to the Plaka. The area has a Turkish atmosphere with many intricate winding cobblestone alleys and lanes dotted with cafes, artifact shops and small restaurants," the curious tourist added. "There's also an excellent view of the Acropolis from many vantage points inside the Plaka. I'm getting a trifle sentimental about leaving this wonderful metropolis so I need to admire the 'city on the hill' one final time. Tomorrow morning it's off to London again and then we'll have to endure our grueling return trans-Atlantic zip back to New York."

"Okay, but please be careful dear!" Doreen advised her still muscular husband. "You never know exactly where an evil-minded terrorist might be lurking in this day and age!"

Tom hailed and took a taxi to the seedy Plaka district, which had a distinct dissimilarity when compared to the rest of the historic city. The narrow streets reminded Farley of the mythical labyrinth, the maze-of-tunnels, home to the lethal Minotaur, a cannibalistic monster that had the body of a man and the head of a bull. The subterranean network of interlocking passages was rumored to lie below King Minos's Cretan palace at Knossos.

After downing a cup of strong coffee at a dingy café, Tom Farley walked up a narrow cobblestone street in the direction of a fortuneteller's stone front business establishment. A dark complexioned woman stood outside her tiny base of operation and beckoned in plain English, "Sir, I speak very good your language. I am Cassandra, fore-teller of the future and predictor of *your* future, Mr. Thomas Farley. Please come inside my humble abode and I shall take great pleasure in advising you of something you need to know."

"How did you know my name?" the vacationing retired teacher asked. "Are you clairvoyant?"

"No Mr. Farley, I know no one by the strange name of Claire Voyant," the gypsy woman sincerely answered. "I already informed you Mr. Farley that my name is Cassandra, in honor of the great prophetess of antiquity."

"How much do you charge for a reading?" the American defensively responded. "I don't take kindly to rip-off artists and price gougers."

"Only fifty of your U.S. dollars is my fee!" the sinister-looking woman responded. "But I will not exactly be giving you a standard reading, Mr. Thomas Farley. I will give you a vital piece of information that is going to save your life many times. Fifty dollars will prove to be more than just a token investment."

"Well then, I don't think I'm quite ready for the family cemetery plot just yet and I'm entirely too young to be pushing up daisies," the ex' social studies teacher awkwardly jested.

"My wife would balk at me spending fifty dollars so frivolously, but in that she's not here right now I'll take you up on your intriguing offer. Here's a crisp new fifty dollar bill with *Ulysses S. Grant's* incomparable stoic portrait featured on the front."

"Whatever you say! But I warn you sir that it is unwise to mock my advice!" the dark dressed grim-faced woman gravely replied. "Now Mr. Farley, heed my important words very carefully. If you' are approached by a vendor selling you a belt having eight special golden buckles be sure to buy it immediately! It is guaranteed to save your life!"

"Is this some kind of scam or trick?" Farley yelled. "I don't like frauds or hoaxes! You don't even have a crystal ball! Is that all I get for my fifty dollars?" the tourist squawked. "I'm going to report you to the Better Business Bureau, if Athens has such an agency!"

"Mr. Farley, that is the extent of my advice," the odd-looking fortuneteller uttered. "Now be gone and soon you will meet someone with the item I have described that will honestly save your life. I encourage you to honor my wise counsel."

'I'll bet this old hag is in cahoots with a quick-talking phony belt salesman, and the peddler's probably going to be *her* anonymous derelict husband!' Farley suspected and theorized. "Okay Cassandra, you craftily won yourself fifty dollars! And since I am superstitious by nature, I'll have to again contribute to your deceitful cause by buying the first belt offered to me in this very eerie but quite refreshing Plaka section."

An elderly whiskered mendicant wearing a dirty white turban accosted Thomas Farley several blocks west of Madame Cassandra's place of business. "Sir, I have a magnificent black leather belt with eight beautiful golden buckles. Each decorative buckle is positioned at separate five-inch distances from the main buckle, which as you can see right now shows the image of the Greek hero Perseus."

"Who are the other heroes represented on the belt?" Tom asked. "Are they as famous in literature as Perseus?"

"Why yes they are sir," the old gypsy amiably replied. "We also have Jason, Achilles, Theseus, Atalanta, Odysseus, Hercules and a mystery face I cannot remember."

"I hate to correct your logic," Farley admonished, "but Atalanta was a female. Therefore she technically was a *heroine* and not a hero. And also Mr. Belt Salesman, you should know that Hercules is the Roman name for the Greek hero Heracles, whom *you* falsely identified as a Greek named *Hercules*!"

"You have great knowledge about this country's heritage!" the vagabond complimented with exaggerated flattery. "Now kind Sir, will you purchase this extraordinary belt from me? It will surely save your life!"

"How much money do you want for it?" Tom nervously inquired. "Don't be too high or I might just walk away and buy my wife a few trinkets instead."

"Three hundred American dollars!" the elderly itinerant sternly replied. "Only three hundred American dollars to save your life!" he inflexibly reiterated.

Such foolish extravagance was contrary to Thomas Farley's parsimonious nature. "That's a little too expensive and completely out of my price range!" the frugal prospective purchaser admitted. "How about if I just buy the belt with only the fake golden image of Perseus on it? What would my cost then be? Fifty bucks cash on delivery?"

"Mr. Farley, the belt is not for sale if that is the arrangement you insist upon," the vagrant threatened in broken accented but very comprehensible English. "If you fail to acquire this belt then you are doomed to die an early very painful death!"

"Well, now that you've put the problem in those exact terms," Tom compromised, "here's three *Ben Franklins*. I'll put this belt around my waist right now so that I am immediately protected from unforeseen devastation or disaster. And Sir, you may keep my old brown belt. It's definitely seen better days!"

"Thank you very much Mr. Farley!" the old scruffy rag picker exclaimed. "You won't regret owning that belt I just sold you, I assure you Sir!"

"How do you know my name?" Tom incredulously asked. "Do you have a cell phone?"

"Let's just say I mentally know it and leave it at that!" the belt huckster mysteriously answered.

After Tom Farley made his peculiar acquisition and donned his shiny-but-gaudy belt, he thought, 'I must be losing my negotiating touch. I allowed that old hawker to out-haggle me! I was born a superstitious fool and have remained one to this very day!'

When the American tourist rounded the next corner, he took another glimpse of the majestic white marble *Parthenon* up on the Acropolis. Then Farley flagged down a taxi to transport him

90

back to the hotel. 'I'll tell my wife I only paid fifty dollars for *my* precious souvenir!' he considered. 'Doreen will still chastise me for being a sucker waiting to be exploited! All Greek chiselers were not ancient sculptors, that's for sure!'

Cassandra met her husband outside a dull dreary poorly lit Turkish restaurant. "The Plaka has been very profitable for us today Demetri!" she acknowledged and reported. "I told the man to visit you and buy the belt and my advice cost him fifty dollars. It's a good thing that my cousin Nicolas at the hotel desk took the picture of Mr. Thomas Farley and wrote *his name* on the back. Otherwise we could have never pulled our little operation off so easily today!"

"Right you are Cassandra!" Demetri agreed. "I would have given Mr. Farley that belt for free just to get it out of our family's possession. Its enchantment can become most dangerous when it is used to its fullest extent!"

"You speak the truth and should be commended for it," Cassandra praised her scruffy-looking spouse. "Now let's go and eat the finest meal we've had in years!"

Inside the hotel lobby Doreen and Betty met-up with a thoroughly fatigued Tom Farley. When he apologized for spending "fifty dollars" for the "tinny-looking" hero' belt, his wife and her new acquaintance both heartily laughed.

"Tom, I had always thought your taste in apparel was a tad more fastidious! I wouldn't give you two cents for that tawdry pieces of garbage!" Doreen criticized. "But since I'm in Betty's company I'll go easy on you for now! You really have horrendous taste Tom Farley! That belt looks like it belongs inside the Hammonton Salvation Army bin next to Wal-Mart! In fact, not even Wal-Mart would sell it!"

"We bought some tee-shirts and nick-knacks at three different souvenir shops!" Betty Ingemi merrily stated to send the conversation into a more positive direction.

"You could have bought the same items on the Atlantic City boardwalk at a third of the rip-off prices you paid here in Athens!" Tom cynically joked.

"Well husband," Doreen blithely interrupted, "at least you didn't squander your hard-earned fifty dollars on a quack fortuneteller over in the Plaka district!"

* * * * * * * * * *

Tom and Doreen Farley were back residing at 127 Woodlawn Avenue late the following night. They required several days of recuperation to get over their jet-lag-fatigue losing seven hours time flying west from London to the United States. But after Doreen had her ten rolls of film developed at the Hammonton Wal-Mart, the wife realized how educational and how rewarding *their* "ultimate Greek adventure" had been.

The former social studies pedagogue wore his pretentious "hero's belt" everywhere except in the shower and to bed. Tom absorbed plenty of good-natured bantering from his critical wife, who made mention of the "disenchanting piece of costume jewelry" on the average of three times every day. Despite the daily humorous-oriented mockery, the sensitive husband remembered Cassandra and the gypsy man's haunting statements and courageously persevered through his wife's occasional benign ridiculing.

The following Saturday the Farleys had the honor of taking their six-year-old grandson Daniel to *Six Flags Great Adventure Amusement Theme Park* in Jackson, New Jersey, forty-five miles northeast of Hammonton. After spending the morning and early afternoon on kiddy rides and meandering through haunted houses with their energetic grandson, the Farleys decided to take it easy on themselves and pursue less stressful entertainment in the late afternoon. "I'll drive the three of us through the adjacent Safari Park," Tom suggested to his mate. "It's got every animal imaginable that lives outside New Jersey and Dan will be thrilled to see them up close wandering about in their simulated natural habitats."

"Great idea!" Doreen concurred. "I think Dan will get a kick out of seeing elephants, bears, tigers and lions up close. Are you sure it's safe?"

"Well there's always an element of risk no matter what you do," Tom cautioned, "but all of the safari park animals are well fed and are used to human contact. I've never read about an incident in the newspapers, and as you know Doreen I'm an avid reader, especially now that I'm officially retired."

Tom drove his 2001 green *Ford Explorer* to the *Great Adventure Safari Park* entrance where he purchased two adult and one child's admission tickets. Dan was delighted with the docile animals that came up to the *SUV* at various intervals, so Farley and other motorists stopped at certain spots to allow camels, alpacas, giraffes, llamas, deer and ostriches to sniff around the vehicle.

"The more aggressive animals are kept at a distance from the tourists!" Tom informed his wife, who was busy documenting a curious camel and a young giraffe lowering their heads to examine the enthralled threesome. "Notice those huge rhinoceroses nonchalantly grazing up on that hill."

"Yes, but there aren't any fences separating the vehicles from the giant creatures," Doreen aptly noted. "It's a good thing that the park has nearly tamed and domesticated their wild animals. Otherwise there might be a lot of problems associated with doing this sort of impromptu itinerary."

A small herd of lethargic Texas longhorns clogged the three-lane one-way road and one of them gently glanced its horn against the green *SUV*. A knot of seven vehicles was caught-up in the congestion but the motorists and their passengers didn't seem to mind the amusing temporary delay.

"I hope that we're insured for dents and scratches," the wife mildly scolded her husband. "Those longhorns could do a real number on a car or *SUV* even if it's by accident."

"That risk comes with the territory!" her husband maintained as Dan demanded, "I want more apple juice!" "Our grandson doesn't seem to be affected by all of the outside commotion! Why don't you just imitate *his* fine example?"

Tom fully halted the *SUV* so that Doreen could take a roll of snapshots of three ostriches and two giraffes strutting around on the *Explorer's* right passenger side while the remainder of the lethargic longhorns slowly stepped past on the left.

"Look at that!" Dan pointed before taking another sip from the straw inserted into his apple juice carton. "The ostrich is so close and so big! I like how he walks around and looks into the cars! He's so funny!"

Just then a male rhino' to the left abandoned its grazing area and approached the startled tourists seated in the seven halted vehicles. At first the enormous creature simply seemed curious, but some unknown factor caused it to become nervous and soon the dual-horned animal became rambunctious and then went totally berserk. It lowered its head and charged the light blue *Mercedes* sedan stopped directly in front of Tom's *Explorer*.

"Quick! Duck down!" Farley yelled to his two passengers. "I'll see if I can get this thing out of here!"

The other five cars took off in all directions but the battered *Mercedes* blocked Tom's means of escape. Farley inadvertently touched his belt buckle and wished that he could exit the area in a hurry. Before the driver could fathom exactly what the consequence of his action was, a tall muscular Greek hero dressed in authentic-looking battle attire appeared brandishing a drawn bronze sword.

"My God Doreen! Is this a staged performance?" the driver gasped to his wife with her head down near the dashboard. "That's Perseus! I would recognize him anywhere wearing his winged helmet and sandals!" But Doreen Farley still fearfully had her head down and her ears covered and interpreted not a word of her husband's exclamation.

The Greek hero swiftly raised his shiny bronze shield with his left arm and his glistening sword with his right hand. And in three piercing thrusts the hostile rhino' let out a ferocious squeal and then plopped to its knees and finally fell prone onto the asphalt three-lane road.

Doreen was still following Tom's earlier command to keep her head down. The anxious driver had an escape opportunity by steering to the right and Farley alertly accelerated out of harm's way, which he instantly took advantage of.

"That weird-looking man killed the rhinoceros!" Dan loudly shouted. "That funny-looking man in the funny clothes killed the rhinoceros!"

Farley looked into the rear-view mirror and observed the Greek hero glimmer and then quickly fade' back into mythology. It was at that very special moment that Tom fully realized the potential and the magical ability of his most exceptional "hero belt."

"Okay Doreen, you can raise your head up now!" Farley imperatively commanded. "That was really a close call!"

"What happened to the rhino?" his wife questioned with her head turned to the rear. "It's lying on the road and not moving!"

"A strange-looking man killed it!" Daniel informed his grandmother in sheer amazement.

"No Dan, that was a park ranger that tranquilized the wild rhino!" the driver corrected. "He just looked strange doing it!"

"Oh well," Doreen concluded, "I guess this trip to *Great Adventure* has been a great adventure after all! I hope no other emergency develops that will put us in jeopardy, rehearsed or not."

"Lightning never strikes twice!" Tom answered in a rather appropriate analogy. "I think we'll be absolutely safe and secure during the rest of our safari expedition. Dan, what did the man you saw look like?"

"Like Hercules in the cartoons I see on TV!" the boy honestly and emotionally replied. "He had on funny clothes! Goofy-looking clothes!"

"Well then Dan, just drink the rest of your delicious apple juice and get pleasure from seeing some neat mountain goats and nifty elephants up ahead!" the grandfather urged.

The following Friday afternoon Tom was returning from his monthly chiropractic appointment in Atco and traveling east on *Route 30* toward Hammonton. A motorist sped by him in a red *Toyota* and tooted his horn. Farley immediately identified the speedster as his cousin Jim Arnold from Egg Harbor.

'It's no secret why Jim's lost his driver's license three times!' Tom recollected. 'My cousin always thinks he's behind the wheel at the *Daytona 500* no matter where he's driving!'

Approaching the Ancora railroad bridge, Tom was horrified to witness Jim's red *Toyota* veer to avoid hitting a dog, crossing the highway and then wildly skidding out of control off the road. The runaway car glanced off a telephone pole, entered a wooded area, caromed off a tree and then turned over on its roof. Engine smoke was billowing up through the damaged hood and the sole occupant's life was suddenly in jeopardy.

Tom Farley was the first rescuer onto the scene. He peered inside the overturned wrecked *Toyota's* smashed windshield and noticed that his cousin had been knocked unconscious from the series of impacts. Flames were now shooting out from the upside-down car's hood and Tom had to act in an instant if Jim Arnold was to be salvaged from death by fire.

The desperate rescuer glanced down at his belt buckle but instead of Perseus occupying the front position, the hero Jason's image and name were now represented. The almost-delirious man wished that his cousin could miraculously evade the jaws of death, and after Farley touched the golden buckle' cameo with his right hand, the mythical hero along with seven husky Argonauts materialized from nothingness onto the Ancora accident scene.

The eight ancient Greeks effectively turned over the crushed *Toyota* in a jiffy, smashed open the driver's side door with their swords and pulled the numb figure from the now-blazing interior. Twenty feet away from the growing inferno Jason and a shipmate gently lowered James Arnold onto the highway's shoulder, and much to Tom Farley's astonishment, the Greek warrior and his loyal contingent momentarily examined their accomplishment and then magically evaporated into thin air.

Several Good Samaritan motorists stopped to render their assistance. One had a cell phone and called *911*. Ten minutes later the dispatched Hammonton Rescue Squad arrived at the spot of the extraordinary incident along with several New Jersey State Troopers. Tom made a statement to the policemen describing what he had observed.

"I was driving east on the *White Horse Pike* when the red *Toyota* passed me. A dog appeared in the passing lane and the car swerved off the highway, clipped a telephone pole, crashed into the tree at an angle and then flipped over," Tom carefully explained to the investigating trooper. "The driver somehow miraculously managed to get out of the vehicle before it caught fire and then he stumbled fifty feet or so until he began losing consciousness. Next the man fell to his knees and finally collapsed along the roadway. That guy was really pretty fortunate to survive such a traumatic ordeal!"

"Thank you for your description Mr. Farley," the second police officer appreciatively stated. "Since you were the only eyewitness, we'll have to rely on your testimony as the sole real tangible evidence we've got. Because the driver went off the road to avoid hitting the mutt, he won't be ticketed for reckless driving or reckless endangerment. But it's amazing what people can perform while under duress!" the trooper claimed. "Any ordinary driver would have been knocked silly from the series of horrible collisions and then would have died in the fire. Mr. Arnold is certainly a very lucky man to be able to elude the Grim Reaper's grasp like he had done!"

Tom's cousin, wearing a neck brace, was cautiously strapped onto the stretcher and then Jim Arnold was gently elevated and expertly placed in the ambulance's interior where a well-trained paramedic had oxygen and an I.V. tube ready for administration. Soon the ambulance's siren was wailing and the red and gray rescue squad vehicle was heading east in the direction of Hammonton's Kessler Memorial Hospital.

On the drive home on *Route 30*, Tom thought about his magical mythological belt and its fantastic golden buckle properties. 'Perseus slew Medusa the Gorgon while wearing the

Hat of Darkness and just last week he shows up at *Six Flags Great Adventure Safari Park* and slaughters an incensed rhinoceros. And then Jason and seven of the Argonauts are no longer in quest of the Golden Fleece. Instead they appear at the location of a serious automobile accident and rescue my cousin from certain incineration.'

Tom Farley stopped for a traffic light at Elmtowne Boulevard, peered down at his waist and turned his belt buckle upwards to study it. Incredibly each of the golden buckles had rotated all by themselves five inches in unison onto the next pants' belt loop. Now the hero Achilles' image was represented on the front belt buckle attachment and presumably was ready to perform some here-to-fore outlandish yet-to-be-known superhuman deed.

Upon reaching his Woodlawn Avenue home, Farley related to Doreen how Jim Arnold had been in a terrible car crash and had sustained several very critical injuries. "I think he'll pull through this one but it was a very close call that was really too close for comfort! I'm now going to notify members of his immediate family about what had taken place near the Ancora Railroad Bridge," he explained to his faithful wife without ever mentioning the intervention of the fantastic belt or the audacious hero Jason accompanied by seven brawny daring Argonauts.

When the next Saturday morning rolled around the retired history instructor drove his green *Explorer* to the Fairview Avenue *WaWa* convenience store to obtain several lottery tickets and a gallon of milk. He pulled into the crowded parking area followed by six rough and tumble bearded and tattooed bikers on their *Harley Davidson* hogs. 'I'm sure glad Jim's gonna' make it through his life-threatening injuries,' Tom considered. 'Now that his internal bleeding has been taken care of all that has to mend is a broken collarbone and a fractured tibia. I'll park my *SUV* in the back of the *WaWa* to keep my distance from those cruddy gruesome-looking bikers.'

Much to Tom's dismay the six bullies also rode to the store's rear parking area', hopped off of their choppers and started merrily conversing among themselves. 'They've blocked me in and now I'll have to politely ask the leader to move his motorcycle so that I'll be able to back out,' Tom conjectured. 'Some people are really egocentric and very inconsiderate of the needs of others.'

"Sir, would you mind moving your bike over a few feet so that I can go in reverse and get out of my parking slot?" Tom respectfully requested.

"Look Mack, I don't move my hog for anyone, especially an ugly jerk like you!" the head honcho answered as his five sidekicks indulged in merriment in response to Tom Farley's obvious dilemma.

"Give the idiot a knuckle sandwich Rat Race!" one of the subordinate bikers implored his antagonistic commander.

"Look, I asked you very friendly-like to please move your cycle!" the *SUV* owner courteously-but-nervously repeated. "I don't want to have any trouble!"

"Listen scum face!" Rat Race boomed. "If ya' got a problem then I can help ya' solve it!" the husky hulk hollered as his huge grease-stained hand grabbed Farley around the throat. "You didn't even go into the store to buy anything and ya' want me to move my chopper so that you can get out! What an idiot!"

Tom had the wherewithal to touch the new golden face on his wondrous belt buckle and his mind prayed that Achilles would hear his silent plea and appear to ward off the hostile motorcycle gang that had "Hell's Children" emblazoned on the back of their cut-off-at-the shoulders denim jackets.

In an instant Achilles in full battle regalia and with a red plume extending out from his bronze helmet appeared along with five of his husky Achaean cohorts. Achilles latched onto Rat Race's neck and flung the hellion over a parked tan *Honda*. The very animated *Trojan War* hero next picked up the defeated biker's motorcycle and flung the object into the air. The *Harley* landed squarely on top of the *WaWa's* roof. When two other bikers were hurled twenty feet through the air and ricocheted off the convenience store's back wall, the other three tormentors ceased their taunting and hysterically sprinted south down Fairview Avenue in the direction of the Hammonton Middle School campus.

Tom looked down toward his stomach and recognized that the hero Theseus was now occupying the front buckle position with Achilles' profile presently rotated to a position parallel to the first pants' belt loop. 'Achilles was a friend of Odysseus in Homer's classic epic poem *The Iliad*,' the mythology connoisseur recalled. '*The Iliad* was the story of the ten-year *Trojan War* fought between the Greeks and the soldiers of King Priam's wealthy city, situated near the Hellespont leading into

98

the Black Sea. Achilles had only one weakness where his body was not protected by armor and that was in the back of his foot,' the history scholar remembered. 'The hero mortally wounded the Trojan prince Hector but was later shot and killed by an arrow from Prince Paris, Hector's younger brother. That's where the terms Achilles heel and Achilles' tendon originated,' Farley's mind recollected and reviewed.

On Sunday afternoon Tom entered his green *Explorer* and drove west on *Route 30*, turning right a quarter-of-a-mile from his home onto Walker Road. 'It's a nice warm weekend afternoon so I'll go out to Tuckahoe Turf Farm and practice hitting some golf balls on the fresh green sod.'

Midway up Walker Road was an animal farm that specialized in raising horses, sheep and cattle, all lazily grazing in various fenced-in pastures. A father had stopped on the road's shoulder and was showing his young son the various species devouring grass and hay. The farm's lone bull was in a nasty mood and broke free from *his* enclosure, charging directly at the shocked man and his petrified son.

Tom anxiously halted his *Explorer*, jumped out of the driver's seat and immediately summoned the services of the hero Theseus. The slayer of the Minotaur in King Minos's dark and treacherous labyrinth instantly entered Tom Farley's reality in a flash and exhibiting the skill of a veteran matador, the daring fellow lanced the ferocious bull's neck with his trusty bronze sword. After the gallant king faded into another dimension, the golf enthusiast dashed over to the thoroughly exasperated man and his sobbing son.

"Sir, are you all right?" Tom earnestly asked. "That crazy bull was about to gore the both of you!"

"Did you see what I saw?" the jittery man stuttered and gasped. "A brave guy dressed like a Roman or Greek or someone like that appeared out of nowhere and decapitated that enraged beast. I think I need a sedative! That was a horrendous nerve-racking experience!"

"I believe your mind was playing tricks on you!" Farley suggested, tongue-in-cheek. "I saw no such thing! The bull caught its neck on the sharp barbed wire fence and ripped its hungry throat open. That's exactly what I saw happen!"

"I insist that an ancient gladiator or someone disguised like that appeared and then disappeared, vanished!" the still-terrified man articulated. "That's what I saw!"

"Are the police going to believe *your* far-fetched version of the story or mine?" Tom convincingly argued with a smile. "Fiction and mythology don't work when the cops are dealing with a real investigation and a possible animal cruelty charge lodged against *you*."

"I see what you mean!" the father acquiesced. "The bull probably did slice its own neck open just as *you* had perceptively observed. I shall corroborate your testimony and I thank you for stopping to assist my son and me. Come on Timmy, let's wait in the car until the police come to report the bull's strange death," the gentleman soothingly recommended to his still whimpering boy. "I'll call them on my cell phone!"

'Theseus kills another bull besides the Minotaur!' Farley mused. The still exhilarated mythology scholar looked-down at his belt and chuckled. 'Atalanta has now taken the mystical belt's front position that had just been vacated by Theseus. I'm certainly glad I had encountered the old gypsy hawker in the Plaka. This fantastic belt is truly worth three million dollars and not a mere three hundred. I would have mortgaged my home simply to own it. I now know I had obtained a real bargain!"

The heroine's image minted on the belt buckle was raised above the background in almost a coined bas-relief' appearance. The great huntress's name was inscribed at the bottom, as were the names of the other ancient Greek personages on the belt, with the exception of the eighth one, a mystery hero with no discernible appellation inscribed. The woman archer was the only female represented of the eight ancient Greek champions evident on Tom Farley's fabulous article of apparel.

'Atalanta certainly was not a city in Georgia,' Tom cleverly imagined. 'She was an expert archer notorious for slaying the fierce Calydonian Boar. And mythology also credits the heroine with killing two abusive Centaurs that persisted in harassing her. And if my memory of mythology serves me correctly,' Tom keenly recollected, 'Atalanta once defeated and humiliated Achilles' father Peleus in a wrestling tournament.'

A whole week passed by in Tom Farley's life without any major incident occurring. The following Thursday morning the ancient history advocate motored over to Hammonton Fleet Bank on Broadway and *Route 30* to deposit his August state pension check. While standing in a short line at a teller's window the bank patron was soon caught in the middle of an armed robbery attempt. Two masked bandits entered the

100

establishment, drew concealed pistols, stepped to the front of the line and demanded that everyone in the building get down on the floor. The three frightened tellers were then commanded to hand over all of the cash in their respective drawers.

While lying on the cold tile floor, Tom Farley confidently touched his golden belt buckle and wished that divine intervention would quickly abort the in-progress-pilfering. Within three seconds a tall woman dressed in a light blue tunic and wearing sandals appeared at the main teller's counter. She quickly withdrew two arrows from her quiver and fired them in rapid succession at the startled bank robbers, and the two masked criminals instantly fell dead from pierced chest wounds upon the tile floor. The beautiful woman then stared at the stunned bank employees and patrons, briefly smiled and soon crystallized and vanished back into antiquity.

After the relieved heroine solicitor rose to *his* feet, Farley incredulously glanced down at his singular belt and noticed that Odysseus was now occupying the front position. 'I know the *Trojan War* hero won't disappoint me and will do a 'top-notch' job!' his rich imagination fancied. 'I hope the King of Ithaca does as well in 2003 AD as he had done scheming up the idea of the Trojan Horse way back in 1184 BC!'

The next several days Tom read verses from Homer's *Iliad* and *Odyssey*. The *Iliad* organized and blended mythological events (and now-accepted history) chronicling the ten-year *Trojan War* and the associated *Odyssey* depicted the series of great adventures that challenged Odysseus in his ten-year "odyssey" getting back to his wife Penelope and *their* son Telemachus on the island of Ithaca.

The following Saturday morning the retired teacher was driving his green *Explorer* south through Hammonton on Bellevue Avenue. When Tom approached the traffic signal at the Egg Harbor Road intersection he heard clanging bells and observed that a woman in a blue van had stalled on the railroad tracks. The descending gates foreshadowed the appearance of a speeding westbound *New Jersey Transit* train and *the gates* further isolated the immobile van from escaping to safety.

Tom rubbed his golden belt buckle with his right hand' fingers and his mind begged that a serious disaster be averted. Odysseus along with twelve Greek warriors appeared alongside the blue van containing the desperate panicky woman and in an excellent example of mass cooperation, the contingent pushed the stalled vehicle through the southern railroad gate, snapping the object in two. The thirteen rescuers predictably quickly dissolved into mythological oblivion after completing *their* terrific heroic deed. The express train zipped by blasting its loud horn on its way to Lindenwold and then rumbling onward to its terminal point, Philadelphia's *30th Street Station*.

'Well now, that just leaves Hercules and the mystery hero to render *their* benign assistance,' Farley thought as he examined the golden image and name 'Heracles' portrayed and minted onto the glistening belt buckle. 'I wonder what will happen when the anonymous unidentified eighth hero does *his* thing?'

A month elapsed without any noteworthy crisis transpiring in Tom Farley's daily activities. Then on a Tuesday afternoon he had accompanied Doreen to Philadelphia for his wife's bi-annual physical examination at *Thomas Jefferson University Hospital*. The couple had driven to Lindenwold and then boarded the *High-Speed Line* for the last fifteen miles into the city. The fast train was really a convenient alternative to having to drive in congestion across the *Ben Franklin Bridge,* spanning the *Delaware* into Pennsylvania, and then having to find a street parking space or high-rise garage near the hospital. "We don't need our *Explorer* vandalized by raunchy city thugs!" the husband commented to his wife.

Doreen's routine examination went smoothly without a hitch. Upon exiting the hospital at Ninth and Walnut Tom and his wife walked arm-in-arm two blocks south to Tenth and Locust. They descended the cement steps and eventually entered the subway station's main section. Much to their dismay the retired educators were accosted on the concourse by a bellicose street gang wielding switchblade knives.

"Okay you two, hand over your money right now or we'll cut ya' both up into sheds and leave ya' bleeding to death!" the inner city gang's chief punk insisted.

"If that's what you want, I promise you that's what you'll get!" the very confident history and mythology aficionado automatically answered. "We'll cooperate with your every demand. Just don't harm my wife! She has a weak heart!"

The seven punks indulgently laughed among themselves seeing that their intimidating presence had instilled fear into their prospective victims' hearts. As the uncouth juvenile delinquents continued their malicious shenanigans, Farley inconspicuously felt his seventh golden belt buckle and the inimitable hero Hercules materialized upon the subway station's concrete platform.

Hercules stared menacingly at his startled delinquent adversaries and soon went right to work. The powerful hero proficiently disarmed and mauled the seven astonished punks, viciously knocking out three of the horrified molesters with devastating body and face blows. The invincible champion then picked up the gang's disrespectful leader and flung the now-apprehensive idiot into the air across the concourse.

The bully was rendered unconscious from his impact with the underground station's opposite tile wall thirty feet away. The remaining two hooligans that had not been incapacitated bolted like Olympic speedsters up the subway steps and into the late afternoon sunshine. Hercules then looked at Tom and his totally astounded wife, winked his right eye in a gesture of friendship and instantaneously faded into mythological oblivion.

"What on earth was that fiasco all about?" Doreen screamed at her thoroughly amused husband. "Who was that person? He looked awfully familiar!"

"I don't know!" her amused spouse fibbed. "He was dressed like Hercules but you never know! Maybe we just witnessed a staged performance by some inner-city theatrical group pretending that they're muggers! Perhaps *they* were simply trying to amaze, shock and entertain us at the same time!"

"You can't tell me that those vile ruffians were doing some kind of improvisation to earn extra credit points for their drama class!" Doreen Farley vehemently protested. "And that wise guy lying over there on the cement and these three idiots at our feet have obviously been punched daffy into unconsciousness. And what was with that guy playing Hercules? He vanished into thin air before either of us could thank him! Theater professors don't teach that kind of violent fantasy wizardry in college!"

"Maybe they're studying urban realism in a *University of Pennsylvania* avant-garde drama class," Tom answered with a smirk on his face accompanied by a mild snicker. "Now let's go down to the lower level and catch the next train back to Lindenwold before these four despicable jerks wake up and decide that they're really street punks looking for some easy prey to harass!"

"This is the second strange incident that has happened to me this summer," Doreen Farley related as the pair advanced down the interior subway steps to the lower platform. "The first was that bizarre rhino' encounter at *Great Adventure Safari Park*. That ordeal too was highly irregular."

"As the esteemed poet Lord Byron once all-too-honestly stated," Tom remarked, "truth is often stranger than fiction!"

"Tell that quote to the police and to a convention of undertakers!" his wife sarcastically commented. "And Tom, when we go to *Caesars World* in Atlantic City with the Espositos next Saturday night, I don't want to hear you mention a single word about what happened today in this dark subway station. Let's both pretend it all was just a grotesque mass illusion! I don't wish to lose two fine friends over you awkwardly describing a bizarre unexplainable event."

The date for dinner and *Caesar's World* casino entertainment had arrived on the September calendar and Howard and Jeanne Esposito brought their *Lincoln Town Car* to pick up the Farleys at 127 Woodlawn Avenue.

"Glad we could get away for once from the restaurant on a Saturday night!" Howard Esposito said to Tom and Doreen from the driver's seat.

"Kenny's going to handle the business's seating and cooking tonight!" Jeanne Esposito chimed in. "He said he could do it on his own so we're giving him the opportunity."

"That's my boy!" the driver amiably agreed with a grin. "He's been anxious all week to see if he could run the operation all by himself. This evening is Kenny's big test! I'm confident he'll be equal to the task."

"I can't wait to sample the giant steak and seafood buffet over at *Caesar's*!" Doreen ecstatically exclaimed. "Tom, did you make sure all the doors were locked!"

"The house is as tight as a drum!" Farley answered in an assuring tone of voice. "But Doreen, I wish you wouldn't have forced me to wear a regular belt tonight. You know how I prefer the one I had purchased in Greece."

"Let's not quibble in front of our more civilized friends," Mrs. Farley suggested with a laugh. "But I must say Tom that the belt you had purchased in Athens is too ostentatious for even a glittery tinsel tourist haven like *Caesar's World*. I hear the place has some new electronic nickel slot machines and I can't wait to give the wheels a spin or two."

The Farley's casino excursion into Atlantic City proved profitable in addition to being a relaxing social experience. Doreen had won three hundred dollars playing the new nickel gaming devices and Tom had gotten lucky at the blackjack tables, amassing a profit of "a hundred and fifty clams."

"Speaking of clams, let's hit the exotic seafood bar," Doreen stated to her spouse. "The buffet was supremely good but I'm still a little hungry and I'm afraid if we hang around the casino waiting to meet up with the Espositos at midnight, then we might surrender all of our gambling winnings back to *Caesar's* coffers!"

The retired teachers strolled across the crowded casino floor and then chatted next to the Seafood Bar where they sampled some steamed oysters along with two orders of cherry-stone clams. The 11 p.m. Philadelphia *Channel 6 Action News* was being broadcast on the overhead television screen and the anchorman announced that a "New Jersey breaking story is unfolding as I speak."

Much to the Farley's utter consternation a remote camera crew was on location outside Tom and Doreen's Woodlawn Avenue home. The pair stood spellbound at the clam bar as the reporter gave her presentation in front of rotating red and blue Hammonton police car and ambulance beacons.

"I'm now standing directly in front of 127 Woodlawn Avenue here in Hammonton where a strange murder has recently taken place. The owners of the house are apparently not at home and local police are attempting to track them down," the female commentator related. "Apparently the dead man now being placed in the coroner's van had just robbed the house. Several hundred dollars in cash have been recovered from the suspect's pockets along with some expensive earrings, necklaces rings and bracelets. And a strange belt with golden images of eight Greek heroes has been discovered next to the dead man's mutilated body," the reporter added. "Apparently the dead suspect had also stolen the weird belt from the house. We'll have additional details to report as police learn more specifics about this rather bizarre incident. Now it's back to the studio with more of *Action News* at 11."

It took Tom Farley a full week to adequately recover from his severe anxiety attack. His disturbed mind hypothesized over and over again what had transpired inside his ranch home when he and his wife were supposedly having fun dining and gambling in Atlantic City. 'I know the belt was probably responsible for the thief's death,' the former owner theorized. 'After breaking and entering the house via the garage's side window, the burglar must have touched the eighth golden image by accident while *he* was exiting my property. But the eighth buckle had no identity etched on it. I'll have to surf the *Internet* and see what pertinent information I can dig up!"

Tom searched and then researched for three consecutive days when finally his assiduous labor came across an illustration that closely coincided with the ancient Greek face engraved on the eighth golden belt buckle. 'Of course!' Farley thought while his mind was swimming in a semi-spellbound state. 'The nameless personage was not an ancient Greek hero at all! *He* was an ancient Greek god, Hades, Lord of the Underworld. Hades just systematically executed and mauled the crook to fill another vacancy in *his* dark morbid mysterious kingdom. No wonder why the gypsies wanted to dispose of that enchanted belt! Let the police keep the mythological belt as evidence,' Tom finally realized and concluded. 'I now know its dangerous significance!'

And at last Farley had accurately interpreted the true functionality of the mystical golden belt. 'It works terrifically for the first seven uses but the eighth one always results in an ugly atrocious bloody death maliciously administered by Hades. I was fortunate that Doreen had persuaded me not to wear the thing to Atlantic City. Otherwise I might not be alive to even be thinking about it!'

"The Oracle"

Robert Kemp never married, was paranoid when around either family or strangers and distrusted everyone with sharing his personal goals, desires and secrets. The introvert's self-concept languished in the thought that he had been fated to live a meager existence as the town clerk of Hammonton, New Jersey, and that the permanency of the *Universe* had decisively and ultimately established *that* particular destiny. Robert Kemp feared the world and everyone inhabiting it, but deep inside his lustful heart the neurotic dreamer strongly craved power, esteem and prestige and all of those abstract qualities' attendant self-satisfying benefits.

'I come from a long-line of losers dating back to over a century-and-a-half ago,' Robert sadly recollected in his modest condominium at 113 Rose Rita Terrace just off Fairview Avenue. 'My family name has been cursed ever since my cowardly great-great-great-great grandfather had sold his farm in tidewater Virginia and then moved his family thirty miles north of Madison, Wisconsin.'

Franklin Kemp had been a hard-working nineteenth century farmer that had raised tobacco on a hundred acre spread near the village of Montross, not far from George Washington's birthplace near the majestic *Potomac* in Westmoreland County. Although not a wealthy plantation owner, Franklin Kemp was able to earn a decent living as an independent grower and as a local crop distributor. But that's when the "Kemp curse" originated in the heating-up cauldron known today as the "Antebellum Period in the American South."

Franklin Kemp correctly sensed that a terrible *Civil War* over the slavery issue was on the horizon so in the late fall of 1858 the worried farmer sold all of his possessions (including his seven slaves) and moved his family from Montross, Virginia to Columbus, Wisconsin to pursue a new life as a respectable dairy farmer. Wisconsin had just become the Thirtieth State of the Union in 1848 so Franklin Kemp had made a strategic decision to escape an imminent conflict based on what he had alertly and accurately perceived as ominous indications of a looming national tragedy, a debacle that would swiftly send the South into economic ruin.

The hard-core Montross supporters of the plantation way of life resented Franklin's unanticipated "Selling-out!" and a mercurial neighbor named Eli Grimmons put a vile curse on the departing farmer and his male descendents to wickedly last for "five long generations." The Kemp family moved from Virginia to Wisconsin, and after purchasing a thriving dairy farm from a distant cousin in December of 1858 three years later the newly acquired homestead mysteriously caught on fire. Franklin Kemp suffered third degree burns while attempting to extinguish the roaring inferno. Ironically the terrible Columbus fire had occurred on April 12, 1861, the same day that southern soldiers bombarded Fort Sumter in Charleston Harbor, South Carolina, igniting the soon-to-be devastating *War Between the States*.

After failing to extinguish the raging Columbus, Wisconsin house blaze Franklin Kemp desperately staggered out of his flaming home and then collapsed to the ground a hundred feet away. Hungry timber wolves soon found the dairy farmer's body and left only a bare-bones-skeleton behind.

Dollie Kemp was totally horrified upon returning from Madison with her four children (Edwin, Vera, Mary and Jeremiah) and discovering her husband's mortal remains picked-clean. Dollie Kemp in her heart suspected that Eli Grimmons accompanied by some other Virginia Confederate rebels had surreptitiously journeyed up to Wisconsin and committed a serious arson to punish her husband for abandoning his Montross neighbors prior to the "*Great War*," but the wife could never prove her gut-instinct theory solely based on a "hate-revenge motive." Dollie borrowed money from Franklin's Wisconsin cousin and dutifully buried her husband, sold all of her assets and moved the family to Baltimore, where relatives would provide security and support despite the war hostilities that were in progress. And Robert Kemp was a fourth generation descendent of Jeremiah, who incidentally was eventually buried in the same downtown Baltimore cemetery as Edgar Allan Poe.

'To my knowledge I'm the only remaining fifth generation descendent of Franklin Kemp,' Robert contemplated while sipping his morning cup of coffee prior to motoring to the Hammonton, New Jersey Town Hall to perform his all-too-familiar public service. "My great-great-great-great-grandfather attempted salvaging his family from a calamitous *Civil War* but he wound-up being burned to death and then devoured by savage wolves. Is there no moral justice in this world to erase a despicable five-generation-curse uttered by an unscrupulous jealous man named Eli Grimmons? Why must I be a passenger in the caboose of this condemned five-car train? If I could ever become rich,' the dreamer wildly speculated, 'then I would get my appropriate revenge on all of my enemies and on all the moral deviates I so desire to punish!' the temperamentally volatile and very vindictive religious fanatic imagined.

As far as Robert Kemp's self-analysis was concerned, the only child of his father (Tyler Kemp) never married because of Eli Grimmons' curse and the very nervous Municipal Clerk now feared that his own demise had been prescribed back in 1858. 'I must reverse the curse and survive this emotional ordeal that my heavy heart must wrestle with every single day!' the pathetic idealist pledged his conscience. 'My doomed great-great-great grandfather Jeremiah Kemp died of pneumonia in Baltimore at the age of twenty-three. And then my great-great grandfather Edwin died in the famous Johnstown, Pa. flood of 1889 when the Fork River Dam east of the city burst during a torrential rainstorm. And next my doomed great-grandfather Emerson perished in a fierce 1907 Kansas tornado. My grandfather Willard was killed in France in 1918 during the fierce *Word War I* Battle of St. Mihiel and my father Tyler expired shortly after being a passenger in a two-bus accident near New York City in 1959,' Robert frightfully recollected and reckoned. 'All of my male ancestors suffered unnatural deaths and now according to Eli Grimmons' ominous curse I'm designated to be the next victim in line.'

The story of Robert Kemp's nineteenth century ancestor Franklin seemed to parallel the story of Oedipus so aptly chronicled and described in ancient Greek literature. The King of Thebes had four children, two male and two female, all of whom suffered horrendous bad luck just like the four immediate descendants of Franklin Kemp had been cruelly condemned by a dastardly curse in a similar bizarre development. As a result of "the Oedipus comparison" Robert became an avid reader and student of Greek mythology and was generally regarded around Hammonton, New Jersey as the town's foremost authority on the obscure academic subject.

The only distant relative of whom Robert Kemp had any awareness of was Dennis Lansing, a shrewd churchgoing South Jersey businessman that would steal and sell the eyes from a dead person simply to achieve a capital gain. Dennis had cunningly conned Robert into investing *his* life's savings of fifty-thousand dollars into what was described and packaged as "a can't miss lucrative enterprise," and soon other investors were convinced to join the pyramid scheme as the new company "Delphi Associates" bought up smaller paper and bag distributorships in the South Jersey towns of Pleasantville, Egg Harbor City, Absecon, Bridgeton, Millville, Newfield and Collingswood. The fledgling corporation had in five years grown into a multi-million-dollar operation and Robert was seriously considering resigning from his Municipal Clerk position and devoting all of his energies to the prospering paper products company.

Delphi Bag and Paper Company was the name of Dennis Lansing's original outlet that had geometrically and miraculously grown to be the South Jersey giant and dominant player in that particular industry. But soon the wily and greedy corporate *CEO* went on a selfish crusade to buy out Robert for a meager hundred thousand dollars and the relentless Dennis Lansing persuaded the weak Delphi Board of Directors to endorse *his* foolproof plan "for necessary consolidation purposes and to save on frivolous non-essential expenses."

With his one-hundred-thousand-dollar buyout along with the three hundred-thousand-dollar "profit-sharing dividend" that Robert had accumulated during Delphi's exceptional first five-years the fledgling entrepreneur audaciously quit his Municipal Clerk's employment and conscientiously founded a similar paper distribution operation in western South Jersey. Kemp successfully established Parthenon Paper Company, followed the progression model developed by Dennis Lansing and soon he had attracted ten anxious investors all ready to proliferate the growth of a newly formed flourishing regional business.

In three short years Parthenon Paper Company had aggressively expanded from the original Berlin outlet and had replicated similar flourishing distribution points in Lindenwold, Cherry Hill, Haddonfield, Glassboro, Swedesboro, Gibbsboro, Clementon and Haddon Heights. But the ambitious entrepreneur's anxiety was reaching a culmination because Robert Kemp daily remembered Eli Grimmons' vicious and effective curse and the fidgety man wholeheartedly believed that his chief competitor Dennis Lansing intended to have him eliminated by some reprehensible nefarious means.

'I'm actually Franklin Kemp's sole male fifth generation survivor besides my totally insidious evil cousin,' Robert painfully meditated, 'and if Dennis can't knock me out of business using standard competition methods he'll probably hire henchmen or hit men to permanently have me erased from this Earth. I must somehow devise a viable countermeasure strategy to erase the hundred and fifty-year-curse and to deftly avoid that despicable Dennis Lansing's notorious wrath. Heaven help my soul if I should fail!'

While he was surfing the *Internet* Robert Kemp, out of sheer curiosity, typed in the words "Curses Lifted" on his favorite search engine. His seemingly innocuous inquiry yielded a plethora of results so the apprehensive researcher refined his selections and chose a specific listing provided by Cassandra, a fortuneteller and spell-breaker that claimed competence in the aforementioned "special areas of client needs." Cassandra's very interesting web site featured and disclosed certain information that immediately intrigued the perplexed visitor's troubled mind. For a stipend of five hundred dollars bad luck "negative elements" would automatically be converted into "good fortune" and for another measly five hundred dollars any curse troubling the *Internet* visitor would be either eradiated or effectively reversed within a month.

'I've always been superstitious and right now I fear that pugnacious Dennis Lansing is going to have me executed because of my rival company being so successful,' Robert logically reasoned. 'He's incredibly ruthless and avaricious. I'll be a total *Internet* sucker and have a hard-earned thousand dollars subtracted from my credit/debit card,' the fretful businessman decided. 'I'm quite desperate and must try anything and everything to escape my family's accursed historical predicament that had its genesis in Montross, Virginia way back in the late 1850s. My family's accursed genealogy must be revised and modified for the better for my own sake.'

The pusillanimous fool eagerly entered his *MasterCard* number onto the readily available "Customer Information Sheet" and then voluntarily provided a detailed narrative of his "Personal Biographical Data" so that an applicable "Personal Horoscope" could be custom-formulated. Next Robert cooperatively described in a convenient blank field the nature of his family's curse that the indispensable Cassandra purportedly would reverse for the total handsome sum of one-thousand-dollars, a paltry recompense for such invaluable services.

'During the *Trojan War* of 1184 BC as described by Homer in his *Iliad*,' Kemp recalled and rationalized, 'Cassandra was the beautiful daughter of King Priam and Queen Hecuba of Troy. But more importantly Cassandra was a prophetess that warned her father to surrender Helen of Troy to the Greeks, otherwise the ruler's city was doomed to destruction. Cassandra's prediction was ignored, the hero Achilles killed her brother Hector and Troy soon fell to the marauding Greeks. In the end Cassandra was abducted to Mycenae by Agamemnon, leader of the Achaean expedition and served as a slave,' the expert on Greek mythology reconstructed in his befuddled mind.

Then Robert's mind pondered some more on the fascinating subject of Cassandra. 'Finally the inscrutable former Princess of Troy was murdered in Mycenae by Agamemnon's greedy wife Clytemnestra and her lover Aegisthus. I must admit that the Greek mythology-Cassandra connection does give my most-recent foolish investment exercise in the *Internet* free enterprise system some degree of credence,' Robert recollected and related from his vast knowledge of ancient legends and modern frivolity. 'In the end Agamemnon was also killed by the lover-conspirators and Clytemnestra's son Orestes and the young man's sister Electra then continued the murder-domino effect by wiping-out Clytemnestra and her lover Aegisthus for conspiring to murder Agamemnon,' Robert remembered. 'I sincerely hope that I'm not now implicated in a similar rash of murders and out-of-control human eradication. My life is already complicated enough with my nemeses Dennis Lansing and with Eli Grimmons' awful awesome curse.'

After carefully submitting his biographical data on the web site information sheet, a brief explanation of his curse affliction and his one-thousand-dollar extravagant expense via credit card to Cassandra's company, Robert Kemp's fancy imagined what the ideal human existence would be for him. 'My life must in the end be a Horatio Alger story,' the delusional dreamer fantasized. 'Now that I have gotten some confidence by virtually going from rags to riches on my own initiative I must neutralize that ever-scheming Dennis Lansing and then effectively invert the wicked Eli Grimmons' pronouncement condemning my ancestor Franklin Obadiah Kemp and his wholly innocent progenies.'

A mere week after engaging in his "impractical *Internet* commercial activity" the emotionally unstable Robert Kemp received an unexpected e-mail from the anonymous self-acclaimed soothsayer Cassandra.

Mr. Robert Kemp:

Thank you for employing my vital services and for providing your detailed statements regarding a certain Dennis Lansing of Folsom, New Jersey and an evil whammy advanced by one Eli Grimmons of Montross, Virginia prior to the *Civil War*. The geographic coordinates you had stated will assist me in alleviating your dire circumstances with Mr. Lansing and resolving your fifth-generation burden with Eli Grimmons' iniquitous proclamation on your predecessor Franklin Kemp and subsequently upon *his* unfortunate descendants.

Now here is what I advise you to do and I strongly suggest that you expedite my counsel with great dispatch. First of all Mr. Kemp, sell your total shares in all of your Parthenon Paper distribution stores in southern New Jersey to Mr. Lansing for a bargain price of a hundred-thousand-dollars, a severe loss of seven-hundred-thousand-dollars in total value.

Secondly Mr. Kemp, after you have appeased Mr. Lansing by disposing of your business assets at a drastic loss, you will then receive via parcel post a box (a smaller version of the one opened by Pandora) that I am certain will change your life most propitiously. I am quite confident that this remarkable gift should more than adequately reward your faith and your trust in my singular problem-solving ability.

May the mighty Powers That Be protect and comfort you for I hereby swear that your destiny has undoubtedly been altered for the better.

Good luck to you Mr. Kemp in all your prospective endeavors.

Sincerely,

Cassandra

The restive man quickly completed all of Cassandra's explicit specifications and then sixty days later certain events materialized that ultimately proved themselves' fortuitous for Mr. Robert Kemp. Dennis Lansing shockingly suffered a harsh fate on vacation in Sicily when he had accidentally slipped on a lip overlooking *Mt. Etna,* tumbled into the volcano's crater and instantly disappeared into a bubbling lava pit. 'My principal enemy has been vanquished by the superior forces active in the invisible *Universe*!' the amazed mythology buff thought after he had read a graphic front-page account of the tragic incident in the *Atlantic City Press.*

And then Robert Kemp reflected some more on Dennis Lansing's violent demise. 'The king-god Zeus had punished Prometheus for giving mankind the gift of fire by having the Titan mercilessly chained on top of *Mt. Etna* and next having a voracious eagle continuously peck away at the giant's liver, which then grew back each morning only to be devoured again the following day. And it's a lot harder for the New Jersey courts to prosecute the whims of the Supernatural as a Defendant for a death occurring thousands of miles away in Italy than it would be for the justice system to put humble little old me on trial if the elimination of Dennis Lansing had occurred here in South Jersey by human involvement rather than by Supernatural intervention,' Robert mused with a prominent smirk on his countenance. 'Cassandra must really have some important clout in the *Invisible World,* an influence that scrupulous lawyers, judges and juries can't even begin to imagine!'

Several weeks later Robert received a fascinating business letter from Mr. Thomas Avery Crowell, the new *CEO* of Delphi Paper and Bag Distributors. The missive invited Kemp to purchase stock in the company and to sit on the firm's Board of Directors. Robert immediately complied with the cordial offer and soon enjoyed occupying an executive's seat on the board of the powerful company that Dennis Lansing had formerly controlled. Talks soon were initiated to consolidate Delphi Associates and Parthenon Paper Company into one unquestionably dynamic and influential corporation that would dominate the entire wholesale paper and bag industry in South Jersey for decades to come.

In May of that year Robert was randomly surfing the *Internet* and out of sheer intellectual impulse typed in the last name "Grimmons" on his favorite search engine. Kemp was astounded to discover that seven brothers and cousins in the Grimmons family had died the day before in a fiery airplane crash outside of Richmond, Virginia while en route to an "extended family reunion" in Montross.

According to the content of a recently released news bulletin, "Byron, Josiah, Zachary, Milton, Barnabas, Simeon and Lazarus Grimmons all perished when flying as passengers aboard a commuter jet owned by the newly formed Icarus Aviation Company. The plane had impacted the earth just prior to a scheduled early morning landing at the *Richmond International Airport*. Details are presently sketchy but more information should be released by the national wire services later today."

'In Greek mythology Icarus was the son of Daedalus and the youth didn't listen to his inventor father's sage advice,' Robert reviewed in his mind. 'The father-son duo was flying from Crete to escape the tyranny of King Minos using specially designed wings that Daedalus had manufactured. Icarus flew too close to the sun and the wax on his wings melted. Soon the irresponsible boy plummeted into the *Aegean Sea* and perished by drowning because of his stubborn egotism!'

'The curse of Eli Grimmons on Franklin Kemp and his descendants has evidently been reversed,' Robert gratefully realized. 'Thank Heaven for Cassandra's magical wizardry. After I receive my special parcel post package from the prophetess I'll send her an additional hundred thousand dollars for 'valuable services rendered'. The remarkable fortuneteller has been the greatest blessing that has ever entered my life. I now have freedom to do anything I so desire without any fear of omnipotent Supernatural Intervention restricting and interfering with my actions.'

As Cassandra had predicted in her e-mail to Robert a special package soon arrived via parcel post at Kemp's Hammonton residence. The recipient quickly unwrapped the brown paper exterior and gazed upon a rectangular amber chest that looked like it belonged somewhere in Greek antiquity. Kemp anxiously unfastened the buckle and lifted the squeaky lid.

Inside the box were the deeds to a lucky thirteen business properties located extensively throughout southern New Jersey. The establishments were thus identified: The Zeus Gun Shop in Egg Harbor City; The Athena Diner in Pleasantville; Hera's Hair Salon in Absecon; Hermes Trucking Company in Millville; The Apollo Theater in Collingswood; The Poseidon Bar and Grill in

Neptune; Hades Well Drilling in Glassboro; The Ares Bakery in Haddonfield; Aphrodite Beauty Products in Cherry Hill; The Olympus Amusement Arcade in Mays Landing; The Hephaestus Copper and Iron Works in Williamstown and the Hestia Dry Cleaners in Berlin had all been inexplicably-but-definitely deeded over to Robert Kemp from anonymous sources.

'The established businesses that I'm acquiring have all been named after various Olympian gods,' Robert instantly recognized and appreciated. 'And I'm familiar with at least six of the enterprises and they are indeed very profitable moneymakers. Cassandra has marvelously performed her magic again! I believe I'll now send my benefactor a two-hundred-thousand-dollar bonus to genuinely express my extreme satisfaction with my present circumstances. I have truly been the beneficiary of wonderful things.'

Kemp felt obligated to substantially contribute to Cassandra's *Internet* web site's address so he went online and diligently searched for it again but his dedicated efforts were to no avail. No evidence of "the Cassandra" that had assisted Robert in the resolution of his myriad vexations appeared anywhere. 'It's as if *she* has evaporated into oblivion! And I now believe that she was actually a divine courier just like the ubiquitous Hermes, a sort of Guardian Angel dispatched to help me with my overwhelming dilemmas,' the *Internet* explorer sorrowfully deducted and mentally cataloged. 'And all I wish to do is reward the Oracle for her phenomenal aid and for the tremendous relief that my formerly encumbered psyche has felt. For the first time in my life I feel inspired and empowered. I never want to feel miserable, exploited and inadequate again!' Robert accurately ascertained. 'And from my personal experience, whoever now says that astrology and mythology are both just a lot of academic absurdity is a foolish dolt of the greatest magnitude!'

As Robert Kemp amassed an enviable fortune from his windfall bonanza he became quite arrogant in his demeanor and forgot what the supernatural powers of the *Universe* had benevolently and mercifully accomplished for him. Soon the investor's new-found superlative wealth and excessive haughtiness made the multi-millionaire practice what the ancient Greeks often called "the sin of hubris." The entrepreneur's extreme pride brought him into direct conflict with the incognito omniscient moral authority that governs space, time and all human punishment.

116

Kemp had abandoned his modest shy disposition and soon boldly financed the operations of radical groups with extreme political and religious agendas that advocated the enactment of swift ideological changes in American society. The financial guru's imminent downfall was accelerated when he hired and subsidized militant Islamic terrorists to kill innocent gays celebrating their vows at a mass wedding in San Francisco. Then the now-insane mogul paid Palestinian and Jordanian suicide bombers large sums to drive vehicles loaded with explosives into American abortion clinics with the expressed purpose of destroying targeted life and property. And then the demented wealthy tycoon employed the services of Hamas fundamentalists (that had crossed the *Rio Grande* from Mexico and who hated both America and Israel) to assassinate liberal politicians that espoused beliefs that threatened traditional American values. Certain liberals that took pro-stances on the issues of abortion, gay marriages and the civil rights of accused anarchists and Al Qaeda sympathizers residing in the contiguous United States were systematically hunted down and "exterminated."

'Ever since I've become a successful American capitalist,' Robert nostalgically contemplated, 'I'll do everything I can to preserve the American way of life I fondly recall from the wonderful '50s, and that includes the pioneering spirit and the foundational tenets of White Anglo-Saxon Protestantism,' the fanatical ideologue confirmed and concluded. 'I profess to maintain, preserve and conserve the core American values of the past that I cherish and treasure so much and I'll even covertly solicit the talents of nihilistic Muslims to achieve my well-defined goals. The Arab radicals want to destroy all of America whereas I simply want to eradicate some of America, especially its corrupt decadent liberal proponents. That's the basic difference in *our* philosophies and approaches. My guns-for-hire are fundamentalist Arabs and I've a proactive Christian fundamentalist.'

While on a business trip to Jupiter, Florida in October of 2004 financier Robert Kemp was brutally murdered and beheaded by what authorities believe to be "zealous Arab extremists." The *FBI* suspects that a wealthy American ultra-liberal billionaire had hired the Middle East gunmen to perform the heinous misdeed and the central Bureau in Washington is currently conducting an intensive investigation into the exact cause and motive for the crime. Even though

Robert Kemp had become carnivorous like a vicious shark stalking for prey, there were still other even larger and much more dangerous predators vigilantly patrolling the hostile dark ocean depths.

"The Amazon Sorority"

The ancient Greek "tragic playwright" Aeschylus (525-456 B.C.) referred to the Amazon culture as "warring men-haters." The female tribe (or cult) amply demonstrated their hostile motives when they had engaged in life-or-death conflict with various heroes and kings. The legendary female civilization is reputed to have lived in *Asia Minor* and their capital city was identified in certain myths as Themiscrya located near the *River Thermodon*. Other Amazon cities cited in historic accounts (one provided by Herodotus) were Smyrna, Cyme and Myrine. The widely heralded activities of these fearless lady warriors were also chronicled in several ancient Greek myths. The race was believed to be the descendants of the war god Ares and the gentle peace-loving nymph Harmonia.

The hero Bellerophon defeated a faction of Amazons in Lycia, a young Priam of Troy thwarted an invasion of belligerent lady warriors in Phrygia and Theseus of Athens repulsed an Amazon attack in Attica and during the battle captured the clan's queen, Antiope. Even the incomparable mighty Hercules had as one of his *Twelve Labors* (the Ninth) the assignment of securing and bringing back the girdle (here, the belt) of Hippolyta, another legendary Amazon Queen. During the champion's incursion the other Amazons charged down a mountainous slope and desperately assaulted Hercules' ship and his crew but the strongest man in Greek mythology immediately killed Hippolyta, believing that the warrior-Queen had been responsible for the ship's siege. According to another mythological account Hercules miraculously escaped the fierce assault with the dead queen's girdle as his trophy.

And concerning the epic *Trojan War,* an episode recorded (outside Homer's classic *Iliad* by Pausanias) that the hero Achilles had killed the Amazon Queen Penthesilea in combat, and then the brave Achaean mourned the gorgeous woman warrior's death. And in another adventure the Amazons are identified as having organized an invasion on the benign people of *Atlantis*, reputed to be the most prosperous and scientifically advanced civilization of prehistoric times.

Amazons were reputed to be highly skilled huntresses that worshiped Artemis, and the women contributed to erecting a wonderful *Asia Minor* marble temple with colorful decorated columns to the goddess of the hunt at Ephesus (now a historic site in southwestern Turkey), which became one of the *Seven Wonders of the Ancient World.*

Sensational myths have often portrayed Amazons as fiercely independent women that removed their right breasts to allow them to aim and shoot their bows and arrows and throw their javelins more accurately. And finally in the *Western Hemisphere,* an old popular Inca myth conveyed to early Spanish conquistadors suggested that a tribe of savage women lived in the dense South American rain forests, hence the creation of the very interesting etymological terminology, the *Amazon River.*

* * * * * * * * * * * *

The state-of-the-art spacecraft *New Horizon II* was zipping at interstellar speed through a seldom-explored section of the *Constellation Virgo.* The two-man crew's mission was to scout the "virgin territory" and to gather information on the unknown fate of the *New Horizon,* which had landed on a planet that the pioneer astronauts aboard had strangely described as *"Amazonia."* All communications between the original *New Horizon Expedition* under the command of experienced Colonel Ralph Clark and Captain Stephen Moran had been terminated because of mysterious causes and Cape Canaveral Control had urgently dispatched a search and rescue vessel manned by Colonel Neil Franks and Captain Thomas Weston to perform an intensive forensics investigation. The second pair of Earth voyagers to journey to *Virgo* was awakened from their suspended animation life simulation chambers by Delta, the astronauts' trusty human-in-appearance all-purpose android.

"Greetings Colonel Franks and Captain Weston!" Delta announced after the dual sealed suspended animation chambers' panels simultaneously opened and the bleary-eyed astronauts began regaining consciousness. "We're now approaching the vicinity of the star *Spica* in *Virgo.* Please be patient gentlemen. The planet described as *Amazonia* by the *New Horizon* crew should be coming onto the *3-D* video screen in just a few of your Earth minutes."

"Excellent preparation Delta!" Colonel Neil Franks declared and commended after he sat up, stretched his arms and vigorously yawned. "You might get to find your idol, your prototype Phi, who as you know is also unaccounted for in addition to our courageous space explorers Ralph Clark and Stephen Moran. Perhaps our hallmark expedition will achieve history and settle a lot of unanswered questions. At least that's my sincere hope."

"Yes," chimed in the now-alert Captain Thomas Weston. "You did a superb job of getting us to our destination Delta. How did you do it? By using Amazonia.com?" the second-in-command jested. "After all my man-made android friend, you've proficiently demonstrated that you're an accomplished space navigator, even when the spacecraft has been put on automatic pilot," Weston facetiously and sarcastically commented. "And that ridiculous understanding, my dear android associate, leads me to my next matter of concern. Why do you suppose that Colonel Clark and Captain Moran referred to the planet they had discovered as *Amazonia*?"

"Because Captain Weston, my early spectrum analysis indicates that most of the planet's surface is covered by thick dense jungle, and this assumption is all speculation of course," Delta specified, "but the heavy concentration of tropical vegetation suggests that this world's surface is analogous to the Brazilian rain forests of South America in and around the *Amazon River*. Probability points in that direction and so I'll stand by my hypothesis and logically advance the proposition that Colonel Clark and Captain Moran had employed the particular nomenclature *Amazonia* for that specific reason!"

"Very well spoken Delta!" Colonel Franks exclaimed to his combination robotic assistant and mechanical subordinate. "We'll soon see exactly how accurate your interpretation of the current reality really is. Captain Weston, let's harness ourselves inside our landing seats because I believe we'll soon be approaching our objective."

"Indeed Colonel Franks!" Delta verified. "The cloud-shrouded planet identified as *Amazonia* is now visible on the overhead space monitor. As you know Colonel our powerful visual scanners can detect and magnify objects that are up to five million miles away. Science and technology have really evolved tremendously since the days of Neil Armstrong setting foot on the moon nearly three centuries ago," Delta reviewed and emphasized. "What a tribute to man's splendid ingenuity!"

"Mission command wants us to provide a comprehensive report on the *New Horizon I's* fate, and remember gentlemen, and I use that term rather loosely Delta," Colonel Neil Franks qualified and laughed, "*that* special commitment is our prime directive. We can't return to Earth until we've determined exactly what's happened to Colonel Ralph Clark, to Captain Stephen Moran and to their versatile android prototype Phi. Now let's have a smooth entry into this uncharted planet's atmosphere and scope-out the general territory where the *New Horizon I* had landed."

"Will do Colonel!" Delta confidently assured his superior. "This planet's just about the size of Earth and our elements' readings indicate that its atmosphere is seventy-eight percent nitrogen with traces of hydrogen and twenty percent oxygen, very similar to the precious air you mortals breathe back home. I don't think you'll be needing oxygen tanks and space suits to do your intended roaming around."

The round saucer entered the *Virgo* world's stratosphere with the bright sun *Spica* intensely glaring through the thick clouds that enveloped and previously had obscured *Amazonia.* Much to the men's elation the *New Horizon I's* still-functioning homing signal had been picked up. The newly arrived spacecraft followed the very discernible distress beeps westward across three hundred miles of majestic-blue-ocean. A few minutes later a beautiful river delta was encountered and fifteen seconds elapsed before a hundred miles of dense lush tropical vegetation was flown over. And then finally near the signal's now-distinct origin the *New Horizon II* hovered over a verdant canyon.

"Their ship's probably being camouflaged by thick jungle growth," Colonel Franks observed and related to Captain Weston. "After Delta lands our discovery craft we'll have to exit and carefully search around on foot. Delta, you stay aboard and perform some basic surveillance and monitoring. The Captain and I will call you via our communication devices if we require your assistance."

"Aye-aye Colonel!" the android respectfully replied. "I see a clearing up ahead that appears to be the appropriate dimensions to initiate a safe landing. Keep your seat-belts fastened! I'm taking us down!"

The *New Horizon II* gently descended and soon smoothly vertically landed in the selected vacant spot situated in the exotic-looking tropical rain forest. The main atomic energy conversion engines were shut off and all systems were placed on auxiliary power. The two astronauts spontaneously disconnected their seat-belts.

"Gentlemen, hope you brought along your sun tan lotion," Delta casually mentioned. "The external temperature is ninety-two degrees Fahrenheit, but the ultra-violet rays are a trifle more severe than the ones that beam down to Earth in your summer season. You'd both better wear your sunglasses or stay in the shade until dusk, if this planet has such a thing as twilight!"

"Thanks for your unsolicited advice you manufactured conglomeration of nuts and bolts!" Captain Weston rankled. "Colonel Franks and I are perfectly capable of reading the instrument panel indicators too so all you were doing Delta was obviating the obvious to us. Now Colonel," the Captain continued, "I strongly suggest we adjust our laser penetration guns to stun mode so that we're ready if we're quickly confronted by any hostile uncivilized humanoid life forms or by any dangerous indigenous animals."

"Yes Captain!" the ship's commander sternly concurred. "I want our search and find recovery mission to be conducted as promptly and as efficiently as possible. As soon as we discover Clark and Moran either dead or alive and retrieve the indestructible Phi," Colonel Franks indicated, "we'll evacuate this tropical paradise and gladly head back to our native planet. I hope there aren't any eagle-sized flies or mosquitoes waiting to attack us out there!"

The two normally cynical space travelers exited the ship's main hatch and passed through the atmospheric equalizer chamber. Then after closing the metal door they conveniently walked down a temporary extended ramp to ground level. Colonel Franks surveyed the general area, keenly located a jungle trail and the intrepid pair entered the alluring rain forest's dense interior. The sounds of cawing and chirping birds occupying various limbs on tall trees filled the air.

"Sounds just like it does back on Earth!" Captain Weston observed and shared. "I expect *Tarzan* or Jane to come swinging by us on a vine any second now. Look Colonel, there's a cliff with a scenic view just up ahead. Let's advantageously use the lookout point to study our immediate environment and to scrutinize the rest of the valley to see if any signs of humanoid habitation are evident."

The men prudently climbed up a hill of rocks from which a hundred-foot-high waterfall cascaded down into the rich green valley. The impressed astronauts cautiously admired their beautiful surroundings and discussed the fabulous Eden that surrounded them. Then Colonel Neil Franks observed something that made him raise his right index finger up to his mouth communicating "Quiet!" to his more garrulous companion. An unsuspecting wild boar was seen foraging for food at the waterfall's base. Colonel Neil Franks and Captain Thomas Weston were simultaneously inspired with the same idea.

"I haven't had the pleasure of munching on fresh roasted pork since we left Earth!" the Colonel anxiously whispered. "Let's take aim and stun that boar before he knows what's hit him. I can taste his savory flavor even though he's a hundred-feet-away down there!" Franks intimated. "Be careful Tom and don't make a sound! I still remember how to skin and gut an animal from when my dad used to take me deer hunting."

The men took their stances and were about to fire their stun rays when suddenly two accurately aimed arrows pierced the boar's flesh and the ferocious beast grunted twice and then collapsed to the ground. A pair of very attractive women scantily dressed in leather cloths dashed to their scene of conquest, tied the dead creature to a six-foot-long pole, hoisted the boar up to their shoulders and then began ambulating towards a formerly unnoticed group of straw huts situated a quarter of a mile away.

"Did you see that?" Captain Weston asked in an astonished tone of voice. "No wonder why Colonel Clark and Captain Moran never re-established communications with Earth. Those primitive dolls that killed that fierce tusked pig were gorgeous-like magazine centerfolds! This unreal place is paradise with a capital P!"

"Yes Tom!" Neil Franks concurred and cautioned. "But remember, those young ladies are pretty deadly with their bows and arrows and they could represent real jeopardy to us if they become antagonistic. Maybe they've captured Clark and Moran and are holding them prisoners. Those women appear to be quite self-sufficient and independent and I'm sure they don't have to rely on men for protection."

"The vanguard team did refer to this place as *Amazonia*, and now we can fully understand why," Captain Weston said. "And maybe Colonel the *DNA* in the boar meat is different than the *DNA* of hogs and pigs back on Earth. Those luscious babes might have fortuitously saved us from intestinal infection. Their intervention into our little hunting gambol might actually have been a blessing in disguise. At least that's my handle on the situation. What do you think?"

"Let's contact Delta and inform him of our activities," the Colonel wisely recommended. "Instead of searching for the *New Horizon I* we'll engage in some dedicated reconnaissance and spy on the Amazon's village. I want to learn as much as possible about them and their customs before we decide to cordially introduce ourselves."

"Very sage and prudent!" Tom Weston commended his superior officer. "There might be more pieces to this jigsaw puzzle than meets the eye. I'm fascinated by these independent-minded Amazons and want to learn as much as possible about their race, especially how men fit into their society scheme, presumably for reproductive purposes," the Captain declared. "But these prehistoric knockout single-breasted women would not look quite as enticing wearing double-breasted suits!"

"You're hilarious but your timing is absolutely lousy," the superior officer aptly criticized. Colonel Franks' hand-held communicator vibrated, indicating that Delta aboard the *New Horizon II* was sending a transmission. The Colonel activated his intricate multi-functional device to receive some pertinent data about *Amazonia* that the android had just gleaned.

"Colonel," Delta began, "I've got plenty of data to report. Please pay attention to my information."

"Go on Delta, we read you loud and clear," Neil Franks responded. "Fill us in on the details."

"Well first of all Colonel, the Amazon women apparently are the dominant humanoids on the planet," Delta revealed. "And I've intercepted some of their messages and deciphered their symbol translations and believe it or not the ladies have some sort of primitive form of mental telepathy whereby they can communicate ideas and certain words without speaking. Does *that* last fact sound too ludicrous to believe? How do you interpret or explain that?"

"Maybe the Amazons are mute," Captain Weston stated into *his* telecommunications device to Delta. "Perhaps their vocal cords are not sufficiently developed to promote speech. Have you been able to detect the existence of any males in the neighborhood other than the Colonel and myself?"

"Yes, there's a tribe of men that inhabit the grasslands over the mountains to our right that the Amazons mentally call *Sapiens*," Delta contributed. "I've learned from their telepathic conversations that the Amazons have an estrus cycle comparable to certain animals back on Earth but it only lasts for around thirty days, one full month a year. During that limited time period the women allow their captive Sapiens out of their prison cells to party and mate before going back to their strict well-disciplined mode of village living and their inflexible division of labor."

"Sort of like *Mardi Gras* back in good old New Orleans!" Colonel Franks drew an absurd parallel. "Everyone involved in the celebration' revels on *Shrove Tuesday* but then on *Ash Wednesday* people become somber and penitent until the end of Lent is finally marked by *Easter Sunday*. The Amazons militant behavior seems quite plausible when viewed in that *Mardi Gras* context. Anything else Delta?"

Static interrupted the essential communication for around thirty seconds until Delta was able to resume his new-found disclosures. "And incidentally gentlemen," the fantastic machine proceeded, "the women have a signal range of sending and receiving mental transmissions of about a hundred-foot-radius so be sure you don't confront them directly or else they'll be capable of reading your secret thoughts. And one final thing," Delta matter-of-factly uttered. "Be back to the ship by nightfall because a strong tropical rainstorm is heading in this direction. The abundant heavy rains quite apparently are responsible for the jungle's dense vegetation. Things could get very torrential out there in a hurry!"

"Have you obtained any other relevant facts?" Captain Weston asked the almost-human machine through *his* communicator. "I must praise you on your scholarly research."

"Why yes, thanks for reminding me," Delta objectively remarked. "The Amazon Queen's name is Evandre, the two principal scouts are Iphinome and Myrina and by all means watch out for wicked Xanthe, who by all indications is the vindictive and spiteful village high priestess. Princess Phoebe is Evandre's obedient daughter and is highly favored as long as her mother holds sway over the tribe and keeps the society in line. And gentlemen," Delta added and warned, "watch out for

126

Marpe, the best archer and huntress amongst the villagers. And there are two other names I've been able to decipher. Clymene is the commander of the archers and Bremusa is the village altar maid and a loyal subordinate of the ruthless Xanthe."

"All right Delta! I'll be glad to see sunset because it's quite sweltering right now and rather uncomfortable standing out here. If you learn anything else significant about these alluring inhabitants, give us a buzz!" the commanding officer abruptly ordered. "This is Colonel Franks over and out!"

The astronauts very methodically clambered down the steep ridge and next followed a narrow trail that led to the perimeter of the Amazon village. Pens of chickens and pigs and neatly arranged corralled pastures of sheep and cows surrounded the thirteen rudely constructed huts, the largest of which was situated in the settlement's center.

"That larger central structure must be either the meeting hall or the temple," Neil Franks surmised and told his trekking comrade. "These women warriors aren't far removed from being barbarians similar to medieval Huns or Visigoths. And obviously the lady hunters are either carnivorous or omnivorous in their eating habits according to the domesticated animals that they keep in their pens."

"And look inside the main hut!" Tom Weston directed as both men crouched down to avoid detection from four serious-faced sentinels conscientiously patrolling the secluded village's circumference. "The Amazons and their Sapien captives are partying in the main hut as if there's no tomorrow. And Colonel," the Captain proceeded, "my growling stomach could use some delicious home-cooked barbecue meat right now, and it wouldn't matter if it were chicken, spare ribs, pork, bacon, porterhouse steak or lamb chops."

"I have a theory about all this," Colonel Franks advanced to his crouched-down avid listener. "After the men have fulfilled their biological usefulness the Amazons either imprison them or kill them off. The women warriors then keep the female offspring and probably sacrifice the male infants to their god or gods. What do you think of my random speculation?"

"I agree with you that the gullible Sapiens are feasting and partying simply to satisfy a temporary need that the Amazons have for replicating their species," Captain Weston agreed, "but we'll just have to keep our distance and observe how this bizarre deck of cards plays itself' out. Gosh Colonel, forget about the gorgeous women! I could use some of that mouth-watering barbecued beef right now!"

Teenage Amazons were serving the main hut revelers portions of roasted lamb, fried chicken, barbecued spare ribs and beef along with succulent broiled pork on silver trays as the epicures relaxed and romanced in male and female pairs on various cushioned bamboo-framed couches arranged in a circular pattern throughout the village's main hut. And after everyone began indulging in the carnivorous feast, something very extraordinary happened. The Sapiens that were voraciously eating pork and spare ribs astonishingly turned into pigs, those that were ravenously consuming chicken meat converted into roosters, those male indulgers that were chewing and swallowing lamb chops transformed into sheep and those remaining unfortunate souls gobbling down beef and steak gradually switched into steers.

"Our eyes must be deceiving us!" Franks gasped to his equally alarmed spying colleague. "The Amazons must have some kind of immunity to the meat that they've been devouring, but the poor Sapiens have been effectively converted into domesticated animals, probably to be eaten later by the cunning female predators."

"The Amazons aren't only carnivorous as we had originally guessed," the repulsed Captain Weston stammered with his stunned mind still dealing with shock, "but they're also cannibalistic, and more than likely all-year-long, too. I hope that Clark and Moran mercifully escaped such a horribly inhuman fate!"

"*Virgo* is the sixth sign of the zodiac," Colonel Franks whispered to his fellow expedition member, "and this insane planet around five hundred million miles distant from *Spica* in *Virgo's* left hand is abounding with lunatic women that are virgins most of their calendar year and then are wildly promiscuous the other thirty days, the last of which we've just witnessed. All of their stealth is designed as a cruel deception to enslave a new batch of men and to transfer their victims into the penned and corralled domesticated animals until more Sapiens are taken into custody next year to participate in the next mating ritual," Neil Franks summarized. "What's your take on the matter?"

"Yes Colonel," answered Tom Weston while breathing and perspiring heavily. "This place is an ongoing insane asylum where craziness is regarded and valued as everyday normal behavior. After what we just witnessed I'm now an avowed vegetarian. And to think that we almost slaughtered that wild boar with our laser beams right after we left the ship. We could have been murderers without our even knowing it," the second-in-command vociferated and attested. Then realizing his inadvertent loudness the Captain lowered his voice's decibel level to a whisper. "Let's get back to the ship before dusk and have safe shelter before that wicked thunderstorm that's approaching converges on the area."

The distraught duo trudged back down the narrow jungle path in the direction of the waterfall that to their knowledge was in the immediate vicinity of the *New Horizon II*. Colonel Franks was preoccupied synchronizing his coordinates in conjunction with those of his intended destination when Delta sent an urgent transmission while Captain Weston was busy examining several bunches of wild orange berries abundantly growing on uncultivated bushes.

"Colonel," Delta objectively said, "my investigation of the region's flora has established that a certain orange berry has properties that can facilitate the onslaught of temporary amnesia. The Amazons refer to the unique fruit as Lotus berries," Delta relayed, "and I'd advise you and Captain Weston to stay away from the strange specimens that short-circuit memory and compel a person to forget, as far as I can determine, their past, their present and their identity."

"Thanks Delta for your timely heads up!" Neil Franks commended. "I'll tell Captain Weston about this new phenomenon you've just described. I'm sure he'll be reluctant to sample the tempting fruit once he realizes….." The Colonel perceptively noticed his partner tossing several of the delectable orange berries into his mouth and then the commander hollered in a panicky voice, "Tom, don't eat those Lotus berries! They'll have a devastating effect on your….."

Before Colonel Franks could finish his declarative sentence Captain Tom Weston staggered for ten feet and then accidentally plummeted into a ten-foot-deep pit that had been very cleverly designed and concealed as a trap (covered with branches and palm leafs) to isolate a wild animal on the prowl.

Thinking instinctively and recollecting a technique mastered in astronaut survival training, Colonel Franks removed his laser gun from his hip holster', adjusted the device to "Laser Ray

Mode," aimed the weapon at a dangling vine and instantly severed the 'wooden rope' from the rain forest tree. Then using the vine as an emergency rescue device the concerned mission-commander managed to hoist his blank-minded but conscious fellow space voyager from the deep hollow.

"Where am I? Who am I?" Tom Weston asked as his mind was swimming around in a complete quandary. "What has happened? Why and how did it happen?"

"Your name is Astronaut Tom Weston and you just accidentally fell into a hole and have momentarily forgotten your identity," Colonel Franks very succinctly and concisely summarized. "You've bumped your head and have lost your memory. You'll be all right once I get you back to our ship."

"Am I a sailor?" Weston answered in the form of a question. "I don't remember sailing on any damned *ship*! How long have I been a mariner? Right now I feel pretty dizzy and giddy! What rank am I?"

"Here, wrap your arm around my shoulder and I'll help you' hobble back to a place of safety," the Colonel advised his almost delirious comrade. "You have several bad lacerations on your arms and legs that require immediate medical attention. I have a physician friend aboard our ship named Dr. Delta who has admirable and enviable medical skills," Franks partially fibbed. "You aren't capable of walking along on your own because of the severity of your injuries. Let's slowly trudge off and then we'll abruptly turn left at that big coconut tree up ahead."

At the rock-laden clearing adjacent to the cascading aqua-blue waterfall Franks and Weston were unexpectedly ambushed and accosted by a band of aggressive-minded Amazons, who were all menacingly pointing their javelins, spears and bow and arrows at the two strangely garbed interlopers. The auburn-haired Evandre then beamed a mental transmission to Neil Franks that the Colonel was able to easily discern and interpret. A viable two-way telepathic exchange of thoughts had been initiated.

'Your friend is hurt!' Evandre observed and mentally stated. 'Come to our village so that our high priestess Xanthe and her altar maid Bremusa can administer healing herbs to your friend's wounds. He seems to be bleeding badly.'

'The skin cuts are only superficial and my friend's injuries appear worse than what they really are,' Franks telepathically

130

transmitted back. 'Thank you ladies for your kind offer but I believe we'll be able to make it back to our campsite without your guidance or assistance.'

'Nonsense,' Evandre's daughter Phoebe curtly interrupted and mentally beamed. 'If you don't cooperate then Iphinome, Myrina, Clymene, Asteria and Marpe will shoot you both dead with their sharp spears, javelins and bows and arrows. Stop acting so defiant! It would be unwise and totally insolent for you to violate my mother's omnipotent will!'

'It pays to have defensive weapons!' Franks conjectured while forgetting that every private thought within a hundred-foot-range could be perceived and translated by the Amazons. 'Oh no, I shouldn't think of anything!'

'What kind of foolish gibberish are you thinking and relaying?' Evandre angrily challenged. 'You two look a lot like Clark and Moran who had recently graced us with their company. I hope for your sake that your fate will be a more favorable one.'

'What has happened to Clark and Moran?' Neil Franks wondered and telepathically asked. 'I must know what has happened to them!' the Colonel reiterated. 'They were our friends and colleagues!'

'We will take you to see them,' the high priestess Xanthe chimed in, 'but first you must accept and taste this roasted meat I am holding on this silver platter as a token of *our* new-found friendship. Here,' the high priestess offered, 'take this food as a gesture of our good intentions.'

Neil Franks considered his alternatives and then pressed a 'magic button' on his multi-functional telecommunications' device. Immediately an impenetrable force field formed and surrounded Weston and him just as the wicked-hearted and cunning Evandre gave a signal for her warriors to hurl their javelins and spears and to shoot their arrows at the space visitors. The objects harmlessly bounced off of the impregnable force field that was protecting the astronauts from the executed attempt that had been resulting in failure. 'I have no desire to be changed into a swine, sheep or cow!' the Colonel mentally protested to his astonished adversaries. 'My advanced magic is much greater than yours is, High Priestess!'

Seeing that the two aliens were impervious to their weapons and had refused to participate in Xanthe's ruse the Amazons stooped and got down on their knees and worshiped the formerly 'inferior Sapiens from afar,' who were now perceived as potent and invincible divine gods.

'I see that you've intelligently figured out our little secret involving the male consumption of meat. Please come to our village and we shall talk and establish an alliance,' Evandre pleaded from her suppliant position. 'We shall show you our venerable sacred goddess and also share with you our honored banquet hall, and I guarantee that you'll come into contact with Clark and Moran. And we'll also show you a frozen statue of 'the Evil One'!'

Before lowering the very effective force field shield, Franks (still holding up a drugged-up Weston) raised his communicator to his lips and sent a communiqué to Delta. "Bring the space shuttle and fly it to the village an hour from now," the Colonel directed the loyal android. "If I raise my right hand into the air use the properly configured laser torpedoes to eliminate as many buildings as you can. Don't delay and be sure to follow these simple instructions to the most minute iota."

'Now what was that message all about, as if I don't already know,' Evandre protested and mentally signaled to the distrustful astronaut. '*You* Alien Stranger do not trust our motives and our words!'

'It's what we call where we come from 'an insurance policy',' Franks attempted explaining as he reactivated the invisible force field. 'If any of you conniving females dare to become antagonistic or treacherous against my wounded companion or me, then your village will be instantly annihilated and so will you too! I trust that you now understand the magnitude of my statement, which is actually a prediction of truth that is yet to happen! Be foolish Evandre and act against me' and then you'll suffer the dire consequences!'

Evandre acceded to the Colonel's demands and the Amazon Queen directed Iphinome, Myrina and Clymene to construct a makeshift stretcher to transport Captain Thomas Weston to the village where soothing medicinal herbs would be administered to his open wounds. The assigned stretcher task was completed in thirty minutes and the odd party meandered west down the serpentine jungle trail in the direction of the medieval-looking Amazon tribal community.

As the short trek to the village proceeded onward, Asteria, Marpe, Myrina and Iphinome carried the improvised stretcher (having two long poles) with the dazed Astronaut Thomas Weston lying on it. Meanwhile Colonel Neil Franks honored his suspicious nature and kept his force field active in case Xanthe, Evandre, Clymene, Bremusa or Phoebe (in that order of distrust) attempted anything nefarious or hostile.

'I'll have to teach these Amazon women common morality,' Franks imagined. 'They need to acquire the rudiments of organized civilization. Their flawed ethical value system is convoluted and needs modifying.'

Evandre sensed the Colonel's private rumination and turned around and looked him squarely in the eyes. 'What is this thing you call morality?' she telepathically inquired. 'The concept is foreign to our traditions and customs. I perceive that it's some kind of weird abstraction that I don't easily fathom!'

'Well for example,' Franks thought and cerebrally hesitated as he and the confused Amazon Queen ambled side by side, 'morality is a sense of doing what is inherently right and what is good as opposed to doing what is wrong and evil. For instance,' the Colonel attempted explaining to his very interested fellow trekker, 'changing men into pigs, sheep and cows is fundamentally immoral and goes against acceptable morality. Those men you call Sapiens have individual dignity and should be treated as your equals. And changing men into animals and then consuming their flesh is the greatest of evils,' Franks endeavored to convey. 'It's what my people call and condemn as cannibalism and it shouldn't be practiced.'

'And where do your people live?' Evandre curiously asked. 'Do you reside in another part of this world? Did you come from the other side of the Sapien savannahs? Or do you reside somewhere over the high mountains?'

'Actually Evandre, the injured man on the stretcher and I originate from another world,' Franks mentally mentioned as he very deliberately pointed to the sky. 'We've come to your planet from another world circling another sun.'

'What is a sun?' Evandre wondered and questioned. 'Is it like a world?'

'A sun is like your large star up there?' Franks indicated while pointing at *Spica* shining brilliantly on the western horizon and presently setting in the late afternoon sky. 'Your sun is actually the closest star to your world.'

'I never realized than a sun was a star,' Evandre mentally divulged. 'I always believed and thought that a sun and a star were two separate things. My people have so much to learn from you. How did you get to our world?'

'A giant white circular ship transported my friend and me to this planet,' the Colonel mentally transmitted to the Amazon Queen. 'A huge ship brought us here! A similar type of ship had transported Clark and Moran to your world, too!'

'I see, that is what Myrina and Marpe saw flying overhead and then the object landed somewhere in the valley,' the lavender-eyed Evandre confidentially informed. 'They then shot a wild boar, returned to the village and told us of the incredible spectacle that they had seen in the sky. I was inclined not to believe them at first,' the Queen shared, 'but I remembered that Clark and Moran had mentally transmitted that they had traveled to my world in a large ship, but I could never understand how outer space could be an ocean since there appears to be no ocean in the sky.'

'Well, space is like an ocean of sorts,' Franks mentally admitted and communicated. 'And tell me Evandre, where are Clark and Moran? Are they still alive?'

'I shall soon show you,' the Queen promised. 'Their bones are resting in Xanthe's temple. They died when fleeing the village to escape Xanthe's wrath. She wanted them to eat boar meat but they stubbornly refused. A volcano over yonder ridge then erupted and there was a tremendous shaking of the ground. The quake caused a terrible rock-slide and Clark and Moran were then crushed to death. That is the truth of what had happened to them.'

After the itinerant safari entered the village Captain Tom Weston's injuries were swiftly attended to in the main hall and then Evandre escorted Franks to Xanthe's sinister-looking but smaller skull-decorated temple-hut. 'Tell me more about what you define as 'not moral',' the intrigued Queen mentally insisted. 'I believe that my people have much to learn from your advanced culture.'

'Well, there's no immediate need for your women to remove *your* left breasts,' Franks pontificated with his personal gratification interests in mind. 'That definitely is not morally correct. And also Evandre,' the divorced Earthling continued and prevaricated while also being aware that Captain Weston was a confirmed bachelor, 'marriage is definitely immoral.'

'What is marriage?' Evandre inquired. 'The elusive term has no meaning in our language. In fact I've never heard that word before!'

'It is when a man and a woman live together for life and have no other mates,' Franks explained as he contemplated his new fantasy existence in his recently discovered strange-but-novel hedonistic Eden. 'Yes Evandre, ideas like marriage, slavery, cannibalism and transforming Sapiens into animals should all be regarded as taboo and immoral.'

'I see,' Evandre answered with a degree of certitude. 'Here is Xanthe's temple,' the Queen informed as the two entered through the only portal. Franks examined Ralph Clark and Stephen Moran's skeletons lying in a pair of rudimentary coffins situated directly below a ten-foot-tall wooden statue of what resembled Artemis, the Greek goddess of hunting.

'Remove the coffins to another hut,' Franks commanded. 'I want to now see and understand what you had previously described as 'the Hut of Evil where the Evil One is kept'.'

Evandre led her 'all-powerful visitor' to the feared Hut of Evil and then Colonel Franks was quite surprised to see the familiar figure of the prototype android Phi standing erect and stationary inside the straw structure.

'His flesh does not decay,' Evandre explained with awe. 'He must indeed be a Sapien god of evil. That's the only feasible conclusion Xanthe had made and described to me. But my people have been afraid to destroy the evil figure because we fear terrible consequences, perhaps in the form of angering the unpredictable temperamental volcano god.'

Franks stepped forward to the 'Altar of Evil' pedestal, opened a metal hatch on Phi's upper left forearm, connected two formerly detached wires and suddenly, much to Evandre's amazement and bewilderment, the android became animated. "Hello Colonel Franks? Who is your female companion? We've never been formally introduced!"

'You *are* magic!' the Amazon Queen thought and related to Phi. 'You are indeed a god of the highest magnitude, either the ultimate evil or the ultimate good.'

"I don't know exactly what you're thinking," the electronically controlled guru answered in a robotic voice similar to that of Delta, "but I evaluate myself as being very fortunate to have found a new home in this sector of the galaxy," Phi rejoiced.

Then Colonel Franks' telepathed something salient to Evandre, who was still quite puzzled by the term "galaxy." 'Now please my dear Amazon Queen accompany me outside so that I may demonstrate my unique magic by giving an important command to a flying object.' Then inside the Hut of Evil perceptive Neil Franks became completely cognizant of the fact that Phi was merely a prototype android and was not able or programmed to intercept the mental transmissions being exchanged between Evandre and himself. "Phi, please follow us outside so that I can properly introduce you to another more recently manufactured robotic mechanism named Delta," Franks commanded.

Five minutes later a streamlined cigar-shaped shuttle-craft with Delta as its pilot glided two-hundred-feet above the ground towards the remote Amazon village. The sleek space jitney was approaching the vicinity from the direction of the *New Horizon II*. The Amazon eyewitnesses were astounded by the aerial phenomenon and all of the female observers hurriedly got to their knees in supplication.

Colonel Franks gave the command over his tele-communicator for the shuttle-craft operator to disintegrate Xanthe's temple housing the ten-foot-tall wooden facsimile of the goddess Artemis. The demolition was readily accomplished (much to the dismay and consternation of Xanthe and the subordinate villagers) and then Delta adroitly landed the shuttle in the center of the tribal community and next, triumphantly exited the wondrous craft.

"Good work Delta," Colonel Franks orally complimented his obedient subordinate. "That was very efficiently done. Now you and Phi please carry the two coffins with the skeletal remains to that adequate hut over there to our left that will permanently replace the former Temple of Evil, and in the future the new facility will be respectfully referred to for all sakes and purposes as the 'Divine Temple of Good'."

A communication transmission was being received from Earth and was being emitted from speakers inside the now-stationary shuttle-craft. "Colonel Franks, Captain Weston," the speaker's voice boomed, "this is General Dickinson at Cape Canaveral. Do you read me? Your exploratory mission has been canceled due to a lack of funding and also because of newly instituted budgetary constraints," the General bellowed.

"It's my duty to order you to return to Earth immediately under penalty of court martial if you refuse to obey my command."

Colonel Franks reached inside the shuttle-craft and flicked off the control panel's "Reception Switch." Then he mentally contemplated, 'I've had more than enough of obnoxious orders, high taxes, perpetual labor, relentless bureaucracy, excessive crime, environmental pollution and Earth's many unbearable hypocrisies. I've found paradise here in this beautiful primitive pristine Eden, and when Captain Weston fully recovers from his amnesia condition,' Colonel Franks sincerely and privately prognosticated, 'we'll both live like kings and even Delta and Phi will be treated like royalty every single glorious day. We've found a new home right here on this marvelous Utopia known to a select few as *Amazonia*. Let the Earth be damned along with all its quarrelsome people and all of *their* ugly distressing complex problems!'

Then a final thought swirled around inside the Colonel's head. 'I gotta' get to *the New Horizon's* control panel and shut off the emergency beacon. Then no recovery ship from Earth will ever be able to locate my little Utopian empire down here on planet *Amazonia*!'

"Greek Statutory Law"

As a youth growing up and going to school in Corinth, Greece, Achilles Greco learned to love Greek Mythology and was especially enamored with the tales that lauded the adventurous heroes' Achilles, (who had killed the Trojan hero Hector), Perseus, (who had slain the vile monster Medusa), Hercules, (who had performed twelve remarkable labors), Agamemnon, (who had led the Achaean expedition against Troy), Menelaus, (whose wife was more famously later known as Helen of Troy) and Orpheus, (who had journeyed down to the Underworld to be reunited with the soul of his deceased bride, Eurydice).

Other great champions that were loved by Achilles Greco were Phaethon, (who flew his father Apollo's horse-drawn chariot too close to the sun), Bellerophon, (who rode mighty Pegasus to slay the monster Chimera), Theseus, (who killed the notorious Minotaur in a dark labyrinth under a palace on the island of Crete), Odysseus, (imaginative king of Ithaca who ingeniously thought up the idea of the Trojan Horse), Daedalus, (an ancient genius who invented framed wings having glued feathers in order to escape the tyranny of King Minos), Oedipus, (who answered the Sphinx's riddle and became King of Thebes) and finally Jason, (leader of the renowned Argonauts that retrieved the Golden Fleece and brought it back to Greece). Achilles Greco also derived much pleasure from reading the wonderful stories that described the incredible exploits of the major *Olympian* gods.

In 1985 Achilles Greco at age twenty-five immigrated to the United States with grandiose dreams of working hard and ascending the ladder of success in the American free enterprise system. The ambitious newcomer started at the bottom of the economic capitalistic way of life as a dishwasher in his uncle's Vineland, New Jersey diner, soon became a cashier, saved every penny he could hoard and in 1989 bought his own small diner/restaurant seventeen miles north in Hammonton.

By 1995 the shrewd entrepreneur and daring risk-taker had mastered the major tenets of capitalism by independently owning six lucrative high-volume dollar-earning diners, and by 2005 the forty-five-year old man had amassed full control of thirteen popular dining establishments situated in various towns all over Southern New Jersey.

Achilles had also profited from shrewdly investing in the stock market, so when the food mogul was approached by a large conglomerate to sell his "lucky thirteen" thriving diners for a handsome thirty-five million dollars, and considering that he' already had accumulated seven million in his "small potatoes' Wall Street portfolio," the shrewd rags-to-riches multimillionaire took advantage of the excellent opportunity, eagerly sold his flourishing enterprises and then optimistically moved to Athens, Georgia where the retiree had purchased a fabulous mansion with magnificent white marble Corinthian columns, which made the impressive palace look like a modernistic Greek temple.

'I never married but I really like entertaining,' Achilles reckoned as he admired the fantastic newly-acquired home on the hill. 'This is my own private *Mt. Olympus* and the former owner's family sold it at a sacrifice price of only five million dollars. And the woman who had lived here also appreciated Greek mythology as attested by the thirteen expensive life-size statues that grace the main library room. This is what I've labored to achieve! My fondest dreams have come true!'

Achilles proudly stood in his fully stocked library and gazed at the handsome mahogany and glass cabinets that housed his exceptional collection of famous authors' works, and without a doubt Greco's favorite volumes were Homer's *Iliad* and *Odyssey* along with a black leather edition of Edith Hamilton's famous literary contribution, *Mythology.*

'And I also really treasure these thirteen fabulous statues, the first being of my namesake Achilles. Then there is Perseus, Hercules, Agamemnon, Menelaus, Orpheus, Phaethon, Bellerophon, Theseus, Odysseus, Daedalus, Oedipus and Jason,' Achilles mused. 'But for some inexplicable reason the Perseus statue is missing Medusa's head in its raised left hand. I wonder why that is so? It was probably broken-off somehow by accident. I should have that deficiency corrected as soon as possible. It really looks incomplete.'

One odd feature of the Athens, Georgia furnished mansion's décor really puzzled and perplexed the normally unflappable Achilles Greco. Three life-size statues of the home's former owners, Mr. Arthur Grimesley, Mr. Joseph Nicastro and Mrs. Joan Sampson stood side-by-side in the entrance foyer, which featured a huge (suspended from the second-floor ceiling) beautiful crystal chandelier. 'I'm rather superstitious and refuse to have the three foyer statues removed,' the tycoon thought, 'but I find the three marble figures both enchanting and mysterious. But what is more peculiar is that the former owners of this mansion all had disappeared without any trace of their whereabouts and all police investigations have ended in futility,' Achilles considered. 'These coincidences are more than strange; they are quite bizarre and almost ominous!'

On Wednesday, June 8th Achilles returned to his Athens, Georgia palace after attending a charity fund-raising function in downtown Atlanta. The hired white limousine pulled into the semi-circular pavered driveway and then stopped under the portico's pavilion. The conscientious chauffeur got out and the driver next promptly opened the back door for Achilles Greco to exit. After giving the chauffeur a generous hundred-dollar tip the lonely tycoon entered his superb mansion only to discover the bodies of three burglars lying dead inside the library. 'This mass murdering could be scandalous!' the alarmed owner defensively thought. 'I'll notify the police and tell them they must conduct a discreet search for clues. I don't want the tabloid press vultures ruining my reputation.'

During the initial police investigation into the unusual "murders" Achilles pointed out to the authorities conducting the probe that a highly irregular phenomenon was quite evident and that it should be delved into. The library's white *marble* Perseus Statue, which was a facsimile of egocentric Benvenuto Cellini's (1500-1571) classic *bronze* masterpiece of the hero holding Medusa's head, had dried blood caked on its' sword. But the police were not as intrigued with the actual discovery as was Achilles Greco.

"We'll do a thorough blood and *DNA* analysis," Inspector Hargrove told the very concerned homeowner, "and off the record, the stains probably got on the sword as a result of some sort of violent struggle, either amongst the three thugs or perhaps from intervention from other criminals that had managed to escape the scene of conflict with their lives. If I remember properly from high school art class," the somewhat curious Inspector surmised and said, "isn't this statue supposed to have a monster's head being held in its left hand?"

"Why yes," Achilles Greco affirmatively answered. "The creature's head has been missing ever since I've been living here! There must be some logical explanation to account for all of these weird and eerie variables that seem to defy explanation. If you need any additional information Inspector Hargrove," the wary and apprehensive homeowner explained, "I'll be more than willing to cooperate. I don't like having murders occurring in my home whether I'm in the house or away from Athens on personal business. But please, keep the media frenzy out of this case."

"Indeed, we fully understand where you're coming from Mr. Greco," Coroner Brent Crawford concurred. "We'll keep you updated on any further findings or quirky developments. At present though, I must confess that this entire matter appears rather baffling, eerily baffling if I may add."

'This investigation all seems horribly frightening,' Achilles fearfully evaluated. 'Three desperate crooks are brutally slain, in fact savagely stabbed to death in my personal library and in addition three former wealthy owners of this house are missing with *their* statues prominently exhibited in the grand entrance foyer. Perhaps I should spend more time vacationing in exclusive European hotels!' Greco conjectured. 'Even the *Athens Acropol* or the *Residence Giorgio* would suffice! But everything else being equal I'd like to see and feel the energy and enlightenment of the splendid *Acropolis* one more time!' Then Achilles snapped out of his reverie. "Thank you officers for your prompt response. Let me know of any future significant discoveries."

The night after the three thieves had been "systematically eliminated" Achilles removed a favorite book from his library's second shelf and began fancifully perusing the story "Perseus and Medusa." Even though Greco had virtually memorized each and every line of the popular myth, the gaudy tale still fascinated his fancy. 'Heroes were half human and half divine characters with gods as their fathers and mortal women as their mothers,' Achilles recalled from his intrigue with mythology.

The hero Perseus was the offspring of a brief love affair between the king-god Zeus and a mortal woman named Danae. A prophet had predicted that Danae's son would eventually kill her father Acrisius, King of Argo, who then a year later had his soldiers place Danae and her infant son Perseus inside a basket that was soon sent out to sea. The basket miraculously stayed afloat and landed on the island of Seriphos, where a kind benefactor named Dictys took the maiden and her child into his care. But Dictys' evil brother Polydictes was the cruel-minded king of Seriphos who feared Perseus's potential to assume the

142

throne as had been foretold by the island soothsayer, so when Perseus became a fearless teenager the wicked king tricked the callow youth into going on a quest to decapitate Medusa's head and to return it to Seriphos as a treasured gift for Polydictes to cherish and revere. And with the help of the benevolent goddess Pallas Athene, who provided the brave hero with a pair of winged sandals and a winged bronze helmet and accompanying shield to make Perseus virtually invincible, the aspiring champion was able to complete his arduous mission and return to Seriphos to gladly turn the ruthless King Polydictes into stone using Medusa's horrible face.

Achilles Greco frequently read other ancient Greek myths such as "Hercules and the Three Golden Apples," "The Legend of King Midas," "Atalanta's Race," "Theseus and the Minotaur," "Psyche and Cupid" and "Baucis and Philemon," and every time the wealthy man got up to retrieve the mail, to use the bathroom facilities or to obtain a drink from the kitchen refrigerator he would return to his library soft leather recliner chair and then recognize that something quite extraordinary had just happened during his recent absence from the room. Each time Greco would re-enter his library and pick up his copy of the *Book of Stories from Greek Antiquity,* no matter which tale he had been reading, remarkably the page in that anthology would always be turned to '145,' the first page of the story "Perseus and Medusa."

'This is all very uncanny, sinister and odious,' the apprehensive man thought. 'It's like being communicated with from a dead person, but every character in the book I'm reading is fictitious and Perseus was undoubtedly a mythological hero that never existed in reality to ever have a chance to become a ghost. My sensibility is really being challenged by this troubling aberrant recurrence,' Achilles determined. 'And it has happened far too many times to be dismissed as merely an anomaly! But in my heart I truly do believe and sense that someone or something is consciously trying to communicate with me, possibly from an unknown occult dimension!'

Then one early October 2005 Friday morning Achilles was casually reading the tale "Pygmalion and Galatea" from Edith Hamilton's *Mythology* collection when the bachelor rose from his chair to retrieve the morning newspaper, which had been tossed onto his front steps beneath the columned portico's pavilion. Upon reentering his mansion and returning to his favorite black leather recliner with the edition of the *Atlanta Journal-Constitution* the rich fellow suddenly became quite distraught. The anthology collection was still closed with the bookmark inserted but the object of convenience had been deliberately moved from page 110 in the story "Pygmalion and Galatea" to page 145, "Perseus and Medusa."

'I'll try an experiment to make sure that my memory and my eyes aren't deceiving me,' Achilles logically imagined. 'I'll read other myths from Edith Hamilton's book and see what results will be yielded.' But much to Greco's astonishment and consternation each time he departed and then returned to his library the bookmark had been deliberately changed to all-too-familiar page 145, "Perseus and Medusa." The ongoing phenomenon was now really tormenting the man's sanity.

Out of curiosity, Achilles conducted similar experiments with other books that contained the common story "Perseus and Medusa," and every time Greco departed and quickly returned to the library, whether he had been reading "The Seven Against Thebes" or "Odysseus and the Cyclops," on each transit the page marker had mysteriously and redundantly been switched to "Perseus and Medusa."

'There must be some feasible explanation, even if it isn't scientific,' the now-superstitious man considered. 'By nature I've always been a cynical and doubting guy, particularly when it comes to religion, metaphysics, the arcane or anything else that involves the theme of supernatural intervention. I certainly won't report this very weird manifestation to my optometrist when I go for my scheduled appointment next Thursday, that's for sure. But I find the whole matter very troubling.'

Late Monday afternoon, October 24th Achilles was bored watching melodramatic cable channel news and was anticipating and thinking about a sensational upcoming November vacation trip to Athens and to Corinth to visit cousins still living on the European Continent. The retired forty-five year old poured himself his second glass of *Southern Comfort* on the rocks and sat down in his favorite library black leather chair to continue reading an imaginative episode of Homer's *Odyssey*, "The Island of Circe." After Achilles Greco visited the bathroom and then returned he immediately noticed that the book he had been reading had been carefully inserted back into the glass display case and that another large volume titled *Bulfinch's Mythology* had been placed on the side table situated next to the black leather recliner, and the new text had been coincidentally opened to the story "Perseus and Medusa."

'I must be hallucinating,' Achilles fearfully suspected and theorized. 'I need to stay away from hard liquor, even something as wonderfully tasty as *Southern Comfort*.' And then Greco's eyes scanned the dimly lit library and they perceived that all thirteen statues surrounding him were that of Perseus triumphantly standing tall and holding his sword in his right hand and nothing in the champion's left. Achilles put his cold glass down on the side table and vigorously rubbed his eyes. His psyche was being tested to its maximum.

'This is absolutely surreal!' the man incredulously thought. 'I now truly believe that this new mansion of mine is haunted! No wonder why the executors of Mrs. Joan Sampson's estate wanted to dispose of the property in a hurry at a bargain price! Now I think I know why!'

And as Achilles Greco further scrutinized the unearthly and illogical spectacle of his "marble gallery," the name Perseus that was now inscribed in stone at the base of each of the thirteen statues suddenly crystallized and then converted to the word "Attica," which was indeed geographic terminology that the still-stunned immigrant fully comprehended.

'Attica is the northern Greek peninsula upon which the city of Athens is located,' Achilles recollected, 'and it extends from the mountains to the *Aegean Sea*. The area's mountains are rich in iron, lead and silver deposits, and the nearby hills are where the white marble to construct the *Parthenon* and other temples on the Acropolis had been gotten,' Greco remembered from his academic studies back in Corinth. 'And many vineyards and olive groves can be found all throughout Attica.'

And then much to Achilles Greco's total bewilderment the "a" on the end of the word "Attica" represented on all thirteen Perseus statues faded into oblivion leaving the word "Attic," which immediately gave the observer an instant inspiration. 'That's the message or clue that the thirteen statues are attempting to communicate!' Greco surmised and concluded with his heart beating wildly. 'I must go up into the attic and search around for whatever the statues want me to find. This entire experience is quite strange and now heading way beyond paranormal. I'm certainly not an ardent churchgoer but it could only be described as being divine, possibly even miraculous!'

Coincidental to the awed man coming to his perceptive interpretation of events, much to Achilles Greco's wonderment the word "Attic" formed back into "Attica," and then the appellation "Perseus" disappeared at the base of twelve of the statues. And as the ceiling lights automatically and simultaneously brightened, further illuminating the library, twelve of the thirteen marble statues then amazingly returned to being impressive depictions of the heroes Achilles, Hercules, Agamemnon, Menelaus, Orpheus, Phaethon, Bellerophon, Theseus, Odysseus, Daedalus, Oedipus and Jason.

'The statue of Perseus that didn't change back to a likeness of itself must be the genuine one that I'm supposed to communicate with,' Achilles cogently hypothesized and considered. 'I'll polish off the rest of this delicious *Southern Comfort* and then maybe I'll have sufficient courage to address Perseus and ask him several relevant questions.'

The half-intoxicated imbiber rose from his soft black leather chair, staggered across the expansive room and felt a trifle ridiculous initiating a conversation with an inanimate marble statue. "Perseus, have you been attempting to communicate with me lately?" the more-than-slightly confused man awkwardly slurred.

"Yes Achilles Greco," the stationary statue replied with only its solid white lips moving. "You finally possessed the wherewithal to figure out the 'Attic' riddle after I had to nearly disclose it to you in its entirety. I only wish that you were a little more intrepid and intelligent."

"What is in the attic that is of such grave importance?" Achilles asked the impeccably formed white marble image. "Is it what's missing from your left hand? Answer me so that I can help solve your problem."

"Yes Master, you must go up into the attic and bring me Medusa's head so that my physical form can again be complete," the statue demanded. "You'll find the severed head concealed inside a bronze box, wrapped in a dark leather bag. Bring the head to me so that the gods' can reattach it to my left hand. Zeus himself has promised to perform that special service for me."

"I'm a little dizzy right now but I'd very much like to step up into the attic to locate the metal box and the leather sack that you've described," Achilles timidly suggested. "May I go find and examine the item that you so desire? I don't have the dexterity right this moment to proficiently handle the head. To be perfectly truthful Perseus, I don't think I'm too physically well coordinated at this time to be able to satisfactorily deliver Medusa's head to you. What do you think I should do?"

"Yes Master Achilles Greco, I insist that you pursue your exploratory folly," Perseus impatiently consented, "but on your second attic venture Master I trust that you'll be sufficiently audacious and sober enough to retrieve the head and bring it back to this library so that I can finally be whole again."

The drunken multimillionaire's curiosity had been piqued. The obedient homeowner climbed up to the second floor guest bedroom, entered it and then opened a door, flicked on the lights and gradually ascended up to the mansion's musty poorly ventilated attic. After rummaging around for several minutes Achilles by chance discovered the alluded to box believed to contain Medusa's head. After opening the squeaky lid the searcher found the designated leather bag. 'I'll only feel the head through the leather material,' Greco nervously instructed his suspicious will. 'It feels awfully grotesque and I can definitely distinguish the solid marble-carved snakes in *her* head that indeed represent hair. I don't want to trip down the steps and have the head roll out of the sack. Next week I'll garner enough mettle to take the head downstairs and personally deliver it to Perseus, or whatever spiritual entity that constitutes the speaking marble likeness of Perseus.'

The now-neurotic wealthy resident meticulously lowered the leather sack back into the bronze box, placed the container next to an old mattress, descended the attic stairs and then switched off the attic lights.

The entire last week of October Achilles Greco occupied his restive mind by working out at a nearby Athens, Georgia Hollywood East Gym (even though the now-paranoid tycoon had his own personal gym in his basement). The beleaguered man also spent time finalizing his much-needed November vacation to Corinth and Athens, Greece to visit distant relatives and boyhood acquaintances. And the remainder of his free time the industrious semi-retired entrepreneur spent narrowing down a list of prospective business associates being considered for investing in a newly proposed suburban shopping mall.

But on *Halloween* October 31st Achilles could not control his resistance to temptation any longer so early that evening he approached the splendid marble statue of Perseus in the all-too-familiar library.

"Perseus, before I go and fetch Medusa's head for you," Greco nervously addressed his very unique statue, "I have a few basic questions to ask you that are dominating and affecting my inquisitive mind. I hope that you and your fellow twelve statues aren't offended."

"No indeed," Perseus's stone lips moved and uttered. "Go right ahead Master with announcing your principal concerns. I'll answer them if I can."

"Who had killed the three bandits that had broken into the house with the intention of probably wanting to rob my mansion of jewelry, silverware, china dishes and other valuables?" the very affluent investor/resident asked. "Do you have any particular knowledge of the crimes that had been committed? Were those men hired to commit robbery?"

"I must confess Master that it was *I* that had performed the heinous deeds," Perseus shamelessly answered. "I wouldn't call my act of protecting your property a crime because as you know I'm a man of honor and integrity and I've always considered eliminating vile humans a sacred duty and not a grievous sin. That's the way we heroes always conducted ourselves in the prehistoric past Achilles Greco," Perseus adamantly maintained and qualified, "you know! And with only three pathetic thugs involved in the attempted larceny, I didn't require any special assistance from my twelve fellow marble champions assembled here in your library."

"Yes Perseus, I now fully fathom your noble motivation to want to protect my estate from vandalism and ransacking," Achilles appreciatively noted. "That swift justice you had practiced was very praiseworthy indeed Perseus! Now tell me honestly," the wealthy aristocrat continued, "did you have anything to do with turning the three former owners of this mansion into stone statues? Are the life-sized statues really the remains of Mrs. Sampson, Mr. Nicastro and Mr. Grimesley standing erect in the main foyer? I can't seem to fall asleep at nights thinking about all of these cryptic things I've just mentioned. Can you please explain the former owners' mystery to me?"

"Certain relevant things I'm not permitted to answer according to specific instructions and guidelines from the incomparable *Olympian* Zeus, and your particular inquiry' is definitely one of them I'll not violate!" Perseus sternly articulated without flinching a muscle aside from his moving lips. "You Master will have to implicitly trust my character and value my judgment in regard to acquiring Medusa's hideous head for my own personal disposal. Are there' any further questions outside the realm of mythology currently pestering your mortal mind?"

"No Perseus, I think you've adequately addressed my two principal ones," Achilles shakily remarked. "Now I believe I do feel valiant enough to stray up to the attic and secure Medusa's wretched wrapped head for *your* own personal disposition. Please bear with me while I attempt performing this very daunting task you've requested."

"Master, I have a word of sage advice for you to strictly adhere to," the statue cautioned and very carefully enunciated. "Remove my magical bronze shield from yonder wall to the left of the stone fireplace and take it with you. In that way when you open the attic box look into the shield and Medusa's face will not have any adverse effect on you!"

"Nonsense Perseus my dear and noble friend," Achilles confidently answered with swagger. "The ghastly horrible head is concealed and wrapped inside a leather sack and therefore my pupils will not come into direct contact with the wretched beast's grotesque face. But thank you for rendering your sympathetic concern anyway!"

Disguising his faltering sense of audacity the stubborn tycoon clambered up the steep second floor steps without even holding on to the wooden banister and after entering the aforementioned bedroom he then flicked on the attic light switch. In the fairly well lit third-floor storage area next to the old mattress Achilles again came across the metal box and opened it expecting to find the leather sack inside. Instead the shocked man momentarily shrieked in terror upon scrutinizing the distorted and disfigured countenance and head of the mythological beast Medusa, and the haughty and defenseless standing examiner immediately was converted into solid marble.

'Another phase of my laborious and difficult mission has been accomplished,' the statue of Perseus gratefully comprehended after hearing Achilles Greco's nerve-shattering spine-tingling shriek from up in the mansion's attic. 'Unfortunately for you Mr. Greco you've solved the very interesting riddle of Medusa's head. You should've heeded my candid instructions and not arrogantly pursued your own cocky solution. Your sin of *Hubris* has been punished. Now all I have to do is trick three more mortal souls into opening the bronze box and have Medusa's face turn them into stone,' the motionless statue of Perseus assessed, 'and then finally my punishment capriciously administered by Zeus will have been successfully completed. Then my yearning soul will be able to at-long-last travel down to *Hades* and there in the eternal underworld finally rest in peace in the fabled *Elysium* daffodil fields. I shall be coming to the banks of the *Styx* soon Charon! Have your barge ready! I shall be coming soon!'

At 7 p.m. an Athens, Georgia mother drove a dark green *SUV* filled with rambunctious trick-or-treaters up to Achilles Greco's mansion's portico pavilion to release the costumed children out of the vehicle to honor the traditional annual *Halloween* ritual. After the four disguised junior visitors vigorously rang the columned palace's doorbell without achieving any satisfactory results, the mother behind the wheel yelled to the disappointed boys and girls, "Jimmy, Janet, Karen, Bobbie, nobody seems to be home tonight! Let's see if we can go next door and get you some candy, cupcakes and some other safe-to-eat *Halloween* treats!"

The four disappointed kids dressed like mini-Greek gods and goddesses dashed back to the *SUV* so that they could try their luck begging for treats at the nearest neighbor's residence. Before the mother drove out of the U-shaped gray-pavered driveway, she asked her oldest son a pertinent question.

"Jimmy, the lights were on in the foyer," the mother wondered and stated. "Did you see anybody moving around inside?"

"No Mommy, what a total bummer!" Jimmy costumed as all-powerful Zeus dejectedly reported in a sad and peeved tone of voice. "There were only *four* white statues standing there' all by themselves."

"Perseus II"

Timothy Higgins hated ambiguity in all his life's activities as much as he despised daily drudgery and intellectual mediocrity. The all-too-perceptive Hammonton Middle School math' teacher typically preferred having clarity and certainty evident in all aspects of his academic and social life. Arithmetical equations easily appealed to his sense of logic because in Higgins' world everything should be weighed, measured and have some standard and predictable numerical justification or equivalency. Science and mathematics normally occupied a much higher plane on the academic hierarchy (in Tim Higgins' objective-oriented mind) than did subjects like English and social studies, which were taught by other 'less serious' instructors on his school's faculty. In Timothy Higgins' very biased educational assessment, math' and science transcended all other traditional disciplines that were imparted to students in the middle school's daily curriculum.

Saturday morning, August 16, 2008 eligible-to-be-married bachelor Timothy Higgins received via U.S. Mail a surprise invitation at his 430 Lincoln Avenue bungalow. The RSVP card requested his attendance at an upcoming party to be held at art teacher Gwen Vickers' condominium. 'Ah, let me see now!' Tim thought. 'The shindig's gonna' start at 8 p.m. next Friday night, August 22nd. I've just finished my summer job managing the peach packing line over at Pastore Orchards so I'm now free to attend the costume party without having to worry about performing any demanding work responsibilities the next morning. The necessity of needing summer employment is definitely the downside of public school teaching!'

Then Timothy remembered that Gwen Vickers was a very good friend of Audrey Duncan, an exceptionally attractive brunette real estate agent that he really wanted to meet. 'I'm sure Audrey's goin' to be at Gwen's bash next Friday night!' Higgins reckoned and then sighed. 'I just gotta' get Gwen to introduce her to me. Audrey's the prettiest girl in all of South Jersey as far as I'm concerned. I know what I'll do! I'll fake everyone out and have the neatest costume at the affair. Everyone's going to get their outfits at the Apex Costume Rentals store over in Berlin and at Ned's Party Apparel over in Mays Landing,' Tim theorized and grinned, 'but I'll trump the other guests by heading over to Bristol, Pennsylvania first thing Monday morning and select some extravagant togs to rent at the Trojan Horse Novelty and Garb Emporium. Although my observation is outside the realms of math' and science,' the savvy schemer considered with an even broader smile forming on his face, 'I had read in the *Philadelphia Inquirer* last month that the Trojan Horse is the best place in the entire Delaware Valley to shop for unique costumes to wear to masquerade parties.'

Tim had spent the bulk of the afternoon mowing his lawn and then after showering, the introverted fellow devoted his recliner chair reverie to contemplating how he would impress the vivacious Audrey Duncan the following Saturday at Gwen Vickers' gala party. 'If I'm a masked King Arthur of Camelot and Audrey comes as Queen Guenevere or if I'm Robin Hood and she arrives as Maid Marian,' the pedagogue mused inside his comfortable air-conditioned den, 'then striking-up a conversation would be quite easy. But then again,' the dreamer continued his fantasizing, 'me being King Louis XVI of France and Audrey being Marie Antoinette would work out perfectly all right too! Say now,' the horizontal occupant of the recliner chair fancifully determined, 'my knowledge outside math' is more extensive than I had ever realized! Watch out Social Studies and English departments! I guess I know more basic history and literature than I ever really gave myself credit for!'

Later that afternoon the fatigued math' teacher fell asleep in his black leather recliner chair and soon had a rather strange dream. Timothy Higgins was standing on a high cliff overlooking a roaring sea when a young enchanting woman in the form of an apparition appeared in his midst, remarkably approaching and then gracefully floating in the air above him. In his subconscious mind's vision the beautiful goddess was clad in a sparkling light blue silk tunic, and after she stared directly into the astonished man's eyes the deity then politely and candidly asked, "Would you rather have a soul of clay or a soul of fire?"

Before Timothy could effectively answer "A soul of fire!" he awoke from his deep sleep, remembering only that a bronze helmet, a bronze sword, a glittering metallic shield and a pair of peculiar winged sandals had instantaneously appeared in the radiant young lady's hands and were (by virtue of gesture) being offered to him.

A minute later Higgins had fully awakened from Morpheus' powerful influence and he curiously rehashed his peculiar subconscious manifestation. That evening while Tim was fast asleep in his electric-adjustable bed the all-too-alluring female specter again appeared holding the four aforementioned special items in her arms, and the enticing lady once more lucidly communicated with the apprehensive man's mind.

"Since I believe you had earlier replied 'A soul of fire!' to my most important question," the mysterious young goddess prefaced, "each day until further notice wear these sandals, this helmet and you may also carry this shield and sword that gores, for certainly, great and wonderful deeds will eventually be yours!" And no sooner had those bizarre words been spoken that Timothy Higgins awoke from his disturbing slumber, his entire body experiencing a cold sweat.

Ten o'clock Sunday morning Tim Higgins picked up his cell phone and dialed Jack McDermott, a close friend and English teacher at the Hammonton Middle School. The caller desired knowing the identity of the attractive young lady (if indeed *she* had an appellation) who had twice paid him a 'mental visitation' after he had dozed off.

"Hello Jack!" Tim began his informational quest. "Have you been invited to Gwen Vickers' masquerade party next Saturday night? I presume you have."

"Yes, and I'm goin' to get the perfect costume," the Language Arts' instructor chuckled and related. "I had a novel inspiration while swallowing down some breakfast cereal. I'd like to attend the party as George Washington's favorite French chum, the honorable Marquis de Lafayette. Of course," the all-too-verbose English mentor added, "I'll have to find an appropriate mask and white wig to wear for the occasion. I think I can get a suitable outfit over at Ned's Party Apparel in Mays Landing. How about yourself Tim? What's your disguising pleasure goin' to be for the big shindig?"

"That's exactly why I've called an authority on literature and mythology such as yourself," Timothy complimented his close faculty colleague without ever mentioning his two similar and unusual dreams. "Was there ever a character or hero in ancient Greek or Roman myths that wore a winged helmet, winged sandals and who carried a magnificent shiny bronze sword and shield?"

"At first I was thinking of the Greek god Hermes, his' Roman name being Mercury," Jack stated without hesitation, "but your very accurate description leads me to believe that you're alluding to the legendary Greek champion Perseus. Have you ever seen the movie 'Clash of the Titans?' It's a modern-day classic and I highly recommend it! Now I'm sure you've seen renditions of the famous statue of Perseus triumphantly holding up the severed head of Medusa, a type of mythological monster called a Gorgon!"

"No, I usually like watching action/adventure war movies and John Wayne westerns," Tim answered almost apologetically. "Mythology, Hercules, the 'Odyssey' and the like hardly ever tickled my imagination. Oh well Jack, you know what I mean. Please tell me more details about this ancient hero...."

"Perseus!" McDermott confidently finished Timothy's awkward statement. "As I was sayin', he's the valiant guy who had slain the ferocious monster Medusa the Gorgon, a hideous creature that had snakes for hair and whose face was so grotesque that her ugliness had the capacity to turn any man that gazed upon her terrible features into a stone statue. In the beginning of the tale," Jack eloquently expounded, "Perseus was visited by the lovely goddess Pallas Athene, better known as Athena, a daughter of Zeus, who was named Jupiter in Roman mythology!"

"Just wait a cotton-pickin' minute Jack! My brain's sufferin' from informational overload!" squawked and objected Higgins. "What did this gorgeous goddess say to the young hero? What was her purpose in coming to him?"

"Well Tim," Jack authoritatively explained, "Pallas Athene wanted to see if Perseus had emotionally matured into a man, had become a proud leader who could exhibit the necessary bravery to slay the sordid-looking Medusa. The compelling goddess asked the aspiring hero if he desired having a soul of fire or a soul of clay, and naturally Perseus responded by saying 'a soul of fire.' Such a strong answer would automatically distinguish Perseus from the mediocre members of mass society, whose weak male inhabitants all lacked courage and who incidentally possessed souls of clay. So you see Tim," Jack academically stressed, "this ancient myth of Perseus, just like many others, had been passed on from generation-to-generation to provide Greek youths with worthy models of behavior to imitate. The stories were like moral tales, or somewhat like Biblical parables, specifically designed to have young people hearing them in hopes that the impressionable youths would strive to achieve certain pre-set ideals in their mortal lives!"

"Thanks a lot Jack for your mastery of literary trivia!" Tim gratefully acknowledged. "If you recognize me dressed as this extraordinary fellow Perseus at Gwen's masquerade party, don't blow my cover! I knew that if anyone could help me out with the right background, I figured it would be you! And I won't tell a blessed soul about your sudden compulsion to be Lafayette. Your name won't be up on the *marquee*! Ha, ha, ha! See ya' at Gwen's big bash!"

"Sure thing Tim! I see you have some understanding of homophones too! Just remember! Only a few more weeks until school starts right after *Labor Day*!" Jack reminded his all-too-serious teaching pal. "Let's make the most out of our remaining days of summer freedom! Take care." Click.

'Jack's a pretty knowledgeable guy when it comes to certain educational things that most people regard as being insignificant minutia. I'll research this mythological character Perseus on the *Internet* but first I'll check him out in my trusty P Encyclopedia,' Tim methodically decided. 'Instead of Timothy Higgins, I think I'm gradually becoming Professor Henry Higgins from the Broadway hit musical and motion picture '*My Fair Lady*' starring Rex Harrison. What an uncanny coincidence! Audrey Hepburn starred in the movie version as Eliza Doolittle and it's now my deepest desire to meet another very special Audrey, Audrey Duncan, at Gwen Vickers' masquerade party.'

The suddenly euphoric math' teacher turned mythology student anxiously leafed through Encyclopedia P until he finally came to 'Perseus.' Higgins impatiently read that heroes in ancient Greek lore were frequently brave-but-brash young lads who often had mortal women for mothers and gods like Zeus or Apollo for fathers, hence they were recognized in ancient Greek civilization as being partially divine: actually, half-human and half-Olympian, all having the distinct opportunity to become immortal deities themselves', of course depending on *their* ability to successfully execute certain fantastic exploits.

'Perseus was the son of Zeus and Danae, whose mercurial-tempered father was Acrisius, King of Argo. The bipolar king was angry that his only-child daughter had become pregnant out of wedlock so he had Danae and her illegitimate son Perseus placed inside a large boat/chest and cold-heartedly sent out to sea,' Tim read and learned from Volume P. 'The two exiled sea travelers eventually landed on the island of Seriphos, where a kind-hearted resident named Dictys took them in.'

As the engrossed Higgins read on, he began empathizing with the accursed Danae and her handsome bold son Perseus, who upon growing up, matured into a splendid specimen of manhood. Dictys' older brother was Polydictes, a cruel vitriolic tyrant that ruled over Seriphos. The evil king wished to have a love relationship with the alluring Danae, but she deliberately spurned her reprehensible suitor and subsequently was assigned to a temple dedicated to Pallas Athene, where the maligned woman became a dutiful servant to the chief priestess.

'Let's see now, this imaginative story is becoming pretty darned interesting,' Timothy assessed as his eyes keenly focused on the words on page 261 of Encyclopedia P. 'Sinister King Polydictes invites Perseus to a celebration at his palace, acts insulted when the poor lad does not bring an appropriate gift as was the custom, and then the calloused Monarch nastily insults and humiliates the innocent adolescent in front of the other invitees. Out of anger at being publicly mortified, Perseus vows that he would venture out from Seriphos and would return with the infamous head of Medusa the Gorgon as his ultimate victory gift to King Polydictes,' Higgins read and comprehended.

Timothy then continued interpreting the encyclopedia article. 'Before getting to confront and kill the awesome Medusa, Perseus becomes a sailor on a merchant vessel and soon is visited on the island of Samos by Pallas Athene, who presents the audacious young man with the sturdy helmet, the winged sandals and the lustrous bronze sword and accompanying shield that the adventurer would need to successfully perform his superhuman assignment. Say,' the reader reasoned, 'could I be Perseus reincarnated?'

The encyclopedia's text stated that in *his* travels, the vernal champion visited three old blind witches that had only one eye to pass amongst themselves, and the crafty cave hags were cunningly tricked by Perseus to give him directions to Medusa's location. Along the way the dauntless hero discovered that wearing the remarkable helmet made him invisible. After arriving at the abominable Gorgon's subterranean lair, Perseus donned his wondrous helmet and then the invisible assassin courageously decapitated the vicious Medusa with his 'invincible and indispensable bronze sword.' The sailor-turned-warrior then placed the bloodstained head with the horrendous-looking vipers for hair inside a goatskin bag and quickly flew back toward dastardly King Polydictes' island, Seriphos.

'Wow! On his return trip Perseus lands inside a troubled kingdom, falls in love with a knockout princess named Andromeda, turns a formidable sea monster into stone using Medusa's head, and finally the dauntless hero takes a ship back to Seriphos with his new love Princess Andromeda by his side. And next,' Tim thought and paused to take a sip of blackberry brandy from his ice-filled glass, 'the intrepid lad arrives back home, enters King Polydictes' palace, and after the evil ruler refuses to abdicate his throne, Perseus dramatically removes Medusa's head from the goatskin bag and turns the diabolical despot into stone. Perseus and Andromeda, along with Dictys and Danae, live happily ever after.'

After fully appreciating the daring Perseus' action-packed mythological biography, Timothy Higgins gulped down the remaining ounce of blackberry brandy from his cold glass, slowly rose from his black leather recliner and then gently placed Encyclopedia P back into its alphabetical slot on his den's filled-to-capacity bookshelf. Finally the curious researcher stepped across the room to further explore the subject of 'Perseus' on his desktop computer. 'Let's first try *Google*!' Higgins decided.

On Wednesday afternoon Tim Higgins hopped into his white 2006 *Nissan Altima* and motored the forty-miles from Hammonton, New Jersey across the *Delaware River*, spanned by the archaic *Burlington-Bristol Bridge,* into Pennsylvania. The Trojan Horse Novelty and Garb Emporium was conveniently located near the corner of Mill Street and Radcliffe where the man in quest of an ancient Greek hero's costume promptly introduced himself' to Mr. Stuart Edwards, Proprietor.

"I'm interested in renting an authentic-looking costume from the ancient Greek era," Timothy stated. "I'm particularly interested in the mythological character Perseus, or in obtaining some outfit similar to the one that he might've worn. Since your store has a reputation for carrying the most extensive costume selection in the whole area," Higgins complimented and flattered the owner, "I figured I'd come across the river here to Bristol and see your inventory before trying anywhere else."

"Why thank you!" Stuart Edwards sincerely replied. "I assure you, you've come to the right place," the friendly businessman suavely added as he escorted his prospective customer to a crowded clothes rack situated in the rear of his establishment. "Here's something from the Roman era, I do believe. Yes, a centurion's garb in quite excellent condition!"

"No, it looks a bit too much like the outfit the villain Messala had worn in the movie *Ben-Hur!*" the fussy visitor observed and declared. "How about the one right next to it? It looks more like it belongs to the ancient Greek period!"

"It's a replica of the warrior's suit worn by King Leonidas of Sparta," Mr. Edwards informatively shared as he allowed his fastidious guest to closely examine the costume's red-plumed helmet. "If I recall, Richard Egan played the proud Leonidas in the thrilling '50s movie *Three Hundred Spartans!*"

"That's a decent disguise for me to consider if you don't have anything else that's more suited to my needs!" Timothy answered while casually admiring the flashy ensemble. "But the red plume on top of the helmet seems a little too ostentatious. Do you have anything more sedate?"

"What did this stouthearted fellow Perseus wear?" Stuart Edwards asked his new-found very discriminating patron. "Perhaps I have something comparable in stock."

"Well, he had an outfit somewhat like this Spartan king's you just showed me," Higgins recollected from his Encyclopedia P and *Internet* readings, "and he carried a bronze sword, a bronze shield, a winged bronze helmet and wore winged sandals."

"Holy cow!" Mr. Edwards gleefully exclaimed. "I have the exact costume you're looking for in my back fitting room. We've never rented that colorful item since it had arrived on the premises three years ago," the proprietor explained. "In fact, I was about to donate the ornate suit to a historical museum but now after hearing *your* inquiry, now I think that the unique item might just be marketable after all!"

After carefully examining the stellar Perseus-like wardrobe getup, which included an authentic-looking breastplate and a standard black-dyed eye-mask, Timothy Higgins readily agreed to rent the splendid costume for the nominal sum of $175.00. Soon after finalizing his amiable negotiation with Mr. Stuart Edwards, the ecstatic leaser was merrily driving his light green *Nissan Altima* south down New Jersey *State Highway 206* heading toward his Lincoln Street residence. After arriving home, while standing in his bedroom, the costume renter could not resist the temptation of trying on the newly acquired ensemble. Upon hanging and buckling the crimson cape around his shoulders, Higgins was astounded to notice that his full-length mirror image was completely marvelous. And upon placing the bronze helmet onto his head, the amazed Perseus II realized that he had immediately become invisible. Several additional hasty experiments utilizing the sensational headgear aptly demonstrated that the helmet's removal miraculously reversed the process with the mirror then capturing and reflecting the disguised fellow's normal physical appearance.

'Now that I know how I can become invisible,' Timothy imagined with his heart rapidly thumping, 'I wonder if I can also fly like Perseus while wearing this fantastic apparel. I suppose that's what the wings on my helmet and those on my sandals are there for.' And with that crazy whim swirling around in his mind, Higgins instinctively leaped up into the air, his head making contact with a large ceiling light fixture, and then the risk-taking daredevil swiftly plummeted to his bedroom's hardwood floor. Soon a stream of blood trickled down his face from his forehead.

'I'm lucky I'm still alive! After I stop the bleeding and put a band-aid on my brow, I'll try experimenting with the art of flying outside,' the giddy fellow supposed. 'None of my nosy neighbors will be able to witness my self-taught lessons because I'll be invisible wearing my magical helmet and winged sandals. I predict that by tomorrow afternoon I'll be able to zoom into the atmosphere and be able to navigate the New Jersey skies like a bird in flight. I know what I'll do. On my first adventure I'll journey seventy miles south down to Cape May on Friday to perfect my basic aviation skills!'

A full day of flying practice afforded Tim the prerequisite talent he needed, and late Friday morning the accomplished Perseus imitator took off from his Lincoln Street backyard sans his black mask, bronze sword and bronze shield. 'I'll honor the local speed limits and not go faster than 70 miles per hour,' the human flying machine decided as he flew above the always-busy *Atlantic City Expressway*. 'I'll just fly as fast as the traffic below! I'll soon be veering on a path above *Route 559* and next zip along at 50 mph from Hammonton to Mays Landing. Then I'll move along to *Route 50* and joyfully take that course until I reach *Route 9*. I estimate that I should arrive at Cape May by noon', that is if my crimson cape doesn't fall off and interfere with my Cape May caper, ha, ha, ha!' the human aviator amused himself. 'I guess that the term 'cape' is really one of those *poly-*

semantic words that garrulous Jack McDermott's always talking about in the faculty room. Yes, while cruising across the sky I gotta' look out for heavy gusts of wind and also I should be on the lookout for errant coveys of birds speeding around in *this* high unnatural environment! And last but not least, I gotta' remind myself to not fly over a thousand or so feet above the ground or else I might become deprived of oxygen and inadvertently fall asleep in the lower stratosphere! I don't want my maiden flight to end in a horrible disaster!'

An hour later, while hovering above several of Cape May's majestic Victorian hotels, Timothy glanced down and his alert eyes perceived a road rage incident occurring outside the popular resort town's historic Congress Hall Hotel. A motorcycle punk was verbally harassing an elderly gentleman with two clenched fists. Invisible Perseus II bravely descended upon the scene of conflict, which was then attracting a crowd of don't-get-involved spectators.

"What's the big idea cutting me off at the intersection!" the infuriated biker screamed at the quivering aged gent. "You stupid old fool! You almost got me killed!"

"I didn't mean to hurt you!" the trembling old fellow replied. "I didn't see you in my rear-view mirror!"

"Look Old Geezer, I'm gonna' give you a good shot in the stomach just so that you'll remember to be more careful rounding turns!" the out-of-control Harley-Davidson hog-freak threatened. "I oughta' grab your driver's license and your car registration and rip them to shreds!"

Just as the incensed bearded maniac was about to administer an injurious blow to the old man's solar plexus, Perseus II skillfully landed and then effectively intervened in the argument, grabbed the suddenly startled mean-spirited biker by the shoulders and next energetically flipped the pugnacious punk into a nearby garbage dumpster. The gathered crowd, seeing the wise guy unpredictably tumble into the nearby trash receptacle while apparently being manhandled by no one, broke out in a boisterous roar of laughter. Remaining invisible, Perseus II leaped up and quickly re-entered the cloudless blue sky just at the same time as a Cape May police cruiser with sirens blaring sped upon the hectic scene.

'Wow! That was really great!' Tim evaluated as he promptly headed north over the marsh meadows up the Atlantic Coast in the direction of the Wildwood Boardwalk. 'I could be like

Superman without any harmful kryptonite hindering my ability and mobility. But I gotta' admit,' Higgins seriously recognized, 'I'm much more powerful than a mere comic strip or fictional cartoon character. I'm none other than Perseus II!'

Timothy adroitly glided over Wildwood Crest and then above the prodigious Wildwood Convention Hall where he and Jack McDermott had attended several '50s rock and roll music revival shows sponsored by a South Jersey oldies' radio station. A minute later the still-exuberant caped crusader was slowly drifting over Morey's Pier and Mariner's Landing, a much-frequented Wildwood amusement and water-slide recreation center extending out into the *Atlantic*. Near the pier's challenging roller coaster ride an observant thug was about to steal an unsuspecting woman's pocketbook that had been loosely dangling from her right shoulder.

The invisible 'freelance law enforcement officer' landed several yards away from the about-to-happen crime, swiftly tackled the alleged hooligan from behind (seconds before the incident could proliferate), kicked and punched the disgusting vermin four times while the confused recipient frantically rolled around on the pier's cement floor, and then lifted the dazed creep up and tossed him onto a nearby amusement ride car that started-up and next moved forward upon a track, in seconds entering the dark confines of the pier's scary Haunted House. As several security guards rushed to the former area of conflict, the invisible champion nobly raised his head toward the sky and casually glided-up into the air.

'I'll catch my breath and gradually maneuver up the shore past Stone Harbor, Avalon and Strathmere,' the somewhat tired recently self-appointed justice advocate thought. 'I definitely don't want to have a soul of clay! On the contrary, I most certainly want to have a soul of fire! Maybe I'll check out what's happening in good old Ocean City, New Jersey. Just like tourist-friendly Wildwood, *that* very special family-oriented beach town has a pretty terrific boardwalk too!"

As Perseus II was nonchalantly flying above Shriver's Candy and Salt Water Taffy Store at Ninth Street and the Boardwalk, the invisible aerial human noticed a female swimmer in trouble just adjacent to the nearby Music Pier. The harried lifeguard on duty was preoccupied rescuing another bather caught in a riptide so naturally Timothy Higgins felt it incumbent upon himself to get involved in the second dire emergency.

Before anyone could even shout a distress call about the second emerging crisis, the contemporary humanitarian swooped down and firmly latched onto the struggling girl's right arm moments before her body was to collide into a pier piling. Several seconds later, Timothy gently deposited the in-shock teenager upon the sandy beach. A team of concerned on-a-mission paramedics was hastening from the crowded boardwalk onto the beach to provide expert medical care. In the meantime, Tim was again gracefully airborne and speeding north toward the popular coastal communities of Longport, Margate, Ventnor and Atlantic City.

'That was really a close call for that pretty blonde-haired girl!' Perseus II noted as he traveled north, accompanied by an occasional sea gull or low-flying egret. 'This vigilante intervention business is becoming lots of fun! I not only could fight crime but also can assist people in distress! Truthfully, I wouldn't mind doing this salvage/rescue stuff until the novelty wears off, which right this very minute appears to be *never*!'

While flying north above Ventnor, in the distance several Atlantic City high-rise landmarks were visible, namely the Hilton Casino/Hotel, Bally's Casino, Caesar's World Casino and the old Atlantic City Convention Hall. 'Say, that's where the Miss America contests were held when M.C. Bert Parks and the national pageant used to be in Atlantic City,' Tim recollected from his exceptional vantage point, 'and I dare not land near Caesar's World and accidentally become visible or unwary witnesses will think that I'm a hired employee working there promoting the place while dressed in this ancient soldier's costume!'

Feeling exhausted from his day's strenuous travails, Timothy Higgins believed that it would be a terrific idea to take a New Jersey Transit train from Atlantic City back to Hammonton rather than to expend additional energy strenuously flying a full thirty miles west. 'There's the train station to my left located right next to the mouth of the westbound *Atlantic City Expressway*, right across from the new Convention Center. And there's the newly constructed underwater car tunnel leading from midtown over to Harrah's Casino, the Trump Marina and the Borgata up near Brigantine. Oh wow, it looks like passengers are boarding the westbound New Jersey Transit to Hammonton. And if I play my cards right,' Higgins conjectured, 'I won't even have to buy a ticket if I just stay invisible!'

As the itinerant hero majestically descended down toward the Atlantic City Train Station he noticed two women walking on the concrete platform about to be accosted from behind by a pair of unsavory-looking assailants toting knives. In an instant the caped rescuer zoomed down from the sky, his legs violently knocking the prospective molesters onto the cement floor, instantaneously rendering both muggers unconscious. The culprits' knives' blades gleamed on the concourse platform several feet away from two listless horizontal human forms.

"Why thank you for preventing those insidious creeps from attacking us!" commended an appreciative Audrey Duncan. "You really saved the day! How could I ever repay you?"

"Why Tim!" yelled the equally excited and bewildered Gwen Vickers before Higgins could ever respond to Audrey Duncan's lavish unsolicited praise. "You came just in the nick of time! How did you ever manage to knock those two thugs out? Are you secretly taking karate lessons? Were you following Audrey and me too, just like *those* two muggers apparently had been?" the art teacher asked as a crowd of curious onlookers began assembling.

"You mean you could actually see me?" gasped the totally shocked Higgins. "How is that possible?"

"Of course we can see you!" the still-addled Gwen Vickers returned, shaking her confused head in astonishment. "Are you joking? Why do you think that you're invisible? And also, why are you wearing that silly ancient Greek costume on this hot summer day here in Atlantic City? Tim, don't tell me!" Gwen laughed. "Are you rehearsing for my masquerade party tomorrow evening? Oh good, here come the police to arrest those two malicious attackers you just knocked out! I hope they get the book thrown at them!"

As four policemen roughly lifted the two uncouth groggy robbers to their feet, Timothy Higgins wondered exactly what had really transpired and precisely how *he* had managed to become permanently visible again. The perplexed fellow thought about Jack McDermott's incessant love of the English language, particularly *his* implementation of homophones. Then instantly Pallas Athene's haunting statement that the goddess had uttered in Higgins' extraordinary dream finally hit home. "Each day wear these sandals, this helmet, and you may also carry this shield and this sword that gores, for great and wonderful deeds will certainly be yours!"

"That's it!" Higgins yelled and then remained quiet out of fear of additional public scrutiny and embarrassment. 'If I substitute the word '*four*' for the word '*for*,' the entire puzzling matter suddenly makes perfect logical sense! '*Four* great and wonderful deeds will certainly be yours!' 'That's precisely how many great deeds I've performed today!'

And upon finally comprehending the true essence of the marvelous riddle, Timothy Higgins fainted and collapsed onto the concrete New Jersey Transit Train Station platform.

"Hurry Audrey! Call 911 on your cell phone!" Gwen Vickers hysterically yelled. "We must get Timmy to the hospital immediately! I think he's entirely run-down and needs some major league intravenous. Hurry! He's scheduled to attend my masquerade party in a little over twenty-four hours!"

"Mythology Economics"

The decline of ancient Greece as a dominant civilization occurred when the power base of the *Western World* shifted from Athens to Rome after the reign of Alexander the Great. Knowledge of the first dynamic ancient cultures had been almost completely eradicated during the infamous *Dark Ages*. But then the miraculous *Renaissance*, the extraordinary *Age of Enlightenment* and the remarkable *Industrial Revolution* drastically altered man's methods of thinking, of working, of recreating and of spiritual believing. By the time of William Shakespeare and Miguel Cervantes, Greco-Roman mythology had diminished in prestige and had virtually vanished, existing as a mere remnant from the past. Soon after the Seventeenth Century, the course of human history had been greatly influenced by the advent of contemporary democracy and by incredible changes in science and technology.

Modern men are no longer fearful, superstitious creatures shuddering in caves during torrential rainstorms. Mortals have evolved into haughty, proud, independent and ambitious beings who can invent computers that are smarter than Apollo, who can build structures that would make grotesque Hephaestus envious, and who can generate atomic energy that would make Zeus's thunderbolts seem like mere electrical child's play.

Archaic beliefs handed-down from ancient bards have now been reduced in importance by modern education. Anything not originating from science and technology is now subject to cynicism and doubt. Materialism and humanism have greatly contributed to the decline and fall of classical wisdom. Homo sapiens don't have time for imperial Zeus, for vindictive Apollo and for whimsical Hera anymore. Instead, the fickle human species reveres plasma-screen televisions, i-Pods, fast automobiles, laptop computers, the *Internet*, music discs and thousands of other fascinating manufactured "material things."

Contemporary mortals have become hedonistic pleasure machines worshiping wealth, mobility and convenience, the triplet decadent offspring of the unprecedented *Industrial Revolution*. Compare those tradition-shattering ideas with what Zeus, Apollo and the other Olympians had to offer primitive man: poverty, travail, sacrifice, punishment, torment and misery. Modern men have little time for ancient gods and *their* mercurial dispositions and capricious propensities. Man's new religion is science, and science has made men selfish, defiant, arrogant and agnostic.

Greek mythology has suffered a very devastating demise oven the span of the last two millennia. Children now prefer believing in fairies, dragons, magic, witches, vampires and demented sorcerers rather than in Apollo, Poseidon, Hades, Ares and Athena. But one of those rare humans that still found interest and fascination with the gods of prehistoric times is a public school educator having the name Franklin Palmer.

During his ten-year tenure as an English instructor at Hammonton High School, Franklin Palmer loved teaching literature, especially his textbook's comprehensive Greek and Roman mythology sections. All decade long the New Jersey pedagogue dabbled and speculated in the American stock market and developed quite an interesting but highly specialized securities' portfolio. The ambitious investor made his equity selections compatible with his intrigue with the mythological characters and places of classical antiquity.

"Some day my many mythology stock market holdings are going to make me a wealthy man," Franklin once audaciously announced at his favorite circular lunch table inside the Hammonton High School faculty lounge.

"The Muslim's 12th Imam will emerge from his deep well and become the next Pope before *that* highly unlikely event ever materializes," Palmer's pessimistic-but-amused veteran English Department Head bluntly answered. "You'll be laboring here in this misnamed mediocre New Jersey insane asylum long after I'm happily retired."

"Yes, I'm going to surprise everyone on this going-nowhere faculty and escape this institutional zoo at least three years before you'll finally decide to make your grand exit," the all-too-proud English mentor curtly predicted to his immediate superior. "I have a permanent evacuation strategy all set to be put into motion so I really don't care if *you* give me poor classroom evaluations or not!"

"If I didn't like you so much I'd write you up for insubordination and for showing a lack of professional respect for your Department Head!" the annoyed Chairman indignantly replied. "Sometimes Franklin, I think you're a tad too verbose for your own good! The next time I have to deal with your rancor I'm going to report your bad unethical arrogant attitude directly to the Principal!"

166

Some of the more prominent corporate entities that populated the opportunistic man's burgeoning Merrill Lynch cash management account (dating from the late 1970s) were Oracle Software, Cyclops Steel, Medusa Portland Cement, Hercules Offshore Drilling, Cerberus Corporation, Chiron Company, Apollo Educational Group, Titan Chemicals, Orion Marine, Juno Cosmetics, Vulcan Materials, Mercury General, Olympic Products, Delphi Financial Group, Chimera Investments Corp. and a fantastic bonanza known as Poseidon Nickel, Ltd.

'Thanks to the nice windfall inheritances I had received from Dad's and Aunt Louise's estates, I intelligently invested in my favorite stocks with mythological references and have parlayed three-hundred thousand dollars into two and a half million,' Franklin recalled as he sat in his magnificent den featuring a very attractive cathedral-style California cedar wood ceiling, a varnished oak-planked floor that featured an expensive Oriental rug, and finally the comfortable enviable room was handsomely highlighted by ten gorgeous full-length Andersen windows.

'I was able to finally quit teaching those six classes a day, four of which were mostly comprised of *junior* anarchists and unmotivated *senior* students. I've had the luxury all these years to remain a bachelor,' Franklin recalled and mused, 'which allowed me the privilege of traveling extensively and of making very prodigious and successful investments that have resulted in amassing substantial dividends. I've been everywhere I've always wanted to visit except Greece,' Palmer considered. 'I gotta' satisfy my urge to travel to Athens, to Delphi, to Mt. Parnassus and to the famous historic pass where the three hundred intrepid Spartans held off the invading Persian army, Thermopylae.'

In April of 2009 the 'gainfully unemployed' former English instructor authorized his travel agent to organize a trip that would make his lingering dream of touring the land of Homer's *Iliad* and *Odyssey* a reality. Franklin's travel agent booked a two-week-long vacation to Greece and the mythology scholar was thrilled at the prospect of witnessing the myriad architectural wonders that were once viewed by renowned cultural contributors such as Socrates, Plato, Aristotle, Demosthenes, Themistocles, Aeschylus, Leonidas, Sophocles, Euripides, Epicurus, Thucydides, Diogenes, Phidias and Pericles. The highly anticipated 'Grecian trek' was formally scheduled for the second and third weeks of June.

Early on Monday morning, June 8th the excited investor in mythology-oriented stocks had his three pieces of baggage loaded into the trunk of a hired white limousine and the courteous Irish-American *Rapid Rover* driver swiftly transported Franklin Palmer from New Jersey across the *Walt Whitman Bridge* and then south on *I-95* into bustling Philadelphia International Airport.

Twelve hours later the United Airlines jet landed at its destination right on time and after obtaining his luggage and passing through customs, the mythology enthusiast hailed a taxi just outside the Athens Airport and sixty minutes thereafter was signing the guest register at the luxurious Electra Palace Hotel situated in the classic city's Plaka District. The edifice was located only two blocks from Syntagma Square and was within easy walking distance of Monasteraki Square.

'The next several days I'll be preoccupied touring the spectacular ancient sites of Athens,' Franklin reminded himself as he and the hotel's chief bellhop entered Room 534. 'The Acropolis seen from my room's window looks phenomenal and just think, Socrates used to walk the Agora almost every day of his adult life. And the *Parthenon* above the market place's ruins is quite breathtaking indeed, despite its rather deteriorated condition. And this magnificent city is where the political sage Plato organized his precocious ideas before writing the *Republic,* the unique principles upon which American democracy had been founded, and upon *that* glorious hill is where the genius Phidias had created his marvelous temples,' Palmer marveled. Then Franklin's inspired and unbridled imagination conjectured some more satisfying nostalgia. 'The Golden Age of Pericles had to be the true birth of what is now called Western Civilization. Maybe this afternoon I'll meander through the Plaka District and casually peruse the myriad shops and winding alleyways.'

* * * * * * * * * * * *

After touring the most popular "tourist-trap" attractions in and around Athens, Franklin surrendered to temptation and rented a *Honda Odyssey* to drive-out to his intended rural Greek destinations, Delphi, Mt. Parnassus and finally, the historic pass at Thermopylae. Although the seasonal climate in *that* mountainous region was rather sultry, Palmer rationalized that the unusually high temperature and accompanying humidity were no worse than that of Savannah or Athens Georgia during mid-June and that the silver *Honda Odyssey* van possessed a 'more-than-adequate air-conditioning system.'

On the journey from Athens out to Delphi the former English teacher's mind fantasized about him luckily finding a suitable Greek woman to marry and eventually take back to the States. 'My heart desires a fine modest lady that has the charm of Hera, the beauty of Aphrodite and the wisdom of Athena. I'll tell her I'm an out-of-luck American pauper looking for a teaching position so that she'll wind-up marrying me for love and not for money. Then,' Franklin persisted in pursuing his behind-the-wheel reverie, 'I'll fly back to Jersey, buy a dilapidated shack in the redneck pine-barrens east of Hammonton and have my new-found devoted wife join me there. We'll live in poverty for one full year until I'm really sure she still loves me,' the mythology buff imagined as he negotiated a bend in the narrow road. 'Then I'll surprise my caring spouse by revealing to her the true nature of our blissful relationship and we'll be able to live in fairy tale fashion, happily ever after.'

Franklin had brought along a versatile Nikon camera, which he wore suspended from an elastic cord around his neck and also the vacationer possessed a small musical device that stored a thousand songs and could be played with or without earplugs, which Palmer readily carried in his pants' pocket. Finally, the high-tech mythology scholar took along several of his favorite music CDs that were currently being alternately played over the well-equipped *Odyssey's* radio/audio system. Everything seemed copacetic and tranquil as the American visitor maneuvered his vehicle along the country road and through the postcard-like hills and picturesque valleys on either side of the scenic road connecting metropolitan Athens with Delphi.

Palmer's fanciful mind then returned its central focus to thinking about more mundane sightseeing circumstances. 'This excursion to Delphi is several hundred miles long and I can't wait to stand at the site where the Oracle went into trances and prophesied the future to the many elite ancient Greeks that sought-out her invaluable advice,' he casually pondered.

But then the enthralled driver's mind contemplated his upcoming travel plans. 'And after leaving the priestess's domain,' Franklin imagined, 'next I'll casually drive onward to Mr. Parnassus, That's not too far from the *Gulf of Corinth* and then I'll motor on to Thermopylae, the scene of the valiant '*Three Hundred Spartans*' waging their last battle against the Persian hordes under the ruthless command of the mighty tyrant Xerxes. I vividly remember *that* '50s Technicolor movie starring Richard Egan in the role of King Leonidas. It was the absolute best in action adventure! They sure don't make that type of excellent film in Hollywood anymore!' Palmer characteristically speculated and determined.

Several dangerous curves along the serpentine-like road caused the wayward adventurer to momentarily be distracted from his ancient Greek daydreaming. 'I'll be staying at the Hotel Amalia in Delphi for two nights and then at the Galini Wellness Spa Resort located not-too-distant from Thermopylae for one evening before returning to Athens. This terrific drive has to be the most exhilarating part of my wonderful expedition,' the extremely impressionable visitor observed. 'It's too bad I don't have my gorgeous Greek woman available as a faithful companion sitting alongside me.'

The easy-listening instrumental classic melody of *Chariots of Fire* was being emitted from the van's audio speakers. As the *Odyssey* rounded an ordinary bend in the road, Franklin was startled and distracted with the appearance of a god-like personage suddenly appearing from behind a rock formation. The amazing newcomer was violently tugging and manipulating the reins of a jewel-studded red chariot attached to four magnificent and powerful white stallions.

After the chariot had wildly collided with the silver van, Franklin swerved his vehicle to the right to avoid further confrontation and impacts. The operator of the fantastic chariot had careened onto a bumpy side dirt road and the *Odyssey* driver caught a momentary glimpse of his frightful adversary in his rear-view mirror. The awesome Greek warrior was using all of his strength to stop his dynamic steeds, and after finally achieving a stationary position, the muscular figure conscientiously removed a golden arrow from his quiver, aimed his dazzling bow at the evading van and within two seconds the sharp object had traveled several hundred feet and punctured the vehicle's left rear tire. The *Odyssey's* brakes were quickly applied and the disabled automobile came to an abrupt halt.

The intimidating white horses, the bigger-than-life brawny driver and the red sparkling chariot all picked-up speed again and the total incredible manifestation astoundingly disappeared from view, swiftly moving along a parallel dirt trail that soon wound its way around the base of a small mountain.

Recovering from his ten-second-long traumatic experience, Franklin Palmer stepped out of his incapacitated vehicle to inspect the extensive tire damage. No sooner had *he* performed that perfunctory task when the anonymous fearless chariot master again appeared atop his riding platform and the bellicose individual began shooting additional golden arrows at the innocent American tourist. Palmer instinctively abandoned his vehicle and fled for his life, dashing at full bolt in the direction of a nearby cave.

The frightened and delirious sprinting fellow frantically entered the dark cavern and his forward progress soon found his body plummeting down a shadowy shaft. Then several seconds later, the pursued escapee awkwardly landed in the center of a huge smelly haystack. The dismally lit physical surroundings quickly dominated the man's rapidly diminishing spirits.

Never before had Franklin Palmer felt so much shock and trepidation. He lay motionless upon the haystack for several minutes, breathing deeply and desperately attempting to clear his mind of its ascending anxiety and fear. Turning his aching head to the left, the terrified trespasser's eyes perceived his immediate environment. Torches inserted within the subterranean cave's walls revealed an obscure but partially discernible labyrinth, the sight of which again caused apprehension to overwhelm the encroacher's now-neurotic cerebral activity.

* * * * * * * * * * * *

'I'm trapped in what appears to be a hostile-looking maze!' Franklin alertly dreaded and assessed. 'Fine sanctuary that above ground cave turned out to be! I'm totally possessed with horror! My worst nightmare was nothing like this! I gotta' try to have reason prevail over emotion!' the paranoid man considered. 'Wait a minute! Those horses were not black so the chariot rider couldn't have been Ares, god of war! I'm not too far from Delphi and Mt. Parnassus, which according to tradition were sacred to the Olympian god Apollo, the patron of music and medicine. Could *that* formidable figure have been the immortal Apollo commandeering that unearthly red chariot drawn by the four intimidating white horses? No, that's impossible! No one in his or her right mind believes in mythology anymore!' the confused mythology expert reckoned.

Palmer then synchronized his disorganized mental state into achieving a more astute perspective. 'But I have to admit that I'm not now in my right mind! Quite frankly I'm quite perplexed! If only I were not so utterly alone!' Palmer regretfully realized. 'If only I had the companionship of my ideal Greek woman to help me endure this hideous illusion, or whatever other type of weird anomaly this new crazy existence happens to be!'

After carefully descending the stench-laden haystack, the petrified trespasser cautiously felt his way laterally a hundred feet further down the dank underground tunnel until his progress came across an isolated cavernous chamber possessing an abundance of very imposing stalactites and stalagmites. Inside the gigantic hollow was a twelve-foot-tall heavily sweating blacksmith who was preoccupied removing a sizzling bronze plate from a forge and then a minute or so later proceeding to assiduously hammer the metal into a roughly rounded shape. Immediately Franklin hypothesized the true identity of the enormous fellow.

'That's Hephaestus, the immense incredible blacksmith god of Greek mythology who obediently fabricated the bronze swords, helmets, shields and breastplates of the other Olympians. His Roman name was Vulcan,' the dictionary authority elicited from his now-disheveled memory, 'and the common words 'vulcanize' and 'volcano' originated from the metalworker's Roman name because the ghastly-looking deity always worked with fire, copper and tin. Those two vocabulary words were on my 'Etymology List' when I had been a struggling high school teacher. And ironically,' Palmer also remembered, 'Hephaestus, the lame and ugly fabricator god was married to Aphrodite, the most glamorous of the Olympian goddesses. I mustn't disturb the bad-tempered giant if I value my safety. Who knows exactly how the unpredictable ogre might react should he discover my unacceptable presence?'

Several hundred feet further down the very shadowy rocky corridor Palmer carefully entered an ominous-looking cavern where he was instantly startled and confronted by a brute of a creature that had the body of a mammoth white horse and the torso and head of a handsome man.

'Don't be alarmed Stranger! I am Chiron the Centaur,' the mythological being mentally communicated in a very effective and graphic thought language. 'I've had many interactions with humans over the eons, those intervals of time that *you* petty mortals call centuries! How can I be of service to you?' the academic wizard asked in vivid idea signals.

'How can I get out of here and get back to my own place and time?' Franklin telepathically inquired while still trying to gather his sensibilities along with his absent courage. 'You see dear Chiron, I need to return to the civilization and history that I had unfortunately left behind when I suddenly stumbled and tumbled into this rather unfathomable pit!'

'To accomplish your desire, you need to subdue and tame four colossal monsters that you'll soon encounter further down the treacherous labyrinth from which you had just departed prior to entering my distinguished bailiwick,' Chiron mentally transmitted to his shocked unexpected guest. 'Then Kind Stranger, after completing your assigned rigorous labor, you'll be allowed to be reunited with your mortal peers in your own time period.'

'I'm not used to being an anachronism! Could I die enacting that unimaginatively difficult task you've just described?' the displaced tourist wondered and communicated.

'Certainly!' the erudite Centaur answered. 'Just call it sort of a necessary occupational hazard! Just pretend that you're Hercules, Jason, Perseus or Achilles, that's all there is to it!'

'What if I refuse to get involved with fighting the four gruesome monsters?' Franklin challenged the great revered sage. 'What would happen then?'

'If that's the case, you'll have offended Olympus and will have incurred the wrath and justice of Lord Apollo, and believe me Inquisitive Intruder,' Chiron emphasized and then paused, '*that* unenviable fate will be much worse than encountering and battling a hundred vicious beasts. Now it is my heartfelt duty to relate that Apollo has temporarily cursed you for having the audacity of nearly knocking him from his jeweled chariot with that odd-looking metallic contraption that you were recklessly operating and steering.'

'Forget the nasty threats Chiron! What advantageous advice could you give me?' the intimidated trespasser cerebrally asked. 'I need all of the helpful guidance your benign counsel could possibly provide!'

'Now then Worried Stranger, I highly recommend that you go away from our chance rendezvous before Lord Apollo loses his patience, or should I say his erratic temper and then maliciously and proficiently decapitates you while utilizing one of his extremely lethal golden arrows!' Chiron mentally related.

'What grudge does Apollo have against me, a mere weak feckless mortal?' the out-of-place man asked.

'My natural intuition tells me that the Great One is not-too-enamored with you or with your disabled self-propelled chariot! On your little jaunt to the aforementioned monster arena you'll soon pass by the Oracle's creepy residence but I prudently suggest that you completely ignore her because she'll only be able to tell you the same basic information that I've already conveyed,' the awe-inspiring centaur mentally transmitted. 'Be gone now from this chamber Cowardly Stranger and learn to control your trembling hands! Be gone while your troubled heart still beats and while living blood still surges throughout your craven veins and arteries!'

Franklin summoned all of his remaining bravery and stamina from the very depths of his heart and the anxious intruder quickly evacuated the eerie cavern realm of the beneficent Chiron the Centaur, even forgetting to say a cursory 'Goodbye' or 'Thank you!' to the eminent purveyor of academic knowledge. Palmer next very quietly stepped past the dusky den of the howling and ranting Oracle of Delphi, who was entirely engrossed in a deep hypnotic state and consequently totally oblivious to the visitor's interloping and intense scrutiny.

'I dare not test Apollo's vengeance!' Franklin concluded with a degree of trepidation affecting his will to advance onward. 'I've already had one serious encounter with that egotistical immortal nutcase and I don't wish to infuriate him again!'

Then other rather troubling thoughts inhabited and disturbed the trekker's very active mind. 'I only hope I have the wherewithal to be able to tranquilize the four evil monsters and then luckily find my way out of this hellish place before I'm somehow permanently terminated. Hey, wait a cotton pickin' moment!' the paranoid trespasser thought during a sudden moment of illumination. 'I happen to have modern technology at my disposal. I can use my Nikon camera, my trusty cell phone and my hand-held musical device to outsmart and tame the four horrendous beasts, whoever they may be! Thank heavens for modern science, even if I am a kind of befuddled misplaced

174

victim wandering around this wicked Hell, oh my God, wandering around this condemned section of Hades!'

Palmer finally conceptualized his precise predicament as he read the foreboding word *Hades* engraved on a shingle tacked above a gloomy-looking portal, the ominous designation vaguely lit by a flickering torch deeply embedded in an obscure side hollow.

The unnerved adventurer instantaneously comprehended that there was no time for meditation or procrastination. Franklin removed his treasured music device from his pants' pocket, touched the master control button and neurotically examined the all-too-familiar main menu. No sooner had he gathered his wits when an inharmonious dissonance of ferocious roars interrupted his introspection. Palmer turned his eyes to the right and his pupils perceived the carnivorous creature Cerberus, who in Greek mythology was the always-hungry, flesh-eating, three-headed dog that presently appeared twice the size of a mastiff and whose sole monotonous responsibility was to loyally guard the dreaded gates of Hades.

Without any hesitation or delay, Franklin pressed several buttons and the remarkable instrument played the rapturous song "Beauty and the Beast" sung by the incomparable Celine Dion. And just like magic, the incensed barking three-headed predator had been expeditiously pacified, its cantankerous disposition soon virtually anesthetized.

'I have to give credit to the ancient minstrel Orpheus for me pulling *that* slick trick off!' Palmer acknowledged his clever plagiarism. 'The hero had journeyed down to Hades to retrieve the soul of his beloved fiancée Eurydice, who had died after being bitten by a poisonous snake's fangs. Orpheus managed to tame the likes of Cerberus,' Franklin lucidly recalled, 'but I must be careful while imitating *his* heroic exploits. His mesmerizing lyrics worked only once and he failed to neutralize Cerberus and also the World of the Dead's other merciless creatures during the sorrowed minstrel's second and even more futile descent into Hades.'

Franklin gallantly trekked onward along the partially dark stone hallway until he arrived atop the summit of an underground ridge. In the distance he could vaguely see the morbid ferryman Charon rowing his arcane barge across the *River Styx* with another deceased soul aboard being slowly transported to Hades' mysterious interior.

'Ah yes,' the observant intruder recognized. 'There's the enslaved Sisyphus over to my left. His eternal punishment is to push a huge boulder up an inclined plane and every time the tremendous rock reaches the top, it obeys the law of gravity and rolls back down to the ground and then poor tired Sisyphus must begrudgingly repeat his irksome labor. And over to the right,' Palmer pessimistically noticed, 'that's the beleaguered old sinner Tantalus, the word 'tantalize' also being on my old English curriculum's Etymology List. That unfortunate starving and thirsty fellow has to stand in a tub. His pathetic hands and feet are shackled to the vat and Tantalus is constantly being tempted with fresh fruit appearing above his head and with clean clear water filling up the tub to waist level. Every time the accursed man reaches for an apple or a peach,' Palmer's mind thought and rehashed with obvious displeasure, 'the luscious fruit suddenly disappears and every time the punished man bends over to drink a mouthful of water, the tempting liquid quickly drains out of the enormous container.'

Soon the extremely nervous encroacher's attention again contemplated his main objective: to successfully escape Hades and its many nightmarish horrors without sustaining any life-threatening injuries. 'I don't want to have to appear before Hades, the King of the Dead and his pallid-faced wife Persephone and then be randomly and arbitrarily judged like poor heartbroken Orpheus had been,' Franklin intelligently decided. 'I'll carefully clamber down this ridge and then hike over to that dimly lit intersection where the three corridor paths converge. Perhaps there I'll be able to tame the three remaining monsters that Chiron had mentioned.'

Upon reaching the juxtaposition of the three dismal subterranean trails, the out-of-place American tourist shrewdly set his next sagacious stratagem into motion. 'I'll play Frankie Avalon's 1959 smash hit song 'Venus' from my hand-held music jukebox. This imaginative scheme might just work in attracting the three on-the-prowl beasts because in mythology Venus happened to be the Roman name for Aphrodite.'

Within two minutes, ferocious growls were heard coming from three separate directions. As soon as the enchanting melody to 'Venus' by Frankie Avalon had finished playing, Franklin adroitly selected the 1962 novelty tune 'The Monster Mash' sung by Bobby "Boris" Pickett and the Crypt-Kickers. 'It's a good thing I've got the tunes displayed on the menu of this music player memorized,' Palmer thought as he exhaled deeply while fearfully standing inside the very dimly-lit alien cavern. 'I'll be sneaky and hide behind those boulders to my right and crouch-down inside what appears to be that small alcove that's apparently naturally carved out of the solid rock wall. And then if I think the time is exactly right,' the mythology wiz presumed, 'I'll audaciously employ my other two improvised weapons, my dependable Nikon camera and my always-reliable cell phone!'

Growling and loud squealing could be discerned as three hideous-but-spectacular monsters, the Cyclops, Medusa the Gorgon and the Chimera all approached the sound of the "Monster Mash's" rhythm and catchy melody. The barbaric one-eyed giant, the venomous fanged Gorgon and the fire-spitting creature (part lion, part goat and part serpent) all were simultaneously lured to the tune being emitted from the electronic battery-operated music device, and the horrendous-looking trio of titanic giants immediately dedicated their malevolent intentions on brutally annihilating one another.

A battle royal of unearthly proportions ensued with all three hideous behemoths gradually inflicting grave multiple injuries upon their equally dangerous rivals. During the culmination of the bloody bizarre altercation, Franklin Palmer valiantly rushed out from his secret enclosure and began wildly flashing his Nikon and his cell phone cameras in alternating pulses. The brilliant light reflecting off the subterranean rocks and walls eerily illuminated Medusa's horrid-looking face, thus immediately converting the antagonistic Cyclops and the extremely truculent Chimera into cold stone.

And then, suffering from massive blood loss, the savage Gorgon's deadly tail ceased its obnoxious rattling as the ugliest face that ever existed accidentally viewed its own freakish reflection being mirrored from an underground pool of water, and seconds later the repulsive-looking creature inadvertently turned herself (including the disgusting writhing snakes growing out of her head) into a gargantuan dolomite formation.

Franklin Palmer had intrepidly survived the very daunting obstacles prescribed in Apollo's very arduous ordeal. The relieved visitor to (and survivor of) Hades' macabre halls slowly made his way back to the morose Underworld's dreary main portal, where the animalistic three-headed canine Cerberus was still entranced (a full half-hour later) by Celine Dion's stellar auditory influence.

Ten meters further down the chilly musky cavern path Franklin's weary eyes gratefully noticed a previously unobserved partially concealed set of stone block steps. But perhaps the biggest surprise of Palmer's surreal modern mythology exploits occurred shortly after he had slowly climbed the hundred dimly lit stone rectangles leading up to the Earth's warm surface.

Positioned directly in the center of a lush grassy meadow was the rented silver *Honda Odyssey*. Inexplicably but undeniably, the vehicle's rear left tire had been supernaturally repaired and the keys were snugly fit inside the ignition.

'Forget about Delphi, Mt. Parnassus and Thermopylae,' the mythology aficionado reasoned while objectively analyzing and reviewing his recent exhaustive adventures. 'Absolutely nothing in Twenty-first Century reality could ever equate with what I had just witnessed and experienced.'

* * * * * * * * * * * *

The following Monday at the *Athens International Airport* Franklin Palmer strolled to a payphone, got contact with an international operator and had her dial the 800 number of Joe DiSalvo, his Merrill Lynch account executive in Atlantic City. 'I've thought this matter through from top to bottom and I've reached my decision. I hope my old Lions Club friend approves of my intended portfolio reorganization.'

After three rings the Merrill Lynch receptionist transferred the long distance call to the appropriate office. Sitting in the center of his spacious office and conversing with his administrative secretary, Joe DiSalvo was pleasantly surprised to be receiving a ring from his most prosperous client.

"Frank, it's good to hear from you! Where are you? The last I heard was that you were on your way to Greece! Are you in the process of buying an ancient temple or something? How about a gigantic marble statue of Zeus?"

"Well Joe, that's exactly where I am right now," Palmer politely verified. "I hope you don't mind receiving this expensive 800 call from overseas. I'm sure that a few transactions in my account today will more than make up for the hefty phone fee."

"Exactly what did you have in mind? Do you want to buy more of Oracle? That stock's got a hot future!"

"No Joe, I want to diversify my entire portfolio so get out your pen and pad and copy this down while I articulate slowly. Keep all of my Oracle assets and sell all of the other mythology stocks," Franklin instructed. "Then buy equal amounts of GE, Bank of America, Wells Fargo, Ford Motors, Alcoa Aluminum, Proctor and Gamble, Coca Cola, Pepsi Cola, South Jersey Gas, Detroit Energy, Florida Power and Light, Duke Energy, IBM and finally Apple Computer."

"Whatever happened with you being enamored with all those amazing mythology stocks?" Joe DiSalvo wondered and asked. "I thought you'd never deviate from that successful pattern! I mean, if it's not broken, don't attempt fixing it!"

"Listen carefully Joe. After much thought I've concluded that my good luck skein with the mythology companies has officially expired, so now it's blue chip dividend stocks all the way to the finish line."

"You must be joking!" the surprised account executive insisted. "This is a radical deviation from your normal buying pattern. Is my hearing becoming impaired or what?"

"These trades I'm making today are all long-term capital gains where I'll only have to pay 15% federal income tax on," Franklin logically explained. "Now Joe, I never again wish to sell stocks I've owned for less than a full year and then have to compensate Uncle Sam a heavy 35% because of short term capital gains. And oh yes!" Palmer remembered and explicitly enunciated into the Athens airport payphone. "Buy some Nikon, some AT&T and some Dell Computer and some Research in Motion too! The NASDAQ stock ticker symbol is RIMM!" Franklin directed his broker and friend from half a world away. "I really like certain camera and cell phone stocks along with those nifty electronic hand-held gadgets that are really popular with the younger crowd!"

"Thanks for giving me all of these fantastic unexpected orders!" Joe DiSalvo exclaimed. "Now tell me Frank, did you get to visit Delphi like you said you would? I understand that the topography in that scenic part of Greece is nothing short of being sensational."

"No Joe, I was in the vicinity but never was able to quite get there," prevaricated Palmer. "Maybe the next time I'm here I'll bring you along too and then you could remind me of my negligence. Truthfully, I think I've finally grown-out of my mythology addiction after all these years."

"Okay Frank. Give me a buzz after you get settled back in Jersey. Have a safe flight back across the Pond. Incidentally, I have a couple of row six tickets to the Billy Joel Concert next month in Philly'. After receiving your call today, I feel obligated to invite you. The treat's on me of course."

"That's a deal Joe! I'll get in touch with you early next week. Thanks for the fabulous concert offer. Have a good one!" Click.

Believing that he had made several judiciously sound investment decisions, Franklin bought a copy of *Fortune Magazine* at an airport newsstand and casually began perusing the periodical's relevant investment articles. A half hour later an announcement informed waiting passengers that the next *United Airlines* plane to Philadelphia International was "now boarding."

After confidently entering inside the jumbo jet, the rich traveler was soon sitting erect in his comfortable first class seat, wondering who would be the occupant of the neighboring seat next to the aisle. Soon the fidgety man's curiosity was satisfied. A tall thin beautiful woman with the elegance of Hera, the pulchritude of Aphrodite and the subtle gentleness of Athena sat down beside the itinerant student of ancient times.

"Hello!" the exotic-looking lady said to the almost-mesmerized American in perfect English, graciously extending her right hand. "My name's Helena Troy."

As far as the enraptured Greek mythology authority was concerned, there was nothing either esoteric or logical about *that* magic moment "I'm Franklin Palmer," the flabbergasted and intrigued American replied. "Pleased to make your acquaintance!"

"Twelve Modern Labors"

Stephen Fischer, a resident of rural Pine Road was quite upset when he had learned that his last remaining aunt had died. Aunt Marie Mayor of Taylor Avenue, Baltimore, Maryland had always favored Stephen and had often doted on him whenever she had the opportunity. In the sixties and the seventies Uncle Henry Mayor and Aunt Marie would frequently visit Steve's hardworking parents at their place of business, Pete's Farm Market on the White Horse Pike in Hammonton, New Jersey.

"I remember when I was a kid that whenever my family visited Baltimore, Aunt Marie and Uncle Henry used to take me to Gwynn Oak Amusement Park and a few times to Trimpers Rides on the boardwalk in Ocean City, Maryland too," Steve told his cousins Jerry and Richard Berkheimer at *their* aunt's viewing inside the huge funeral home on Bel Air Road in the Overlea section of the city. "I'm sure going to miss her and her kindness towards me. But ever since Uncle Henry passed away Aunt Marie had become a recluse. Certainly not the person I remember her being in her earlier days."

"She never had a driver's license and after Uncle Henry passed on, Aunt Marie had to rely on the rest of the family for transportation around Baltimore and for simple things like groceries and taking care of her property," Jerry Berkheimer respectfully explained. "And she had a very large lawn to maintain too. My brother and I cut it at least once a week every weekend during the spring, summer and fall for ten consecutive years."

"And Aunt Marie was so meticulous and fastidious," cousin Richard Berheimer added. "Her house was almost like a museum and everything in it had to be exactly right all the time. The story goes that *our* grandparents had lived in Alpena, Michigan and grand-pop was an industrious timber man who leased forestland from the government. At one time he had over fifty lumberjacks working under his employ. Anyway," Rich continued with his glorified narrative, "a wicked fire burned-down the whole logging camp and also the nearby dwelling, or should I say 'homestead,' and the family lost everything because people didn't carry any insurance back in those days in the early 1900s. And so…"

"And so later the family came east by train from Michigan to stay with relatives here in Baltimore," Jerry Berkheimer informed his New Jersey cousin Stephen Fischer. "That is, after both grand-pop and grandmother died of tuberculosis in Alpena so Aunt Marie was the eldest of seven children and she by necessity became her brother and sisters' substitute parent, raising *your* dad Uncle John, *our* mom, your Aunt Vera, and also Aunt Tina, Aunt Elsie, Aunt Lillian and Aunt Catherine. Times were exceptionally tough back then," Jerry stressed and then paused. "We just gotta' believe that Aunt Marie's teenage life was ruined because she had assumed adult responsibility at too young an age."

"Yes, things were certainly hard in the so-called 'good old days," Stephen Fischer evaluated and shared with his cousins. "But if I recall from family gossip, after Aunt Marie had married Uncle Henry, he soon became a construction engineer and the two traveled and lived all over the world, including Egypt, Italy, France, Spain and Greece. So there was some enjoyment in Aunt Marie's life despite all of the early adversity she had suffered and endured, and I suppose she always made a big fuss over *us* when we were kids because she and Uncle Henry never had any children of their own."

"I understand that the three of us are going to be pall bearers," Jerry informed his brother and his cousin in a low voice so as not to disturb the other mourners. "It's only right that we can carry Aunt Marie to her final resting place considering that she had carried us around when we were infants."

Two months after the Baltimore funeral of Aunt Marie Mayor Stephen Fischer received a certified letter in the mail from the office of Byron Tucker, Esquire, of Baltimore, Maryland. In the legal missive the attorney stated that his firm had been assigned to administer and execute the will of Marie Helen Mayor and that Stephen's inheritance from the woman's estate was a large Grecian urn with a classical Greek hero and his various adventures painted on all sides from top to bottom. "You'll be receiving your extraordinary item via UPS delivery, and the package will be shipped next Tuesday," the lawyer indicated in his letter. "This unusual-but-exquisite gift represents your entire inheritance."

Stephen Fischer felt dejected upon reading the surprising news. 'I always understood that Aunt Marie believed that I was her favorite nephew,' the disappointed recipient of the Grecian urn thought. 'I suppose that *that* all changed when Uncle Henry had died and then Jerry and Rich began taking care of her property and doing errands for her. After all, I was here up in New Jersey and they were only a mile away from Overlea. And besides,' Steve continued his train of concentration, 'Aunt Marie probably exhausted most of her savings with medical and hospital expenses and nursing home care. I recall that she had spent one full year in a convalescence home. Jerry and Rich probably inherited her brick ranch home and the remaining cash was more than likely divided among *my* other seven cousins living in the Baltimore vicinity. I suppose there's much merit in the old adage 'Don't count your chickens before they're hatched!'

The following Friday afternoon (right on schedule) the familiar local brown UPS truck pulled into Steve Fischer's U-shaped asphalt driveway and delivered a rather heavy package labeled "Fragile: Handle With Care." After thanking the cheerful driver the new owner of the Grecian urn carried the carton into his house and decided that he would open it after supper. At eight p.m. Fischer used a sharp knife and carefully sliced open the intricately wrapped cardboard shipping box, folding the four flaps back to the sides. Inside a well-insulated inner container was a "hideous-looking" urn with the Twelve Labors of Hercules painted in vertical circles from top to bottom. Stephen casually examined the strange gaudy item and shook his head to express his personal dissatisfaction.

'This object was probably obtained when Aunt Marie and Uncle Henry spent two years living in Greece, both years residing just outside Athens I believe,' Fischer conjectured as his eyes studied the odd-looking object. 'This baby's definitely going into either the attic or the cellar. I wouldn't wish this grotesque-looking artifact, if indeed it is an ancient artifact on my worst enemy, or on my all-too-fortunate cousins Jerry and Richard Berkheimer, as far as that's concerned.'

Stephen poured himself a generous amount of *Southern Comfort* over fresh ice cubes and began imbibing the delicious caramel-flavored liquor. Out of curiosity, reaching up to his bookshelf, the homeowner grabbed a seldom-read volume on the subject of ancient Greek mythology and randomly thumbed through the pages until he came to a heading that appropriately read: "The Twelve Labors of Hercules." As the slightly depressed man gulped down several more ounces of *Southern Comfort* his eyes and attention alternated between what words he was reading and what images and scenes were represented on the "rather ugly" recently acquired Grecian urn.

'Let's see now,' Steve pondered after pouring his second potent glass of *Southern Comfort*, 'it states here that the hot-tempered hero Hercules had killed his wife and out of sheer anger had burned his house down with his dead spouse still inside. As a punishment for his wicked deeds, King Eurystheus of Mycenae assigned Hercules the task of performing twelve super-difficult labors to atone for his egregious misdeeds,' Fischer comprehended and visualized. 'In his initial labor Hercules' first choked to death the vicious Lion of Nemea, the carcass of which he immediately returned to King Eurystheus to keep as a coveted souvenir. The second superhuman task was to travel to a place called Lerna to kill the nine-headed Hydra that terrorized anyone that accidentally came close to its native swamp. Whenever a head of the Hydra was chopped off,' Stephen laughed while reading his book and drinking more of his tasty whiskey, 'another one would instantly grow back in its place. But then Hercules seared each of the nine necks off with a burning brand so that the heads eventually could not sprout-out again. Pretty ingenious solution for a brawny guy like Hercules to creatively solve such a challenging dilemma, ha, ha, ha! Hercules had invented cauterizing! Ha, ha, ha!'

After swallowing down another mouthful of his favorite liquor, Stephen continued his spontaneous analysis of Hercules' twelve arduous labors. 'The third obligation was capturing a wild stag that was sacred to the hunting goddess Artemis, the fourth detail was to kill a great boar and the fifth command was to clean the filthy stables of Augeas that contained thousands of ill-tempered horses and cattle possessing loose bowels. What a smelly mess *that* terrible environment must've been!' Fischer giggled as he read and drank some more. 'Hercules used his great strength to change the course of two rivers, making the separate diversions flow and flood right through the stables as if they were teabags. And the sixth demanding labor was to chase away a flock of huge predatory carnivorous birds using *his* trusty bow and arrow. Say, these labors are not only funny, they're quite interesting too!'

After refilling his glass of *Southern Comfort* and replenishing his ice cube supply, Stephen Fischer continued with his academic-but-whimsical investigation into the Twelve Labors of Hercules. 'The seventh labor which appears both in the book and on this oddball urn was that Hercules had to journey to Crete and capture King Minos's legendary monster the Minotaur and then put the wild beast on a boat and transport it to King Eurystheus' palace in Mycenae. The next grueling project of Hercules was to kill Eurystheus' enemy King Diomedes and to disperse *his* hostile man-eating stallions out of their stables. The ninth tough labor was to steal and bring back the girdle of the Amazon Queen Hippolyta, which the Greek hero had cunningly accomplished using both charm and guile.'

Then the urn owner assessed the remaining three scenarios. 'These fantasy stories, or should I say 'extraordinary myths,' are absolutely intriguing,' Stephen admitted. 'Ancient people probably were totally bored with the difficulties of everyday life so they invented this crazy outrageous fiction making-up what we today call mythology to entertain and inspire one another.' Next the nearly intoxicated Fischer imbibed the balance of his mellow *Southern Comfort* and groggily struggled through the three remaining labors: the tenth job was to bring back the cattle of Geryon and in the process the hero formed the Pillars of Hercules, now Gibraltar (then Calpe) in Southern Spain and Abyla in Northern Africa with the wine-dark Mediterranean Sea flowing between the two landmark rock masses directly into the Atlantic Ocean. In Hercules' eleventh labor he had to retrieve and bring back the Three Golden Apples of the Hesperides and also briefly hold up the sky for the very demanding Titan known as Atlas. 'And finally,' Fischer conscientiously read and paraphrased from the informative text, 'there was a private expedition the strong fellow had made down to the underworld.' The now-inebriated reader and urn scrutinizer proceeded to learn about Hercules courageously trekking-down to Hades for the purpose of releasing the champion Theseus from the Chair of Forgetfulness and next single-handedly capturing and bringing the ferocious three-headed dog Cerberus up from Hades and then proudly taking the savage cur directly to King Eurystheus in Mycenae.

The overly indulgent drinker closed the Greek Mythology book and slid it onto the coffee table in front of the cranberry leather couch upon which Stephen Fischer was sitting. 'I'm a trifle dizzy and fuzzy-headed but I'll be all right! I actually enjoy being in this happy state of mind!' Then the lonely businessman thought about his downtown Hammonton pharmacy, about his separation from his wife Michelle and about her gaining custody of their children Maryann and Justin. Fischer then recollected how Michelle (instead of receiving alimony) was drawing a thousand dollar a week settlement salary from the drugstore business. 'I know of a guy living down Stone Harbor named Ernie who owns seven drugstores all over South Jersey and three of his thriving establishments have already been bought out by *Rite Aid*,' Stephen reasoned. 'Ernie's my idol and I'll model my future life after his! I'll be the next drugstore tycoon in New Jersey, just wait and see. All I have to do is start accumulating available bankrupt pharmacies! Ha, ha, ha!'

And then Stephen Fischer focused his attention on the Herculean Grecian urn that he had just obtained by virtue of inheritance. Staring at what his now dull mind perceived as a 'bad-conversation piece,' the totally soused contemporary "apothecary" spoke sarcastically to the urn, "Oh mighty and intrepid Hercules! If you're dwelling inside this horrendous-looking Grecian vase please have the courtesy of showing yourself! Ha, ha, ha! I dare you to come out of that ceramic pottery jug, or whatever the heck it is!"

A puff of light green smoke wafted-up and eddied out of the urn and then a gaseous two-legged form leaped-out onto the den's Oriental rug, and next the archaic-looking muscleman gradually grew from a mere foot high to a remarkable height of nearly seven foot tall. The bearded fellow (actually a splendid itinerant/anachronism) sported a frown on his weather-worn tan countenance that immediately intimidated the shocked and startled possessor of the Grecian urn. Hercules was indeed a tremendous sight to behold.

"What's going on here?" startled Stephen Fischer nervously stammered. "Who are you? You look a lot like the illustrations of ancient Hercules I had seen in a book I've recently viewed and you also bear a peculiar resemblance to the strong fellow repeatedly painted on that Grecian urn! Are you the legendary Hercules?"

"Indeed I am!" the incomparable giant bellowed in a booming voice that made the hanging light suspended from the wooden cathedral ceiling shake. "And I'm here in *your* reality because you had just summoned me. Actually, I haven't had decent employment in over a hundred years so I'm really chomping at the bit to attempt some brave act requiring plenty of strength

186

and dexterity. What is your name Master? Are you a king or potentate? Perhaps a powerful wizard or alchemist?"

"My name's Stephen Fischer and I *am* some sort of an alchemist," the homeowner answered, sobering-up from his *Southern Comfort* fantasy adventure in a hurry. "Tell me now Hercules, why did you kill your wife and burn your house down according to the weird myth I had just read?"

"That's personal business between King Eurystheus and me," the hero loudly responded as the hanging lamp again began vibrating. "As you can plainly see and discern, I can speak many languages including yours. That particular natural ability came with the terrible curse that has kept me captive inside that miserable urn since ancient times. Now then, do you wish to learn more about our relationship, or should I say about our unique partnership?"

"Sure, anything you say," Stephen reflexively acceded and complied. "After all, I am your Master and my secret wish is probably your command."

"Not exactly!" the huge hero disagreed. "Well anyway, I still have to endure two additional Masters after you Stephen Fischer before I'm finally liberated from my three millennia incarceration," the mighty Hercules informed his almost mesmerized new Master. "And just like I had obediently performed exceptional deeds to satisfy my moral debt to the very vindictive King Eurysthesus," the champion elaborated, "I'm presently committed to enact twelve new labors for *you*. All you have to do Master is utter the code word 'Heracles' and I'll appear and assist you out of a crisis or problem. Is that information perfectly clear?"

"But what does 'Heracles' mean?" the intrigued owner of the urn asked.

"Heracles is the Roman name for the Greek appellation Hercules!" the immense strongman explained. "Are you dense or what?"

"Have you ever met Aladdin's genie?" Stephen frivolously inquired, lacking something more rational and more appropriate to communicate.

"Who is Aladdin and what's a genie if I may ask?" Hercules wanted to know.

"Never mind! It's all totally irrelevant to our basic relationship!" Stephen smartly replied.

"Okay about that!" the massive figure vociferated almost loud enough for distant Pine Road neighbors to hear. "Now remember this essential instruction Stephen Fischer. If you urgently require my vital services, just say the name 'Heracles' and I'll show up and gladly help you out of your predicament, just out of sheer boredom. Now I suggest that you not drink any more alcoholic beverage and that you sip-down a cup of hot black coffee and then take two aspirins before retiring to bed. And don't take a hot or cold shower either. You might slip and fall down in the tub or cubicle, and if you're unconscious, you can't possibly summon me to your rescue to help you out of your quagmire. And besides that," the inflexible Hercules emphasized with a stern expression featured on his visage, "I'm a little deficient in administering medical aid! I should've taken a few fundamental lessons from Hippocrates! And finally Master, I'll dutifully perform twelve special labors for you!"

And after announcing those marvelous words, recommendations and explicit directions, the famous hero instantaneously shrunk down to one foot in height and then quickly jumped high into the Grecian urn, his inimitable laugh echoing out of the top of the wondrous object.

* * * * * * * * * * * *

The following Monday afternoon Stephen Fischer left his Bellevue Avenue Towne Pharmacy in his manager's charge and drove ten miles north on two-lane State *Highway 206* to the popular local eatery, the Pic-A-Lilli Inn, frequented by South Jersey pineys, black leather jacketed motorcycle enthusiasts and in-need-of-a-bath deer hunters. 'The Pic-A-Lilli has great hot wings and baby back pork ribs!' the hungry apothecary thought as he passed the popular Red Barn breakfast and lunch spot on his left. 'And not too many people from Hammonton go there so I'll just enjoy a great dinner sitting at the bar before the noisy supper crowd arrives. It's too early for *Southern Comfort* so I'll just settle for a couple of *Coors Lights*.'

All during his ride up *206* the 'chemist' contemplated his 'almost surreal' encounter with Hercules. 'That weird visitation had to be some sort of aberration, a phantasm of sorts,' the prospective tavern patron assessed. 'I don't place too much credence in it whatsoever, simply because I was partially drunk during the entire strange encounter. Greek mythology went out of vogue over two thousand years ago. Perhaps I'll need psychiatric care if the perplexing illusion happens again,' the driver of the brand new white Nissan Maxima mused. 'I don't want my delicate psyche haunted by disturbing hallucinations.'

The hot wings and the pork ribs were delectable, and on his way back from 'Indian Mills,' upon passing Atsion Lake to his right, Fischer remembered something that he felt needed to be addressed. 'I want to get an estimate for new tile in my hall bathroom. I'll take *County Route 536* through the pine barrens and meet-up with my former brother-in-law at his place over in Waterford to discuss the price and installation,' the full-bellied driver decided. 'It's six p.m. and Ollie's probably just getting home for dinner. I'll pull over and give him a call on my cell phone. I don't want to get a traffic ticket from an overly ambitious backwoods cop on patrol. Pretty soon even game wardens and forest rangers will be giving motor vehicle citations in this money hungry state!'

After steering his white Nissan Maxima onto the deserted road's shoulder Stephen opened his cell phone but much to his frustration, the battery was too weak to transmit a signal. And then the driver's acute hearing detected a hissing sound. 'Oh no! Of all the bad luck! When I pulled over to make the phone call I got a flat tire. Pretty soon it'll be dark and now I can't call Triple A for road service. Sometimes it doesn't pay to be too law-abiding!' the demoralized driver regretted and concluded. 'I knew I should've driven down to *Route 30* and taken the Pike west to Waterford. This lousy shortcut through the forest has proven to be a veritable nightmare. Twilight's setting in and it's quickly getting dark out. Damn it! I used to know how to change a tire back in the sixties but these new-fangled crank jacks are completely alien to me.'

Stephen disgustedly exited the comfortable automobile and evaluated the damage to his right front tire. He angrily opened his trunk and removed his lug wrench. 'Tire's only get flat on the bottom!' he mused, trying to think in a more positive and constructive frame of mind.

A junkyard hound-dog was wildly barking several hundred feet away and *that* fearsome sound was the only sign of any possible human habitation on the desolate country road. Remembering his 'mental manifestation' in his home's den regarding the inherited Grecian urn, Fischer instinctively mumbled the name 'Heracles' and much to *his* surprise, the notorious hero from antiquity appeared upon solicitation.

"You require my immediate assistance Master?" the brute of a man asked. "This metallic mode of transportation you've been utilizing seems to be debilitated. How may I help you?"

"If you can," the amazed owner of the Grecian urn said, "lift up the right front side of my vehicle, er, I mean my modern chariot while I change the tire and put a donut, er, I meant to say new tire onto the front wheel. Can you do that?"

"Easier done than said!" the exceptional seven-foot-tall physical specimen answered. "But only as long as I don't get my cherished lion-skin dirty. This furry itchy outfit is the only haberdashery I have, you know!"

Within five minutes the flat tire had been successfully replaced with the donut, thanks to Hercules' incredible strength and inexhaustible energy. The fantastic show-off even held the front of the car two feet off the ground with only one hand during the whole tire change. And after the first labor had been comprehensively completed, the fabulous marvel instantly disappeared into thin air. The changed tire along with its flat counterpart represented the only evidence of the hero's former presence in that back-road setting.

'One down and eleven to go!' Stephen recalled and counted. 'After visiting Ollie over in Waterford I'll take my Nissan over to AT Auto Clinic first thing tomorrow morning. I dare not tell Anthony or Lou about how I managed to change the tire in the dark on a deserted country pine barrens' road. There're entirely too many skeptics and cynics in this modern age! Who says that magic and mythology are obsolete?'

Three nights later a terrible spring storm descended on Hammonton and at three a.m. a bolt of lightning (accompanied by a loud thunderclap) scorched a tall oak tree situated next to the jinxed pharmacist's Pine Road abode. The trunk of the enormous tree uprooted and the bulk of its weight crashed down onto Fischer's house and violently penetrated the roof with jagged limbs entering Stephen's bedroom. Immediately the aroused and frightened bed occupant summoned his new-found servant 'Heracles.'

"Yes Master, what can I do for you?" the fearless hulk requested. "You're quite lucky that my indispensable services are available twenty-four hours a day, seven days a week."

"Are you mentally retarded or what? Hercules, can't you see that I'm trapped in my bed and have nearly gotten killed by this humungus tree crashing down through the ceiling!" the flustered act-of-God victim yelled. "And besides that, I'm getting all wet! Act quickly and get me out of this room right away and then remove the encumbering tree limbs before the entire roof collapses and crushes me right into the floor!"

"Do you have an axe?" Hercules calmly asked. "The job can be done in a jiffy if I have the proper implement!"

"Yes, but a chain saw can do the task a lot quicker!" the still startled resident insisted.

"Forget this modern technology stuff that I don't know how to operate!" Hercules petulantly replied. "You can't teach an old mutt new tricks you know! A simple ordinary axe will do just fine. I'll easily perform the perfunctory task you've mandated before you can recite the Greek alphabet from alpha to omega! But make sure the axe isn't a toy hatchet!"

"Okay, go quickly into the garage. That's the room where I park my car, er, I mean my white chariot," Stephen anxiously instructed and clarified. "You'll find an axe in the corner of the garage near the laundry room door, er, I mean right near the particular door leading into the house!"

Astonishingly, Hercules was able to chop the invasive tree into small parts and then mechanically chuck the heavy chunks through the huge hole in the ceiling and roof directly into the back yard in a matter of ten minutes. Stephen was freed from his entrapment and when he turned around to gratefully thank his salvager, Hercules had already disappeared without a trace of ever being there to render *his* inimitable assistance.

'I don't know if having Hercules around is a curse or a blessing!' Stephen pensively thought. 'I'd have him repair the roof but I don't want to expire another wish. I don't know if it's a coincidence or not but ever since I've gotten the Grecian urn I've experienced a horrible bad luck skein. Perhaps the urn *is* cursed. I've never had a tree plummet through my bedroom ceiling before! It'll cost me a small fortune to get a carpenter here and fix the devastation. Oh well, I guess I should consider myself fortunate to still be alive! Thank God the heavy rain's stopped!' But then the still jittery homeowner had a change of heart and mind. He again summoned Hercules to start repairing the damaged roof at daybreak.

"No problem Master!" Hercules agreed to undertake the simple project. "I'll easily do this side job. I promise that I won't charge you for overtime! And I'll even give you a small bonus in the meantime. Is there anything else of a minor nature that requires my attention before I get started on this elementary-type roof repair project?"

"Yes Hercules, you can carry the heavy desk that the furniture store had delivered yesterday from the side screen porch into the computer room, er, I mean into the spare room at the other end of the hall," Stephen ordered. "I'm sure that *that* additional minor job I've just mentioned will be minuscule and picayune compared to slaying a nine-headed dragon, er, I mean Hydra, or venturing down to Hades, or holding up the sky for Atlas while he performed a special favor for you by skillfully retrieving the three golden apples!"

And as had remarkably been demonstrated before, Hercules (with facility) completed his assigned roof labor and attendant desk transport favor and then magically vanished in a puff of green smoke without ever waiting around to be thanked or acknowledged.

* * * * * * * * * * * *

Three days later the Pine Road resident was preoccupied inspecting certain materials left off by a tractor-trailer to be used to erect a white picket fence in his well-manicured backyard. 'Why should I pay three workmen four hundred dollars each when I could economize and have Hercules do the required work for gratis?' the parsimonious pharmacist considered. 'After all, I still have nine labors remaining and my temporary Greek genie will efficiently and competently get the job done.' So without any additional thought the owner of the inherited urn said the magic name "Heracles."

"Hercules, I want you to construct this white picket fence around the perimeter of my back yard," Stephen commanded his Grecian urn servant. "It would take three workmen an entire day to finish the job. How long would you' estimate that it'll take you? Six hours I would guess."

"A half hour at the most," the muscular fellow replied and promised. "The building of the fence isn't even a Promethean task let alone an arduous Herculean task. This third labor will be like stealing milk and honey from a baby."

192

"Make sure you don't allow any of my nosy neighbors to see you in action," the wary homeowner imperatively insisted. "I don't want them to report any suspicious activities to the police. I've had enough personal trouble lately without having any unnecessary added aggravation!"

"Allay your fears Master!" Hercules persuasively exclaimed. "Confidentially, whenever I do a labor you'll be the only one who'll be able to witness my stellar performance. All that any other people in the vicinity will see is a puff of green smoke appear and then later again form and finally vanish. Yes, smoke without mirrors is my personal motto!"

A week after the white picket fence had been "professionally completed" Stephen Fischer stepped-out of his Bellevue Avenue pharmacy and ambled two blocks to the Hammonton Post Office on the corner of Central Avenue and Third Street. Three hooded Ku Klux Klan members were distributing literature in front of the post office, the phony subject matter describing the hate organization's opposition to asbestos that had been recently discovered in the demolition of a local municipal building. The six-foot-seven hooded Klan leader attempted handing the harried local businessman a pamphlet.

"Get that freakin' brochure and then shove it where the sun doesn't shine!" the apothecary strenuously objected. "You're just trying to give some legitimacy to your offensive hate propaganda and using asbestos as a vehicle to accomplish your sinister goal."

"Watch your tongue Buddy!" the burly surly Grand Dragon shouted in Stephen's face. "You could've just declined my solicitation courteously rather than become so damned belligerent."

"I don't have to stand here and argue with you three losers!" the livid pharmacist countered. "Go advocate your discrimination and your violence tactics somewhere else! Your vile primitive philosophy belongs in an earlier century!"

The three insulted Ku Klux Klan members grabbed their vocal critic and began jostling him around. Fischer immediately uttered the name "Heracles" and the superhero obediently appeared and very expertly tossed the first Klan member onto the post office's slanted roof, the second one was flung into a nearby maple tree and the third one hurled onto the flagpole of the Hammonton Police Station situated next door to the Post Office. A crowd of twenty spectators watched the melee develop and progress but all the stunned bystanders could see were three bodies shooting out in different directions from the central point of conflict in front of the town Post Office. Thus the fourth sensational labor had been successfully consummated.

That afternoon Stephen drove his shiny white automobile to the Bank of America office situated on the corner of Broadway and *Route 30,* (the White Horse Pike) to make a business deposit. Two armed masked bandits entered the establishment and ordered all customers to get down on the floor. Fischer confidently whispered the name "Heracles" and the dependable ancient Greek showed-up in a second, grabbed the first confused crook and swiftly tossed him into the bank's opened vault. And then in the blink of an eye the invisible invincible muscleman latched onto the second culprit and flung the criminal through a thick pane glass window, knocking the dangerous thug unconscious. Then Hercules gave Stephen Fischer a wink that only *he* could perceive before the servant of the urn crystallized into the oxygen, hydrogen and nitrogen gas around him. Labor Number #5 had been satisfactorily performed.

The following week was uneventful with the charmed pharmacist going about his daily routines without any significant complications or difficulties. On Monday Fischer did his standard laundry and dry cleaning visitation. On Tuesday Stephen enacted his evening grocery shopping at SuperFresh and ShopRite. His biweekly haircut was done on Wednesday at Salon FX, and the Hammonton resident's Thursday evening Bruni's "extra-thick" tomato and cheese pizza was greedily consumed. And then predictably the owner of the Grecian urn played cards and drank beer with "the boys" on Friday night at the Sons of Italy Lodge on North Third Street.

On Sunday afternoon Fischer drove his impeccable Nissan Maxima to the town's gravel carnival grounds on North Third Street and boarded a bus headed for the Showboat Casino on the boardwalk in Atlantic City. The Hammonton Lions Club was sponsoring the trip (and a fundraiser) earmarked for its sight and hearing projects, and being a past president of that noble organization Fischer wholeheartedly supported the event.

Midway between Hammonton and Egg Harbor the chartered bus veered off the White Horse Pike and skidded into a ditch, just barely missing a telephone pole. Several passengers were shaken up but no one had been seriously injured from the jolt of suddenly stopping. Before anyone could exit the tilted vehicle

Stephen softly uttered the name "Heracles," and the genie-like giant showed-up and with dispatch pulled the bus (much to the passengers' astonishment) back onto the shoulder of the highway, thus allowing the driver to again pilot the large vehicle eastward towards Atlantic City. Labor #6 had been officially consummated.

The following week Steve and his best buddy and pinochle partner Mark Benedetto drove to South Philadelphia to attend a Philadelphia Phillies and New York Mets baseball game at Citizens Bank Park. In the seventh inning Fischer excused himself to the Men's Room on the stadiums' second level and inside the crowded quarters was accosted by several irate and burly Mets' fans, who' took umbrage with the Hammonton man's red Phillies cap. Soon a loud verbal altercation ensued.

"Give me that hat so I can spit into it and hurl the crummy thing into that trash can!" the first obnoxious and drunk Mets' fan yelled. "That red hat's an abomination!"

"Yeah Creep! Do as my pal says or else you'll wind-up in the trash can too!" the second nasty Queens punk directed. "I always said you Phillies' rooters were garbage!"

Before Fischer ever complied with the rude jerks' orders the fellow casually articulated the name "Heracles" and in the next thirty seconds both two hundred and fifty pound now-addled bullies had been simultaneously elevated off the tile floor (seemingly against the laws of gravity) and then hastily thrown over two lavatory stalls, landing directly upon the seated and defenseless bodies of two other taken-by-surprise Mets' fans. Fischer shrugged his shoulders while staring at other Mets and Phillies fans (standing with their mouths agape) inside the men's room and then after conducting his bathroom business, the triumphant fellow nonchalantly returned to his box seat rejoining Mark Benedetto, who never learned of the incredible 'Men's Lavatory incident.' Deed #7 had been effectively executed.

On the following Saturday morning in June Stephen decided to drive to Atlantic City and use his fifty dollar cash coupon at Bally's Casino before the valuable comp' would expire. While walking along Pacific Avenue Fischer was solicited by a rather obese blonde prostitute. The anxious gambler refused her offer and then the hooker's pimp leaped-out from behind a parking attendant's small building and wielded a knife pointed directly at the pedestrian's chest. The prospective Bally's patron muttered the name "Heracles" and two seconds later a ball of green smoke formed, suddenly distracting the astonished pimp brandishing the sharp blade. The invisible servant next lifted the struggling scoundrel off the ground, stepped over to a black hearse that had stopped at a traffic signal, opened the back compartment's latch and next energetically deposited the puzzled exploiter inside before hastily slamming the door shut. Consequently Labor #8 had become history.

Tuesday evening' June 26th arrived on the kitchen calendar and Stephen Fischer motored east on *Route 30* to engage in his weekly ritual of grocery shopping at SuperFresh and at ShopRite. June traditionally meant blueberry season to Hammonton area farmers, the community advertising itself as "The Blueberry Capital of the World." At nighttime many immigrant Mexican farm laborers would hang around outside the Wal-Mart and the next-door SuperFresh stores having nothing better to do with their idle time.

While casually pushing his loaded shopping cart out of the SuperFresh chain store Stephen noticed five Mexicans desperately attempting to break into his prized white Nissan Maxima. "Hey you! Stop or I'll call the police!"

"Look here Gringo, shut your mouth or you'll be pushin' up daisies in the nearest cemetery!" the chief instigator threatened in broken English as his on-a-mission companions continued to manipulate the door handles. Without wasting another precious second Stephen pronounced the noun "Heracles!" and before anyone could say "enchilada" or "hacienda," five over-matched and totally surprised dizzy Mexican aggressors wound-up in the nearby Salvation Army Deposit Bin. Hence Labor #9 came to fruition.

* * * * * * * * * * * *

On Sunday afternoon July 22, 2007 Stephen Fischer was driving north up *State Highway 206* to again consume some scrumptious hot wings and pork ribs at the notorious Pic-A-Lilli Inn. 'I only have three more Herculean labors to use to my benefit,' the possessor of the Grecian urn comprehended. 'I'll have to employ discretion and choose how I should wisely use my last several emergency Greek hero interventions. But honestly,' the pharmacist pondered and evaluated, 'I've never had such unexpected arguments and disputes with bellicose people cropping-up before I owned the ornate gaudy-looking urn. Oh well, there's placid Atsion Lake on my left and I'll be at the Pic-A-Lilli in less than two minutes.'

Inside the popular establishment the jukebox was playing loudly and boisterous pineys and raucous bikers were preoccupied with pool and air hockey games on the available tables, and several locals were busy taking turns aiming darts at a wall target board. Stephen sat down upon a black bar stool and gave his order to the accommodating waitress on duty. An attractive biker girl and her scruffy-looking escort were seated at the far corner of the crowded bar and sharing drinks and laughs with a group of tattooed men wearing cut-off blue denim jackets with the designation "Renegades" emblazoned on the back.

After consuming his spicy meal and downing three brown bottles of *Coors Lights* the bashful self-disciplined Hammonton businessman paid his bill, left a generous tip and then exited the lively tavern. Fischer's path was followed by a bevy of drunken bikers, one' of whom shouted a derogatory criticism in Stephen's direction.

"Hey Jerk, what's the big idea of making goo-goo eyes at my girlfriend!" the mean-looking scar-faced dude hollered in front of his amused peers, who were egging him on with his bullying taunts. "Me and my Harley friends are gonna' make mince meat outa' ya' whether ya' answer me or not!"

Eight mean-looking bikers (that looked like they hadn't taken baths or showers in months) quickly surrounded the suddenly beleaguered Fischer, who soon abandoned his generally lackadaisical attitude. "Heracles!" Stephen said loudly enough for his un-illustrious new-found adversaries to hear.

"What did you call me?" the acrimonious bully instigator asked. "You're gonna' be road kill Buddy!"

A wild brawl instantly ensued with bodies flying all over the place as the invisible Hercules assiduously attacked his unwary opponents and knocked their bodies over parked cars and Harley Davidsons. Several bearded pineys who loved fisticuffs got into the fray and they too were appropriately mauled and disposed of by the incomparable Greek strongman. In less than a minute eleven tough guys and their previously vociferous dates were sprawled all over the inn's parking lot, moaning and groaning and gasping for air. Stephen Fischer then sauntered over to his white Nissan Maxima, matter-of-factly climbed inside, nonchalantly fired-up the engine and slowly backed out as if nothing irregular had ever happened. Labor #10 had been brutally fulfilled.

* * * * * * * * * * * *

The lazy hazy days of summer were coming to a close. In late August Stephen had taken a few automobile excursions over to the Ocean City and the Wildwood boardwalks with Mark Benedetto, but no incidents of any consequence had transpired with ill-tempered self-appointed destructive enemies. But the roller coaster on Hunts Pier had stalled at the top of the steep first hill and soon Hercules had been summoned to free the amusement ride (with the two Hammonton natives aboard) from its encumbrance. Thus, much to Stephen Fischer's disgust and Mark Benedetto's relief, Labor #11 had been enacted.

On Labor Day Stephen received a call from his sister Anne, who had just purchased an ultra-modern duplex in sunny South Padre Island, Texas. The conversation between the siblings was cordial but quite surprising to Fischer.

"Steve, how would you like to fly down here from Philly' to South Padre?" Anne invited her older brother. "It's a really neat place. Phil and I would love to have you as our guest. It's only twenty miles north of the Mexican border, the beaches are phenomenal and the summer crowds ought to be gone so we'll practically have the whole island to ourselves. And as you might not know, South Padre Island is called the 'Shrimp Capital of the United States'."

"South Padre Island!" Steve imagined and stated. "Isn't that the new Fort Lauderdale where the college kids go on their spring break?"

"Yes, but that's just in March and April and you'll be down here in September when the entire resort has been nearly evacuated by tourists and the Gulf's water temperature should be in the high seventies and low eighties," Anne convincingly framed her invitation. "It'll be like a week in paradise. You'll be going from the Blueberry Capital of the U.S. to the Shrimp Capital!"

"Are there any direct flights from 'Philly?" Fischer wanted to know.

"You'll have to take Continental Airlines from 'Philly to Houston," Anne specifically explained. "That'll be around a three and a half hour flight. And then you'll have to fly Continental from Houston to Brownsville, another full hour in the air. Phil and I will pick you up at the airport once you land. And then South Padre is only twenty or so miles north of Brownsville. You won't even have to rent a car."

"Great info'! I'll book plane reservations for the week of September 25th to October 2nd," Fischer related as he circled the important dates on his kitchen wall calendar.

"Terrific!" Anne exclaimed. "Phil and I can't wait to see you. He's driving down from our California home in Palm Springs and should be here tomorrow afternoon. I'll call him on his cell and tell him the good tidings. So long Steve. And as the classic song goes, 'I'll see you in September'." Click.

The next few weeks elapsed rather quickly for Stephen Fischer, who then boarded Continental Flight 177 at precisely 2:05 p.m. from the D Concourse of Philadelphia International Airport. In another ten minutes the southbound jet was taxiing down the runway and seconds later ascending into the air. The first hour and a half of the flight was not inordinate but then suddenly somewhere over Tennessee three Muslims dressed in conventional western-style business suits and ties stood up and began screaming commands while holding and waving switchblade knives and Korans.

"Okay you American pigs, be prepared to die and sacrifice yourselves to Allah!" the leader of the hijackers arrogantly yelled. "In case you're wondering one of your pilots in the cockpit is a Muslim associate of ours' and the entire plane is now under our control!"

"And if you're curious about how we had smuggled our weapons aboard with all the tight airport security," a Muslim accomplice bellowed, "the knives were strategically placed under our seats by Arab security workers at the 'Philly Airport."

"Heracles!" Stephen Fischer softly said amidst gasps and delirious cries coming from the mouths of hysterical passengers and flight attendants. In another ten seconds the invisible indestructible Greek hero began flinging the terrorists' bodies all over the anterior part of the airplane, breaking their skulls open with his pummeling blows. And then the relentless ancient Greek champion easily cracked open the cabin door with his powerful right fist and savagely molested the shouting Arab co-pilot, who was then violently strangled, dying instantly from a broken neck and a fractured cranium. Thus the twelfth and final Herculean labor had been accomplished.

* * * * * * * * * * * *

The national newspapers and the major TV and cable networks covered the incredible jet plane incident and no passengers interviewed could logically account for the "very extraordinary salvation from impending disaster." Stephen Fischer eventually recuperated from his trying ordeal and after returning home from glorious South Padre Island on October 2nd, the somewhat disappointed man was pleased to receive a phone call from his Baltimore cousin Eleanor Damysen.

"Hi Steve," Eleanor began. "I have a favor to ask of you. I hope you can oblige."

"If I can render assistance I'll be more-than-happy to help," Fischer suavely answered. "What's your pleasure?"

"Well Steve, Aunt Marie Mayor had left me a funny-looking Grecian urn that I understand is quite similar to the one that you had inherited," Eleanor awkwardly prefaced. "So since I'm not the least bit interested in keeping my artifact, or whatever it is, and since you have a matching one in your care, would you be interested in obtaining the second urn. If so, I'll wrap it carefully and send it to you via UPS. You could have it by early next week."

"Is the character represented on the external paintings Heracles, er, I mean Hercules?" the befuddled but suddenly intrigued apothecary inquired. "That's the one that I have. It features Hercules!"

"No, I asked around and checked the illustrations or paintings or whatever they are in a reliable encyclopedia and they all seem to be renditions of an ancient Greek hero named Achilles," Eleanor informed her now-inspired New Jersey cousin. "You know, the guy with the heel!"

"Well Eleanor, to tell you the truth I'm not exactly enamored with *my* Grecian urn either," Stephen replied, feigning disappointment. "But I'll suffer through having another atrocious-looking urn if it'll make you satisfied that a dependable person such as myself will safely keep and loyally guard Aunt Marie Mayor's set of hideous-looking urns."

"Marvelous Modern Mythology"

Dr. Bertram Novac was finishing-up his end-of-semester lecture to a self-motivated graduate class in his second-floor University of Pennsylvania Logan Hall classroom. The eminent world-renowned Anthropology Professor was reaching the culmination of his presentation on the subject of how the ancient Greeks had misconstrued the nature of dinosaur fossil remains and ascribed their origin to the existence of mythological creatures and monsters. The lecturer's dissertation held his captivated audience both alert and spellbound.

"Certainly the ancient Greeks that were glorified in Homer's *Iliad* and *Odyssey* and also in many classic myths were believed to have battled bigger-than-life monsters such as the Nine-headed Hydra giving Hercules a difficult time, Scylla and Charybdis going-up against Odysseus, the Sphinx threatening to eliminate Oedipus with not answering correctly its puzzling riddle, Medusa the Gorgon challenging the dauntless Perseus, the Minotaur confronting Theseus and the Chimera waging combat against the hero Bellerophon," Professor Novac eloquently stated, "and I hereby claim that those imaginative myths depicting man challenging and defeating wretched creatures all have a very plausible explanation. The embellished tales all attest to ancient man's inability to draw the exact conclusions from physical evidence and from indirect observations. Their hypotheses were completely erroneous because the people of ancient cultures lacked advanced science to fully comprehend their surroundings."

A perceptive student sitting in the small auditorium's second row raised his right hand to clarify something that remained nebulous in *his* understanding of the distinguished professor's profound statements. "Dr. Novac," *U of P* senior Demetri Callas respectfully addressed his anthropology mentor, "I'm a little confused and I don't exactly fathom what you mean but you certainly have my attention. Could you give the class several concrete examples to illustrate your thesis?"

"Why certainly!" the accommodating instructor answered. "The fossils of prehistoric animals like dinosaurs for instance were around in ancient Greece and very visible to anyone coming across them, especially on the island of Seriphos, but quite evident most anywhere else from Athens in Thessaly down to Sparta in the Peloponnesian Peninsula. Upon finding these colossal-sized dinosaur bones embedded in mountain ridges and marble quarry pits," Dr. Novac elucidated, "the ancient Greeks had no workable frame of reference and little scientific basis to accurately classify them. Consequently then, since dinosaurs, mastodons and the like were not animals living alongside ancient man in the prehistoric humans' natural environment," the professor proceeded, "the Achaeans and the Minoans conjured-up exotic myths explaining what they thought the dinosaur and mastodon bones represented. Hence my dear students, you have Minotaurs, Gorgons and Cyclopes evolving out of dinosaur and mastodon skeletons and fossils scattered all over. And this practice probably held true for the Mesopotamians and the Egyptian cultures as well. The horrible creatures found in popular myths were probably based on false assumptions and deductions the Greeks had made about the prehistoric fossils that were quite prevalent in their physical environment."

"I see!" Demetri realized and exclaimed to the amusement of his fellow graduate students. "Those crazy elaborate myths and wicked monsters you had mentioned were created by the Greeks to explain the existence of what seemed to be to them very confusing bones of unknown origin. They never knew about the Brontosaurus, the Trachodon, the Allosaurus or the fierce Tyrannosaurus and the like so the Greeks invented creatures and incorporated them into their folklore. That's quite academically interesting Professor Novac, and now the scenario you've described all makes absolute logical sense."

"And furthermore," Dr. Novac suavely elaborated, "when the stories were passed on as oral tradition from one generation to the next, and considering that all of this creative fabricating was happening before men knew how to write and accurately record events as actual history, let's say before 1,000 B.C., individuals added and subtracted details and the stories gradually became grossly amplified and exaggerated. The monsters and creatures became even larger and more formidable and ostensibly more evil with the retelling of the myths by each subsequent generation of storytellers and bards. And even though mythology significantly contributed to the birth of literature," the erudite speaker emphasized, "its totality unfortunately was being interpreted as fact and truth and then ultimately incorporated into the Greek religion, into the Greek value system and also into the Greek morality."

202

The 9 p.m. bell rang indicating the end of the fascinating lecture session. The twenty-nine students in the second floor *U of P* Logan Hall classroom stood and left the temple of learning all abuzz and quite impressed with the sophisticated knowledge their ears had just heard. Demetri Callas, a third generation Greco/American had been particularly influenced by Professor Bertram Novac's very enlightening presentation.

* * * * * * * * * * * *

In early June of 2005 young Demetri Callas was touring Sicily with his mother's brother, Nikos Mitropoulos, an acclaimed educator in his own right. The *U of P* graduate student's uncle was a prestigious literature professor at *Princeton* and Dr. Mitropoulos was also recognized as the foremost authority on ancient Greek civilization, proficiently speaking several dialects of the language of Demosthenes and Homer besides sporting an international reputation for being an avid big game hunter. Dr. Mitropoulos was sitting behind the steering wheel of a rented car driving his favorite nephew along the rugged eastern coast of Sicily from Messina through Catania, their destination being the ruins of Syracuse.

"I suppose to Archimedes and to his contemporaries Syracuse was known as Siracusa," Dr. Nikos Mitropoulos explained to his passenger as he steered the rented red *Volvo* around a series of mountainous bends overlooking the dark blue *Mediterranean Sea.* "I love this rough terrain between *Mt. Etna* and Syracuse. And it's very scenic starting south from the *Strait of Messina.* No wonder why the ancient Greeks were attracted to and colonized this area of the island around 700 B.C."

"I guess the Romans had conquered and then took control of Sicily later on," Demetri added, trying to impress his uncle with his knowledge of history. "Just what my college history professor often said, 'Greek culture and Roman rule of law'."

"Generally correct Nephew!" the driver replied with a broad smile. "Sicily was a popular crossroads in ancient times and in addition to Roman occupation the island was also ruled by Carthage and by the Saracens, whom you may more readily know as Muslims from Northern Africa. That's why the Sicilian natives even to this day are distrustful to government rule of any kind," Nikos communicated. "People here have a code of ethics called 'omerta,' which means that they'll refuse to report any sort of irregular activity including crime to the government. That's why Demetri, the Mafia has thrived on Sicily for over a century. The people here have traditionally resented foreign rule, and even today they're skeptical about the Italian government on the mainland. Their antipathy to foreign rule dates back over two millennia to Rome's domination."

"Weren't the Cyclopes described in Homer's *Odyssey* supposed to be residents of this island?" the all-too-inquisitive Demetri asked. "I recall my Anthropology Professor stating that."

"Yes, very good again Nephew!" Nikos Mitropoulos amiably complimented. "The individual Cyclops that Odysseus and his men had encountered was very independent-minded and acted hostilely to the visiting Achaeans just like the natives of this island had treated the Romans. As you can plainly determine Demetri this particular business of the Sicilian natives despising foreigners goes back a very long time."

As Nikos carefully steered his rented red vehicle through Catania Proper he answered Demetri's curious inquiries about ancient Syracuse's most popular resident. Nikos was very happy to educate his precocious nephew about Archimedes, one of the acclaimed sage scholar's most revered and respected personages of ancient *Western Civilization.*

"Archimedes lived from 287 to 212 BC," the prestigious self-appointed expert began as he adroitly negotiated a difficult curve, "and the inimitable fellow was perhaps the most accomplished inventor and mathematician of his era. The genius was the founder of what we now know as experimental science and perhaps his most important invention was the Archimedean Screw', which as you know functioned by raising water from one spiral of a large screw up to the next groove. The Egyptians used that same basic principle to drain and irrigate land along the *Nile.* The great inventor also refined the use of the lever and the pulley, which as you know are employed in the operation of simple machines."

"Sounds like he was a pretty amazing guy," Demetri readily admitted. "But didn't Archimedes conduct some sort of nifty experiment involving a crown. I recall reading that he put it in water and….."

"Well Nephew, here's what I think you're attempting to explain," Nikos interrupted his verbose eager-to-learn young companion. "A fellow named Hiero was King of Syracuse who had his doubts about a crown that he suspected was not made of solid pure gold. Archimedes thought that if the crown had some silver being intentionally substituted for gold, then since gold has a different volume per pound than silver does, the resourceful experimenter figured he could therefore establish the existence of silver by quantifying water displacement."

"Exactly what do you mean?" Demetri queried. "I don't quite get the water part!"

"Well, my astute inquisitive Nephew," Nikos answered as he nonchalantly negotiated another precarious curve, "when Archimedes was taking a bath one morning he had an inspiration. He recognized that some of the water spilled over the sides of the tub. This process is called displacement. Archimedes reasoned that the volume of spilled water would be the same as the volume of *his* body if the tub was absolutely filled to the brim."

"I believe I get it now!" Demetri excitedly exclaimed. "It's really quite remarkable and rather simple at the same time! Archimedes put the king's crown in water and found that the goldsmith that had manufactured it had used some silver because of the difference in volume between a pound of silver and a pound of gold. The King was right thinking he had been cheated. That's when Archimedes shouted out...."

"Archimedes shouted 'Eureka'!" Nikos yelled as he pounded the steering wheel with his left fist. "It's meaning is 'I have found it'! And that's when Archimedes got the idea to explore and define the laws of buoyancy in water that submarines honor even to this day. And besides that," the renowned literature professor continued, "Archimedes discovered the functionality of Pi, being the first one to figure out that 3.17 diameters of any circle always equals the circumference of the given circle being studied. Hence," Professor Mitropoulos continued, "the equations for the area and for the circumference of any given circle can easily be mathematically determined. Now you know why Archimedes is one of my favorite ancient Greeks along with Homer, Aristophanes, Socrates, Plato and Aristotle."

"Didn't Socrates teach Plato and wasn't Aristotle a student of Plato?" Demetri inquired as he stared at an oil tanker in the dark blue *Mediterranean*. "I think I remember those historical facts from one of my high school teachers."

"Well that's quite true Nephew, but the three philosophers did have their fundamental differences," the driver pointed-out to his callow protégé. "Socrates was a moral philosopher mostly concerned about ethics and about what is right and what is wrong. Plato was more concerned about determining what form of government was most advantageous for the people and he concluded that it was the idea of a *Republic*," the sagacious speaker clarified. "And then Aristotle diligently classified science into the different categories that we study today: biology, anatomy, chemistry, astronomy and physics. That's the major distinctions among and between Socrates, Plato and Aristotle."

"Not to change the subject," Demetri injected into the dialogue, "but why are you smuggling those two rifles you've concealed in the trunk? Do you think we're going to encounter some ferocious tigers or some wild panthers up here in this secluded mountainous terrain?"

"You never know!" the amused uncle heartily laughed. "Actually the rifles are for a little off-the-beaten-path target practice. I brought along a dozen tin cans in a brown paper bag for us to shoot at when we get bored of being bounced around on remote bumpy country dirt roads. In fact my dear Nephew I think I'll take a detour off of this coastal highway and get in a little target practice en route. I gotta' keep my marksmanship up to world class levels. You never know when the skill will come in handy!"

* * * * * * * * * * * *

As Nikos Mitropoulos drove his rented automobile up a steep incline he attentively listened to Demetri telling him about Professor Bertram Novac's theory accounting for the origin of mythological monsters being imagined by means of ancient Greeks viewing and subsequently misunderstanding the exact nature of prehistoric dinosaur and mastodon fossils. The driver was fascinated by Demetri's revelation.

"That sounds quite logical!" Nikos praised as his red *Volvo* ascended along the bumpy dirt road higher into the mountains. "Oh no! The car's being enveloped in fog. I'm going to stop right here Demetri. We'll get out our rifles and do a little target shooting as soon as this wayward low cumulus cloud drifts across the mountaintops. I can't back-up because visibility is too bad and I don't want to risk damaging our vehicle with us in it tumbling off a cliff. We'll just have to wait this one out," Nikos decided and urged his young companion. "I was so busy speaking and then listening to your rendition of Professor Novac's theory that I completely lost track of the gradual change in atmospheric conditions."

The occupants exited the car and Nikos removed the rifles and a box of shells from the trunk and then handed one of the weapons to Demetri. "Take along the tin can bag, the two flashlights and please shut the trunk," the uncle directed. "We'll hang-out nearby and do some basic target practice until this low-drifting cloud passes. That's one very distinct disadvantage of being temporarily stranded in the mountains. You have to contend with the whims of Mother Nature."

"Look!" young Callas hollered. "There's an opening in the side of that nearby hill big enough for a person to squeeze into. How's your spirit of adventure Uncle?" the youth rhetorically asked. "How about if we take along our flashlights as well as the guns and conduct a little amateur exploring."

"That's fine with me!" the elder answered in sheer admiration of his nephew's initiative. "Maybe we can catch a glimpse of some beautiful stalactites and stalagmites. I'm especially intrigued by unusual rock formations almost as much as I savor Archimedes, Socrates, Plato, Aristophanes, Aristotle and Homer."

The two momentarily inconvenienced men soon escaped the fog that had enveloped them by leaning down and carefully stepping into what turned-out to be a limestone hollow. The duo very cautiously meandered through a long narrow winding tunnel that soon led to a huge chamber having a vast arched cathedral-shaped rock ceiling. Much to their utter amazement and bewilderment a blazing fire was flickering off the distant walls. Nikos then whispered an intelligent suggestion to his now-almost-mesmerized nephew.

"Let's turn off our flashlights," the uncle strongly recommended. "There's sufficient illumination ahead for us to further investigate. And I also detect light being admitted into the cavern through that giant circular-shaped opening in the front of the cave. Quiet Demetri! I think I hear movement. Someone's approaching the entrance right now!"

"Uncle, look at the giant primitive-looking chair and the goats, sheep and rams kept in the enclosed pens. And over there is a colossal bucket brimming with milk. Do your eyes see what mine' do? Is this a grotesque illusion or are we hallucinating?"

Before Dr. Nikos Mitropoulos could render a reply a vast shape ducked-down and awkwardly entered the enormous cave. The two-legged creature had a form as large as a mountain crag and the hideous brute was as ferocious-looking as any twenty-foot-tall one-eyed primate monster imaginable. The awesome creature then rolled an immense circular stone to fully cover the cave's entrance, thus preventing any of *his* non-penned animals from escaping. However the awesome one-eyed giant dressed in animal skins appeared to be injured, bleeding profusely from his singular foot-long eye situated directly above his dirty nose. But apparently (from studying the awesome creature's behavior) the powerful ogre's sense of smell had become keenly accentuated with his loss of vision.

"Who are you that have come uninvited into my cave?" a tremendously loud dreadful voice thundered in an ancient Greek dialect that Nikos Mitropoulos immediately recognized. "Identify yourself! Are you more scurrilous plunderers arriving from Troy?"

"We're your guests who have come in peace?" the cowering literature professor unconvincingly answered the barbaric-looking giant. "Are you the Cyclops known as Polyphemus, son of Poseidon the sea god?"

"Yes," the enraged creature responded in a highly perturbed tone of voice. "I was just blinded by a hostile Greek named Odysseus and now I suspect that you're one of his men that failed to leave my cave," the grotesque-looking creature accused as he began feeling around the back of the cavern for whom he believed to be his new-found tormentor. "Ah hah!" Polyphemus shouted. "I now smell that there are two of you!"

"Don't come any closer!" Nikos shouted-up as Demetri trembled, expressing his genuine fear. "We have weapons that can kill you!" the elder intruder intrepidly yelled as he handed his frightened nephew two shells and motioned for him to load *his* gun.

"Do you think that I'm stupid?" the deformed giant bellowed. "Your puny swords and spears could scarcely cut a scar into my thick skin. I seek revenge for your sly Captain Odysseus blinding me! I shall dash your brains out upon the ground and then promptly devour each of you intruders for supper!"

"Cannibalism goes against the laws of man and God!" Nikos boldly hollered up to his formidable very imposing adversary. "If you dare attempt grabbing me I swear that you'll die!"

Not heeding the trespasser's threat the wounded Cyclops reached down with his right hand and barely missed making contact with his tormentor's head. Demetri and his uncle simultaneously raised their rifles and fired two shells into the creature's forehead, making the already encumbered clumsy giant moan from pain. But soon Poylyphemus's knees wobbled and in another moment the savage freak-of-nature collapsed to the ground, screaming in agony from his recently inflicted head injuries.

The two daring encroachers flicked-on their flashlights and hightailed it through the winding tunnel-labyrinth back to the rear entrance to the cave (that was only big and wide enough to accommodate human-sized wanderers). And upon exiting the limestone mountainside Nikos hastily opened the *Volvo's* trunk, recklessly threw the two rifles and ammunition inside and then quickly slammed the hatch shut. Next the fearful fleeing interlopers hurriedly opened the sedan's front doors and quickly leaped inside. Nikos turned on the ignition and quickly put the auto' in reverse.

"The fog's lifting just in time!" the alert driver noted to his petrified passenger. "If Homer's description is correct Polyphemus lives in a colony of Cyclopes and his neighbors obediently come to his rescue. That's why we have to hightail it out of here. A single one-eyed monster was more than enough for us to wound and escape!"

Demetri finally regained his sensibilities and now had the capacity to mentally focus and to logically speak. "I might watch too much science fiction on TV but I think that the fog cloud was some sort of mysterious time portal that for thirty tense minutes had dramatically transported us over three thousand years back into ancient history. Say Uncle!" the youth exclaimed as Nikos frenetically maneuvered the *Volvo* into an improvised K-turn and then instantly headed back down the bumpy dirt road leading to the coastal highway. "Dr. Novac's hypothesis about the monsters of mythology was totally erroneous. Our bad Cyclops experience back there in that dank dreary cave certainly disproves it."

"I now seriously believe Demetri that there exists some phenomenon called 'modern mythology', which you and I both have witnessed and miraculously survived! I only wish that I had brought along a camera to catch the entire Cyclops confrontation on film! Then you could've taken it to Dr. Novac and have him try and explain it all in a plausible manner!"

"We now know that mythology is just as valid as history is," the restive rider intelligently realized and articulated, "but we'll never be able to duplicate or verify that truth and no one will ever believe our bizarre testimonies. We would be the laughing stock of the academic world if we dared share our exploit involving Polyphemus in any university lecture hall."

"Sometimes reality seems like fantasy and sometimes the pattern operates in reverse," the still-nervous driver noted as the red *Volvo* finally approached the paved coastal highway. "Demetri, what did you ever do with the bag of tin cans we were going to use for target practice once the fog lifted?"

"I accidentally left then in the Cyclops cave during our hasty departure," the nephew remembered and related. "I guess that old Polyphemus's one-eyed comrades will be puzzled when the blind fellow finds and shows the tin cans to his belligerent neighbors. Those inbred imbeciles won't be able to identify the purpose of the metallic material comprising the strange anachronisms from the future!"

"You're assuming Demetri that Polyphemus will be able to survive his gunshot wounds to the forehead," Nikos logically declared. "But from our recent thrilling escapade I've learned two very salient facts."

"What are they?" the vernal passenger curiously asked his esteemed summer vacation guardian.

"That the hero Odysseus described in Homer's *Odyssey* was a real person Demetri and that contrary to what your knowledgeable Professor Bertram Novac maintains," Dr. Mitropoulos declared, "the mythological Cyclops was also really an honest-to-goodness true-to-life historical character."

"Accidental Coincidence"

It was April Fools' Day and Hammonton, New Jersey' CPA Troy Rogers was extremely stressed. The April 15th IRS tax deadline was looming only two weeks away and the conscientious accountant's phone was constantly ringing with worried clients inquiring about their estimated or already tallied income tax burdens. 'I should run away to the South Pacific for the rest of my life or else join the French Foreign Legion if the organization still exists!' the harried "numbers' cruncher" lamented and fantasized. 'It's a good thing I have a trusty secretary/assistant to help me through these especially rough times. Mrs. Cheryl Penza's a terrific aide and I can't afford to lose her steadfast allegiance. In fact, in appreciation of her loyalty I've decided I'm going to offer her a two thousand dollar raise effective May 1st!'

The phone rang inside the anterior office and Cheryl put the caller on hold and immediately relayed the message to the overwhelmed tax law authority, who was disgustedly staring at a stack of alphabetical order folders that had been accumulating over the past week upon his cluttered desk.

"Troy, it's Phil Caruso on Line 1," Cheryl announced in her normal pleasant tone of voice. "What should I tell him? He insists on talking to you."

"Tell that neurotic insurance salesman I just stepped out of the office to mail some important tax returns at the post office," the fatigued CPA instructed. "Tell Phil his tax return will be done within two days and that I'll get on the horn to personally convey the dreaded bottom line to him. That feasible explanation ought to stave off that annoying worry wart's incessant curiosity for at least forty-eight hours."

"Okay Boss," the cooperative office assistant concurred, "but I've also just got paranoid Hector Russo on Line 2. This time he's a little over the top, insisting that he's one of your biggest accounts and he's demanding that I get through to you or else he's going to take his coveted business elsewhere."

"Put the petulant maniac through Cheryl!" the assets and debits expert directed. "I can't afford to lose that nutcase fanatic as a customer even though his nasty mercurial temper is undeniably on the reprehensible side."

Cheryl Penza immediately honored her employer's command and transferred the call to *his* desk.

"Hello Hector! How's your seven hundred acre blueberry crop looking for this coming season?" Troy Rogers greeted his significant account subscriber. "I'll bet that pretty soon the honey bees will be buzzing around doing their vital field thing!"

"Don't try soft soaping me!" the vitriolic and volatile blueberry farm mogul yelled. "I've got a seven million dollar a year fruit operation going for me and if I need to scrape-up more than a quarter of million bucks in a hurry to pay off that legal crook Uncle Sam, I have to know how much I owe the greedy thief pretty damned soon so that I can sell stocks in my UBS cash management account, which incidentally isn't performing too well because of the terrible economic recession that's currently plaguing the country."

"Hector, I'm working diligently on your complex statistics and I promise you I'll have the ballpark data in your possession by noon tomorrow," the numbers guru committed and vowed. "Now my preliminary evaluation is that you won't have to pay a penny over three hundred thousand! But truthfully," Troy Rogers qualified, "I'll be able to provide a more thorough and comprehensive analysis of your tax liability situation no later than four p.m. tomorrow, Greenwich, England time!"

"Stop being such a dumb preposterous sanctimonious Ignoramus!" prominent blueberry grower Hector Russo squawked and protested. "If I was standing next to you right now I'd be inclined to beat the living daylights out of you after first making you swallow your front teeth! I used to be a middleweight boxer in the Navy before I inherited my father's fifty acre farm and expanded it to over fourteen times its original size!" the blueberry empire agriculturalist egotistically bragged. "Now then Mr. Troy Rogers, CPA, get my tax information to me by noon tomorrow or else I'm gonna' find myself a more reliable and less difficult tax accountant to handle my personal money affairs! Ya' know Troy, it's wise guys like you that really get my dander up and make the world a rather lousy place to live in!" Click.

'I think that the inimitable Hector Russo should read the book *How to Win Friends and Influence People!*' Accountant Troy Rogers concluded as he gently placed his land-line phone back into its charging cradle. 'It's amazing how that belligerent Idiot could've ever become a successful influential businessman! Market conditions of supply and demand I suppose, especially when the great demand for fresh-picked New Jersey blueberries tremendously exceeds the available supply.'

Cheryl Penza again buzzed her perturbed Boss. "Troy, it's Cynthia Harper on the line and she wants to speak with you about her upcoming social event."

"All right," the beleaguered professional financial genius answered, shaking his head. "But from here on out, I'm not taking any additional calls today. Fact is Cheryl, I'm literally drowning in a sea of responsibility. Oh, hello Cynthia!"

"Troy, I just want to remind you that you've been invited to my masquerade party that's slated for this coming Saturday night but I haven't yet received your RSVP," the vivacious tanned blonde-haired hostess stated. "Are you attending my affair or aren't you? I assure you it'll be a real gala happening that you'll definitely regret missing!"

"Why Cindy, of course I'm going to be there! I wouldn't miss it for all the gold bullion in Fort Knox!" Troy communicated and exaggerated. "But honestly Cynthia, I've been deluged with a colossal workload this tax season and I must've inadvertently forgotten to contact you. Please accept my genuine excuse! I sincerely apologize for the grievous oversight."

"Well Troy, I just want you to know that Rita Maimone is going to be a special guest at my party and I've picked-up gossip around town that she has her eyes on you and I've also heard through the local grapevine that you've taken more than a casual interest in her," Cynthia Harper confided and then giggled. "That luscious revelation alone oughta' be sufficient motivation for you to get your rear end in gear. Exactly what costume are you going to be wearing? As a personal policy I really don't like having any costume duplications at a masquerade party, you can understand my position, don't you?"

"Wow Cindy! I'm more than thrilled that Rita will be there, fancy mask and all I presume," Troy "Buck" Rogers gleefully exclaimed. "And by the way, thanks for the confidential information! I'll treasure it and promise to keep my intel' source a secret!"

"Well Troy, here's a bit of indispensable news you can count on. She'll be wearing an exquisite Marie Antoinette outfit and won't be hard for you to identify!" Cynthia Harper voluntarily revealed. "But the big question is, what will *you* have as a suitable disguise so that I'll be able to recognize you when you enter the front door?"

"I plan to arrive as a distinguished Egyptian pharaoh so that you'll easily be able to confirm my attendance," the CPA disclosed and joked. "Possibly Ramses II or King Tut!"

"Great! I don't have any pharaohs on my list!" the talkative party-giver enthusiastically divulged. "And Troy, don't forget to have your vizard on Saturday night!"

"What's a vizard?" the bewildered accountant asked.

"It's a type of mask Silly! William Shakespeare himself often used *that* cool word 'vizard' in many of his comedy plays! See you at my place Saturday at eight!" Click.

Troy Rogers placed the phone into its cradle a little harder than usual. 'Oh mercy me!' the CPA mentally anguished and languished, holding his aching head. 'It's Monday and I forgot to order a King Tut or Ramses II outfit for Cindy's big masquerade party. I know what I'll do! There's a historical costume rental store over in Mays Landing inside the Hamilton Mall and it's only twenty miles away. Cheryl's not yet meltdown material and she's definitely not too argumentative during the all-too-vexing tax season! And besides, my Girl Friday is very dependable and can keep her calm composure even during a major crisis!' Troy Rogers determined. 'I'll temporarily put her in charge of the office and let her diplomatically contend with all of the relentless mounting duress while I'm out of the vicinity preoccupied on my weird in-quest-of-a-disguise shopping expedition!'

* * * * * * * * * * * *

Troy Rogers pulled his dark blue Lexus out of the Vine Street parking lot located next to Columbus Park and then made a left turn onto Egg Harbor Road. Soon he passed by Hammonton Lake Park and the Little League and Babe Ruth League baseball complexes. Several miles later on his all-too-familiar route was the blinking Red Traffic Light. After stopping at the four-way signal, a right was made onto County Road 559, better known to local motorists as Weymouth Road', and after the Lexus ascended the Atlantic City Expressway overpass, the two-lane highway then meandered in a snake-like fashion left and right past the 1,300 acre Atlantic Blueberry Plantation, the largest cultivated blue fruit farm in the world. 'In five more minutes I'll be heading east on Route 322, the Black Horse Pike' and I'll be halfway to my destination,' Rogers reckoned.

214

The Alpha-minded CPA had his immediate itinerary already sketched-out in his belabored mind, for ever since his' childhood days Troy had always been a stickler for honoring minutia and enacting details. 'I'll park my car in the Hamilton Mall lot, take the center mall escalator up to the food court for a couple of slices of pizza and a Coke and then hasten over to the Acme Costume and Tuxedo Rental Store to obtain my gaudy pharaoh's garb for Cindy Harper's posh party.'

Fifteen minutes later the stressed-out man was sitting at a Food Court table staring at his rather mediocre lunch. 'Not exactly an Epicurean banquet but nevertheless these two tomato and cheese slices are adequate junk food substitutes,' Troy imagined as he began gobbling-down his fast food meal. After downing his two savory pizza slices and his medium-sized cola, the pressed-for-time accountant took the convenient escalator downstairs to the mall's main corridor. A right hand side amble soon had Troy Rogers stepping into the desired retail rental place of business.

"Hello," a tall thin mustached clerk behind the counter amiably greeted the new arrival. "I'll bet you know exactly what you want without browsing around. May I help you?"

"Yes, I've been invited to a very special masquerade party extravaganza and I'd like to go as an ancient Egyptian pharaoh, possibly either King Tut or Ramses II," Rogers concisely stipulated. "Ever since I was in middle school I've been fascinated by ancient Egyptian culture, the Nile River, the pyramids and especially Cleopatra. You seem to have a vast inventory here on your racks. I believe that I've come to the right place!"

"Yes you have Sir, but regrettably, our only pharaoh ensemble has already been rented and will not be returned until late Thursday morning," the suave store employee informed his disappointed visitor. "But Sir, I promise you that our dry cleaner can get the pharaoh getup spruced-up and shipped to your door via UPS no later than Friday afternoon, that is to say, if you luckily live in either Atlantic or Cape May County."

"Well now, I do live in Hammonton, Atlantic County," Troy stated, his overall demeanor suddenly reflecting mild relief. "But how can I be certain if the pharaoh outfit will fit me if I don't have the opportunity of trying it on for size."

"That's quite easy to explain Sir," the pleasant store attendant insisted in a mellow tone of voice. "It states right hear in the company catalog that the pharaoh costume is specifically tailored to fit any man ranging between the heights of five foot eight inches and six foot two and who weighs anywhere between one hundred seventy and two hundred and ten pounds," the salesman indicated. "Here is a glossy representation of the particular item on this page presented in vivid color. Notice Sir that the handsome black' mask accompanies the exotic looking apparel and headdress. And if I may add Sir, it's at no additional charge. Now then, after viewing this color photo', what do you think about you impersonating Ramses II? Isn't the costume rather intriguing?"

"It's very outstanding, extremely top notch!" Rogers commended the persuasive salesperson. "That's my personal opinion. Exactly how much will it cost me to rent all of the Ramses II paraphernalia Friday through Sunday."

"A real bargain Sir. Only a hundred bucks plus ten dollars to cover the UPS express delivery," the clerk recited. "I say only a hundred smackers simply because the costume was not in stock when you had stepped through the store's main entrance to make your inquiry. I'm proud to say that *that's* our strict company discount policy. What's your pleasure Sir?"

"Okay, here's the hundred dollars up front," the convinced customer said, handing the clerk a crisp Ben Franklin note. "And here's an Alexander Hamilton to cover the express freight delivery charge. I believe you'll now need my residential address and phone numbers, both land-line and cell."

"Yes Sir, I'll gladly take down that pertinent information and give you a copy to keep as a receipt. Now I only have one further question. Is your girlfriend or wife going to the grandiose party as Cleopatra?"

"No," Troy laughed and grinned, shaking his head in mild amusement. "She's actually going to the shindig as Marie Antoinette."

"Sounds like a definite conflict in historical eras to me," the congenial fellow behind the counter chuckled. "Oh well Mr. Rogers, I guess it could've been even more problematic like Adolph Hitler and Dolly Madison or diabolical Ivan the Terrible escorting dangerous Lucrezia Borgia, ha, ha, ha!"

At six p.m. Friday evening a brown UPS truck pulled into the CPA's Walnut Street ranch home's asphalt driveway and the carrier delivered a large package from the Acme Costume and Tuxedo Rental Store, Hamilton Mall, Mays Landing, NJ. Five

216

minutes later the excited recipient quickly unwrapped and opened the string-tied cardboard box but then suddenly became highly upset upon discovering and examining its mistaken contents.

'Oh no!' the vastly disappointed resident thought. 'Those incompetent imbeciles sent me an ancient Greek warrior's regalia instead of the elaborate Ramses II getup.' The man's frustration became more heightened upon him calling the Hamilton Mall store.

"Sir, we're sorry for the unusual rare mix-up!" an apologetic voice on the other end stated. "Wilhelm, the fellow who had rented you the pharaoh's costume is away on vacation in St. Thomas, Virgin Islands so obviously he's not available to speak with you about the matter. But from what I can determine," the sympathetic Acme employee related, "three costumes had been simultaneously sent to the wrong customers, your pharaoh outfit to someone else, the Greek warrior one that you've accidentally recently received and a third one inadvertently addressed to an altogether separate party. I'll speak to the owner and arrange an appropriate refund for you because of the oddball shipping error."

"Never mind the trivial explanations!" Troy angrily and vehemently protested. "I'll wear the pathetic Greek thing you've sent me, bronze sword, helmet, sandals and all to the masquerade party tomorrow night, but with truth as my witness, I'm never going to recommend or do any further business with your irresponsible company ever again!" Click.

Slowly regaining his emotional composure, the Walnut Street resident sat at his computer desk and typed in "Greek heroes" into the Google search box. After perusing the faces of battle uniformed Odysseus, Hercules, Agamemnon, Menelaus and Ajax, Troy Rogers' eyes eventually focused upon the graphic color illustration of the magnificent champion Achilles.

'This is without a doubt the exact guy I'm going to impersonate!' Rogers concluded. 'It says here that Achilles was the mightiest of Greek warriors during the Trojan War, a ten year conflict that happened around 1184 BC as chronicled by the supposedly blind poet Homer in his narrative epic poem the *Iliad*.' Rogers reflected for a moment and then continued reading the language presented on his desktop computer screen. 'And this tragic hero figure Achilles in spiteful revenge had killed Hector, the King of Troy's son because Hector had previously killed Achilles' best friend Patroclus. But,' Rogers paused and gasped before resuming his remarkable reading session, 'later in the adventure tale saga King Priam's younger son Paris accurately shot an arrow and killed Achilles by hitting him in his most vulnerable area, the heel of his foot. Hence, that part of the human anatomy is now called the Achilles tendon. Oh my God!' Troy Rogers realized. 'The Trojan King Priam's son Hector in the *Iliad* bears the same name as Hector Russo, my unsavory nemesis in real life!' the superstitious CPA keenly evaluated. 'What a truly oddball set of coincidences with the names Troy, Hector and Achilles all seeming to spontaneously be intersecting.'

* * * * * * * * * * * *

Saturday evening eventually arrived, and after admiring his new-found appearance in the living room mirror, Achilles (alias Troy Rogers) climbed into his dark blue Lexus, meticulously exited his circular driveway onto Walnut Street and then proceeded to turn left onto Third. The driver's mind was still troubled and distracted by the peculiar shipping error. The disgruntled motorist was heading his 'chariot' toward downtown Hammonton and soon Troy had to slam on his brakes when a huge dump truck going south on Fairview Avenue rumbled through a yellow traffic signal. Instantly Rogers' automobile was then unexpectedly and violently rear-ended by a shiny black Mercedes.

Immediately two cursing masked men, one dressed as a Greek warrior and the second aggressive fellow as a Trojan Prince swiftly evacuated their respective vehicles. The enraged pair soon confronted one another.

"See here you arrogant clumsy Fool!" Troy wildly screamed at the Prince Paris impersonator. "You were recklessly speeding and smashed into the back of my car. If you weren't going so damned fast you rambunctious Fool, and also speeding recklessly and deliberately tailgating me, then this unnecessary collision would've never occurred!"

"Don't give me any stupid crap or I'll decapitate you with your own sword!" the infuriated man (regally dressed in the Trojan apparel) bellowed as he pointed to Troy's bronze weapon. Then getting an impulsive evil inspiration, the incensed maniac removed an arrow from his quiver, inserted it into his bow and aimed the primitive weapon at an astonished and suddenly intimidated Troy Rogers, who instantaneously turned and frantically fled onto a North Third Street home's front lawn.

The truly out-of-control and greatly irritated Prince Paris pretender shot his arrow, which accurately pierced the back of Troy Rogers' right foot. The victim fell to the turf with a thud, agonizing, crying and then writhing about in excruciating pain as the arrow recipient futilely held his wounded lower right appendage.

* * * * * * * * * * * *

Hammonton Chief-of-Police Henry Passarella sat behind his town hall office desk and was in the process of seriously reviewing and assessing the report of the outlandish Saturday evening traffic accident at the corner of Third Street and Fairview Avenue. The Chief was conversing with Sergeant Fred Ingemi, the equally confounded on-duty investigating officer handling the case. The two guardians of the peace were carefully putting together the complicated pieces of the strange sociological/mythological puzzle.

"Fred, you've written here in your report that Hector Russo, oddly dressed as Prince Paris of Troy, shot and wounded Troy Rogers in the right heel while using a primitive-looking bow and arrow, and you've also indicated that Mr. Rogers at the time of the incident was dressed as the Greek hero Achilles. And," Chief-of-Police Passarella proceeded with his oral analysis and interpretation, "a witness to the accident/crime, blueberry farmer Skeeter Bertino had been traveling as a passenger in Hector Russo's black Mercedes and Officer Ingemi, your unusual report states that the third party had been dressed as an Egyptian pharaoh named Ramses II! What kind of an insane anachronism is this incredible incident Sergeant?" Chief Passarella bellowed. "The bizarre set of events will easily make national tabloid journalism news along with bad-publicity cable chatter once the ravenous Philly' newspapers and TV stations grab a-hold of this thoroughly demented story! Don't *you* get it? Our respectable town will soon become the laughing stock of the entire nation!"

"At least the two principal participants were driving cars and not riding in ancient war chariots!" Sergeant Ingemi humorously articulated, much to his superior's mounting chagrin. "It seems Chief that all three subjects were en route to a masquerade party

219

down on Central Avenue given by that blonde knockout dame Cindy Harper. I surmise that since all three men were wearing masks," Ingemi hypothesized and nervously stated, "I believe that Troy Rogers and Hector Russo didn't recognize one another even though they actually knew each another in real life!"

"And also Fred, the corresponding hospital report explicitly states that Mr. Rogers' injury is only minor and that the doctors in the Atlantic Care Emergency Room have determined that the arrow wound is only superficial," the Chief read and disclosed. "Thank God for *that* minor miracle!"

"That's right Hank!" Sergeant Ingemi confirmed in a more personal tone of voice. "Troy Rogers will not be hobbling around for long and fortunately, he won't be a cripple for life. He'll be able to make a full recovery and be back on his feet without crutches in less than a week," the officer disclosed to his boss. "I've also learned from interviewing Troy Rogers in his hospital room that he plans on suing that detestable bully Hector Russo for attempted manslaughter. And once the shrewd accountant wins the accident civil case in the local municipal court," Sergeant Ingemi predicted, "then Troy will be filing a felony criminal lawsuit at the county level, and if he wins that particular litigation," the presumptuous policeman elucidated, "Rogers will be awarded a gigantic settlement by an empathetic jury and will possibly wind-up with perhaps half of Russo's prosperous blueberry farm empire. Being wounded by a non-poisonous arrow might actually be a blessing in disguise," Fred Ingemi divulged and punned.

"What unbelievable irony!" Chief Passarella exclaimed. "Hector Russo should've stopped his rage at just shooting-off his big mouth! Now he's in real deep hot water for thinking that he was Prince Paris of Troy shooting-off an arrow at his avowed ancient Greek foe Achilles, alias Troy Rogers, coincidentally wounding him in *his* right heel. Now Fred," Chief Henry Passarella emphasized to his loyal and obedient subordinate, "I hope that you don't think that you're almighty Zeus and then angrily hurl a million volt lightning bolt in my direction just two weeks before I can enjoy my long-awaited retirement from the Hammonton Police Force!"

"Excavations"

As an impressionable seventh grader at the Hammonton Middle School in early December of 1975, Jeremy Ingram was greatly influenced by his effervescent social studies teacher, Mr. Charles Galinas. The history instructor had mentioned to his usually lethargic fifth period' students the story of Heinrich Schliemann (1822-1890), a German entrepreneur that had become wealthy making lucrative business deals in Russia during the *Crimean War*.

Schliemann had accumulated sufficient wealth to enable the industrious businessman to retire and pursue *his* childhood ambition: to prove once and for all that Homer's *Iliad* and *Odyssey* had been actual historical events and not mere myths and legends as had been widely believed throughout the Nineteenth Century civilized world. Later more scientific archeological expeditions in 1891-'94 confirmed beyond a shadow of a doubt that *Level VIIa* was "the Troy" that Heinrich Schliemann had amazingly discovered.

After researching the subject of Heinrich Schliemann more extensively in the New Jersey town's middle school's library, thirteen-year-old Jeremy Ingram was fascinated to learn more about the conscientious Nineteenth Century' businessman turned renowned amateur archeologist. Young Jeremy discovered that in 1870 Heinrich Schliemann had excavated a mound around four miles from the Hellespont and had officially found seven cities buried on top of one another. One of the lower levels Schliemann impetuously identified as *"Troy II,"* the ancient domain of wealthy King Priam described in Homer's classic epic poem the *Iliad*.

'The *Trojan War* had happened around 1184 BC,' Jeremy remembered reading from a library encyclopedia in 1975. 'I want to become an even more famous archeologist than Heinrich Schliemann! Who knows what other ancient treasures besides Troy lie under the Earth?' the young man conjectured. That spark created by Mr. Charles Galinas back in 1975 was the impetus for Jeremy Ingram to dedicate his entire adult life to initiating significant breakthrough anthropological and archeological explorations.

"There was no romantic love affair between Paris, Prince of Troy and Helen, wife of King Menelaus of Sparta," Dr. Jeremy Ingram explained to his fellow accomplished archeologist

Professor Gregory Lawler inside an Italian restaurant near the *University of Pennsylvania* campus.

"Just about every educated person in Philly' now understands that," Dr. Lawler readily admitted. "The Achaens were ruthless marauders and they invented this fanciful romance story about Paris abducting Helen from Menelaus to make it appear to history textbook writers that *they* were justly raiding Troy to capture back Menelaus's gorgeous wife."

"Yes Greg, your logic is generally accurate," the now internationally famous archeologist complimented his affable colleague. "Agamemnon of Mycenae efficiently organized a thousand ships to specifically plunder Troy's wealth and not to retrieve Menelaus's beautiful wife from Prince Paris. *That* was the actual real cause of the war. The popular myth is in reality an ancient rendition of a romantic fairy tale."

"That's where Odysseus, Achilles, Ajax and other dauntless greedy Greek hero-kings collaborate and join forces with Agamemnon to defeat Troy," Dr. Lawler indulgently laughed. "Didn't Schliemann also find Mycenae?"

"Right again!" the foremost archeologist concurred showing a more-than-mild degree of animation. "Even back then the Greek monarchs unified against a common enemy even though *their* kingdoms supposedly functioned as independent and autonomous city-states. And old Heinrich was my personal inspiration to become the world's most celebrated archeologist of my time, thanks to my seventh grade social studies teacher. What goes around comes around I guess! Teachers influence pupils that then become future teachers!"

A *U of P* graduate student rushed into the crowded off-campus restaurant, anxiously glanced in all directions and was relieved to locate his eminent adviser's booth. The young scholar then quickly advanced to Jeremy Ingram's favorite side table and announced his purpose in interrupting the distinguished men's late lunch.

"Professor Ingram, excuse me!" Darren Hall rather nervously began. "But an important call just came into your office and your secretary sent me over here as a courier. Expedition Team F has just found what appears to be remarkably preserved ruins outside Smyrna, Delaware just as *you* had predicted."

"Thank you Darren," Ingram courteously answered his more-than-enthusiastic subordinate. "Don't worry one sweat bead! I'll dispatch a more experienced team out to that particular dig site

222

right away. I believe Smyrna '*is near Izmir*'!" the *U of P* department chairman rhymed while fabricating an imaginative ancient history pun.

After the excited graduate student messenger exited the bustling restaurant, Jeremy Ingram and Gregory Lawler resumed their casual academic conversation. Lawler was especially curious as to how Ingram always knew the precise coordinates where the next major discovery would take place. He listened intently to his friend's extraordinary revelation.

"First of all Greg, as you know the government is keeping all of my recent digs top secret confidential information, not for public disclosure," Jeremy reminded his *U. of P.* department' associate. "The last thing we want to do is have us to talk to the merciless print media. And the TV news shows are just as carnivorous and just as ruthlessly ravenous as the newspaper and magazine journalists are. Stay away from the hypocrites because the brutal vultures only want to exploit you and me for *their* own financial advancement and for their own reputation enhancement."

"I'll remember your solemn words of wisdom!" Greg Lawler promised his mentor. "But how did you know about Smyrna, Delaware and what clued you in to Hannibal, Missouri, Ionia, Michigan and Eureka, California?"

"Well Greg," Jeremy modestly replied with a broad grin, "actually a site right outside good old Philadelphia was my first big claim to fame."

"I recall that event now that you've mentioned it!" *Penn'* Professor Greg Lawler admiringly answered. "I apologize for carelessly overlooking *that* very obvious memorable discovery. How could I be so negligent?"

Ingram conveyed to his loyal friend how a village in Turkey and another one in ancient Palestine both bore the name Philadelphia as described by Greek and later Roman historians. "I followed a wild hunch and dug in several places in Montgomery County and in Chester County. Then a boy from Conshohocken accidentally found an ancient gold coin near the Schuylkill River and the rest is top-secret archeological non-public history," Ingram explained. "All I did was equate the ancient Philadelphia in Asia Minor and also the other one in Phoenicia with Philadelphia, Pennsylvania and the rest just automatically happened."

"Well, Phila-delphi is Greek for *City of Brotherly Love!*" Lawler remembered and stated. "I wonder if any Quakers ever lived in Mycenae, Sparta or the Athens of Pericles and Phidias's time," the genial fellow jested. "But seriously now Jeremy, what got you involved with the crucial Ionia and Eureka digs?"

Dr. Ingram revealed to his trusty friend that *he* had followed several strong premonitions to make the great temple and column discoveries in Ionia, Michigan and the marvelous ancient Greek ruins excavated near Eureka, California. The two situations were very similar to *his* Philadelphia' approach.

"I have always been intuitive and have learned to trust my inner compass," Jeremy related just prior to asking the harried blonde waitress for "a check please." "And then Greg, using the logic I had employed on the successful Conshohocken dig, I then took my best *r and d* team out to Ionia, Michigan. I knew all about Ionic columns and after news of our presence circulated among the area residents," the Project Director explained, "a lady presented me with several ancient Greek artifacts she had coincidentally collected about three miles away."

"Did a parallel thing happen in Eureka too?" Dr. Lawler curiously asked his idol.

"And with the Eureka Project," Jeremy continued in a soft tone of voice while leaning across the table, "who would have thought that Eureka, California would have any connection with Sicily? I thought of what Archimedes had reputedly shouted at the Greek colony of Syracuse when *he* inadvertently had discovered the theory of water displacement by slinking down inside a bathtub," Professor Ingram recollected and laughed. "That's how Archimedes understood that the true volume of a golden crown could be assessed if it was placed in a container of water with the excess spilling over the sides representing the actual mass of the golden object. Then of course, Archimedes yelled...."

"Eureka! Meaning 'I have found it'!" Greg Lawler marveled and chuckled with admiration while gaining the attention of several dozen other restaurant patrons. "And following *your* train of thought, Hannibal crossed the Alps with elephants and fought the Roman legions while representing the city of Carthage in Northern Africa. I wonder if Mark Twain had ever imagined that ancient ruins might be buried right outside his Hannibal, Missouri doorstep?"

224

"But in each instance," Jeremy clarified, "my instincts only brought me in proximity to the buried ruins. Then some formerly obscure citizen would hear of my search and come forward with a vital piece of pottery or some primitive cutting tool and cooperatively show me where it had been found," Ingram qualified. "So Greg, it was the everyday concerned average American that patriotically led me directly to the site where we then had to make our grid."

And next Jeremy related to his colleague how thanks to Hannibal, Missouri, Carthage, Missouri soon equated with Carthage, Northern Africa and how Palestine, Texas coincided with ancient Palestine, the home of both Bronze-Age Israelites and Philistines. And after those tremendous finds ancient Greek ruins were located outside Syracuse, New York, which matched up with the Greek colony on what is now Sicily. "And so Professor Lawler, Archimedes came full circle from his inadvertent connection with Eureka, California and his indirect association with Syracuse, New York. And Greg, don't be astounded if we find similar ruins in Smyrna, Georgia as we do in Smyrna, Delaware!"

"Well, how do these incredible coincidences happen? I mean what causes them?" Greg Lawler impulsively questioned. "I thought that only early Eskimos resided in North America after the last *Ice Age* retreat around ten-thousand years ago. The nomadic hunters crossed a narrow inter-continental land' bridge connecting what is now Siberia with what is now Northern Alaska. The rest of the migration is now recorded history."

"Or the rest is actually distorted or erroneous history," Ingram suggested to his protege. "The only thing I can offer is that the Feds in Washington are more nervous about the weird ancient and modern parallels than they are about the mysteries of crop circles, alien abductions, cattle mutilations and *UFOs*. To be perfectly honest Greg," Ingram firmly elaborated, "no one in America can realistically account for the recurrent ancient ruins' phenomena. And if it weren't for the contributions and the leads from commonplace Americans, no one including you or me would ever know about the fantastic discoveries near Ionia, Michigan, Carthage and Hannibal Missouri, Philadelphia, Pennsylvania, Eureka, California, Palestine, Texas and now nearby Smyrna, Delaware."

"Are we driving out to Smyrna, Delaware?" Gregory Philip Lawler asked his eminent mentor. 'I think we could take *I-95* south past the airport to Wilmington and hit *Route 40*, and then turn off at *Route 13* heading east across the Delmarva Peninsula towards Dover. I believe there's some kind of prison located in Smyrna if my memory serves me correctly."

"No Greg, you and I are soon jetting down to Jupiter, Florida to meet up with Team D. If my instincts are again accurate, we'll more than likely be re-discovering one of the *Seven Wonders of the Ancient World*, the inimitable *Statue of Zeus*. I had reckoned that since Zeus became Jupiter in Roman mythology, then Jupiter, Florida would predictably yield us either the colossal sculpture or the *Ancient Wonder's* fabulous ruins."

"But what about the important information Darren Hall just delivered?" Lawler innocently challenged. "I suppose you think the young messenger was really Hermes or Mercury disguised as Darren Hall!"

"Right now Greg, Jupiter, Florida is more paramount than Smyrna, Delaware is," the world's leading authority on prehistoric ruins insisted. "And the only reason that the government is both sponsoring and subsidizing *my* twenty-six teams on *their* secret digs across the United States is because the bureaucrats in the nation's capital want answers that are not readily forthcoming. If I am not mistaken," Ingram hypothesized and declared, "*we* are mince-meat if you and I can't calculate a suitable answer to the complex puzzle soon. In archeology, we can't have *our cake* (archaic) and eat it too!" Jeremy Ingram joked.

"What's with Washington?" Dr. Lawler asked while laughing heartily. "Why are the bureaucrats so paranoid and neurotic?"

"It is a lot easier for the bureaucratic yahoos in the Administration to regurgitate shallow explanations to the Russians, the Germans, the French and the British than it is to honestly admit that our esteemed American methodologies are a failure," Dr. Ingram explained. "In politics, the lack of an immediate answer translates into embarrassment. Then that sign-of-weakness eventually means that our core beliefs have been defeated, that our mother and apple pie values, that *our* great institutions and *our* envied American way of life are indeed quite fallible. And therefore Greg, *our* free enterprise democratic society is vulnerable to harsh world criticism."

The dedicated professors left the restaurant and walked to their respective townhouses, packed their suitcases in less than half an hour, caught a cab not far from the *University of Pennsylvania's* landmark *Benjamin Franklin Statue* and at 6.p.m. had already filtered through tight airport security and were seated comfortably aboard a *Boeing 737* taxiing off the tarmac onto the takeoff runway.

Aboard the smooth flight from *Philadelphia International Airport* to its Miami, Florida counterpart the eminent travelers discussed their priority first-class seating on jets. Eventually Greg Lawler changed the subject to a more "shop-related topic."

"Jeremy, this flight is jam-packed with many decent tax-paying passengers," Lawler noted. "I truly feel sorry for the two anonymous people that were cruelly bumped off the plane at the last minute so that *we* could get down to Florida in a jiffy. I hope it wasn't a romantic couple en route to a pleasurable Miami Beach honeymoon. That type of power manipulation would make me feel very guilty if lovebird honeymooners had become disappointed because of *us*."

"Forget about what you'll never find out!" Greg's objective-minded companion rationally advised. "Now I can't wait to learn the name of the next formerly nondescript American that will come forth and provide us with indispensable information about where we should be digging! Oh stewardess," Ingram beckoned, "please bring us two more *Southern Comforts* on the rocks. Whiskey always makes me relax and think better!"

On the two and a half hour flight's last leg the determined experts discussed the impeccable *Statue of Zeus* at Olympia, Greece and how a replica/duplicate was destined to be uncovered in or near Jupiter, Florida.

"The statue was enormous in size, perhaps even over thirty-five-feet high. According to the most accurate documentation," a half-inebriated Jeremy Ingram sanctimoniously lectured to his audience of one, "Zeus was carved out of ivory and was regally portrayed sitting on a resplendent golden throne."

And next, passionate scholars Ingram and Lawler engaged in an academic dialogue on two other stellar *Wonders of the Ancient World,* the *Temple of Artemis*, goddess of hunting at Ephesus in Asia Minor, and the enormous marble tomb *The Mausoleum* at Halicarnassus, just south of Ephesus that had been constructed to contain the remains of the wealthy King Mausolos, who had commissioned the finest Greek architects and sculptors to complete the magnificent Asia Minor' undertaking.

"And don't forget the nearby bronze *Colossus* on the island of Rhodes assembled to honor Helios, the land's sun god," a half- intoxicated Greg Lawler indicated to his fellow first-class passenger. "Some ancient reports claim that the gargantuan bronze statue was so enormous that merchant ships were capable of sailing right between the huge figure's two feet anchored on separate well-engineered island' pedestals."

The now-jovial pair rounded out their intellectual exchange by briefly commenting on and discussing King Nebuchadnezzar's majestic *Hanging Gardens of Babylon*, built just off of the Euphrates River and next the incomparable *Lighthouse at Alexandria*, Egypt, the ancient world's premier beacon that guided Mediterranean Sea mariners safely into the city's harbor.

"Nebuchadnezzar authorized the *Hanging Gardens* to make his new wife from a foreign land feel more at home in desert Babylon," Ingram recollected and verbalized, "and the *Lighthouse at Alexandria* was an architectural masterpiece. Unfortunately a terrible earthquake in the region brought the edifice crumbling to the ground. Entrepreneurial snorkel and scuba divers are still retrieving some of its remains from the harbor."

"Well, that just leaves the Egyptian *Pyramids at Giza* as the only *Ancient Wonder* left to discuss," Greg slurred before mildly hiccuping. "They're actually the only *Wonder* that has survived the erosion of time and that are still in existence. Jeremy," the less famous and less experienced anthropologist prattled, "but now something dramatically salient has just occurred to me. If *your* astute paradigm on this *Seven Wonders'* subject is consistent with your theory about your other significant finds," Lawler indicated, "then the *Pyramids* should be located adjacent to Cairo, Illinois, another bronze *Colossus* will miraculously *turn up* like *a turnip* off the coast of Rhode Island, the *Hanging Gardens* will be unearthed in the vicinity of Babylon, New York, and the replica *Great Egyptian Lighthouse* in the vicinity of Alexandria, Virginia will miraculously show up across the Potomac from those numbskull government bureaucrats you and I both immensely despise."

"That's why I've scrupulously dispatched teams A, B, C, and E to scout out those specific areas," Jeremy divulged to his still astounded companion. "The more I penetrate into this riddle the more complicated and perplexing it becomes. The entire problem is sort of a mental *Gordian Knot* if you know what I mean and I gotta' instantly become a contemporary Alexander the Great to systematically unravel it!"

"But tell me, how do ancient Greek, Babylonian, Persian and Egyptian ruins get buried inside the continental United States?" Greg Lawler asked in relation to the ever-expanding labyrinthal puzzle. 'It's like we're foolishly going up against inexplicable supernatural forces here!"

"That's precisely why you and I have been delegated by the government clowns to find out the elusive answer," the chief official on the new Jupiter, Florida expedition finally informed Lawler. "Greg, our outstanding reputations depend on our ability to investigate this rash of outlandish coincidences. After we have the Jupiter Police Department cordon off the area of the giant ivory and gold *Zeus Statue*, we'll furtively conduct our academic examination of the matter."

"'Many scholars believe that history repeats itself!" Greg Lawler realized and exclaimed. "You don't think that civilizations might regenerate and repeat themselves too on different world continents? Now that's a rather spectacular theory, isn't it?"

"I'd hate to disappoint you good buddy," the planet's greatest ancient ruins' researcher answered, "but I've considered *that* unique prospect at least a thousand times. Now fasten your seat belt. We're scheduled to land in Miami in fifteen minutes."

"What would Heinrich Schliemann have done under similar circumstances?" Dr. Lawler humorously asked.

"Old Heinrich would have gone back into the business of selling war' supplies and afterward, tour the world on his personal luxury yacht living off of his handsome profits," Ingram wryly replied.

The slightly dizzy pair was warmly met at *American Airlines* Luggage Carousel #2 by Cindy Noto, the brilliant and gorgeous captain of Jeremy Ingram's elite G Team. After removing their suitcases from the rotating "luggage merry-go-round," the three cleared the "Arrival Flight Security" check station personnel's scrutiny. After flashing her government assigned credentials, Cindy then escorted her feeling-no-pain bosses to her vehicle parked in a high-rise airport customer garage.

"Cindy, what's going on at Jupiter that hasn't yet been uploaded into my laptop computer?" Jeremy asked. "What has Team G got to currently report?"

"We've dug up at least half of the *Zeus Statue* and it looks as bona fide as if it had been sculpted twenty years ago in Fort Lauderdale instead of 2,300 years ago in Olympia," the slender female informed as she exited the airport and headed her rented car north toward a connection leading to the *Florida Turnpike*. "It's nice that the government covers all our expenses such as cars and money earmarked for food allowance," Miss Noto opined. "Team G's biggest headache right now is to keep the public and the press away from the restricted area according to standard team policy. Luckily, the statue is buried and well preserved in a swampy grove section southwest of the major population pockets along the coast."

"Have you been in contact with *our* other teams in operation all over the country?" Greg asked the astute driver from the back seat. "What can you tell us?"

"Well, there's been several artifacts discovered late this morning around both Troy and Rome, New York," the pretty blonde post-graduate student disclosed. "And I understand from the *Internet* grapevine that some interesting items that appear ancient in origin have been unearthed by *your* expeditionary units in Bethlehem, Pennsylvania, Athens, Georgia and Sparta, New Jersey. Dr. Ingram, why are all of these extraordinary coincidences happening? Is the past resurrecting itself?" Cindy asked. "Have ancient civilizations been going through some kind of regeneration that defies reason? What's *your* off-the-record handle on these mind-boggling paradoxical events?"

Jeremy Ingram was temporarily baffled and reticent on the matter so his best friend took up the slack while the *CEO* contemplated all of the various ramifications.

"Dr. Ingram and I have been noticing the same patterns that you have just described for the past several years," Greg Lawler matter-of-factly declared from the back seat, "and we're just as addled as you are. We're both contemplating resigning our positions and recommending to Congress having the vivacious Cindy Noto appointed the new head of the department answerable to the arcane Washington political establishment! Now Cindy, get us to that *Best Western* as quick as you can!"

* * * * * * * * * * *

The following morning Jeremy Ingram and Greg Lawler had sufficiently sobered up to allow Cindy Noto of Team G to drive them out to the sensational "Jupiter Zeus dig." Along the way the trio compared observations, assumptions, analysis, interpretation, theories and hypothetical conclusions. The three researchers were fully cognizant that the "sacrosanct scientific method of reasoning" had been soundly challenged and diminished and also its reputation humbled by an uncanny combination of amazing coincidences, serendipity, mystery and befuddlement.

"I suppose our team in Sparta, New Jersey has found ruins dating back to the *Peloponnesian War* and that the *Parthenon* has been detected protruding from underground somewhere on the perimeter of Athens, Georgia," Jeremy laughed while camouflaging his overall mental quandary.

"Professor Ingram, your guess is nearly accurate!" Cindy gasped in admiration. "The next things that probably will turn up in Athens, Georgia are the bones of Thucydides, Socrates and Plato. Have you any answers to these exceptional findings that defy my understanding of *Archeology 101*? Are the defunct Olympian gods making a comeback or some kind of divine encore appearance?" Cindy rambled on. "And now I just learned from an e-mail written by our Midwest R Team that ancient Greek columns have been located in Corinth, Mississippi! I suspect that they're genuine Corinthian columns. Please tell me what is responsible for all of these fantastic finds?"

"Cindy, if I had any authentic definite explanations to give," Jeremy honestly confessed, "I would certainly be providing them. *We* just have to now record the data, measure the objects, grid out the locations, keep the public and the press away and hope that the mystification somehow solves itself'. So far," Ingram proceeded, "the series of dubious events has transcended both Dr. Lawler's and my limited intelligence. Remember Cindy, success is often a thousand little steps and not one giant leap as the general public imagines!"

"But there must be a simple feasible answer," Greg suggested from the back seat. "Dr. Ingram and I have been hopping all over the country Cindy as if we were hyperactive sugared-up kangaroos attempting to accumulate evidence, but the more statistics we gather, the greater the mystery becomes! But please remember Miss Noto, the menace of pneumonia was finally conquered by penicillin originating from simple bread mold. Something similar might accidentally appear and become a decisive factor in this abnormal series of ruins' scenarios."

"Oh, there's my cell phone ringing again!" Cindy Noto noticed and articulated. "Dr. Ingram, could you please answer it and see what is materializing in the ever-changing archeological world?"

The famous archeologist complied with Miss Noto's request. "Hello! Yes, this is Dr. Ingram speaking. You've found exactly what over in New York?" the amazed-but-exasperated anthropologist/archeologist yelled. "Greg and I will be hunkered down here in Jupiter until this evening and then I promise you that Dr. Lawler and I will book a flight up to New York as soon as possible. Thank you for the update! Goodbye."

"Who was that?" Cindy and Greg asked in unison. "What's going on now?" Lawler then apprehensively inquired.

"That was Mike Templeton from Team K up in Jericho, New York, doing some constructive preliminary surveillance on several leads," the head investigator related. "Since Jericho is not that far as the crow flies from Rome and Troy, New York and from Sparta, New Jersey, Greg, you and I will be jetting back north to gather more pertinent information about *this* ever-growing perplexity. I truly wish that I were just as sagacious as the rest of the world gives me credit for being," Dr. Ingram confided. "I now feel like someone psychologically classified between a moron and a dunce!"

"Here's the swampy terrain area where the mammoth Jupiter *Zeus Statue* has been discovered," Cindy pointed out with her right hand index finger. "I guess it's now one of the *Seven Wonders of the Modern World!*" the driver uttered in awe.

'Let's get out and look around," the Project Chief commanded from the front passenger side seat. "We'll interrogate the natives and record our myriad facts as usual. God Greg! If only we had an augur, a prophet or a soothsayer in our midst to tell us exactly *what on Earth* is going on across the country! Where's someone like Laocoon when we really need him? Cassandra, where are your dutiful descendants?"

"Jeremy, you mean what *under the Earth* has been going on!" an alert and now sober Dr. Lawler logically corrected. "Things would make a lot more sense if our Jupiter Team was to nonchalantly dig up Cleopatra and King Tut buried at the base of the reincarnated *Zeus Statue*," Dr. Lawler facetiously answered.

* * * * * * * * * * *

The pair of archeologists boarded the *United Airlines* morning flight from *Miami International* to New York's *Kennedy International* as first class passengers, again bumping ordinary citizens that had paid premium money and had expected to be treated like airline' royalty. Jeremy Ingram and Greg Lawler had a subdued in-depth dialogue about recent developments.

"The next thing we'll know, the *Roman Forum* will be dug up in Cicero, Illinois after we methodically extricate the Agora and the Acropolis from Athens, Georgia," the second-in-command stated. "No *Southern Comfort* doubles on *this* special *odyssey*. Say Jeremy! I just recognized something germane! Everything in this jigsaw puzzle seems to be remotely connected! *Odyssey* comes from the Greek hero Odysseus, and while we're shuttling around New York State like two snakes or chickens searching for our decapitated heads, we might as well send a team up to Ithaca and look for Odysseus's palace and Penelope and Telemachus's smoldering skeletons too."

"You're joking but in reality, you're actually not too far off the mark!" the avant-garde archeologist smartly answered. "I've given-up teaching graduate-class courses next semester to devote my energies exclusively to solving this very demanding renaissance of ancient civilizations' riddle."

"Jeremy, let's summon the stewardess and order two more cups of coffee to shake the cobwebs out of our cerebrums!" Greg Lawler proposed. "And what if the duplicate *Pyramids* that will turn up in Cairo, Illinois are soon also discovered outside Memphis, Tennessee? How could we explain *that* wild parallel to a closed session of Congress?"

"And what if the established pattern is suddenly broken and we suddenly locate a third set of Great Egyptian *Pyramids* in Jericho, New York?" Ingram promptly challenged. "That distinct possibility could not only upset the applecart but send it wildly spinning into the air indefinitely while deftly defying Newton's widely accepted Law of Gravity!"

Greg Lawler apologized to his superior that *he* was originally from Los Angeles, was weak in small-town geography and didn't have a clue as to where Jericho, New York was. "Is it near Buffalo, Syracuse, Troy or Ithaca? I know a mathematics professor at *Cornell* we could visit in Ithaca!"

"No Greg, Jericho's on Long Island, in fact not far from *Kennedy International*," the *U of P* department head clarified. "The town is pretty close to Hempstead but actually nearer to

Hicksville. And here's the principal reason why I changed horses in midstream and decided to go to Jericho right now. We're not next trekking up to Troy, New York or to Sparta, New Jersey as we had previously considered. Our next stop after Jericho will be Cairo, Egypt where, if my dependable instincts are again correct, I now firmly believe the solution to this queer chain of incidents can be found."

"Inside the *Pyramids*?" Lawler automatically asked.

"No Greg, inside the *Sphinx*!" Jeremy Ingram seriously answered. "I told you that I honor what my intuition dictates, didn't I?" the secret study's Chief Executive Officer rhetorically asked. "Well Dr. Gregory Lawler, I'm now convinced that *we* have to get the Administration in Washington to obtain overnight permission from the Egyptian government for us to explore the eternal *Sphinx*. Ironically, the world's future might hinge on harebrained bureaucracy's capacity to respond to a prospective emergency!"

"Do you mean Armageddon and that the Four Horsemen of the Apocalypse are finally on their way?" Lawler gasped. "The end of the world is imminent? I hope it all ends with a bang and not a whimper!"

"I wouldn't be that drastic or fatalistic," the now calm and collected Jeremy Ingram advised and maintained. "Let's just say I'm at a casino' roulette wheel and my gut feeling tells me that black is gonna' come up on the next spin. Archeological history started in Egypt and I think that's where human civilization and culture is also destined to end. That's why Greg we're leaving for Cairo at the first opportunity as soon as you and I receive preferential treatment clearance from the *White House*."

Both archeologists realized that sphinxes were prevalent in ancient civilizations. The Greek Sphinx possessed the head of a woman and according to mythology resided on a cliff outside the city of Thebes. The Sphinx would ask a difficult riddle of anyone who passed, and the venomous creature would then kill and violently devour the individual that couldn't satisfactorily answer the tricky question.

"Of course! Every college history student is knowledgeable of *that* crazy myth," Greg chuckled. "The Sphinx would ask each unfortunate itinerant, 'What walks on four legs in the morning, two legs in the afternoon and has three legs in the evening?' The answer of course was '*a man*' because *he* crawls as an infant in the beginning of his life, walks on two appendages in adulthood and finally requires the aid of a cane when encumbered with old age!"

"That's absolutely right and you win yourself a kewpie doll!" Jeremy verified and laughed. "And when Oedipus was on his way to Thebes he correctly answered the Sphinx's riddle and the monster became so angry and insane that she leaped in despair off of her perilous cliff and committed suicide. And Greg, between you and me," an amused Jeremy Ingram added, "that's who I feel like *I* am being reincarnated into! I feel as if I'm Oedipus reborn trying to solve a very irritating recurrent riddle!"

"And don't forget the Avenue of Sphinxes on the east bank of the Nile at Luxor," Lawler reminded his brilliant boss. "It leads to the temple of Amon-Re at Karnak and was built during the reign of Amenhotep III, circa 1400 BC. Incidentally, that subject was the theme of my Masters' thesis. Say Jeremy," Lawler prattled, "do you think there's any relationship between Thebes, Greece of Oedipus's time and Thebes, the Egyptian city of antiquity on the Nile? Now *that's* another unique parallel we might have to analyze!"

"Maybe something significant will be found below the *Luxor Hotel and Casino* in Las Vagas!" Ingram cleverly uttered with an accompanying grin.

The two experts were quite familiar with the *Great Sphinx* at Giza. The object's head and its body were carved out of solid rock and its paws and long arms were meticulously constructed out of stone blocks that could withstand severe and often inclement desert wind storms. The prodigious *wonder* had marvelously survived normal deterioration caused by the residual effects of time and of nature's elements.

Both Jeremy and Greg had memorized in their intensive college preparations that the massive Sphinx is 66 feet in height and is 240 feet long. Its face has a diameter of 13 feet, 8 inches and parts of its nose and eyes are missing because of relentless desert windstorms. But then Jeremy revealed several incredible theories to his already beleaguered colleague.

"Unlike the legendary Greek Sphinx which featured the head of a woman," Jeremy said to his rather bewildered companion, "the Egyptian *Sphinx* had the head of a man, possibly an ancient regional king before the land ever had powerful conquering Pharaohs. The local king represented Horus, who as you know was a deity that guarded temples and tombs to ensure that the monarchs and their nobility would safely make the arduous trip from life to death," Ingram elucidated. "But now I'm going to tell you Greg the essence of the hunch we're going to be implementing without the government's knowledge or approval. Legislators and politicians are too pragmatic and don't like endorsing what *they* would evaluate as flimsy impractical theories. But unlike the bureaucratic dolts, you and I have the wherewithal, the imagination, the courage and the resourcefulness to know and to believe otherwise."

"Exactly what is this esoteric hunch you've been evasively alluding to?" Greg Lawler insisted on knowing. "Divulge it now or forever hold your peace!"

"Did you ever hear of the religious psychic Edgar Cayce?" the *University of Pennsylvania* distinguished scientist surprisingly asked his loyal traveling mate.

"Sure!" Greg Lawler instinctively acknowledged. "Cayce would go into a deep trance and soon assume the identity of a person living in the past. He would then under hypnosis mumble strange messages that sounded a lot like the versed prophecies of Nostradamus. His litanies under hypnosis were cryptic in nature and amazingly made absolute sensible utterances when interpreted in a chronological historical perspective!"

"You're smarter than the average forest animal!" Ingram playfully congratulated his main apostle. "Well anyway, please never tell anyone this item Greg, but when consternation entraps my intelligence, I often consult the non-scientific realm of metaphysics for guidance. That's where the predictions of Edgar Cayce now come into this equation."

"Okay Einstein, you've adroitly baited me!" Lawler quite reactively praised. "What on Earth does a dead psychic like Edgar Cayce have to do with taking a sidebar trip to the famous Egyptian *Sphinx*? Your spontaneous response ought to be excellent science fiction material!"

"Edgar Cayce once went into a deep trance and claimed that the answers to antiquity would be found in one of the *Sphinx's* arms," Jeremy disclosed. "And according to the prophet's remarkable prediction, a comprehensive physical library written in an unknown ancient language exists in the *Sphinx's* left or right arm and that the books contained therein will adequately explain the history of mankind hundreds or maybe even thousands of years *before* the advanced Egyptian civilization ever appeared on the earth."

236

"Wow, you might've hit on something greater in significance than discovering Noah's Ark!" Greg Lawler exclaimed while nearly foaming at the mouth. "Your erudite theory may possibly be the greatest single anthropological breakthrough ever! Only *you* could decipher this mysterious code that is in progress! Please give me more pertinent details!"

"Well Greg," Ingram authoritatively continued, "sagacious Edgar Cayce quoted that there existed advanced ancient cultures that had preceded the *Pyramids* by thousands of years. His extraordinary prophecy was discarded and dismissed by Western Civilization's hypocritical closed-minded egotistical scientists, who generally believed that religion and religious people were quickly motivated to sensationalism and were easily affected by a need to propagate *their* own selfish agendas. But Greg, my acute judgment presently suspects the contrary!"

"What makes you place merit in *that* particular antithesis besides your reputation for being a practicing contrarian?" Lawler queried.

"No one knows who actually built the *Sphinx* or when it was designed," the "Old World" master very deliberately enunciated. "We have also possibly fallaciously assumed that the Egyptians had assembled the *Sphinx* simply because it is situated right in front of the *Pyramids*. I propose to you that Egyptian kings built the *Pyramids* because *they* were awed and wanted to pay tribute to the *Sphinx* that had already been there for centuries," Ingram ecstatically editorialized. "I am suggesting to you that Khufu and Khafre had respectfully commissioned *their* immense burial tombs to honor the *Great Sphinx*, which to the early Pharaohs was a profound enigma left over from a previous unknown advanced civilization."

"Many leading scientists now think that the *Sphinx* and the pyramids were built during different eras but are afraid to come public out of fear of ridicule from their peers and from the press," Professor Greg Lawler contributed. "But your Edgar Cayce theory does have an element of credence based on the notion that the *Sphinx* had not been built by the Egyptians, who then constructed the *Pyramids* to supplement the remarkable product of an earlier much more dynamic civilization. What a fabulous proposition!"

"And with revolutionary sophisticated x-ray scanning equipment and with modern adaptable *MRI* technology," Dr. Ingram confidently declared, "you and I can now make those

Sphinx's appendages transparent and either verify or disprove Edgar Cayce's claim that an extensive library preceding the *Pyramids* exists in one of the structure's arms, directly behind one of the paws."

"And we know that the *Pyramids* were really modified Mesopotamian ziggurats. As you know my dear Professor Ingram," Lawler judiciously remarked, "it is always far easier to borrow than to invent and the clever Pharaohs were no exception to that rule. They acquired the ziggurat' design from the Mesopotamians and then filling in the various ramp levels, made a smooth-surfaced matrix exterior. My mind is staggered by all of these new stupendous considerations!"

"After we visit Jericho, New York," Ingram euphorically indicated to his loyal companion, "we'll obtain the latest diagnostic equipment and be the first modern humans to observe precisely what is inside the *Sphinx's* arms. I hope that Edgar Cayce doesn't have us both cavorting and gallivanting around the Sahara and the Nile participating in some insane wild goose chase!"

* * * * * * * * * * *

Mike Templeton warmly greeted Jeremy Ingram and Greg Lawler at the designated *Kennedy International' United Airlines* arrival gate and after encountering and overcoming the normal airport security and luggage repossession routines, the thorough and efficient neophyte drove the two journeymen to a Long Island' *Ramada Inn* several miles from Hempstead.

"Another ordinary *Ramada Inn*," Lawler complained to his department *CEO*, "and if it's not another ordinary *Ramada Inn* it's another *Econo-Lodge, Comfort Inn, Hampton Inn, Quality Inn* or *Holiday Inn Express*. I wonder what it's like to have a normal life and stay in the same residence and sleep in the same bed every night?"

"There's a word to describe that sedentary mundane existence and it's spelled b-o-r-i-n-g," Jeremy indulgently laughed. "Greg, your frivolous pursuit of a lackluster nondescript existence places you in the same category as most every university science professor. They're mostly fleas on dogs' backs," Ingram asserted, "and those host canines happen to be government agencies and bureaus and also exorbitant student tuitions. Please remember my dear Dr. Lawler, in the initial phase most great contributions to science are labeled 'preposterous' by the jealous, cynical and un-inventive educational establishment. It is only after a *crazy idea* becomes accepted practice that recognition is finally given where credit is due!"

Mike Templeton steered the rented blue Buick LeSabre into the *Ramada Inn* parking lot. "Okay gentlemen, tomorrow morning we zip on over to Jericho to examine some pottery samples and pretend we're in Jordan."

"Don't you dare make light of our serious mission!" the Project Director chastised the jovial chauffeur from the front passenger side. "That particular city's been in existence longer than Damascus has been and Jericho's first settlement dates back to around 8,000 BC."

"Over 10,000 years ago," interrupted Dr. Lawler. "The Egyptian *Sphinx* was probably already twenty thousand years old at that prehistoric time!"

"Let's get settled into our accommodations and Mike," Jeremy added, "thanks for getting us *Ramada Inn* reservations on such short notice."

The next morning the three on-a-mission men enjoyed a sumptuous hardy breakfast in the *Ramada's* main dining room and then motored east in the direction of Jericho. It was a crisp late summer day and the scientists were eagerly anticipating interviewing Mrs. Marie Mento, the middle-age woman that had stumbled across several artifacts whose origin Michael Richard Templeton had skillfully identified as belonging to the ancient city of Jericho.

"This could be the *genesis* of something big you've hit on Mike!" Greg Lawler exclaimed. "It might even be as terrific as the landmark *Rosetta Stone* discovery!"

"Greg, you might have hit the nail on the head by accident!" Jeremy dually complimented and criticized from the front seat. "Genesis might be accurate if it's the *Biblical Genesis* of Moses you've referred to!"

Mike Templeton's rented automobile entered a dusty dirt trail and the novice stopped the vehicle close to an old frame house that had been built besides a strange-looking hill, which was not characteristic or consistent with any other terrain found anywhere on Long Island.

"This certainly looks like some sort of geological anomaly," Dr. Lawler observed and stated to his illustrious superior. "This landscape aberration is incompatible with any other land formation east of the Appalachians."

"You're finally correct about one thing," Dr. Ingram sarcastically-but-affectionately chided his best friend. "Watch your *appellations* when in Jericho."

"Hello Mrs. Mento!" Michael Templeton graciously saluted. "I'd like to have the privilege of introducing you to my two employers, Dr. Jeremy Ingram and Professor Gregory Lawler."

"Pleased to make your acquaintance Mrs. Mento!" Jeremy suavely said.

"Thank you!" Mrs. Marie Mento shyly replied. "Thank you for coming out here so quickly!"

"Now Mrs. Mento," Professor Lawler chimed in, "please be so kind to show us exactly where you had located the rare artifacts."

"Why certainly, it will be my pleasure!" the cooperative woman answered. "We just moved into this house last week. It's been abandoned and unoccupied for the past three years. The objects were found just around the side on the large hill, right behind the back yard."

The four ambled around the corner of the much-in-need-of-repair home and then Mrs. Mento noticed her five-year-old grandson examining a strange-looking horn he had incidentally found among the out-of-place hill's rocks and stones.

"Joshua, put that dirty thing down!" Marie Mento bellowed. "Now Grandson, you don't know what kind of germs that odd-looking ram's horn has all over it!"

Jeremy Ingram immediately discerned both the gravity and the danger of the situation. "Listen to your grandmother Josh! Put the dirty ram's horn down right now!"

"No!" young Joshua vehemently protested. "I won't put it down!"

"Joshua, do as your grandmother has suggested," Jeremy nervously stated as he slowly inched closer to the boy to confiscate the filthy ram's horn. "Obey your grandmother's wish!"

The stubborn five-year-old lad raised the ancient horn to his lips and defiantly blew into it with all of his might. A low rumble was quite discernible until the ominous noise soon ascended to a much more perceptible pitch that sounded exactly like overhead thunder.

And when Joshua blew his horn at Jericho, the walls came a-tumbling down, and the walls came a-tumbling and a-crumbling down!

"Ice Ages"

In early December of 1975 Jeremy Ingram had been an impressionable seventh grader at the Hammonton Middle School where he was greatly influenced by his effervescent social studies teacher Mr. Charles Galinas. The New Jersey history instructor had mentioned to his usually lethargic fifth period students the amazing story of Heinrich Schliemann (1822-1890), a German entrepreneur that had become exceptionally wealthy making lucrative business investments in Russia during the *Crimean War*.

Schliemann had accumulated sufficient expendable wealth to enable the industrious businessman to retire and then energetically pursue *his* greatest childhood ambition: to prove to the world once and for all that Homer's *Iliad* and *Odyssey* had been actual historical events and not mere myths as had been widely believed throughout the Nineteenth Century civilized world. Soon his scientific archeological expeditions confirmed to cynics that *Level VII-a* in Asia Minor was "the Troy of Priam" (that he had against all odds) discovered.

After researching the subject of Heinrich Schliemann more extensively in the middle school library, inspired thirteen-year-old Jeremy Ingram was fascinated to learn more about the life of his new-found hero, the German dreamer turned investor turned amateur archeologist. Young Jeremy discovered that in 1870 relentless Heinrich Schliemann had excavated a mound around four miles from the Hellespont and had officially found the remains of seven cities buried on top of one another.

'The Trojan War had happened around 1184 BC,' Jeremy remembered in 1975 while reading from a library encyclopedia. 'I want to become an even more famous archeologist than Heinrich Schliemann! Who knows what other ancient treasures besides Troy lay under the top layer of Earth's dirt?' the young man conjectured.

And *that* wonderful spark created in 1975 by Mr. Charles Galinas had been the very impetus for Jeremy Ingram to dedicate his entire adult life to pursuing significant breakthroughs in anthropological and also archeological exploration. A decade and a half later the inspired scholar became a revered professor at a major Philadelphia college.

* * * * * * * * * * * *

"There was no romantic love affair between Paris, Prince of Troy and Helen, wife of King Menelaus of Sparta," Dr. Jeremy Ingram again explained to his fellow accomplished archeologist, University of Pennsylvania Professor Gregory Lawler, who had heard *that* story analysis from his superior's lips at least a dozen times.

"Most every educated person attending the conferences here in Charleston understands *that* elementary truth you just cited," Dr. Lawler readily admitted. "The Achaeans were ruthless marauders and they had invented that fanciful romance story about Paris abducting Helen from Menelaus to make it appear to history textbook writers that the moral and ethical Greeks had justly raided Troy to capture back good old Menelaus's gorgeous wife."

"Yes Greg, your normally suspect logic is basically accurate this time," the internationally acclaimed archeologist complemented his truly affable colleague and assistant. "Agamemnon of Mycenae had efficiently organized a thousand ships to plunder Troy's riches and his design was not to retrieve Menelaus's beautiful wife from sex-starved Prince Paris. That greedy raiding aspect was the real cause of the Trojan War. The popular myth is in reality an ancient rendition of a romantic fairy tale."

The men continued consuming their delicious dinner inside Charleston's Cypress Restaurant on East Bay Street, only several blocks from the South Carolina city's exquisite historic district. After swallowing-down another mouthful of his Maryland-style Crab Soup appetizer, Professor Gregory Lawler gave his take on the Greek heroes of antiquity.

"I'll tell you Jeremy, that's where Odysseus, Achilles, Ajax and the other dauntless-but-egotistical Greek hero-kings collaborated and joined forces with Agamemnon to defeat Troy," Dr. Lawler remarked and then indulgently laughed. "Didn't your incessant-minded idol Schliemann also find Mycenae?"

"Bravo! You're right once again!" the planet's foremost archeologist concurred, waving his right hand above his head to show a more-than-mild degree of animation. "Even way back then the avaricious ancient Greek monarchs unified against a common enemy even though their separate kingdoms functioned as independent and autonomous city-states. And oh yes Greg,"

Jeremy pompously and facetiously lectured, "old Heinrich was indeed my personal inspiration to become a dedicated archeologist and I owe my entire career and success to my seventh grade social studies teacher who had illuminated my academic path and showed me the light. What goes around comes around I guess! By *that* comment, or should I say 'cliché', I mean that teachers certainly influence confused students, who then eventually evolve into and become future teachers!"

"You're scheduled to deliver the keynote address tomorrow afternoon at the Renaissance Hotel over on Wentwerth Street," Dr. Lawler deliberately said to his traveling *University of Pennsylvania* companion to get off the mundane subject of seventh grade social studies teachers. "According to the city map back at our hotel room, the Renaissance is only five blocks from the Hampton Inn where we're staying over on Meeting Street. It's within easy walking distance if the weather permits, and the casual quarter mile stroll ought to wear off some of tomorrow's high-calorie lunch."

"Right Greg," Jeremy confirmed while checking his wristwatch. "And while we're flitting about downtown Charleston, our very capable graduate school assistant back in Philly', you know, Agnes Ross, well she highly recommended that *we* just have to eat at Hank's Restaurant down near the waterfront not far from the historic marketplace and also we gotta' have a breakfast at the Hominy Grill on the west side of town right after we drive around the *Citadel's* military campus. Agnes says and swears that the really excellent breakfast place absolutely has the best apple cinnamon French toast she's ever sampled."

"And besides cramming our gluttonous stomachs full at those terrific eateries you've just mentioned," Dr. Lawler reminded his fellow Cypress Restaurant diner, "there're plenty of cultural things to see right here in Charleston and vicinity. First of all we have to take the ferry over to Fort Sumter and see where the *Civil War* actually began. And interestingly enough," the overzealous Professor chuckled, "the natives down here still erroneously refer to the War Between the States as 'The War of Northern Aggression,' an odd observation in that the Southern troops aimed and fired their cannons on the Union soldiers defending Fort Sumter. And then," Lawler continued his pretentious monologue without even taking a deep breath, "there's the much-advertised carriage ride that goes around the entire historic district. I especially want to see the antebellum-style stately mansions that line the Battery Park area, including the noteworthy John Calhoun mansion. And the classic architecture in many of the homes, museums and churches in Charleston show a definite Greco-Roman influence with more than a plenteous amount of Doric and Corinthian columns in rich supply."

And after thoroughly discussing how the two rivers that geographically border Charleston were each named after a rich Southern gentleman/settler named *Ashley Cooper*, and after mutually vowing and committing to touring the ancillary sights of interest, namely Sullivan's Island, the Isle of Palms and Folly Beach, the men were finally served their Key Lime pie desserts.

"Yes, Sullivan's Island!" Dr. Lawler robustly exclaimed. "Maybe you don't know this, but I have a master's degree in literature. Sullivan's Island was the setting for Edgar Allan Poe's great novella 'The Gold Bug'."

Jeremy Ingram was not at all impressed with his friend's literary-world braggadocio. "And Greg, there's two other places I want to visit before we depart Charleston," the prestigious archeologist insisted. "Agnes mentioned that the exotic Magnolia Plantation is a must see. It's around twelve miles from downtown on the other side of the *Ashley River*. All we have to do is take the Calhoun Street Bridge to get there in a mere half an hour."

"Yes, I saw a brochure about that semi-tropical garden paradise while perusing the pamphlet rack back at the Hampton Inn lobby," Dr. Lawler added. "It's a scenic thousand acre rice plantation that's still partially operating after all these years. There's also a well-preserved mansion on the premises, not to mention alligators inhabiting the many nearby swamps. I read where the management of the property has had ramps built in the water for the large reptiles to bask in the sun because the gators used to meander out onto the various asphalt tram trails so that the cold-blooded creatures could absorb the heat ascending from the blacktop right into their carnivorous bodies."

"Pretty intelligent solution to the alligator-tourist problem," the renowned guest lecturer stated. "And Greg, did you know that the Spanish moss on all of the live oak and bald cypress trees and also growing on some of the palmettos isn't really a parasitic moss at all. It's really an independent growth that just happens to thrive all by itself on those various kinds of indigenous vegetation, but the term's a definite misnomer. It's not a moss at all."

"You're just a veritable treasury of irrelevant scholarly information!" quipped and laughed Dr. Lawler. "Perhaps you should change your first name to Encyclopedia and your last name to Britannica!"

* * * * * * * * * * * *

That evening Jeremy Ingram was in a rare philosophical mood and the Renaissance Hotel guest lecturer naturally shared his historical sentiments with his affable Hampton Inn roommate, Professor Gregory Lawler. The famed archeologist was in the process of citing how both Charles Darwin and Albert Einstein had dramatically affected and changed the world outside of their separate scientific and mathematical realms.

"Exactly what do you mean Jeremy?" Professor Lawler inquired and mildly challenged. "For instance, how did Charles Darwin impact the world outside the domain of his theory of natural selection? I mean, humans in civil society don't act like animals and don't feel a need to physically survive by being the fittest!"

"After Darwin had made his Evolution Theory public by publishing his classic work, which incidentally had been organized following his tedious study of the unique animal species populating the Galapagos Islands," Ingram said to his educational associate, "social scientists began devising imaginative theories of political development regarding the existence of an *evolutionary theme* advancing throughout history. For example Greg, according to those social revisionists," Ingram staunchly maintained, "in the time of the ancient Greeks, power concentrations *evolved* from aristocracy existing under many city-state rulers to monarchy under King Agamemnon. And then just before the *Revolutionary War*, Thomas Jefferson took the theory one step further when King George's monarchy eventually *evolved* into Constitutional democracy. And then good old Vladimir Lenin…"

"Boldly claimed that democracy would naturally *evolve* into socialism and then the Russian crackpot Joseph Stalin hypothesized that socialism's next alteration would be to characteristically *evolve* into communism. I plainly see now what you're driving at! But Jeremy," Dr. Lawler continued prattling, "what about Albert Einstein's mathematics' equations influencing human society?"

"Well Gregory," the stellar archeologist proceeded with his typically creative discourse, "Einstein's Theory of Relativity really upset the societal apple cart. Mr. Einstein indubitably proved that Isaac Newton's Laws of Gravity were not absolute truths as originally had been thought for several centuries. Instead, everything in the universe, everything in the galaxy and everything in the solar system is *relative* and not absolute. And so as a result of Albert Einstein's revolutionary discovery," the young genius confidently claimed, "your monkey-see-monkey-do social scientists believed that they could engineer a similar cultural theory whereby…"

"Whereby all areas of human behavior and all human values are *relative* and not absolute," Dr. Lawler realized and stated. "Of course, I clearly comprehend your astute observations now, but at first your Einstein statement seemed entirely obscure. Sometimes you impress me with your esoteric and erudite declarations that when thoroughly explained, don't seem so esoteric and so erudite any more, but conversely, your analysis then appears rather simple and easy to understand!"

"Okay Professor, we now have a long and arduous next few days ahead of us. Let's get some sleep before we'll be waking-up the local roosters!"

At 2:15 a.m. Dr. Gregory Lawler woke-up, and while attempting to slightly turn the side table clock so that he could see the correct time, by mistake the man accidentally touched a button on top of the clock and then instantly, loud rock and roll music blasted out of the clock radio, which the absent-minded Professor had thought was only a table timepiece. Then Lawler clumsily fumbled in the dark to activate the table lamp located alongside the clock radio.

"Nice going Indiana Jones!" Jeremy Ingram sleepily chided, holding back his strong inclination to laugh. "Why don't you wake-up the entire second floor while you're at it! Things could've been a lot worse ya' know! You could've had a dissonant rap music station thumping through the speakers!"

"Sorry Boss!" the very embarrassed and florid-faced Dr. Lawler apologized. "The next time I have to use the bathroom I'll do it in the dark without knowing what time of night it is! Who cares if I trip and break my neck?"

Another disruptive interruption occurred an hour later when the wake-up buzzer atop the clock radio unexpectedly blared because Gregory Lawler had accidentally set the timer for 3:15 a.m. when he had been fumbling to turn-off the clamorous rock and roll music an hour earlier.

"If this were amateur night at the local comedy club you'd surely win top prize hands down!" the bleary-eyed archeologist mildly balked and criticized. "Now let's get some much-desired sleep and whatever you do Greg, don't fidget with any more electronic gizmos. Just like good old Rip Van Winkle had aptly thought up in the Catskill Mountains, 'I need my beauty rest'!"

* * * * * * * * * * * *

Jeremy Ingram's cell phone rang at precisely 7:15 in the morning. Mike Templeton, an enterprising West Coast archeologist affiliated with several top government excavation projects was on the line and happened to be extremely excited about several "unbelievable discoveries" that had just been located.

"Well Mike, at least you had the decency to call me at 7:15 eastern time here in beautiful Charleston, but right now it's only a little after 4 a.m. out there in my favorite U.S. metropolis San Diego," Jeremy deliberately grunted into his hand-held phone, feigning being slightly disturbed. "Listen-up Mike; there's two things I totally despise: exaggeration and hyperbole! Now after telling you those two specific truths, what's so important that you had to call me so early in the morning before I've even had a chance to wash my face, brush my teeth and take two aspirins."

"Jeremy, ya' gotta' hear all of this!" the young man shrieked into his cell phone with a sense of urgency. "Last night several of our advance teams dug-up sensational evidence that you'll never believe in a million years!" Templeton's bass voice boomed. "A replica Parliament Building and an intact Big Ben duplicate have just been unearthed in Antarctica and only two hundred miles away another of our units has found a more-than-marvelous duplicate of the Eiffel Tower, yes, still all in one piece."

"Please forgive my lingering chronic allergies Mike but just yesterday," Jeremy calmly answered before clearing his throat, "one of our select digging groups working in conjunction with the Moscow Natural History Museum located a structure in Siberia very much akin to the Egyptian Sphinx. It's apparently guarding three pyramids that are situated not too far away. These types of phenomena have been occurring all month," Dr. Ingram conveyed to his astonished subordinate, "and the government's been trying to keep the incredible finds out of media scrutiny. What's next? The Hanging Gardens of Babylon being unearthed in Alaska I suppose?"

"But Jeremy, er, I mean Dr. Ingram, what's going on? Why all of this science fiction stuff evidently coming to a culmination? Is the Apocalypse rapidly approaching?" Mike Templeton nervously questioned. "How could civilization, the exact same civilization be occurring, or should I say be reoccurring, that is I mean, being repeated or re-invented, or whatever you want to call it! If my mind had a heart, my brain would be having a major coronary right now!"

"Professor Lawler and I are working on several possible theories," the knowledgeable scientist related and then coughed three times in succession, "and when we have all of the vital details ironed-out, I promise I'll get back to you with some feasible explanation! Just keep me posted Mike about any new significant revelations! Right now my mind is a little fuzzy, sort of in a temporary quandary."

"Okay Boss! Will do! I'm beginning to feel as thrilled as your undaunted hero Heinrich Schliemann probably did over a century ago in Asia Minor! I hope to be in contact with you again real soon! I'll keep burning the midnight coal!" Click.

"More fantastic cultural parallels!" Dr. Lawler exclaimed before yawning heavily and stretching his arms while still lying horizontal in his queen-sized bed. "Now I don't endorse the practice of eavesdropping but I had overheard young Templeton's voice. The neurotic chap was all bent out of shape about a facsimile Big Ben and Parliament Building being identified near the South Pole. Jeremy, I want you to give me your unabridged audacious opinion. What do you make of all of these corroborative remnants of unknown past cultures being dug-up one by one?"

Jeremy slowly explained that "Chuck Darwin" and "Al Einstein" probably had been faced with similar "perplexing conundrums" prior to the scientific wizards formulating their rather incredible theories. Ingram then mentioned to Dr. Lawler how the discovery of the Burgess Shale cliff in Northwestern

Canada had completely revolutionized geology and how it had rearranged man's perception of natural history.

"When the fossils of prehistoric clams, huge mollusks and other sea animals were discovered on top of mountain ridges and even in the high Himalayas," Dr. Ingram expressed to Dr. Lawler, "scientists, I mean those researchers of different areas of pursuit such as archeologists, geologists and anthropologists had to radically modify their assumed understandings of not only the Earth's history but also of mankind's brief tenure on this ever-changing Earth!"

"Well Jeremy, many expeditions to various mountain tops have proved that some extraordinarily powerful force had to push sea level up thousands of feet for the ocean animals' fossils to be so high-up on ridges like the Burgess Shale discovery to which you've just alluded. The serious documentation of those dynamic observations eventually led to the modern-day Theory of Plate Techtonics!"

"Correct Greg!" Jeremy promptly confirmed, showing a trace of rare emotion exhibited in his voice. "Any elementary school student studying a bold relief classroom globe a hundred years ago could've seen that South America and Africa could easily fit together like giant jigsaw puzzle pieces. And that's precisely how the Asian mountains rose from the ground or sea level up to the height of Everest in the Himalayas. It was not an isolated find, that's for sure! The sea fossil evidence on the summits of the Himalayas were soon connected to the similar discoveries associated with the fabulous Burgess Shale animal fossils up in Canada's Pacific Northwest!"

"Yes Jeremy," Dr. Lawler appreciatively agreed, finally sitting-up on his bed in his pajamas and nodding his head in the affirmative. "It's a known fact that the plates on which the continents rest move apart about one inch a year, but over the span of millions of years the various land masses sitting upon the floating plates had managed to drift thousands of miles apart. And when two plates carrying a pair of continents collide, that's when...."

"That's when India moving at an inch a year gradually smashed into southeastern Asia and as a result, the Himalayas rose thousands of feet from under the sea into the air, and that's also why ocean animal fossils are quite abundant on those lofty mountaintops," Dr. Ingram finished. "But the whole land-mass grinding/impact process probably took eons to complete!"

"Well then," Professor Lawler frankly proceeded with his evaluation, "what's your outlandish theory about all of these mind-boggling discoveries that your myriad expeditions are digging-up all over the world? Have you managed to combine knowledge from archeology, natural history, geology and anthropology together to synthesize some heretofore unimaginable ingenious hypothesis?"

"Yes Greg, I have, and I'm now ready to share its essence with you!" Jeremy communicated to his eager-to-know traveling companion. "Prepare yourself for something rather alien to traditional thought that might totally defy all human reason! Oh no, there's my blasted cell phone ringing again!"

Cindy Noto, a very conscientious *University of Pennsylvania* archeology doctoral candidate was on the line calling from Iceland. She excitedly reported to her supportive thesis paper sponsor that world history was literally repeating itself with the on-the-spot unearthing of an enormous Colossus of Rhodes bronze statue only ten miles outside Reykjavik and that a Temple of Artemis along with an unscathed Acropolis and a splendid Parthenon had just been found in very superb condition in Greenland.

"Just hang in there Cindy," Jeremy encouraged the euphoric doctoral candidate. "Here's something tangible and worthwhile you could write your thesis on. According to testimony given by another of my students, Kelly Greene," Dr. Ingram related to his enthusiastic intern assistant, "replicas of the pyramids and a duplicate Egyptian Sphinx have just been excavated in Siberia. Now confidentially Cindy, I suspect and believe that survivors from the lost civilization of Atlantis had built the Sphinx and that a library housing the secret history of the ancient world is stored inside either the Sphinx's left or right paw, or perhaps there are two separate and distinct archives, one inside each paw. Anyway Cindy," Jeremy objectively elucidated, "the Egyptian government will not allow us to open-up the original Sphinx's paws but I do think we can convince the Russians to cooperate and give us permission to explore what is perhaps the greatest archeological discovery of all time!"

"Gee Jeremy, er, I meant to say Dr. Ingram!" the very beautiful Cindy Noto ecstatically yelled. "My research paper will make me almost as famous as you are! You're a doll for giving me this special once-in-a-lifetime opportunity to make a name for myself!"

"Glad I could help you in earning your doctorate degree!" Dr. Ingram genuinely answered. "I know that your paper will make a great contribution to both science and to general knowledge! If you learn anything else, don't hesitate to get in touch with me! See you in sunny San Francisco next week for the upcoming big Archeology Convention! Bye now Cindy!" Click.

"How about some tasty breakfast over at the Hominy Grill?" Dr. Lawler graphically hinted before hearing his stomach growl. "I'm so hungry I could eat a pregnant stegosaurus!"

"Good idea!" Dr. Ingram replied. "But instead of prehistoric dinosaur meat, I think I'll prefer sampling the apple cinnamon French toast that Agnes Ross had strongly recommended. Then as we academically discuss current developments over our sumptuous breakfasts, I'll merrily share my latest theory with you and then see what you think of it."

* * * * * * * * * * * *

The two famished Charleston conventioneers were cozily seated inside the Hominy Grill indulging in their delectable hotplate orders of apple cinnamon French toast, cornbread, orange juice and savory coffee. Dr. Lawler was glibly commenting about how lucky he and Dr. Ingram were to have arrived at the popular breakfast/brunch place fifteen minutes before a long irregular patrons' line had formed outside the establishment's main entrance.

"Yes Greg, and the shrimp dinners we had enjoyed over at Hank's Restaurant and the fine meals we had gobbled-down at the Fleet Wharf and also at the Cypress Restaurant over on East Bay were terrific dining delights," the normally introspective Dr. Ingram opined. "Now Professor, just think about the many fantastic advancements mankind has made, not only achievements in the food industry but also progress in industry in general. Just twenty-thousand years ago," Dr. Ingram said, "Neanderthal and Cro-Magnon men were crudely drawing animals on cave walls, believing in magic, foolishly thinking that if they drew the animals as perfect as possible, then their artwork would make the two-dimensional ox or the flat-surfaced wild deer appear the next morning in three dimensions to be hunted and killed for food."

"Exactly and very cleverly put," Dr. Lawler amenably agreed, "and humans certainly have been a remarkable species these last ten thousand years, ascending from mere scavengers to the rank of hunters and then moving up to farmers, and finally rising to a nobility where mankind now dominates the entire planet. Science and technology have fantastically led to a plethora of exceptional accomplishments like the invention of the wheel, the bow and arrow, hammers, saws, knives, screwdrivers, shovels, automobiles, forklifts, radios, telescopes, microscopes, televisions, computers, the list goes on and on. And most of those wonderful tools and accessories were specifically created in the last three hundred years."

"Truly impressive but perhaps not totally unprecedented!" Dr. Ingram qualified.

"What do you mean?" Dr. Lawler inquisitively asked. "Is this the introduction to your new Theory of Civilization Regeneration?"

"Why yes it is," the widely-acclaimed archeologist declared. "My latest hypothesis has a lot to do with what I believe is the shifting of the Earth's poles every twenty-five thousand years or so. Now the last ice age ended around 10,000 BC so *that* cessation has given mankind approximately twelve thousand years to get its act together and develop civilization to its present sophisticated level."

"And you claim that before the last catastrophic Ice Age had descended onto the various continents," Dr. Lawler postulated, "similar sophisticated cultures like that of Atlantis had existed?"

"Exactly!" Jeremy argued and maintained. "There have probably been hundreds, maybe thousands of Ice Ages since the world was formed some four and a half billion years ago. And there's substantial concrete geological evidence that as recently as 650 million years ago a mile-thick blanket of ice had covered the entire planet. Then almost miraculously, volcanic action sent heat venting through the ice cover and into the atmosphere, thus creating a novel green house gas that then gradually melted the ice."

"I now see your drift of thought," Gregory Lawler said and paused to gulp down the remainder of his tangy orange juice. "The ice melting eventually caused the great greenery of the planet to happen with the advent of the Cambrian Ecological Period. Colossal swamps similar to today's Okefenokee in Georgia and the Everglades in Florida appeared all over. The lush vegetation in time gave evolving animals a fighting chance to exit the cold seas and then live as voracious reptiles and amphibians on the warm land masses."

Jeremy Ingram was just in the midst of disclosing his scholarly exposition. "Then of course around 200 million years all the way down to 75 million years ago the Earth had its notorious Jurassic Period when scores of plant-eating and carnivorous dinosaurs roamed the continents and ruled over all other animated life forms. And when the much-discussed giant asteroid slammed into the edge of what is now Mexico's Yucatan Peninsula," Dr. Ingram vociferated and emphasized, "then *that* violent collision was the end of the great reptilian era and soon the new environmental reality gave mammals a fair chance at ascension, of course eventually leading-up to the rise of apes and later primitive men."

Much to Dr. Lawler's amazement, Dr. Ingram went on to profoundly discuss the "Mini Ice Age" that had occurred in the 1770s, which remarkably had enabled George Washington and his troops to cross the frozen *Delaware River* to surprise the Hessian soldiers at Trenton and conversely, which also nearly decimated Washington's army at Valley Forge. "During several of those Mini-Ice Age years the sun hardly ever shined brightly in the summer months of July and August. But my principal point Greg is that we've been having Ice Ages of all kinds and of all sizes throughout the entire course of human history."

"Well now Jeremy, you've taken the curious position that the last major Ice Age had ended around twelve thousand years ago, that it in fact actually corresponded to the destruction of Atlantis and that there had been previous human civilizations that had populated the Earth, possibly even long before the last major Ice Age started over 100,000 years ago!"

"You're a quick read Sir Gregory, and definitely a credit to your noble profession!" Dr. Ingram complimented his very savvy colleague. "As you well know, the thick sheet of glacier that had descended down from Canada had slowly traveled as far south to what is now New York City. Then when the massive ice sheet retreated back north, it ripped-out boulders and rocky land above what is now present-day Michigan, thus forming the Great Lakes when the remaining ice masses over time melted inside the deep cavities that had been formed."

"But your theory is advancing the idea that human civilizations have risen and fallen between the major Ice Ages!" Dr. Lawler reiterated. "And you're conjecturing that this ebb and flow of scientific and cultural development has been primarily caused by the Earth shifting on its axis, thus radically changing polarity and playing havoc with geographic climates every twenty-five thousand years or so!"

"Excellent analysis!" Jeremy Ingram commended. "Perhaps *that* pattern recurs every hundred thousand years or so, I'm not quite sure. Now here's an interesting addendum, or should I say 'appendix' to my theory. The Mayan calendar and the French prophet Nostradamus have both predicted that a cataclysmic change is going to alter human life on Earth during the winter solstice, December 21st, 2012. On that targeted day the Earth and the planets of our solar system will be in alignment with the exact center of the Milky Way Galaxy. The gravitational pull on the Earth might be so tremendous that...."

"That the North or the South poles will shift to what is now the Equator because the particular Milky Way-Earth positioning occurs once every twenty-five thousand years," Dr, Lawler gasped before swallowing down some cold water to revive his dizzy thought processes. "Perhaps Mike Templeton was right after all! The Four Horsemen of the Apocalypse might just be galloping their steeds around the closest corner and heading at full speed in our direction!"

"Or perhaps another possibility is that a rather huge celestial object, perhaps a remote planetoid, could approach the Earth and cause the relevant axis shift when acting in unison with the Milky Way alignment!" Jeremy speculated and suggested. "A cosmic magnetic pulse could cause the molten liquid inside the Earth's core to swirl around, thus resulting in a life-threatening polarity shift! Yes Dr. Lawler, I do believe that I like the nomenclature you have cooked-up to describe my new hypothesis: The Theory of Cultural Regeneration! But in the final analysis, I meant to say 'in summary', *we* might all soon fall victim to our own Galaxy's 'Earth destruction timetable' when its set into motion!"

"Move over Newton, Darwin and Einstein!" Dr. Lawler out-of-character yelped, getting the attention of other more disciplined Hominy Grill breakfast patrons. "I had always suspected that you were *bipolar*, ha, ha, ha!"

The archeologists' intense conversation was instantly interrupted with the familiar ringing of Dr. Ingram's cell phone. On the line was one of his more ambitious understudies, Karen Richardson calling from California.

256

"What's that you're saying?" Jeremy asked the caller above the abundant static being transmitted. "Speak louder please Karen! You say you're having big tremors in San Francisco and you're calling from San Jose?" The telephone communication was then disrupted and within seconds the electronic transmission lost.

"Gregory," Dr. Ingram said with his jaw open and his mouth agape. "Are you ready for survival of the fittest? I think that perhaps December 21st, 2012 is happening a couple of years prematurely!"

"Olympus Lives, Part II"

On December 31, 2100 AD supreme Greek deity Zeus impetuously convened his conference of Olympic gods within his fabulous palace situated inside the protection of Thessaly's resplendent Mt. Olympus. The essential purpose of the conclave was to review vital strategy on how to control the dominance of the prolific human race and how to encumber mankind's fantastic ever-expanding technology. According to the assembled gods, especially stubborn Almighty Zeus, mortals were supposed to revere and worship the Olympians and not defiantly challenge and rival *their* omnipotent power.

"This scheduled meeting will come to order," King God Zeus bellowed above the chatter of the congregated gods. "It is my distinct understanding that the overwhelming opinion of this council is that those uncouth vile humans should have the opportunity at a second chance to worship *me*, er, I meant to say *us*. But first the despicable mortals must abandon their errant ways and then willfully go back to *our* former master/servant relationships that were quite popular in ancient times. What progress has been made during the last earth century in successfully engineering *that* important development to happen? Hermes, my most trusty dependable messenger god," Zeus eloquently stated and paused, "I call upon you to be our first stellar speaker who will adroitly articulate your highly anticipated report."

"These are the exact goals of my thinking, that is to say how *we* will sufficiently thwart the advancement of the mortals' remarkable science and technology," Hermes nervously began his dissertation. "First and foremost Lord Zeus, we shall reduce mankind's ability to communicate words and languages, either verbally in personal conversation or by radio, cell phones, video conferencing, television or by ordinary Internet transmissions. I maintain that in the future only primitive sign language will be tolerated or permitted to be practiced down there on good old terra firma."

"Honorable Hermes, have you gone completely insane?" Athena, goddess of wisdom and rebellious daughter of Zeus argumentatively asked. "Reveal to us your clandestine scheme. What do you intend to do? Cut all of the humans' ears and tongues off and make the entire species deaf mutes? Even though you're the speedy Messenger God, you're ideas are not too swift!"

"Quiet my impulsive Daughter," Zeus yelled from the head of the gilded-gold palace table. "Your irritating attitude is less acceptable than a bad case of indigestion, that's for sure! Kindly show more basic respect for your elders!"

"But Father, Hermes sounds like he's doing a zany stand-up Aristophanes-type comedy routine!" Athena audaciously insisted. "He's obviously jealous and envious of how the people living on Earth manage to send billions of messages and frequently gossip certain random stupidity over the Internet. And he's spiteful too because he's neither listed on Facebook nor on MySpace."

"Athena, I patiently warn you, stop rudely interrupting Hermes!" Zeus boomed. "Give the poor fellow a chance to advance beyond his rather strange preamble. Must I remind you! Our distinguished winged relative's presence warrants our total concentration. Now please continue with your dignified presentation dear Hermes."

The somewhat paranoid messenger god cleared his throat and then referred to some hand-written notes that had been scribbled upon a wrinkled piece of Egyptian papyrus. "Your Highness, I strongly recommend that all televisions, computers, radios and telephones be banned, and in the area of transportation," Hermes proceeded with elaborating upon his very peculiar outlandish recommendations, "all airplanes, helicopters, motor-scooters, automobiles, trains, trucks along with motorcycles and buses should be eliminated or destroyed in addition to other significant things like e-mail and post office snail mail. Only I and my cadre of nutcase aerial couriers will be allowed to flourish in the area of message delivery. Needless to say," Hermes embellished, "I've spent a whole ten decades developing these most excellent logistics, of which I feel I should be satisfactorily rewarded with a substantial title promotion and also Lord Zeus, a much better and less-encumbering job description!"

"I see!" Zeus reluctantly answered. "I fully comprehend your impeccable logic. No more mass media to influence the mindless masses, no newspapers, no magazines and certainly no more books. What you say makes superior sense!" the King God concurred with his jittery subordinate. "We'll also abolish all mints and bureaus of engraving and printing, thus depriving the craven mortals of everyday commerce and eliminating a basic medium for exchanging necessary goods and services. Using Athena's oddball terminology," Zeus prattled, "the *deaf mutes* will have to barter everything in their material world, employing manufactured objects, and most certainly, not trading with paper money, credit cards and minted coins. Could you imagine a trip to another village on donkey or on oxcart and having to exchange a chicken for toll passage across a bridge or paying two shirts and a brassiere for a watermelon and a length of salami at the neighborhood grocery store? What a complicated awkward scenario would then prevail! I think *your* innovative plan is in-genius!" Zeus commended Hermes. "I believe that I shall elevate your current miserable status to that of Chief Ambassador to Hades, ha, ha, ha!"

"Yes my Lord," the flattered messenger god humbly replied, bowing and obediently nodding his head. "Humans will exclusively engage in bartering and their vulnerable existence will once again be reduced to the mere pursuits of building fires, of searching and hunting for food, of building crude rudimentary shelters, of wearing primitive bearskin clothes and of using obsolete flint stones for tools. Men and women will be relegated to a subsistence level of functionality. I just knew that my constructive ideas would meet with *your* imperial approval."

"Ah yes!" Zeus emphatically expressed. "No more textbooks from which to study dangerous revolutionary theories, and no more electronic encyclopedias, almanacs or medical journals to peruse either. Cable news will finally confront its ultimate demise and all broadcasting over the crowded airwaves will eventually cease. Everything will go back to *Neanderthal times* way before that numbskull Prometheus taught men how to ignite and conveniently preserve the gift of fire. Say Hermes, *that* wonderful appellation I had just mentioned could be the name of the mortals' next defunct newspaper, The Neanderthal Times! Ha, ha, ha!"

"You're both apparently overlooking one very important thing!" callow Athena adamantly protested to Zeus and to Hermes. "How are you two savants going to accomplish all of your stated lofty impractical goals? I simply mean," the sassy and annoying girl persisted and rankled, "we'll have to wait a full five hundred years for humans to gradually self-destruct in a future cataclysmic atomic war! In the final analysis, I find Hermes's insane flimsy objectives to be both silly and ridiculous!"

"Daft Daughter, have you forgotten that I could easily annihilate the entire human race with a series of fifty billion lightning bolts going off like spectacular fireworks!" Zeus loudly exaggerated. "In fact my opinionated impudent Daughter," the aggravated Father vociferated, "as you already know I'm quite ambidextrous and can skillfully hurl rounds of electrical flashes simultaneously in all directions with both hands!"

"Once the shrewd mortals discover where the lightning bolts are coming from," Athena obnoxiously quipped, "then they'll promptly neutralize you and all of us with one of their many devastating doomsday bombs! We'll all be instantly blasted right into oblivion before we can ever chant *'the Pretty Parthenon Positioned on the Acropolis'* three consecutive times!"

"Yes dear Husband," Hera, Zeus's wife interrupted in defense of *their* never-aging teenage goddess Athena, "I wholeheartedly agree with our daughter's most brilliant claim. In your extreme haste to dramatically punish the humans, you might just accidentally short-circuit yourself and in the process, also stupidly electrocute the rest of us innocent victims up here inside Mt. Olympus as well. And if I may add, pathetic Hermes is an absolute total dunce who, without a doubt, in psychological terms, must be severely mentally challenged! What good are glorious goals without competent methods of ever achieving them?" Hera loquaciously asked her grim-faced spouse. "Truly Husband, how could the ends justify the means without the existence of any relevant means in the first place?"

"Well Wife Hera, perhaps your caustic assessment is to a degree correct," Zeus partially apologized, showing an iota of rare humility. "Hermes, I believe that you should go back to the old drawing board and revise your approach on how we Olympians could effectively liquidate humanity before they successfully liquify us. Then after your prolonged meditation is done," Zeus instructed, "conscientiously report your genuine findings to this eminent committee at our next slated gathering a century from this precise date."

According to tradition and past practice, Poseidon, awesome god of the sea, was the second immortal on the agenda to address the gods' council. Weary-looking and fatigued, Old King Neptune sported a stern-but formidable expression upon his light green countenance. The bearded fellow's colossal tail slowly flapped against the solid bronze floor, thus immediately gaining everyone's astute attention while sending random loose fish scales all across the chamber.

"Brother Zeus, Olympians, and assorted family members, lend me your eardrums," Poseidon began, deliberately mimicking Mark Antony speaking at Julius Caesar's funeral. "I have been deeply contemplating how to eliminate this very vexing human vermin problem for quite some time and to be perfectly honest, I'm enthusiastically anxious to contribute to *our* in-progress conspiracy."

"Brother, get on with your informative oration," Zeus politely demanded. "Explain your proposals in detail. And kindly make your spiel short and sweet, exactly how my pinky feels and tastes after I dip it into a goblet of pure honey."

"Yes Uncle Poseidon," Athena boldly chimed-in. "Get into the swim of things before we all drown in a sea of despair from your drab oratory. Bring us some good tidings in addition to your usual unfavorable tides. Truthfully Uncle, get your mediocre act in gear. I wanna' go surf the *Internet* and float around in a chat room right after this frivolous meeting is over!"

"Daughter, I strongly advise you to bite your tongue before I instruct Ares and Hephaestus to physically remove you from this very serious parlay," Zeus threatened his rather annoying offspring. "If you can't act your age, then I urge you to act your dress size. Now before Athena gives me any indignant backtalk, please get on with your recently organized proposals, Brother."

"Before I commence with my sensational sea stories, I must convey to all of you in attendance a rather amusing anecdote," Poseidon prefaced his planned narrative. "I was casually swimming along beneath the chilly Baltic Sea, minding my own business, when all of a sudden three Russian SCUBA divers intrusively plunged into the salt water and the absurd reckless fools were instantaneously impaled upon the triple prongs of my ancient trident spear. What a delicious unexpected tasty snack I then enjoyed and savored!"

The totally bored audience suddenly found great levity in Poseidon's utterances and all except Athena cheered and laughed rather indulgently.

"Are *you* nothing more than a savage barbarian? Didn't you commit the sin of cannibalism?" super-sensitive Athena asked.

"Since the repulsive humans are not gods and therefore are biologically of another species," Poseidon lucidly clarified, "I definitely was not guilty of committing cannibalism! *Sin* is a problem that only the humans have!"

When the abundant laughter inside the enormous chamber finally subsided, the sea god became much more solemn upon delivering his next even more profound statement.

"My fellow Deities, I've thought at great lengths about how I could ambitiously frustrate the reprehensible mortals, and my best solution would be by having me and my aquatic staff wildly generating ten thousand tremendous tsunamis all at the same time, occurring all around the world, and as a result of *my* intense labor," Poseidon hypothesized and adamantly stated, "*our* joint efforts will have instigated massive havoc developing on every affected continent. What a tremendous catastrophe my historic deed will have wrought! Yes, *my* legendary history causing widespread histrionics! And naturally, I'll gladly claim full responsibility for all the gross sordid mayhem!"

"Your dynamic actions would devastate every seacoast from pristine California all the way around the globe to highly polluted New Jersey!" Hera gasped and exclaimed. "Every fish and every ocean creature imaginable will be violently washed ashore somewhere."

"And every crazy quixotic environmentalist would be at wits end because you Poseidon would have made their prediction that the oceans will die from accumulating pollution in another hundred years prematurely come true a full century before-hand," Zeus commended his favorite gruesome sibling. "I must admit Brother, despite your hideous appearance, you're much smarter than the average crustacean."

"And such a worldwide tidal wave calamity would kill all of the ocean tuna so then there'll be no more chicken of the sea!" Athena facetiously joked, much to her father's disenchantment. "Obviously then, sharks and whales will wind-up on dry land in Pennsylvania and octopuses landing in Central England, and sea food restaurants all over the globe will have to swiftly close their battered doors to throngs of hungry and angry already-dead patrons!"

Poseidon then acknowledged to his colleagues that he had a huge grudge against the insubordinate insolent human race because quite recently two U.S. submarines had surreptitiously picked him up on their sonar screens and upon converging on the underwater Olympian, the dual ships separately collided with the god's three-pronged spear, bending out-of-shape all three sharp tips and consequently, leaving the distressed sea deity absolutely defenseless.

"Don't worry about *that* triviality Brother," Zeus empathized and expressed. "I'll commission obedient Hephaestus to forge you a new solid bronze trident. Your misadventure with the atomic submarines must have been quite traumatic indeed. Have you fully recovered from that nerve-wracking escapade?"

"Well Brother Zeus," Poseidon recollected and shared with the now-alert council, "my tender ego had been damaged to a far greater extent than was my greatly damaged trident. For you see, at that particular moment I had been flirting with six gorgeous mermaids when the unanticipated submarine attack had occurred, and confidentially, I haven't seen scales or fins of any of the beautiful nautical beauties since!"

"I guess the six sirens didn't shriek-out any sirens!" Athena quipped.

The chagrined King discreetly ignored his daughter's inane remark. "Well Poseidon," Zeus replied in a calmer tone of voice, "I think that you ought to sever every underground trans-ocean cable as a much-deserved punishment to these depraved brazen humans. *That* specific reprisal ought to stifle their capacity to communicate their gibberish from continent to *continent*, and therefore your dramatic retribution would render the whole defiant species totally in*continent,* ha, ha, ha!"

After the general raucous cackling and chuckling inside the majestic palatial chamber had diminished, Hera courageously spoke-up. "But the relentless mortals will still have their sophisticated space satellites orbiting the Earth along with their cell phones, their computers, along with their Nooks and Kindles. I predict that they'll not be affected in the least."

"Yes Uncle Poseidon, and you're lucky that some off-course cruise ship didn't drop its heavy anchor directly upon your thick skull," Athena casually admonished her father's readily-perturbed brother. "Then your rusty crusty bronze crown would be embedded right into your dense cranium!"

"Please master the art of diplomacy," Zeus chastised his brash offensive daughter. "You're still not too old to receive a royal spanking from me! You're truly becoming a despicable juvenile delinquent right before my eyes!"

"Daddy, stop being so pugnacious and hostile! Haven't you ever heard of child abuse!" Athena petulantly replied. "In many ways the contemptible mortals have written benign laws that are much more civilized than those arbitrary and capricious rules governing Mt. Olympus. I gotta' admit, I wish I had Constitutional Rights to protect me from *your* mean-spirited ruthless vengeful personality!"

"Well now Hera," Zeus arrogantly commented, completely rejecting Athena's most recent temper tantrum, "I can readily knock the space satellites out of the sky with my mighty lightning bolts. The humans of the various nations will be blaming each other for the sudden interruptions, and then as a result, numerous atomic wars between the scientifically advanced countries will ultimately trigger the downfall of the deplorable human race," the King Deity haughtily lectured. "Russia will accuse America of diabolically attacking it, Israel will fault the Palestinians and India will suspect Pakistan for deliberately perpetrating the all-too-abundant chaos. I just hope that I have enough energy volts in me to adequately finish the hugely difficult electrifying task."

Hera was next on the event's docket to offer her pragmatic solutions to the dilemma of mankind's phenomenal ascension and the race's present overshadowing of the emotionally distraught Olympians. The Queen of the Gods desired to avoid any direct verbal confrontation with mercurial-minded Zeus, who just like herself had been guilty of myriad extra-marital love affairs. Hera's ultra-courteous rhetoric was very direct and to the point.

"As you are well-aware Lord Zeus, I had been principally responsible for promoting Women's Liberation in America in the early 1900s," Hera boasted and revealed, "and ever since my direct intercession, the male-female power equation has been drastically altered because of my valuable input."

"Yes, if I recall the situation," Zeus sagely injected into the dialogue, "Women's Rights led to the female gender acquiring the privilege to vote and soon thereafter, feminine temperance leaders and their boisterous lady minions created the wicked societal scourge known as Prohibition. Since alcohol was no longer available for retail consumption," Zeus pontificated, "the American economy quickly tanked into a Great Depression and as usual, women made men's lives miserable and unbearable during that horrible period of economic austerity."

"Daddy, you're a true male chauvinist pig of the highest caliber," Athena vehemently alleged. "When you aren't having illicit and immoral sex with a vivacious female mortal, you are despising all of us ladies including your latest sex partner! Your promiscuous behavior must change for the better.”

“One more atrocious peep out of you Young Lady and I'll feel compelled to instruct my crazed hit men Ares and Hephaestus to gouge-out your twinkling peepers!” the Imperial King nastily hollered. “Quite frankly Athena, I've grown sick and tired of your juvenile antics and semantics! Now then Hera, proceed with your eloquent articulation.”

“Well Husband, Women's Liberation has produced several factors that support *our* dedicated campaign of weakening and dismantling the entire human race,” Zeus's shrewd wife explained. “Divorce is now rampant throughout the modern democratic world with one out of three discordant marriages ending in ultimate separation. And the rise of lesbianism has also affected family disintegration,” Hera deftly emphasized. “Soon the total Western World culture will have been contaminated by divorce and ample homosexuality, and slowly-but-surely the complex fabric of organized society will become tattered and tarnished, and soon thereafter the whole disgusting civilized structure will rapidly deteriorate.”

“Yes Mother,” Athena obstinately opined, “abortions abound everywhere because a woman in the United States now has the right to choose. And most of the time the woman will choose killing her unborn baby because she's basically narcissistic without a strong moral conscience to guide her decision-making. Mom,” the girl goddess addressed her very patient parent, “you sure know what to do to promote the downfall of mankind. But quite frankly, I'm sure as Hades glad that I wasn't aborted by some fanatical women's lib' advocate! I wasn't born yesterday you know, and I really resent you and father treating me like I'm some sort of mentally handicapped toddler about to enter elementary school kindergarten!”

Both Hera and Zeus paid little heed to Athena's arrogant rant. The sophisticated Queen of the Greek Gods then, with her husband's tacit approval, resumed her grandiose testimony, much to the utter dissatisfaction of garrulous Athena.

“Contemporary Earth females have recently ascended to positions of power in both politics and government,” Hera patiently reported, “and the White House's Oval Office is now often referred to as the Ovary Office. And to further efficiently corrupt American society, the ultra-formidable ladies' rights movement is currently proposing an original Ant-*Disarm*ament Day, the annual event appropriately titled Venus Di Milo Day."

"My good Wife," Zeus judiciously declared from his opulent golden throne perch, "to backtrack a degree, the development identified as Prohibition was actually the beginning of the detrimental Underground Economy, which evidently violates all of the laws of standard taxation. When people don't pay their fair share of the revenues," Zeus concluded and communicated, "the ruling government loses its much-needed strength because it doesn't obtain enough tax money to keep vital services and programs going. You're a most brilliant genius after all my good Wife, and I sincerely commend your efficacious and remarkably grand efforts! Now kindly tell the council, what have you been doing in regard to the birth control issue? If humans stop reproducing, eventually the race will dwindle-down and again will be subordinated to the stringent Laws of Olympus fiat. Please review the bold elements of *that* particular ongoing debacle to us."

"Inside certain major pharmaceutical companies women scientists are now in the process of contaminating male sex-drive pills that when taken, the male testicles will begin to shrink and after several months, they will completely atrophy," Hera proudly and slowly enunciated. "Castration will have become totally obsolete and male sterility will incisively dominate the world scene."

"But if you truly believe in the principle of gender equality," Zeus conjectured and cleverly stated, "then female birth control tablets and sex stimulus pills ought to be prevalently ingested too! Wouldn't you agree with my fundamental premise?"

"Yes Husband, similar products are being invented for women too," Hera concurred and indicated. "After three months of taking the sex and birth control pills women's breasts will automatically deflate to pre-pubescent sizes, their wet pink vaginas will become noticeably pale and dry and will then start to wither away and finally, their cherished ovaries will gradually shrivel-up, dissolve and soon disappear."

"Holy Acropolis!" Athena shrieked. "I'm not ever taking any of those terrible pills you've just described Mother. Honestly, I haven't had the pleasure of experiencing sex yet, and I refuse to die as a lousy frustrated four-thousand-year-old teenage virgin. And besides," the girl goddess elaborated, "I can't wait until the right guy, er sorry, the right adolescent god comes along so that *we* can roll over and over in the clover together, and then I could finally get this dumb virginity business behind me!"

"Haughty naughty Daughter, I find your reprehensible drivel intolerable!" Athena's beleaguered father mentioned from upon his high seat of authority. "If you don't shut your bothersome trap right this moment I'm going to pour a whole bottle of those delicious birth control pills down your hyperactive throat before you can ever count to two! Is that warning perfectly clear?"

Silence permeated the ornate palace throne room. Zeus grunted three times to communicate his utter displeasure and then being pleased by the notion that humans will soon not be able to rapidly reproduce, the Mighty One called-upon Artemis, goddess of hunting to confidently address the somewhat receptive assemblage.

The professed virgin hunting goddess Artemis stood and immediately apologized to Zeus for missing the last council meeting because she had been on a personal expedition pursuing wild boar and ferocious monsters in the Ethiopian wilderness. The young self-conscious deity proposed (in rambling speech) that only married men and women could and should have children. "No child should be born out of wedlock. And I insist that only married men who strongly desire kids should be able to achieve erections, and also," Artemis neurotically shared with her now thoroughly lethargic listeners, "all forms of homosexuality, including lesbianism, ought to be banned. Men will return to their original role as hunters of savage animals and women will again be assigned to the monotonous job of picking wild berries off of bushes near their caves and sewing and stitching together furry clothes using dependable animal ligaments for thread."

But since most of Artemis's weird ideas were incompatible with the council's primary goals of destroying humanity, her impromptu verbal oration was abruptly terminated by Zeus so that the Omnipotent One could hear some more appropriate and more relevant suggestions from Hephaestus, the astounding dark-skinned lame god of metallurgy. The swarthy awesome-looking fellow rose from his immense bronze chair and spoke his strong opinions on how continuous volcanic activity could essentially bring about the demise of the "very perplexing" human race.

Fifty-foot-tall Hephaestus, the notorious lame and grotesque-looking blacksmith god, ironically was married to voluptuous

Aphrodite, the goddess of beauty, their odd relationship proving the common fact that even in mythology, opposites do indeed attract. Always featuring a despondent-looking pessimistic facial appearance, the frightful god of the forge was indeed extremely skeptical in nature, his negative mind and heart possessing an actual inferiority complex about mankind's vast array of scientific accomplishments.

"Hephaestus, I want you to construct me a doomsday bomb," Zeus commanded from his elevated throne. "The abominable humans are working on one and so should we."

"You my fellow Olympians have already been constructed out of immortal flesh and bones," the hideous dark-skinned crippled god phlegmatically answered, "and yes, for your information Zeus, doomsday bombs do consist of ingredients existing outside the realm of my very limited knowledge. It's impossible for one discouraged overwhelmed god, assiduously laboring in his mediocre dingy workshop to realistically compete with millions and millions of human scientists energetically discovering and inventing in a plethora of laboratories around the world."

"Well then, what specific advice do you offer in terms of stifling the incessant advancement of mankind?" Zeus rebuked and rankled, exhibiting glaring bulging eyes and an exaggerated frown upon his visage. "What lethal forces could be summoned from the bowels of the Earth that would instantly place all of humanity in jeopardy?"

"As the council is well aware," Hephaestus mumbled and grunted, "my revered Roman name is Vulcan, and naturally, the word 'volcano' has its unique etymology genesis coming from *that* obscure appellation. In conjunction with Poseidon's plan to cause ten thousand enormous tsunamis," the dreadful-looking lame deity continued, "I'll also be able to contribute by activating a thousand volcanic eruptions to transpire exactly while *your* destructive lightning bolts are igniting forest fires on all vulnerable continents. Lord Zeus, *our* combined efforts will generate an inimitable calamity of an incomparable magnitude! It'll be, well, to use oddball terminology often spoken by the humans, it'll be analogous to triple-teaming the unwary dumbfounded mortals! Soon their entire population will be soundly eradicated!"

"Marvelously stated noble Hephaestus!" Zeus lauded and applauded."Since the dastardly lowlife refuse to be *our* compliant slaves, let them all die for all I care! I'm looking forward to being your warring comrade during *our* fantastic triple-threat endeavor!"

"Yes All-Powerful Omniscient Lord Zeus," Hephaestus affirmatively concurred. "You, me and your brother Poseidon could be like, as the humans say, Larry, Moe and Curly, er sorry Boss, I really meant to say Manny, Moe and Jack."

"Wow!" Athena yelled from her flimsy seat located in the chamber's posterior. "*You* should institute a college of higher learning called Hephaestus University and then in a short four years, all of the weirdo humans attending the infamous academy could easily graduate *magma* cum laude!"

"What would those victimized unlucky lackluster mortal students be diligently studying at Hephaestus University?" Zeus facetiously questioned his all-too-talkative daughter.

"How to use the *lava*tory!" Athena sarcastically replied. "As you all very well know, the Latin root *lava* means 'to wash,' and early soaps and detergents were produced by using grounded pumice coming from volcanic lava."

After the heavy levity within the underground chamber ceased, Zeus leaned forward and commented to his awesome blacksmith god, "Yes loyal Hephaestus, what you had achieved with Pompeii in 79 AD was truly a monumental act of magnificent devastation. And that's not to readily forget what sensational eruptions you had employed at Santorini, at Mt. St. Helens and at Crack-a-finger, er, I meant to say Krakatoa over there in remote Indonesia. Educate me now Good Handicapped Friend, have you any other pearls of wisdom to share with us?"

"Of all the occupations of the mortals, I mostly despise and detest the greenie environmentalists with great animosity, even though their impractical policies tend to stymie both industrial and economic growth and development," the terrible-looking husband of Aphrodite verbally related. "I intend to have intense carbon monoxide spewing into the atmosphere from one thousand volcanically active mountains, killing all of the victims who incidentally breathe in the odorless toxic fumes, that is, within a ten mile radius of each individual crater explosion."

"Indeed," Zeus summarized, nodding his head in animated approbation, "I had read in one of the mortals' science textbooks that carbon monoxide is a highly poisonous gas whereas, carbon dioxide is not. What an incredible difference the absence of that one atom of oxygen makes in the admirable chemical arrangement, the volcanic death formula fortuitously being all to our illustrious regal advantage, ha, ha, ha!"

"Yes Omnipotent Zeus, each simultaneous volcanic eruption will positively be a *carbon*-copy of the one before!" the blacksmith god persuasively finished, showing an unusual trace of zany humor in his inane commentary.

"Well, it's a good thing that Mt. Olympus contains no active volcano, otherwise we'd all be blown right through the stratosphere and swiftly propelled vertically into outer space!" Zeus generalized and responded. "Maybe I'd be exploded all the way to Jupiter and my luscious wife all the way to Juno!"

Aphrodite and Apollo were next due to speak in consecutive order, but Aphrodite had recently stealthily evacuated the dazzling jewel-laden chamber to powder her tender nose and thus, exhausted Apollo, who had been preoccupied dozing-off (since the handsome god had been riding his sparkling gem-covered chariot while arduously pulling the eternal sun from horizon to horizon for 1,200 months straight) had been designated to speak. But noticing Apollo's deep sleep, Zeus had the dissatisfaction of introducing Dionysus, the intoxicated god of wine, merriment and out-of-control orgies to *his* unimpressed distinguished cohorts.

"Greetings and salutations,. my fellow Olympians," the drunken fool prefaced his exposition. "Oh how unfortunate! I regret that I have no wine left in my goblet to propose a meritorious toast to this all-too-worthy conceited council!"

"You're a pathetic inebriated lush!" Athena rebelliously accused. "Allow me to revise my language with a few relevant descriptive adjectives: you're a totally pathetic, disgusting, idiotic, hypocritical inebriated lush!"

"I'm very complimented by your excessively delicate nomenclature!" Dionysus amazingly volleyed back, sounding almost sober. "Most certainly, an exotic tropical rain forest is lush, a botanical garden is lush and a rich posh wall tapestry is also lush, so callow Athena, I'm deeply flattered to be in such beautiful comparative company and therefore, I graciously accept your elegant words of genuine praise. Should I afford *you* the courtesy of a curtsy?"

"Extinguish your asinine dual linguistic folly this very second!" Zeus ineffectively reprimanded Athena and Dionysus. "If each of you two underlings want to make yourself into a spectacle, then first figure out how to become separate

272

eyepieces. Now then Dionysus, alias drunken Bacchus, I'm fairly anxious to hear what warped words of utter lunacy you have to convey!"

"First of all Lord Zeus, I think that we need the psycho humans to build more marble-pillared temples in their various communities so that the more devout mortal winos can worship me, er, I meant to say, diligently worship *us*. But all harmless jesting aside," Dionysus frivolously disclosed and stammered before loudly and indiscreetly hiccuping three times, *"here's* where I'm determined to outline my impeccable solution to the human menace, a genuinely fierce diabolical problem that's quite apparently pestering us all."

"Where's this evasive answer to the conundrum of which you've just flaccidly alluded?" Zeus demanded knowing. "How can we best dispose of mankind and effectively make the dangerous human race into a veritable forgotten anachronism?"

"The only real major difference between the common words where and here is the letter W," Athena's errant tongue spouted-out. "Hasn't Dionysus ever studied elementary school geography? He probably thinks that the Alps are in America and the Rockies are in Asia Minor!"

Everyone in the room immediately and vigorously chastised the young goddess by raising their forefingers to their lips and in unison saying "Shhhhh!" After Zeus stated that he would physically expel Athena from the sacred conference room if she persisted with her "unjustified "juvenile delinquency outbreaks," the All-Potent Ruler signaled for Dionysus to recommence with his insane-type drivel.

"As everyone here knows, female virgins among the women of the Earth are as rare as pandas and tigers thriving in downtown Antarctica," the dizzy giddy fellow oddly uttered. "Therefore, illegitimate children are rather plentiful in most every country, and indubitably, the general inferior population is burgeoning all over the globe," the all-too-comedic god stuttered and slurred before again egregiously hiccuping and burping. "And the worst part of the whole bizarre scenario that I'm now accurately and methodically depicting is *this* particular indisputable and undeniable observation. The repugnant tasteless humans are procreating without ever drinking good vintage wine. Much to my horror, most of the amorous pinheads drink quantities of cold beer, vodka, rye, bourbon, gin, brandy, rum, champagne and nauseous scotch whiskey before ever even contemplating having decent pleasurable sexual relations!"

"I must confess Dionysus, those obscure *points* you just mentioned are indeed designed for pinheads," Zeus intentionally chided his lowly peer, "but I feel compelled to call you, my devilish Dionysus, an absolute pinhead if you don't get directly to the point!"

"I advocate and advance *this* rather special creative theory," the mentally-disoriented god stated and then involuntarily belched. "All illegitimate children, and believe me, there are countless millions of the little buggers scampering around, should be spared from the ultimate holocaust that's currently being engineered by this supreme council, and then after being salvaged from obliteration by treacherous tsunamis, lethal lightning bolt volleys and violent volcanoes," Dionysus editorialized and then thrice regurgitated on the formerly impeccable floor, "all of those unwanted kids, instead of being put up for random adoption, the little annoying tykes and toddlers will be provided for in nurseries and orphanages located right here inside the safety of good old Mt. Olympus."

"Wouldn't *that* absurd enterprise be an expensive proposition in regard to costly maintenance, food, clothing and shelter?" Zeus intelligently argued. "Our budget has no substantial gold coin reserve deposits to ever begin to satisfy such an extravagant impractical expense allotment."

"Why must we raise an unruly mob of these unwanted boys and girls?" Hera logically asked Dionysus. "Have you lost your scruples? Your implausible idea makes no sense whatsoever!"

"Because dearly beloved Queen," the playful clown-god replied, this time vomiting-up some partially digested red wine from his stomach, "in the future we gods will need a loyal human military to protect, defend and worship us. It's all that wonderfully simplistic, don't you agree! The legions of illegitimate children will proudly serve in the Olympian army and from the outset they will be indoctrinated into worshiping and adoring us!" Dionysus elucidated and then again hiccuped, the echo resonating off the solid gold walls and ceiling. "But may I postulate my Queen that all illegitimate military personnel that are identified to be confirmed and dedicated alcoholics be fully exempted from the regular military service and that the new-found numbskulls should become *my* personal servants, assigned to merrily accompany me as I blithely journey from party to party during my numerous exploits, joyous jaunts and exciting escapades."

"Astounding, yes, astonishingly astounding, you delusional drunken imbecile!" Zeus euphorically exclaimed. "Your truly keen speculation is even better than the prodigious tsunami and volcano recommendations. Keep up your matchless drinking addiction Dionysus! You are much more of a viable genius when you're plastered than when you're in almost sober condition! Now my fellow deities," Zeus ordered, turning his attention to the remainder of his eminent audience, "I hereby solicit your unanimous indulgence. Let's all stand and merrily drink to the health and wealth of our great venerable and totally soused salubrious colleague, the most-venerable god of wine."

"Who put this sugary soda-pop in my goblet?" Athena petulantly protested, much to the amusement of everyone in her company. "How am I ever going to grow into an irresponsible adult if no one here treats me like a responsible teenager? How am I ever going to learn how to practice adultery like most of you feckless fools do daily if no one ever shows me how to be initiated into the drab club?"

"Be quiet or else I'll by proclamation commission you to one of Dionysus's dank dismal orphanages," Zeus warned his irascible daughter with a shallow grin evident upon his otherwise grim face. "Since you are illegitimate already Athena, perhaps then you'll find your perfect mortal mate while suffering under Dionysus's cruel jurisdiction! But by all means Daughter, don't be radically surprised when you easily outlive your doomed-by-nature mortal husbands!"

Apollo, god of medicine, music and the sun, awoke from his deep slumber and was now prepared to wearily address the council of gods. The handsome deity stood tall and then in a firm convincing voice, very deliberately announced his motives and tenets to Zeus and to the other revered family members reticently sitting behind parallel rows of golden tables.

"Lord Zeus," the radiant-looking sun god initiated his preamble, "basic economics is the glue that holds the mortals' science, technology, governments and culture together. If we could drastically weaken and collapse the world stock markets, starting with the New York Stock Exchange and the technology-oriented Nasdaq," Apollo asserted, "then the rich aristocrats among the mortals will be sufficiently vanquished and soon the contemptible race will once again be humbly obligated to serve and worship us, the mighty gods of antiquity."

"Redistribution of wealth, the elimination of decadent materialism, the abolition of the middle-class," Zeus considered and maintained as the Potent One pensively stroked his thick white beard. "Make no mistake about it. Men again will become poor, ignorant, uneducated and dependent upon the gods for subsistence. Holy Hades, Apollo! We Olympians could once again command *their* absolute obedience and servitude!"

"This entire fiasco sounds like twentieth century socialism and communism revisited," Hera candidly contributed to the weird discussion. "Marx, Lenin and Stalin's philosophy now being resurrected and rejuvenated, just like Victor Frankenstein's grotesque monster in that insightful novel by Mary Shelley I had eagerly read a full century ago."

"With no more free market systems in play, there'll be *no* more upward social and financial mobility. Ambitious students getting out of high schools and colleges will either be Stalin grads or Lenin grads with no prospect of any meaningful job security in sight," jested Athena. "Capitalism will cease to function! Prosperity will stop prospering! Progress will soon come to a grinding halt!"

Before Zeus could again chastise his all-too-provocative daughter, Apollo deftly shifted his stilted presentation into second gear. "I must confess My King, I'm a tad spiteful and jealous of the humans' unique attainments, especially in the field of medical research. If we could hinder the rampant growth of the pharmaceutical companies, and successfully do away with all chemists and alchemists," the god of medicine clearly articulated, "and finally reduce the population of the bloated medical profession, including all nurses and disorderly orderlies, then men will have no alternative other than to once more have to worship us and pray to us for such personal favors as miracles along with soliciting *us* for their painful recuperation from sundry illnesses and terminal diseases."

"I don't wish to demean or ridicule your integrity Apollo, but your rudimentary ideas are good and sound, but conversely, they are a little too vague and they also lack definite clarity," Zeus evaluated and communicated. "Try being more cogent. Could you now be more focused and thus, competently expound on your fuzzy hypothesis, making your supposition more lucid and more palatable for me to judge."

"Yes Apollo, your peculiar statements are as clear as mud and as smart as a large sack of square rocks," Athena snottily critiqued. "And Folks, there's no way in Hades that I'm going to apologize to Apollo!"

"Time is also a vital factor in limiting the mortals ability to think and create," the god of music emphasized while not paying any noticeable attention to Athena's gross buffoonery. "Take away the humans' leisure-time vacations and throttle their propensity to listen to harsh rock and roll and rap music and then my Fellow Deities, the easily influenced dull doltish creatures will quickly become irritated, despondent, and consequently, fully disdainful to one another."

"But wouldn't *those* cited means of obnoxious musical entertainment commonly referred to as rock and roll, rap and hip hop all by themselves make the men and women of the Earth want to kill each other?" Hera intrepidly piped-up. "It seems that by getting rid of rap music, you're erroneously doing something inordinate that is counterproductive to *our* main goals and objectives."

"Don't you dare get rid of rock and roll, heavy metal, rap and hip hop music!" Athena theatrically pleaded to Zeus and Apollo. "If you do that extremely mean-spirited thing, I'll have to take advanced anger management rehabilitation classes over at the yet-to-be-built Hephaestus University!"

"Do you have any other utilitarian statements to render for the good of the order?" Zeus requested of Apollo. "Please be brief and concise with your concluding rhetoric."

"Well Lord Zeus, I've been furtively collaborating with Ares to instigate an extended war between Iran and North Korea on one side and Israel and Europe on the other. Indeed the fearsome god of war has been a staunch ally of mine ever since the time of the blind bard Homer," Apollo convincingly reminded the council. "Our combined synergies could lead to a superb global nuclear war and the dramatic conflict could bring about what the mortals have aptly described as Armageddon!"

"Is there anything else?" an unimpressed Zeus asked the very virile muscular sun god. "Do you have any other plan in your cerebral arsenal that accidentally happens to transcend mundane mediocrity?"

"Yes My Lord," Apollo reflexively answered his volatile-tempered master. "After two centuries of difficult intensive experimentation, I've perfected a rather mysterious ingredient and confidentially, I now secretly desire to mischievously contaminate the world's fresh water supply with my new chemical compound. When the mortals inadvertently drink their faucet water," the ancient alchemist declared, "the magical item that I will have added will clog-up the mortals' intestines and then immediately thereafter, it'll rapidly seal-up their delicate anus cavities. Frantic people all over the world suffering from excruciating lower digestive tract agony will either implode or explode because they won't be able to excrete solid wastes from their blocked bowels."

"What a remarkable feces, er, I mean thesis!" Zeus promptly congratulated Apollo. "I guess what really matters in *their* future altered reality is the humans' inability to defecate fecal matter! Ha, ha, ha!" Zeus chortled. "Waste management will definitely be more than a fanciful environmental issue! Nice work Apollo! I'll instruct Hephaestus to begin constructing for you a glorious new chariot as a token of my utmost appreciation for your steadfast loyalty."

"No more fresh water for me!" Athena re-actively screamed out, much to everyone's mental dissatisfaction. "From now on it's Coke and Pepsi, orange juice and vodka and a healthy full enema a day for me!"

Ares, the bold and daring god of war, rose from his golden chair and his formidable presence was instantly recognized by Lord Zeus. "As you all well-know, dear Family, I'm very skilled at the art of mental suggestion. I nonchalantly plant a toxic idea into men's minds and soon thereafter, the afflicted nutcases go around murdering and performing other atrocious felonies upon one another. Right now I'm devoting my cultivated powers to having mortals viciously pulverize and pummel each other while fighting over certain natural resources like coal, steel, uranium, oil, water rights and food," Ares eloquently elaborated. "I estimate that within a mere decade the frenetic humans will have efficiently exterminated one another because of the onslaught of myriad droughts, famines, diseases along with horrendous pestilence invasions."

"Indeed Ares, these puny men, who now arrogantly rival our shrunken authority, are blatant butchers of the lofty culture and knowledge that *we* had benevolently taught them over three thousand years ago. Their once admirable allegiance has abandoned us, all of *this* horror happening when we stopped being vigilant and ceased being wary of their subversive activities. Is their any remedy to their unending defiance?"

"The trump card that we hold Lord Zeus is the fact that the licentious mortals have matured scientifically over the past three millennia but the bizarre charlatans are still emotionally primitive dolts, the exact same psycho' creatures that they were during the epic time of Odysseus, Achilles and Agamemnon. The erratic lunatics have recklessly turned on us, and now, thanks to *our* rational scheming, they're about ready to betray one another all over the inhabited world."

"Ultimately, the unreliable dunces will return to respecting our benign tyranny," Zeus pragmatically predicted. "The whole race desperately needs our despotism in order to pacify their regrettable affinity for perpetual anarchy. Even today my dear Ares, despotism and totalitarianism govern over the plurality of the mentally-sick human species. It's just a matter of time," Zeus prognosticated, "until *we* will be bona-fide substitutes for their ruthless communist and brutal authoritarian regimes. Yes, I can imagine it all quite vividly in my superlative mind. The destiny along with the demise of the Homo-sapien race splendidly dovetailing into a massive and final self-fulfilling prophecy!"

"Yes King Zeus!" Ares verified out of force of habit. "Let's not procrastinate any further! Make war and not love; that is my vowed motto! Those totally inadequate humans occupying the Earth don't actually care if it's a minor venial sin or an egregious mortal sin. They just love to sin, period!"

"Just wait a minute!" objected Aphrodite from her golden seat, a brief minute after she had returned from the adjoining luxurious goddesses' lounge. "Ares, you have those interactive relationships arranged all in reverse order. Humans should make love, not war!"

"Regardless!" the thoroughly upset Athena avidly and strenuously protested. "Your last comment Uncle Ares really *mars* my day! As I've said at these preposterous conferences several times before," the child goddess defiantly stressed, "I'm still a virgin and crave having sex, since I have been starved and deprived of it by my promiscuous parents' edict. And to top it all off," Athena aggressively balked and squawked, "I'm quite disconsolate from the whole ordeal! I'm over three thousand years old now and haven't yet gone through puberty! How many times must I tell you adult hard-heads *that* lousy unsavory detail? And I still periodically get acne too even though I've yet to get my first period!"

"Daughter, my overall patience for your persistent diatribes is running thin!" Zeus loudly complained. "If you want to have a role model to imitate, then I suggest that you ought to direct your tiny pupils in the direction of our next terrific facilitator, the glamorous and vivacious Aphrodite."

The flirtatious goddess of love and beauty stood erect with a glittering diadem situated upon her silky auburn hair. Her smile revealed stunning pearly white teeth and the goddess's matchless pulchritude was both devastatingly alluring and mystically enchanting. Even comely Hera felt a chill of envy speed through her heart as her jealous eye's scrutinized her major rival's most excellent celestial appearance.

Before Aphrodite could ever utter a syllable, totally crocked Dionysus unexpectedly sang out, "Oh, you beautiful doll, you great big beautiful doll!"

"You're about as hilarious as the Battle of Gettysburg and World War II packaged together!" Athena hollered at the devil-may-care god of wine.

"What about me being as funny as the infamous Battle of Troy?" the inebriated immortal jester rebutted.

"Not quite as amusing as the Trojan War, no way!" Athena rambunctiously finished. "That war had class, much more class than you'll ever have!"

As demure Aphrodite started her public speech, Zeus quietly motioned for Ares and Hephaestus to unobtrusively leave the jewel-laden chamber to retrieve and then carry back a large cage into the secret conference room, the aforementioned enclosure to be utilized to incarcerate an unsuspecting Athena if she were to intentionally incite another unwarranted ruckus.

"I've been quite busy working with Hera and with Artemis to make all women into dedicated lesbians," Aphrodite related her bombshell message to her mostly shocked listeners. "Men will soon go bonkers not having any sexual intercourse at their disposal and then naturally, they'll become exceedingly frustrated, and I predict that they'll abandon their straight lives as husbands and boyfriends and will in short time become practicing homosexuals also, just like the lady dykes and the independent lesbians. All relationships between men and women will become contentious, if not vitriolic. I assure you

280

Lord Zeus, in the future the simple word *gay* will no longer mean 'happy'."

"Didn't your past exploratory experiments with pornography work?" Zeus questioned the knockout goddess. "I mean, what man in his right mind doesn't value graphic pornography?"

"That's precisely my basic point," Aphrodite confidently countered. "Throughout the eons men's sexual fantasies have been fascinated by huge breasts, by succulent nipples, by wet pink vaginas, by erect clitorises and by puffy vulva. When everyone eventually becomes homosexual, that is, according to my imaginative design, human society will rapidly degenerate into absolute turmoil. Lesbians will quickly honor their need for survival, transform into contemporary Amazons and ostensibly declare open warfare on the emotionally depressed men," Aphrodite expeditiously affirmed. "Puzzled males will soon become both terrorized and petrified upon being exposed to womens' hostile uncontrollable scorn. The incensed females will capture and torture the enraged-and-distraught men, steal their sacred sperm and then oversee the process of human conception with female eggs being impregnated inside laboratory Petri dishes. The sample female eggs will then be implanted inside men, who will then have to suffer the intense pain associated with childbirth while concurrently experiencing my novel and innovative sex-role reversal technique!"

"Well then my cunning Aphrodite, what would be the exact purpose of all of this abnormal lesbian business?" the contemplative King of the Gods wanted to learn.

"Let's say that an adopted boy has two lesbian parents," Aphrodite proposed. "The accursed kid will automatically become confused because he won't know which lesbian is his father and which one is his mother. And furthermore," the goddess of beauty proudly contended, "let's say that an old-fashioned man with a frigid spouse wishes to have an affair with his neighbor's wife, but living next door to him are two professed lesbians. It'll take the befuddled fellow forever to decipher precisely which one of the avowed lesbians is the neighborly wife for him to aggressively romance."

"Honestly and truly, I totally sympathize with these already described victimized men Aphrodite, and not wishing to undergo any excruciating childbirth myself, I can't condone or endorse the radical principles advanced by your proposed quack project," Zeus decided and divulged. "I'm fully aware that I'm a dye-in-the-wool male chauvinist pig, but I believe your general scheme smacks of what those demented mortal psychologists identify as Venus, er I meant to say *penis* envy!"

"Let there be a multitude of mothers engaged in laborious childbirth!" hooted a disheveled-looking Dionysus. "And those unfortunate infants entering into Aphrodite's weirdo world situated inside jet planes will all be airborne, ha, ha, ha!"

"One more unsolicited snicker out of you and you'll be thrust into this *heavy metal* cage!" Zeus irritably shouted at Dionysus as *he* pointed to the sturdy barred object recently transported into the throne room. "I shall see to it *you* waggish moronic imbecile that you'll be behind bars and not inside bars becoming excessively intoxicated with your flamboyant whimsical mortal companions! And also, I firmly caution *you* Athena; I don't want to hear any nonsensical jargon about *heavy metal* either!"

Zeus searched around for his set of earplugs but his brief quest was to no avail, quite obviously since brazen Athena was listed as the next presenter on the meeting's agenda that had been elegantly printed on formal scrolled parchment. After being officially announced by Hermes, Athena briskly stepped to the front of the capacious chamber to directly confront and address her obdurate father.

"Here's my first explicit idea to curb the awesome dominance of mortal power," Athena more-than-discourteously stated. "Since I've been denied the privilege of maturing through puberty, I propose that all teenagers living on Earth be denied *that* nifty part of growth and development also. The general purpose of my keen strategy is that the targeted kids would grow old without ever even having hair clusters forming under their arms and in other distinct body places. According to my clever calculations," the girl goddess verbally estimated, "the vulgar human species will die-out in less than a century since the process of reproduction would be permanently curtailed."

"And how will you deprive the affected adolescents of readily available sexual knowledge?" Zeus austerely asked his flighty-minded daughter.

"I'll take measures to make sure that they have thirteen years of kindergarten before graduating as total illiterates from high school, actually without any evident skills or abilities," the on-a-mission girl/goddess equivocated. "Let's forget about all of this theoretical gender-neutral stuff for a moment! And besides thirteen consecutive years of kindergarten, I'll also implement the policy that boys will always be required to wear colorful skirts and dresses and conversely, girls will be clad in ordinary boys' apparel right through their entire non-academic education. I have my personal reason why I intend to do these things; I mean Daddy, how am I to ever find out if I'm straight or if I'm a valid lesbian if I never have the chance to enter puberty?"

"Would you also have it that girls will wear letter-man sweaters and black leather motorcycle jackets and that it would be mandatory for boys to play with dolls?" Hera curiously asked her always-defensive progeny, the mouthy goddess prodigy.

"Yes Mother, and it will also be compulsory for young girls to play with tin army soldiers and miniature toy tanks and on the flip side of the bronze coin, boys will all have cute little doll houses and exquisite children's kitchen tea cup sets along with baby cradles to ambitiously rock during their leisure time. And no more Boy Scouts exclusively for boys. The Boy Scouts will be for girls only, and the Girl Scouts will be a viable training ground for horny-but-sexually inhibited boys."

"What about the dastardly scourge known as urban rap music?" Zeus queried. "What about *that* dissonant nuisance?"

"The kids residing all over the world will all talk in catchy hip-hop rhyme patterns, which will eventually make them revolt against their parents' assumed authority. Boys and girls will quickly become derelict delinquents and their lack of discipline will ultimately come into conflict with their parents' arbitrary behavior rules."

"That is the most abominable aggregation of suggestions I've ever heard!" Zeus verbally exploded from his raised golden throne. "Your perverted ideas aren't worth an ounce of sand in Hades or a gram of ice in the remote Land of the Lost!"

"Look Daddy-o, I resent your sanctimonious opinion of me and I demand right this very minute that the council vote on whether or not my imaginative recommendations are satisfactory?" Athena bravely replied in an insistent tone of voice. "I'm tired of listening to your loose dictatorial tantrums Father! I want this entire assemblage to hereby acknowledge that I do have a singular mind of my own and that I intend to use it with impunity from now on! And besides that, I'm pretty damned durable too! While exploring the humans' remarkable realm, I learned a lot! Bring on your next Ice Age Big Daddy! Off the record Pop, I've survived many *Blizzards* at a place the mortals call Dairy Queen, ya' know!"

Being at his wits end, Zeus gestured with his right hand and the subtle movement dispatched Hephaestus and Ares to latch onto Athena, handcuff the ornery brat with bronze manacles and then very forcefully toss the rebellious young lady into the barred cage located immediately to the right.

"I'll have to make an example out of you, sassy-mouthed Daughter!" Zeus angrily exclaimed. "Hephaestus," the Chief Deity next commanded as helpless shrieking Athena squirmed and gyrated in a wild frenzy inside the locked strong metal cage, "here's some duct tape to wrap around my dysfunctional offspring's uncontrollable mouth. At least the misguided humans have invented something worthwhile that's relatively practical and quite useful!"

After *that* rather difficult assignment had been accomplished, Zeus had additional instructions that he directed toward Hephaestus and Ares, much to the alarm of appalled Hera, to the other spellbound assembled gods and also to the remaining petrified goddesses.

"Now I want you two musclebound lugs to lug the bronze cage containing my shrill-mouthed cagey rambunctious daughter into your workshop Hephaestus," the livid King of the Gods bellowed, "and then it is my imperial decree that Athena be dipped into a vat of hot red nail polish up to her neck for twenty-four Earth hours at a nasty temperature of one hundred and ten degrees. Is my simple declaration perfectly clear to you two knuckle-headed nincompoops?"

"Yes Master!" Hephaestus and Ares chanted in chorus while nodding their dual gigantic heads. "Yes Master!" the all-brawn mini-brained duo mechanically reiterated.

After hysterical-but-mute Athena had been swiftly conveyed out of the fabulous throne room while violently wriggling and gyrating inside her square bronze barred containment, Hades, sinister Greek god of death and lord of the bewildering underworld, was selected to be the final speaker to deliver a narrative to omnipotent Zeus and his now-skeptical council. Used to being in an atmosphere of complete dark silence, the shady morose-looking fellow stood and waited for all whispering and chattering among his peers to terminate.

"Well now my good brother Hades," Zeus very respectfully acknowledged, "do you have anything scintillating to say to *our* honorable gathering? And please don't aggravate or excoriate my bland character like my belligerent daughter had just attempted to do! And by all means Brother Hades, even though you aren't a Roman Catholic acolyte, I don't want to witness any demonic demonstrations originating from you!"

Just as the pallid-looking god had reported a hundred years prior, the Area of Atonement was the sector of Hades where the principal growth and development was still occurring. The famed punishment district had to be tripled in size since the last council session had taken place, the additional construction recently being completed to accommodate the billions of new souls that required "final residency" within the dark depressing after-world. Thousands of horizontal and diagonal tunnels had to be recently excavated and burrowed deep into the Earth's mantel in order to provide sufficient space for the newly arrived souls. "The more indecency that occurs on Earth among the mortals, the more the Area of Atonement must be expanded," lugubrious-faced Hades solemnly reported to Zeus. "My labor and responsibility is exceptionally hard since the multitude of deceased men and women have, over the past hundred years, become extraordinarily sinful in their baneful misbehavior," the pessimistic Hades sadly reported in a rather melancholy tone of voice. "Truthfully Brother, I am greatly overwhelmed!"

"Is that crazy singer fellow still down there in your gloomy realm sitting by the dock of the bay?" Zeus curiously inquired, for lack of a better thing to say.

"Yes my Lord, that very inconsolably morbid spirit Otis Redding is still down there chronically moaning on the bank of the River Styx while sadly watching macabre Charon row his shadowy barge across the quiet channel from the noisy Land of the Living to the lonely and silent Kingdom of the Dead."

"Does anything in particular right this minute make you extremely angry?" The Chief Greek God asked his thoroughly inanimate younger brother.

"Yes, please have everyone blow-out all of the candles on the tables and extinguish the fires emanating from the abundant wall sconces and torches," Hades politely asked his fellow deities. "The bright lights greatly hamper my super-sensitive vision."

"Okay Brother, we've now complied with your modest request," Zeus cooperatively answered a minute later. "But ignoring the environment found here inside Mt. Olympus, is there anything on Earth that gives you displeasure?"

"Why yes," Hades ruminated and then softly commented. "What really irks me is the fact that the Dead Sea is in Israel and that the notion of Death Valley is in California. Those aggravating designations ought to be part of *my* underworld and not geographically located anywhere else on this evil planet's surface. Other than those two annoying circumstances," Hades qualified and related, "thank the Universe that everything else on Earth, aside from the great incidence of death and genocide, is generally copacetic with me!"

"Well Courageous Brother, you have my expressed allegiance and my supreme support in all of your noteworthy daily endeavors and immediate concerns," Zeus sympathetically remarked. "Now then dear Hades, let's be mutual friends in the art of problem-solving. What the Hades can this dynamic council do to assist you in your pledged commitment to providing vital necessary services for the dead? And please don't say something off the proverbial wall that will quickly bankrupt our limited treasury!"

"You could have all of the gods including myself instantly drop dead so that all of this crazy and boring eternal immortality existence nonsense stuff could finally come to a sudden abrupt bittersweet end!"

Zeus felt compassion for the plight of the sorrowed Hades so he diplomatically overrode his own conscience and refused to ostracize the somber god of death from the enormous council assembly room. Instead, the King of the Gods rose from his golden throne and spoke his singular mind.

"Under my aegis, I vow and swear that the humans will ultimately be defeated and that Olympus will ascend to splendid prominence once again," Zeus declared, receiving a robust round of applause from the council. "First and foremost, it will be mandatory to ban the exercise of *free will* among mankind so that *we* can easily conquer our extremely militant mortal foes. Also, alien human religions will be abolished and there will be no more Christians, Muslims, Greek Orthodox, Greek Unorthodox, Buddhists, Hindus or proselytizing atheists. Furthermore, I proudly decree that there will be no more Constitutions, Bill of Rights or Communist Manifesto. In the future," Lord Zeus stipulated, "free speech will be a misnomer, a lost relic from a forgotten antiquity, and the hapless humans will once again be in a prehistoric mindset and have to again start their primitive civilizations from scratch."

After a moment's pause, the inimitable King God continued with his sage analysis. "Now Hades," Zeus regally stated, "we have approximately thirty billion souls in Hades already, and with the forthcoming planned destruction of mankind, we'll have about eight billion more spirits to accommodate. To facilitate the end of their chaotic era," the King of the Gods blustered, "we'll have Poseidon's traumatic tsunamis and Hephaestus's invincible volcanic explosions and concomitant earthquakes, and since I am the designated Lord of the Atmosphere, after I administer my flurry of disastrous lightning bolts and then systematically remove all oxygen from the lower air," Zeus emphasized, "and since the remaining nitrogen will kill-off everyone else including those loathsome bothersome environmentalists, thus my very potent retribution will completely expire the full measure of those ungrateful troublesome human creatures once and for all. And I'll very scrupulously salvage the orphans and the hordes of illegitimate children just as delirious Dionysus had constructively suggested, and when I feel fully motivated, I'll train-up an army of loyal mortals to gladly serve *our* every whim and fancy."

Lord Zeus hesitated before concluding his summary with a rather stark closing remark. "Finally my beloved fellow gods and goddesses, I'll make it occur that the periods of global cooling and global warming that will soon follow will gradually extinguish the few remaining humans that had fortuitously escaped my original premeditated vengeance. I hereby promise you Brother Hades, with every fiber and cell inside my immortal body, that man's impending horrible demise will come by freezing, by drowning, or by being wildly electrocuted or by being swiftly incinerated with hellfire," the Lord God enthusiastically thundered. "And finally my devoted Fellow Deities, it gives me great pleasure to announce that this very fruitful meeting is now officially adjourned!"

About the Author

Jay Dubya is author' John Wiessner's pen name and also his initials (J.W.) John is a retired New Jersey public school English teacher and he had taught the subject for thirty-four years. John lives in southern New Jersey with wife Joanne and the couple has three grown sons.

Author Jay Dubya has written zany adult satires *Fractured Frazzled Folk Fables and Fairy Farces and FFFF and FF, Part II. Black Leather and Blue Denim, A '50s Novel* and its sequel, *The Great Teen Fruit War, A 1960' Novel and Frat' Brats, A '60s Novel* are adult-oriented literary endeavors constituting a trilogy.

Pieces of Eight, Pieces of Eight, Part II, Pieces of Eight Part III and *Pieces of Eight, Part IV* are' short story/novella collections featuring science fiction, paranormal and humorous plots and themes. *Nine New Novellas* is the companion book to *Nine New Novellas, Part II, Nine New Novellas, Part III* and *Nine New Novellas, Part IV.* And *So Ya' Wanna' Be A Teacher* is a satirical autobiography describing the author's thirty-four year educational career in American public schools.

Ron Coyote, Man of La Mangia is adult humor and the work is an imaginative satire/parody on Miguel Cervantes' *Don Quixote,* published in 1605. *Mauled Maimed Mangled Mutilated Mythology* is a work that satires twenty-one famous ancient tales. *The Wholly Book of Genesis* and *The Wholly Book of Exodus* are also adult satirical humor. *Thirteen Sick Tasteless Classics, Thirteen Sick Tasteless Classics, Part II, Thirteen Sick Tasteless Classics, Part III* and *Thirteen Sick Tasteless Classics, Part IV* are adult satirical rewrites of famous short fiction.

John has also authored a trilogy of young adult fantasy novels, *Enchanta, Pot of Gold* and *Space Bugs, Earth Invasion. The Eighteen' Story Gingerbread House* is a new collection of eighteen diverse and creative children's stories.

Jay Dubya likes '50s rock and roll music and he also enjoys pop' songs by the Beach Boys', Fleetwood Mac, the Eagles, the Rolling Stones, ELO, John Mellencamp and by John Fogerty. When not writing or listening to music, Jay Dubya likes watching 76ers basketball and Phillies and Yankees television baseball games.

288